DEBBIE MACOMBER

Perfect Partners

mira

Recycling programs
for this product may
not exist in your area.

ISBN-13: 978-0-7783-3157-5

Perfect Partners

Mira
22 Adelaide St. West, 40th Floor
Toronto, Ontario M5H 4E3, Canada
www.Harlequin.com

Printed in Lithuania

MIX
Paper from
responsible sources
FSC® C021394

Also available from Debbie Macomber and MIRA

Blossom Street

The Shop on Blossom Street
A Good Yarn
Susannah's Garden
Back on Blossom Street
Twenty Wishes
Summer on Blossom Street
Hannah's List
"The Twenty-First Wish"
   (in *The Knitting Diaries*)
A Turn in the Road

Cedar Cove

16 Lighthouse Road
204 Rosewood Lane
311 Pelican Court
44 Cranberry Point
50 Harbor Street
6 Rainier Drive
74 Seaside Avenue
8 Sandpiper Way
92 Pacific Boulevard
1022 Evergreen Place
Christmas in Cedar Cove
   (*5-B Poppy Lane* and
   A Cedar Cove Christmas)
1105 Yakima Street
1225 Christmas Tree Lane

The Dakota Series

Dakota Born
Dakota Home
Always Dakota
Buffalo Valley

The Manning Family

The Manning Sisters
   (*The Cowboy's Lady* and
   The Sheriff Takes a Wife)

The Manning Brides
   (*Marriage of Inconvenience* and
   Stand-In Wife)
The Manning Grooms
   (*Bride on the Loose* and
   Same Time, Next Year)

Christmas Books

A Gift to Last
On a Snowy Night
Home for the Holidays
Glad Tidings
Christmas Wishes
Small Town Christmas
When Christmas Comes
   (now retitled *Trading
   Christmas*)
There's Something About Christmas
Christmas Letters
The Perfect Christmas
Choir of Angels
   (*Shirley, Goodness and Mercy,
   Those Christmas Angels* and
   Where Angels Go)
Call Me Mrs. Miracle

Heart of Texas

Texas Skies
   (*Lonesome Cowboy* and
   Texas Two-Step)
Texas Nights
   (*Caroline's Child* and
   Dr. Texas)
Texas Home
   (*Nell's Cowboy* and
   Lone Star Baby)
Promise, Texas
Return to Promise

CONTENTS

LOVE 'N' MARRIAGE

One

Stephanie Coulter sauntered into the personnel office at Lockwood Industries, the largest manufacturer of airplane parts in North America, carrying a brown paper bag. Her friend Jan Michaels glanced up expectantly. "Hi. To what do I owe this unexpected pleasure?"

In response, Stephanie placed the sack on Jan's desk.

"What's that?"

Stephanie sat on the corner of her friend's desk and folded her arms. "Maureen sent books. It seems I've been allotted the privilege of delivering your romances."

"I take it Potter is still sick?"

"Right." The entire morning had been a series of frustrations for Stephanie. Her boss was out with a bad case of the flu for the third consecutive day. For the first couple of days Stephanie had been able to occupy herself with the little things an executive assistant never seemed to find the time to do. Things like clearing out the filing cabinets, updating the on-line calendar and reorganizing her desk. But by the third morning she'd run out of ideas and had ended up writing a letter to her parents, feeling guilty about doing it on company time.

"Old Stone Face is out, as well," Jan informed her.

The uncomplimentary name belonged to the executive assistant to the company's president, Jonas Lockwood. In the two years Stephanie had been working for the business, she'd never known Martha Westheimer to miss a day. For that matter, Stephanie had never even visited the older woman's domain on the top floor and doubted that she ever would. Martha guarded her territory like a polar bear protecting her cubs.

The corner of Jan's mouth twitched. "And guess who's working with Mr. Lockwood in the interim? You're going to love this."

"Who?" Stephanie mentally reviewed the list of possible candidates, coming up blank.

"Mimi Palmer."

"Who?"

"Mimi Palmer. She's been here about a month, working in the mail room, and—get this—she's Old Stone Face's niece."

"I can just imagine how that's working out."

"I haven't heard any complaints yet," Jan murmured as she opened the paper bag. "But then, it's still early." She took out the top book and shot a questioning glance in Stephanie's direction. "Are you sure you don't want to read one of these? The stories are great, and if you're looking to kill time…"

Stephanie held up both palms and shook her head adamantly. "That would look terrific, wouldn't it? Can you imagine what Potter would say if he walked in and caught me reading?"

"Take one home," Jan offered.

"No, thanks. I'm just not into romances."

From the look Jan was giving her, Stephanie could tell

that her friend wasn't pleased with her response. She knew that several of the other women at Lockwood Industries read romances, and often traded books back and forth. To be honest, she didn't see why they found the books so enjoyable, but since she hadn't read one she felt she didn't have any right to judge.

"I wish you wouldn't be so closed-minded, especially since—" Jan was interrupted when the door burst open and Mr. Lockwood himself stormed into the room like an unexpected squall. He was tall and broad-shouldered and walked with a cane, his limp more exaggerated than Stephanie could ever recall seeing it. She remembered the first time she'd seen Jonas Lockwood and the fleeting sadness she'd felt that a man so attractive had to deal with the twisted right leg that marred the perfection of his healthy, strong body. His appearance was that of a cynical, relentless male. As always, she couldn't take her eyes away from him. His dark good looks commanded her attention any time he was near.

He paused only a second while his frosty blue gaze ran over her in an emotionless inspection, dismissing her. She wasn't accustomed to anyone regarding her as though she were nothing more than a pesky piece of lint. His attitude infuriated her. She hadn't exactly been holding her breath waiting for the company president to notice her. Still, she found him intriguing, and subconsciously had expected some reaction from him once they met. He revealed nothing except irritation.

"Michaels, couldn't you find me a decent replacement for even one day?" he roared, completely ignoring Stephanie.

"Mr. Lockwood, sir." Clearing her throat, Jan got to her feet. "Sir, is there a problem?"

"I'd hardly be standing here if there wasn't," he gritted. "Why would you send me that nitwit woman in the first place?"

"Sir, Miss Westheimer recommended Miss Palmer. She told me that Mimi Palmer is highly qualified—"

"She's utterly incompetent."

He certainly didn't mince words, Stephanie mused.

"I specifically asked for a mature executive assistant. Certainly that shouldn't be such a difficult request."

"But, Mr. Lockwood…"

"Older, more mature individuals approach the office with businesslike attitudes and are far less emotional."

That had to be one of the most unfair cracks Stephanie had ever heard. She bristled involuntarily. "If you'll excuse me for interrupting, I'd like to point out that a qualified executive assistant is able to adapt to any situation. I sincerely doubt that age has anything to do with it."

His sharp eyes blazed over her face. "Who are you?"

"Stephanie Coulter."

"Miss Coulter is Mr. Potter's executive assistant."

"Do you always speak out of turn?" He eyed Stephanie with open disapproval.

"Only when the occasion calls for it."

"Can you type?"

"One hundred words a minute."

"Computer skills?"

"Of course."

"Follow me."

"But, Mr. Lockwood…" Stephanie felt like a tongue-tied idiot for having spoken out of turn.

Ignoring her, he imperiously addressed Jan. "I'm sure Ms. Coulter is willing to prove just how qualified she is. She can work for me today. What you tell Potter is no concern of mine." He turned abruptly, obviously expecting Stephanie to trot obediently after him.

Her gaze clashed with her friend's. "I guess that answers that."

Grinning, Jan pointed in the direction of the elevator. "Good luck."

Stephanie had the distinct feeling she was going to need it.

Walking briskly down the wide corridor, she arrived just as the elevator doors parted. She stepped inside, holding herself stiffly.

Jonas Lockwood moved forward and pushed the appropriate button, then stepped back. Stephanie noted that he leaned heavily on the cane. She had trouble remembering the last time she'd seen him use one. More often than not, he walked without it.

The elevator rode silently to the top floor, and the doors swished open to reveal his huge office, which occupied the entire top floor. Half of the area was taken up by an immense reception area with a circular desk in the center.

"This way," he said.

Speechless, she followed him, taking in the plush furniture in the gigantic office. The view of Minneapolis was spectacular, but she didn't dare stop to appreciate it. Mimi Palmer was sitting at the large circular desk, sniffling. A man Stephanie didn't recognize was pacing the area near the desk. He glanced up when Jonas and Stephanie approached, and frowned. He was ruggedly built and of medium height. She guessed his age to be around forty-five, perhaps a bit older.

"Jonas, I'm sure the young lady didn't mean any harm," the other man said, gesturing toward Mimi.

Jonas ignored the other man the same way he'd ignored

Stephanie only moments earlier. He stepped in front of Mimi and shot a furious glance in her direction. "She may have ruined six months of negotiations with her incompetence."

"I'm sorry, s-so sorry," Mimi said, still sniffling. "I didn't know."

"Not only does she keep an important call on hold for fifteen minutes while she makes a pot of coffee, she insults the company president by demanding to know the nature of his business, and then claims I'm not to be bothered and hangs up on him."

Mimi covered her face with her hands. "I was only trying to help."

Jonas snorted, and Mimi let out a sob.

Stephanie moved forward. "Mimi, stop crying. That's not doing anyone any good. Unless you can help here, I'd suggest you go to the ladies' room and compose yourself." She turned to Jonas. "Tell me whom to contact and I'll do whatever is necessary to smooth matters over."

"Phinney," he said, not sounding at all pacified. "Edward Phinney."

"I tried to call him back, but I couldn't find his phone number," Mimi said on her way out of the office.

Jonas Lockwood glared at Mimi's departing back.

Stephanie had a fairly good idea what might have happened. "Under pressure, she might have had trouble spelling it." Sitting at the desk, she went through the Rolodex until she located the *Ph*'s. Within seconds she located the card. "I'll return Mr. Phinney's call and explain."

"I would prefer to do it myself," he barked.

"Fine." She pulled the card free and handed it to him.

"Now, how can I help you?" She directed her question at

the middle-aged man who stood in the center of the room with his mouth hanging open.

"I'm Adam Holmes."

"Mr. Holmes," Stephanie acknowledged briskly. "As I'm sure Mr. Lockwood explained, his executive assistant is ill for the day, but I'll be happy to help."

He opened his leather briefcase. "I'm here to drop off a few papers for Jonas to read over."

Stephanie took them from his outstretched hand. "I'll see to it that he receives these as soon as he's free."

"I don't doubt that for an instant," he said with a low chuckle. "Tell Jonas to contact me at my office if he has any questions."

"I'll do that."

The phone beeped, and Stephanie reached for the receiver. "Mr. Lockwood's office," she said in a crisp, professional voice, then wrote down the message, promising that Mr. Lockwood would return the call at his earliest convenience.

While she was writing down the information, Adam Holmes raised his hand in salute and sauntered toward the elevator. She watched him go. There was a kindness to his features, and the spark in his dark blue eyes assured her that he was far from over the hill.

The phone rang twice more while she sorted through the mail. She wrote down the messages and put them in a neat stack, waiting for Jonas to be off the line so she could give them to him.

Mimi reappeared dabbing at the corner of her right eye with a tissue. "I made a mess of things, didn't I?"

"Don't worry about it." Stephanie offered the younger woman a warm, reassuring smile. "This job is just more than you're used to handling."

"I'm really not very good at this sort of thing."

"It's all taken care of, so don't worry."

"Aunt Martha said I wouldn't have any problems for one day."

"I think your aunt seems to have underestimated the demands of her position."

"I...think so, too," Mimi said. "Would it be all right if I went back to my job in the mail room? I don't think I'll be any good around here."

"That'll be fine, Mimi. I'll tell Mr. Lockwood for you."

At the mention of their employer's name, Mimi grimaced. "He's horrible."

Stephanie watched the young blonde leave, furious with Old Stone Face for having put her niece in such an impossible position. An hour later, however, Stephanie found herself agreeing with Mimi's assessment of their employer. He *was* horrible.

A couple of minutes after Mimi's departure, Jonas had called her into his office. She had taken the phone messages and the mail with her.

"Take a letter," he said, without glancing up from his huge rosewood desk.

She was too stunned by his cool, unemotional tone to react quickly enough to suit him.

"Do you plan to memorize it?" he said sarcastically.

"Of course not..." Stephanie didn't fluster easily, but already this arrogant, unreasonable man had broken through her cool manner. "If you'll excuse me a moment, I'll get a pad and pen." She hadn't used her shorthand skills in a very long while. But apparently this was the method he used with Martha and was most comfortable with, so she would adjust—just as she'd told him a good executive assistant would do.

"That's generally recommended."

No sooner had she reappeared than her employer began dictating his daily correspondence. He barely paused to breathe between letters, obviously expecting her to keep pace with him. When he'd finished, he handed her a pile of financial reports and asked her to update the computer records.

"How soon will you have the letters ready?" His expressionless blue eyes cut into her. The impatience in his gaze told her that as far as he was concerned, half the day was gone already, and there was business to be done.

"Within the hour," she replied, knowing she would have to draw on every skill she'd learned on the job to meet her own deadline.

"Good." He lowered his gaze in a gesture of dismissal, and she returned to the other office, disliking him all the more.

Her fingers fairly flew over the keys, her concentration total. Jonas interrupted her three times to ask about one thing or another, but she was determined to meet her own deadline. She would have those letters ready on time or die trying.

Precisely an hour later, smiling smugly, she placed the correspondence on his desk. She stepped back, awaiting his response. Meeting the deadline had demanded that she stretch her abilities to their limits, and she anticipated some reaction from her employer.

"Yes?" He raised his head and glared at her.

"Your letters."

"I see that. Are you expecting me to applaud your efforts?"

After all the effort she'd gone to, that was exactly what she had expected. After his derogatory remarks, she felt that her superhuman effort had shot holes in his chauvinistic view of the younger assistant's abilities, and she wanted to hear him say so.

"Listen, Miss Coulter, I'm paying you a respectable wage. I don't consider it my duty to pat you on the back when you merely do what you're paid to do. I have neither the time nor the patience to pander to your fragile ego."

Stephanie felt her face explode with color.

"If you require me to sing your praises every time you complete a task, you can leave right now. Is that understood?"

"Clearly," she managed, furious. This was a rare state for her; she thought of herself as even-tempered and easygoing. Never had she disliked any man more. He was terrible. An ogre. She pivoted sharply and marched into the reception area, so angry that she had to inhale deeply to control her irritation.

Rolling out her chair, she sat down and took a moment to regain her composure.

She hadn't been back at her desk more than fifteen minutes when the intercom beeped. For one irrational instant she toyed with the idea of ignoring him, then decided against it.

"Yes, Mr. Lockwood?" she said in her most businesslike tone.

"Take lunch, Miss Coulter. But be back here within the hour. I don't tolerate tardiness."

Stephanie sincerely doubted that this man tolerated much of anything. Everything was done at his convenience and at someone else's expense.

Grabbing her purse, she took the elevator down to the floor where Human Resources was located. Jan was at her desk, and she raised questioning eyes when Stephanie walked in the door.

"Hi, how's it going?"

Slowly shaking her head, Stephanie said, "Fine, I think." The lie was only a small one. "Is he always like this?"

"Always." Jan chuckled. "But he doesn't push anyone half as hard as he drives himself."

Stephanie wasn't entirely sure she believed that. "He gave me an hour for lunch, but I think I'm supposed to show my gratitude by returning early."

"I'll join you." Jan called a coworker to say she was taking her lunch hour, then withdrew her purse from the bottom drawer and stood.

Although Stephanie hated to admit it, she was full of questions about her surly employer, and she hoped that Jan would supply the answers. For two years she'd only seen him from a distance, and she had been fascinated. From everything she knew about Jonas Lockwood, which wasn't much, she wouldn't have expected him to be so surly. Those close to him were intensely loyal, yet she had found him rude and unreasonable.

By the time they arrived, the cafeteria was nearly deserted. Stephanie doubted that many employees took lunch this late.

They decided to share a turkey sandwich, and each ordered a bowl of vegetable-beef soup. Jan carried the orange plastic tray to a table.

Stephanie tried to come up with a way of casually introducing the subject of Jonas into their conversation without being obvious. She couldn't imagine any executive assistant, even Martha Westheimer, lasting more than a week. Finally she just jumped right in. "Why does Mr. Lockwood find young assistants so objectionable?"

"I haven't the slightest idea."

"You know—" Stephanie paused and took a bite of the

sandwich "—he'd be handsome if he didn't scowl so much of the time."

Jan answered with a faint nod. "I think he must be an unhappy man."

That much was obvious, Stephanie thought. "Why does he walk with a limp?" The problem with his leg couldn't be age-related, since she guessed that he was probably only in his mid-thirties, possibly close to forty. Figuring out his age was difficult, since he'd worn a perpetual frown all morning.

"He had an accident several years ago. Skiing, I think. I heard the story, but I can't remember the details. Not that he'd ever let anyone know, but I'm sure his leg must ache sometimes. I can tell because he usually goes on a rampage when it hurts. At least that's my theory."

From the short time she'd spent with him, Stephanie guessed that his leg must be causing him excruciating pain today. She'd noted the way he'd leaned heavily on the cane while in the elevator. Maybe there was a chance that his temperament would improve if the pain eased. But at this point she doubted it would make any difference to her feelings toward the man.

Part of the problem, she realized, was that she was keenly disappointed in him. For two years she'd been studying him from a distance. Perhaps she'd even romanticized him the way that Jan and others romanticized men in the books they read. Whatever it was that had fascinated her from afar had been shattered by the reality of what a hot-tempered, unappreciative slave driver he was.

Jan finished off her soup. "Will you stop by after work?"

"So you can hear the latest horror stories?"

"He's not so bad," Jan claimed. "Really."

"He's the most arrogant, insufferable man I've ever had the displeasure of knowing."

"Give him a day or two to mellow out."

"Never."

Finished with lunch, Stephanie deposited their tray and refilled her coffee cup to take with her to the top floor. When she arrived, the door between the two offices was closed, and she hadn't the faintest idea if Jonas Lockwood was inside or not. Setting the coffee on the desk, she read over a stack of financial reports and cost sheets he'd left on her desk, apparently wanting her to update them. Taking a sip of coffee, she turned one sheet over, her eagle eyes running down the columns of figures.

"Welcome back, Miss Coulter." The gruff male voice came from behind her. "I see that you're punctual. I approve."

She bristled. Everyone who worked with the man seemed to think he was wonderful, but that certainly wasn't the impression she had. He made her furious, and she struggled to disguise it.

"I would suggest, however, that you stop wasting time and get busy."

"Yes, sir." She tossed him an acid grin. For just an instant she thought she caught a flicker of amusement in his electric-blue eyes. But she sincerely doubted that someone as cold as Jonas Lockwood knew how to smile.

As the afternoon progressed, the one word that kept running through Stephanie's mind was *demanding*. Jonas Lockwood didn't ask, he demanded. And when he wanted something, he wanted it that instant, not so much as one minute later. He tolerated no excuses and made no allowances for ignorance. If he needed a dossier, she was expected to know what drawer it was filed in and how to get to it in the most expedient manner. And she was to deliver it to him the instant he asked. If she was a moment late, he didn't hesitate to let her know about his disapproval.

The phone seemed to ring constantly, and when she wasn't answering it, she was tending to his long list of demands.

Just when she got back to updating the financial report, the buzzer rang.

"Yes." If she didn't get this finished before the end of the day, he would certainly comment. He didn't want a mere executive assistant, he required Wonder Woman. Her low estimation of Martha Westheimer rose quite a lot.

"Bring me everything you can find on the Johnson deal."

"Right away." She moved to the cabinet and groaned as her gaze located three files, all labeled Johnson. Not taking a chance, she pulled all three and set them on his desk. She noted that he was rubbing his thigh, his hand moving up and down his leg in a stroking motion. His brow was marred by thick lines. He seemed to be in such pain that she paused, not knowing what to say or do.

He glanced up, and the steely look in his eyes grew sharper. "Haven't I given you enough to do, Miss Coulter? Or would you like a few more tasks that need to be completed before you leave tonight?"

Rather than state the obvious, she returned to her desk. Sitting at the computer, she couldn't get Jonas out of her mind. There was so much virility in his rugged, dark features, yet for all the emotion he revealed, he could have been cast in bronze. No matter what, he wasn't a man she would be able to forget.

Five o'clock rolled around, and she still had two short reports to finish. It didn't matter how much time it required, she was determined to stay until every last item he'd given her was completed.

"Hi," Jan said, stepping off the elevator at five-thirty and greeting her. "I've been waiting for you."

"Sorry." Stephanie rested her hands in her lap. "I've only got a bit more to do."

"Leave it. I'm sure Old Stone Face doesn't expect her desk to be cleared when she comes in tomorrow morning."

"It isn't what she expects, it's what Mr. Lockwood demands. I've never met anyone like him." She lowered her voice. "Everything has to be done at his convenience."

"It *is* his company."

Stephanie shook her head. "Well, listen, I'll trade you bosses any day of the week."

"Is that a fact, Miss Coulter?"

Stephanie managed to swallow a strangled breath. She turned and glared at Jonas, despising him for eavesdropping on a private conversation.

"That will be all, Miss Coulter. You may leave."

She opened her mouth to argue with him but decided she would be a fool to give up the opportunity to escape when it was presented to her. "Thank you. And may I say it was a memorable experience working for you, Mr. Lockwood."

He'd already turned and didn't even acknowledge her statement.

"However—" she raised her voice, determined that he hear her "—I'd prefer working for a more mature individual." She wondered if he even remembered his earlier derogatory comments about executive assistants. "A man over forty is far less demanding, and a thousand times more reasonable and patient."

"Stephanie..." Jan hissed in warning.

"Good day, Miss Coulter." He'd turned to look at her, and if possible, the icy front he wore like an impenetrable mask froze all the more.

"Goodbye, Mr. Lockwood." With that, she retrieved

her purse and marched out of the office, Jan following in her wake.

"Wow, what happened this afternoon?" Jan asked the minute the elevator doors closed, her eyes sparkling with curiosity.

"Nothing."

"I can tell."

"He wasn't any less objectionable after lunch than he was before. Mr. Jonas Lockwood is simply impossible to work with."

"Obviously you two didn't start off on the right foot."

"I'm a fairly patient person. I tried to work with the man. But as far as I'm concerned, there's no excuse for someone to be so rude and arrogant. He has no right to take out his bad mood on me or anyone else. There's simply no call for such behavior."

"Right." But one side of Jan's mouth twitched as though she were holding in a laugh.

"You find that amusing?"

"No, not really. I was just thinking that you could be just the woman."

"Just the woman for what?"

"For ages the female employees of Lockwood Industries have been waiting for a woman exactly like you, and for the last two years you were right here under our noses."

"What are you talking about?"

"Jonas Lockwood needs a woman with nerves of steel who can stand up to him."

"Martha must be able—"

"Not in the office."

"Then what are you talking about?"

"Someone to bring him down amongst us mortals. A few of us feel what he really needs is to fall in love."

Stephanie couldn't help herself. She snickered. "Impossible. Rocks are incapable of feeling, and that man is about as emotional as marble."

"I'm not so sure," Jan commented. "He works so hard because this business is his life. There's nothing else to fill the emptiness."

"You don't honestly believe a mere woman is capable of changing that?"

"Not just any woman, but someone special."

"Well, leave me out of it."

"You're sure?"

"Absolutely, positively, sure." Although the thought of seeing Jonas Lockwood humbled was an appealing one, Stephanie was convinced it would never happen. He was too hard. A man like that was incapable of any emotion.

"Oh, I forgot to tell you."

"Tell me what?" From the look on Jan's face, Stephanie could tell she wasn't going to like her friend's next words—and that Jan hadn't forgotten at all.

"Martha Westheimer telephoned this afternoon...."

"And?" Already Stephanie could feel the muscles between her shoulder blades tightening in anticipation.

"And she's apparently recovering."

"Good."

"But, unfortunately, not enough to return to work. It looks like you'll be working with Mr. Lockwood another day."

"Oh, no, you don't," Stephanie objected. "I'll quit before I'll work with that man for another minute."

Jan didn't speak for a moment. "In other words, you're willing to let him assume everything he said about younger assistants is true?"

Two

"Good morning, Mr. Lockwood." Stephanie looked up from her desk and smiled beguilingly. After a sleepless night, she'd decided to change her tactics. Her mother had always claimed that it was much easier to attract flies with honey than with vinegar. In working with Jonas Lockwood that first day, she'd been guilty of giving him a vinegar overdose. Today, she'd decided, she would fairly ooze with charm and drive the poor man crazy. With that thought in mind, she'd been humming happily as she'd dressed for work.

"Morning." He showed no reaction at all to her good-natured greeting.

"There's coffee, if you'd like a cup." She'd arrived an hour early to organize her desk and her day, and making coffee had been part of that.

"Please." He carried his briefcase into his office.

She realized that his limp was barely noticeable this morning. Jan's theory about his leg tying in with his disposition could well be proven within the next ten hours.

He was already seated at his desk, going through his mail, by the time she brought in his coffee. He didn't look up. "I would have thought you'd consider making coffee too menial a task for a woman in your position."

"Of course not. A good executive assistant is responsible—"

"I get the picture, Miss Coulter." He cut her off and continued to scan the mail, his concentration centering on the neat stack of letters she'd previously sorted. "I'll need you to accompany me to a luncheon meeting and take notes."

"Of course," she replied sweetly. "Are there any files I should read beforehand to acquaint myself with the subject?"

"Yes." He listed several names and businesses, but for all the notice he gave her, she could have been a marble statue decorating his office. "One last thing." For the first time he raised his eyes to hers. "Contact personnel and find out how much longer Ms. Westheimer will be out." His tone told her that day couldn't come soon enough to suit him.

It was on the tip of Stephanie's tongue to tell him that his precious "mature" executive assistant couldn't be back soon enough to suit her. "Right away." Her tone dripped honey.

The piercing blue eyes narrowed fractionally. "I think I liked you better when you weren't so subservient. However, I'm pleased that you finally realize the nature of the position."

She was so furious that she wanted to explode. Instead, she smiled until the muscles at the sides of her mouth ached with the effort. "It's my pleasure."

His eyes sharpened all the more if that was possible. "Good to know, Ms. Coulter."

It took every ounce of self-control Stephanie possessed to disguise her irritation. She'd never before had to deal with such a difficult man. But with everything that was in her, she was determined not to give in to his dislike of her.

They worked together most of the morning, dealing with the mail first. If Jonas spoke to her, it was in the form of clipped requests. They had a job to do, and there was no room for anything else. Not a smile. Not a joke. No unnecessary communication. He seemed to look at her as a necessary piece of equipment, like the computer. She was there to see to the smooth running of his business—nothing else. She hated to sound egotistical, but that puzzled her. She knew she was reasonably good-looking, and yet Jonas treated her with as much emotion as he would his briefcase. She was both amused and insulted.

In every other office where she'd been employed, she'd seen herself as part of a team. With Jonas, she was keenly aware that she was only a small spoke in a large wheel, and Jonas Lockwood was the wagon.

Once back at her desk, she took a minute to contact Jan before tackling the long list of requests Jonas had given her.

"Jan? Stephanie here. I won't be able to meet you for lunch."

"Do you want me to bring you back something?"

"No, I'm attending a meeting with Mr. Lockwood."

"Hey, that's great. He's never taken Old Stone Face with him before. You must have impressed him."

"I sincerely doubt that. I don't think a rock could make an impression on him."

"Don't be so sure," Jan said, a smile evident in her voice. "By the way, did you give any thought to what I said yesterday?"

Stephanie could only assume Jan was referring to the challenge of making Jonas Lockwood fall in love. The idea caused her to smother a small laugh. "Yes, I did. You're nuts if you even think I'd attempt anything so crazy."

"He doesn't need to be put in his place as much as to find

it. And from what I saw yesterday, you're just the woman to help him with that."

"Maybe." However, Stephanie sincerely doubted that someone as unemotional as Jonas Lockwood was capable of falling in love. Part of her wanted to rebel at the way he treated her. Rarely had a man been so indifferent toward her. With her even features, smooth ivory skin and soft golden hair, she was aware that men found her attractive. Jonas's blatant indifference was a surprise. When he looked at her, all she felt was a chill that cut straight through her bones.

"Steph? Are you there?"

"Oh, sorry, I was just thinking."

"I hope that means what I think it does. Listen, I'd like to get together with you soon. There's something we—I— want to talk over with you."

"If it has to do with you-know-who, forget it!"

Chuckling, Jan said, "I'll see you later."

"Right."

Replacing the receiver, Stephanie wheeled her chair to face the computer. She worked with only a few interruptions for the next two hours. Forty minutes before the scheduled luncheon, she read through the files Jonas had recommended in order to familiarize herself with the people she would be meeting, and tucked her tablet computer in her purse so she would be ready to take notes.

She felt mentally prepared and alert when he appeared. She stood wordlessly and followed him into the elevator. Well aware that he was a man who didn't appreciate unnecessary conversation, she kept her comments and questions to herself. She would have her answers eventually.

A limo and driver waited outside the building, and the driver held open the door for them as they approached.

She climbed inside, her fingers absently investigating the smooth leather interior of the limo. Almost immediately, Jonas opened his briefcase and took out a file.

She eyed him curiously. She might have a low opinion of him as a human being, but his knowledge and business acumen were beyond question. He was a man born to lead. In working with him these two days, she had witnessed his swift, decisive nature. When he saw something, he went after it by the most direct route. Life had no gray areas for a man of his nature—everything was either black or white, with no middle ground.

She found her gaze wandering to his hands. They were large, with blunt nails, and short wisps of dark hair curled out from the French cuffs of his shirt. He could be gentle— his hands told her as much. The thought of his large hands stroking her smooth skin did funny things to her breathing. The ridiculousness of the notion made her shake her head. A funny sound slid from the back of her throat, and he glanced up momentarily.

Quickly, she turned to look out the side window, wondering what was happening to her. She didn't even like this man.

As the limo pulled up to a huge skyscraper, Jonas announced, "As I said earlier, I want you to take notes during the meeting. When we return, format them for me and give me your impressions of what happened."

Stephanie opened and closed her mouth in surprise. She was his assistant, not his analyst. But she knew better than to question the mighty Jonas Lockwood. She would do as he asked and accompany it with a smile. She would give him no reason to find fault with her.

They rode the elevator to the twenty-first floor of the Bellerman Building. The heavy doors slid open, and Jonas directed her into the meeting room at the end of the long hallway. Ten chrome chairs upholstered in moss green were strategically placed around a long rosewood table. He claimed the seat at the end and motioned for her to take the chair at his side. She was faintly surprised that he wanted her so close at hand. Since she was an assistant and only there to take notes, she had expected to sit in a corner and observe the proceedings, not find herself right in the middle of them.

Lunch was served, and what followed was a lesson in business unlike anything she had learned in her four years as an executive assistant. There was a layered feel to the meeting. She took meticulous notes of everything that was said, but several times she wondered at the underlying meaning of the words. She was impressed by the role Jonas played. He appeared to be in complete charge of the subjects that were discussed, though he rarely spoke himself, determining the course of the meeting with a nod of his head or a small movement of his hand. At first glance, anyone looking in would assume that he was bored by the entire proceedings. The man was unnerving.

At precisely two, it was over. She looked up from her tablet and flexed her tired shoulder muscles. As the other men stood, the sounds of briefcases opening and closing filled the spacious room.

"Good to see you again, Lockwood." As the man sitting on Jonas's right spoke, his gaze slid over Stephanie with a familiarity that left a bad taste in her mouth. "Leave it to you to have the most beautiful woman in Minneapolis as your executive assistant."

Jonas's cutting blue gaze shifted to rest momentarily on her. "She's only a substitute. My regular assistant is ill this week." He didn't give her a moment more of his attention as he stood and reached for his cane, leaving her to follow him.

Fuming that he had treated her so dismissively, she reached for her purse. He hadn't noticed anything about her but her secretarial skills. She was a woman, and if Jonas Lockwood didn't recognize that, it was his problem, not hers. Even so, she was offended by his comment, and she stewed about it all the way back to Lockwood Industries.

The phone rang ten minutes after she was seated back at her desk. "Mr. Lockwood's office."

"Steph, it's Jan. I talked with Martha Westheimer this afternoon, and I have good news."

"I could do with some," Stephanie grumbled.

"She'll be back Monday morning."

"And not a minute too soon."

"How'd the luncheon meeting go?"

"I… I don't know." She hadn't yet sorted through her notes deeply enough to analyze what had transpired. "It was interesting."

"See, he's already having an effect on you."

"He?" she said, teasing Jan. "I can't possibly believe you mean who I think you do."

Jan's answer was a smothered giggle. "Don't forget to meet me at five-thirty. On second thought, I'll come up for you."

"Fine. And thanks for the very *good* news. I could do with a lot more."

The remainder of the afternoon was surprisingly peaceful. Stephanie fleshed out her notes and added her observations, then printed everything out and placed it on Jonas's desk.

He was writing something, but he paused and glanced up when she didn't immediately turn and walk away. "Yes?"

"I just wanted to tell you that Ms. Westheimer will be back on Monday morning. It's been an education working with you for the past couple of days."

He leaned back in his chair and looked at her steadily. "Not a pleasure? You filled in nicely. Quite a surprise, Miss Coulter."

She supposed that this was as much of a compliment as she could expect from such a man. "Now that's something I'm pleased to hear," she said, smiling despite the effort not to.

"I'm convinced you'll do well at Lockwood Industries."

"Thank you." She felt obligated to add, "And if ever you need a replacement for Ms. Westheimer..."

"I'm hoping that won't happen again any time soon."

Not as much as I am, Stephanie mused. "Good day, Mr. Lockwood."

He'd already returned to his work. "Good evening, Miss Coulter."

Her heart was pounding by the time she met Jan. For an instant there, she could almost have liked Jonas Lockwood. Almost, but not quite.

"I take it the afternoon ran smoothly."

"Relatively so," Stephanie confirmed.

"Are you ready to talk?"

"It depends on the subject. Jonas Lockwood is off-limits."

"Unfair," Jan objected. "You know I want to discuss our infamous boss. Come on, I'll buy you a drink and loosen your tongue."

"That's what I'm worried about."

"Stop complaining. Don't check the olive in a gift drink."

"What?" Stephanie asked, laughing.

"Oh nothing, I was just trying to make a joke. You know

the old saying about checking the teeth in a gift horse? It's Friday, and it's been a long week." Folding her jacket over her arm, Jan led the way down the elevator and through the wide glass doors of the Lockwood Industries building. The Sherman Street traffic was snarled in the evening rush hour, and Jan wove her way to a small lounge a couple of blocks from the building.

Three women waved when they entered. Stephanie recognized one, but the other two were strangers.

"Hi, everyone. This is Stephanie."

"Hi." Stephanie raised her hand in greeting.

"Meet Barbara and Toni," Jan continued. "You know Maureen." She sat down and looked at the others. "Well, what do you think, ladies?"

"She's great."

"Perfect."

"Exactly what we want."

Taking a chair, Stephanie glanced around the small group, shaking her head in confusion. "What are you guys talking about?"

"You!" All four spoke at once.

"Does this have something to do with Jonas Lockwood?" Already she didn't like the sound of this.

"You didn't tell her?" Toni, a brunette, asked Jan.

"I think we'd better order her a drink first."

Still shaking her head, Stephanie glanced from one expectant face to the other. Barbara had to be over forty, Toni in her mid-thirties, Maureen younger, and Jan, Stephanie guessed, was near her own age of twenty-four.

The waitress returned with five glasses of sparkling wine.

"Now, what's this all about?" Stephanie asked, growing more curious by the minute.

"I think we should start at the beginning," Jan suggested.

"Please," Stephanie murmured.

"You see, we all read romances. We're hooked on them. They're wonderful."

"Right. And Jonas Lockwood makes *the* perfect hero, don't you think?" Barbara added.

"Pardon?" To Stephanie's way of thinking, he made *the* perfect block of ice.

"Haven't you noticed his chiseled leanness?"

"And those craggy male features?"

"I suppose," Stephanie muttered, growing more confused by the minute. To ease some of the dryness in her throat, she took a long swallow of her wine. It was surprisingly refreshing.

"He's got that cute little cleft in his chin."

Now that was something Stephanie hadn't noticed.

"The four of us have decided that Mr. Lockwood is really an unhappy man," Maureen, who was a redhead, continued. "His life is empty."

"He needs a woman to love, and who will love him," Barbara said.

"That's an interesting theory," Stephanie said, reaching for the wine for a second time. She had to watch how much she consumed, or the four of them would soon be making sense.

"It's obvious that none of us can be his true love," Toni added.

"What about you, Jan?" Stephanie pointed her drink in her friend's direction.

"Sorry, but you know I'm in a serious relationship. I'm expecting Jim to propose within the next year."

"Only Jim doesn't know it yet," Maureen piped in. Everyone laughed.

"But what has all this got to do with me?" Stephanie had to ask the question, even though she was sure she already knew the answer.

"You're perfect for him—just the type of woman he needs."

"The quintessential heroine. Attractive and bright."

"Spunky," Jan tossed in.

"I can't believe what I'm hearing," Stephanie protested. "I don't even like the man."

"That's even better. The heroines in the novels seldom do, either. Not at first, anyway."

"I think you ladies are confusing fantasy with reality."

"Of course we are. That's the fun of it. We're all incurable romantics, and when we see a romance in the making it's simply part of our nature to want to step in and help things along."

"We've even thought about writing one," Toni informed her.

"But why me?"

"You're perfect for Mr. Lockwood, in addition to being exceptionally attractive."

"Thanks, but…"

"And you don't seem to lord it over those of us who aren't," Barbara murmured.

"But that doesn't explain why you chose me to weave your plot around."

"Mr. Lockwood likes you."

"Oh, I hardly think—"

"All right, he respects you. We all noticed that this afternoon when you left for the meeting. He wouldn't take you along if he didn't value your opinion."

Stephanie shook her head wildly. "Do you know what he said? A man commented on what an attractive executive assistant he had, and your hero Lockwood told him I was only a substitute, as though he'd had to scrape the bottom of the barrel to come up with me." Finding the situation unbelievably hysterical in retrospect, she giggled. It took her a moment to notice that the other four were strangely quiet.

"What do you think, Maureen?" Jan asked.

"I'd say he's definitely noticed her. He's fighting it already."

"Oh, come on. You've blown this all out of proportion."

"I don't think so." Jan reached for her purse, and withdrew a copy of Stephanie's employment application. "I did a bit of checking. You had two employers in the two years before you came to us. Right?"

"Right." Stephanie's hand tightened around her wineglass as she shifted uncomfortably.

"Why?"

"Well." She paused to clear her throat. "I've had some problems with the men I've worked with."

"What kind of problems?"

"You know." Embarrassed, she waved her hand dismissively.

"Men making advances?" Toni suggested.

"They all seemed to think I must be interested in off-duty activities, if you catch my drift."

"We do," Jan said. "Stephanie, there are laws against such behavior."

"I know, and I probably could have filed a lawsuit but it was easier to look for another job and avoid the hassle." She felt bad about that, but at the time it had seemed the more practical solution.

"It's always hard to know how to handle something like that," Jan said giving her shoulder a squeeze.

"I did make sure my replacement understood the reason I was leaving."

"Good move," Maureen said.

"Yes, she's heroine material, all right," Toni added with a nod.

Unable to hold back a laugh, Stephanie said, "You ladies don't honestly believe all this, do you?"

"You bet we do," all four concurred.

"But why does it matter to you if Jonas Lockwood is married or not? Maybe he's utterly content being single. Marriage isn't for everyone."

Jan answered first. "As I explained, we're all incurable romantics. We've worked for Mr. Lockwood a lot longer than you. He needs a wife, only he doesn't realize it. But we're doing this for selfish reasons, too. It would help the situation at work for everyone if Mr. Lockwood had a family of his own."

"Family?" Stephanie nearly choked on her wine. "First you have me falling in love with him, then we get married, and now I'm bearing his children." This conversation was going from the ridiculous to the even more ridiculous. To be honest, she was half tempted to practice her feminine wiles on Jonas Lockwood just for the pleasure of seeing if he would crumble at her feet. Then she would have the ultimate pleasure of snubbing him and walking away. But this clearly wasn't what Jan and friends had in mind.

"You see," Barbara inserted, "we feel that Mr. Lockwood would be more agreeable to certain employee benefits if he walked in our shoes for a while."

Dumbfounded, Stephanie shook her head. These women were actually serious. "I think a union would be the more appropriate way to deal with this."

"There isn't one. So we're creating our own—of sorts."

Stephanie still didn't understand. "What kind of benefits?"

"More lenient rules regarding maternity leave."

"Extra days off at Christmas."

"Increased health benefits to include family members."

Lifting the blond curls off her forehead, Stephanie looked around the table at the four intense faces studying her. "You're really serious, aren't you?"

"Completely."

"Utterly."

"We mean business."

"Indeed we do." Jan raised her hand and called for the waitress, ordering another round.

"I'm really sorry, but despite what you might think I'm not heroine material." The waitress delivered another round of sparkling wine, and Stephanie waited until the woman had left before going on. "A man like Mr. Lockwood needs a woman who's far less opinionated than I am. In two days, we barely said a civil word to each other."

"The woman who loves him will need a strong personality."

"She'll need more than that." Stephanie couldn't imagine any woman capable of tearing down Jonas's icy facade. He was too hard, too cold, too unapproachable.

"Say, I didn't know you spoke French." Jan glanced up from Stephanie's application, her eyes growing larger by the minute.

"My grandmother was French. She insisted I learn."

"Then you're bilingual?"

"Right."

All four women paused, regarding Stephanie as though she had suddenly turned into an alien from outer space. "Hey, why are you all looking at me like that?"

"No reason." Barbara lowered her head, apparently finding her drink overwhelmingly interesting.

"So your grandmother was French?" Toni asked.

"Yes, I just said so. And why do I have the feeling that you four have something dangerous up your sleeves?" She glanced from one grinning face to the other. "What does the fact that I speak French have to do with anything?"

"You'll see."

"I don't like the sound of this," Stephanie muttered.

"Be honest. What do you think of our idea?" Barbara asked bravely.

"You mean about finding a woman for Mr. Lockwood?"

The others nodded, watching her expectantly.

"Great. As long as that woman isn't me."

"I think it's fate," Jan said, ignoring Stephanie's words. "This couldn't be turning out any better than if we'd planned it."

"Planned what?"

"You'll see," all four echoed.

Monday morning Stephanie arrived for work early. She'd spent a peaceful weekend planting a small herb garden in narrow redwood planters and placing them on her patio. Living in a small apartment didn't leave much room for her to practice her gardening skills. The year before she'd rented a garden space through the parks department. This year she'd decided to try her green thumb on herbs.

Jan was at her desk when Stephanie arrived at coffee-break time. As much as possible, she had tried to blot out Friday evening's conversation with Jan and her friends. It appeared that the four had some hideous plot in mind. But she'd quickly squelched that. Even imagining Jonas Lockwood in love was enough to amuse her. It would never happen. The man had no emotions. That wasn't blood that ran through his veins—it was ink from profit-and-loss statements. He wasn't like ordinary humans.

"Oh, I'm glad you're here," Jan said.

"You are?" Already Stephanie was leery. "Ms. Westheimer's fully recovered, isn't she?"

"Yes, she's here. At least, I assume she is. I haven't heard any rumblings from above."

Stephanie felt a sense of relief. The less she saw of Mr. Jonas Lockwood, the better.

"I've made arrangements with your boss for you to be gone next week."

"Arrangements?" Stephanie repeated surprised. "What are you talking about?"

"Do you want to get together at lunch?" Jan asked, ignoring Stephanie's question.

"Jan, what's going on?"

"You'll see."

"Jan!"

"I'll talk to you later." She glanced at her watch. "I'd tell you, honest, but I can't...yet."

Disgruntled, Stephanie returned to her office, pausing on the way to question Maureen, who gave her a look of pure innocence. Stephanie didn't know what her friends had up their sleeves, but she was certain it involved Jonas Lockwood.

The remainder of the morning ran so smoothly that Stephanie was surprised to note that it was lunchtime. Truthfully, working for anyone other than Jonas Lockwood was a breeze. Mr. Potter, her grandfatherly boss, was patient and undemanding, a pleasant change from the man who'd barked orders at her as though she were a robot. And Mr. Potter was free with his praise and approval of her efforts. Getting a compliment from Jonas Lockwood was like pulling teeth.

She had lunch with Jan, Maureen and the two others she'd met Friday evening, so there wasn't an opportunity to corner Jan and ask her to explain her comment about arranging for her to be out of the office the following week.

The group was fun-loving, quick-witted and personable. Stephanie was grateful when no mention of their infamous employer entered the conversation. In fact, she was more than grateful. Despite all her intentions to the contrary, she had been thinking a lot about Jonas.

Later that afternoon, on her way back up to her office after delivering a file to accounting, she unexpectedly ran into the big boss himself. She was waiting for the elevator, checking her makeup with a small hand mirror, when the doors opened and she found herself eye to eye with him.

"Good day, Miss Coulter."

Caught entirely by surprise, she didn't even lower the tube of lipstick, her mouth open as she prepared to glide the color across her bottom lip. She was too stunned to move.

"Are you or are you not taking the elevator?"

"Oh, yes," she mumbled, hurrying in next to him. She quickly stuck her mirror and lipstick inside her purse, pressing her lips together to even out the pale summer-rose color.

He placed both hands on his cane. "And how are you doing, Miss Coulter?"

"Exceptionally well. Everyone I've worked with *lately* has appreciated my efforts."

"Perhaps your skills have improved."

She felt like kicking the cane out of his hands. The man was unbearable. "As you suggest," she said with a false sweetness in her voice, "things have definitely improved."

His mouth quirked upward in something resembling a

smile. "I admit to missing your quick wit. Perhaps we'll have the opportunity to exchange insults again sometime soon."

A joke from Jonas Lockwood—all right, an almost joke. She couldn't believe it.

"Don't count on it." The elevator came to a halt at her floor, and the door swooshed open. As she stepped out she said, "Perhaps in another lifetime, Mr. Lockwood."

"You disappoint me, Miss Coulter. I was looking forward to next week." The doors glided shut.

Next week.

She'd let Jan get away without explaining earlier, but she wasn't waiting another minute. She hurried to Jan's office.

"All right, explain yourself," she demanded, placing both hands on the edge of her friend's desk.

"About what?" Jan was the picture of innocence, which was a sure sign she was up to something.

"I just saw Mr. Lockwood, and he said something about next week. I don't like the sound of this."

"Oh, I guess I forgot to tell you, didn't I?"

"Tell me now!" Stephanie straightened, a strange sensation, akin to dread, shooting up and down her spine.

"Mr. Lockwood's traveling to Paris on business."

Crossing her arms, Stephanie glared at Jan suspiciously. "That's nice."

"The interesting part is that he would like a bilingual assistant to accompany him."

Knowing what was coming, Stephanie tightened her jaw until her teeth ached. "You can't possibly mean…"

"When Mr. Lockwood first approached Human Resources about it, we couldn't think of anyone appropriate, but since that time I've gone through our personnel records, and when I found your application…"

"Jan, I refuse to go. The man and I don't get along."

"When I mentioned you to Mr. Lockwood, he was delighted."

"I'll just bet."

"Your flight leaves Sunday night."

Three

The jet tilted its wings to the right, slowly beginning its descent. Stephanie stared out the small window, fascinated by the breathtaking view of the River Seine far below. Her heart pounded with excitement. Paris. How her grandmother would have envied her. As a young French war bride, Stephanie's grandmother had often longed to revisit the charming French city. Now Stephanie would see it for her.

"If you would tear your gaze from the window for a minute, Miss Coulter, we could get some work done," Jonas Lockwood stated sarcastically.

"Of course." Instantly she was all business, reaching for a pad. This was obviously the only level on which she could communicate with him. Not once since they'd taken off from Minneapolis-St. Paul International Airport had her employer glanced at the spectacular scenery. No doubt he would have considered it a waste of valuable time.

"I've reserved us a three-bedroom suite at the Château Frontenac," he informed her coolly.

She silently repeated the name of the hotel. "It sounds lovely."

He glanced down at the report in his lap and shrugged one muscular shoulder. "I suppose."

It was all Stephanie could do not to shout at him to open his eyes and look at the beauty of the world that surrounded him. At times like these she wanted to shake him. The mere thought of anyone—much less her—even touching him produced an involuntary smile. He would hate being touched.

She looked across the aisle at Adam Holmes, who had accompanied them. His role in Jonas's plans had been left to conjecture, but she suspected that he was an attorney.

"It looks like we're in for pleasant weather," he said conversationally. His dark eyes narrowed fractionally as he gazed out at the ground below. For most of the trip he had carried the conversation. He was both friendly and articulate, a blatant contrast to the solemn, serious Jonas.

A little surprised, Stephanie glanced up, unsure whether Adam was addressing his comment to her. Jonas didn't respond. Of course, she would have been shocked to learn that any type of weather interested her employer.

"I would guess early summer is the perfect time to visit Paris." In reality, she wondered how much of the city she had any chance of seeing. Her one hope was that she would be able to visit the Champs de Mars and view the Eiffel Tower, built for the 1889 World's Fair. High on her list were the twelfth-century cathedral of Notre Dame, and the Arc de Triomphe. She'd spent a year in France as an exchange student in high school, but apart from a quick trip through the airport, she hadn't seen anything of Paris.

The plane began its final descent, and she clicked her seat belt into place. Casually Jonas put away his papers and closed his briefcase. As soon as they landed they would be going through customs and she would be expected to step into her role as translator. Although she spoke fluent French, it had been a while since she'd had the opportunity to use it, and she hoped she was up to the task.

To her surprise, everything went without a hitch at customs, and her confidence grew. They moved from the terminal to the waiting limo with only minimal delay.

The driver held the door open, and she climbed inside the luxurious automobile. Jonas and Adam followed her, and they were soon on their way.

At the hotel they were escorted to their rooms and their luggage was delivered promptly. While she unpacked her clothes, she heard Jonas and Adam discussing the project. Apparently they would be meeting a powerful financier in the hope of obtaining financial backing for a current project. Lockwood Industries, the largest North American manufacturer of airplane parts, was apparently ready to buy out their French counterpart. If the deal progressed as expected, Lockwood Industries would become the largest such manufacturer in the world. There also seemed to be the possibility of Lockwood establishing branches in several European cities.

"Miss Coulter."

"Yes." Responding instantly to the command in Jonas's voice, Stephanie stepped into the doorway of her room.

"We have a lunch reservation downstairs in ten minutes."

"I'll be ready. I just need a few minutes to freshen up."

"Of course."

He was already turning away, and she doubted that he'd even heard her. He'd often given her that impression. Returning to her assigned room, she glanced in the mirror. Several tendrils of soft blond hair had escaped from the coil at the base of her neck. Rather than tuck them back, she pulled out the pins and reached for her brush. Unbound, her hair curled naturally to her shoulders. Normally when she was working she preferred to keep her hair away from her face. It gave her a businesslike look, and she felt that was particularly important around Jonas.

"Miss Coulter."

Jonas again.

Her brush forgotten in her hand, she moved into the large living room, where Jonas and Adam were waiting.

"Yes?"

For a moment the room went still as Jonas caught her gaze. Their eyes met and locked. His narrowed, and an expression of surprise and bewilderment flickered across his face. Something showed in his eyes that she couldn't define—certainly not admiration, perhaps astonishment, even shock. His mouth parted slightly, as if he wanted to speak, then instantly returned to a stern line.

Adam's face broke into a spontaneous smile as his lingering gaze swept her appreciatively from head to toe. "I don't think I realized earlier how attractive your assistant is, Jonas."

The muscles in Jonas's jaw looked as though they were frozen solid. He ran an impatient hand through his hair and turned to reach for his briefcase.

"You wanted me?" It was hard to believe that breathless voice was hers. She sounded as though she'd been running a marathon. She couldn't be attracted to Jonas. He was the last person in the world she wanted to have any romantic feelings for. Normally she was a levelheaded person, not the sort who let her emotions carry her away. Not that Jonas Lockwood was worthy of a moment's consideration. He was arrogant and…

"We'll meet you downstairs." He interrupted her thoughts, his voice cool and unemotional.

"I'll be there in a minute."

"Take your time," he said dismissively, clearly doing his best to avoid her.

She turned to go back into her room, but not before she caught the look Adam directed at them both, disbelief etched clearly on his smooth, handsome features.

After closing the door, Stephanie sank onto the edge of her bed. There must be some virus in the air for her to be thinking this way about Jonas Lockwood. For a moment she'd actually found him overwhelmingly, unabashedly appealing. She'd been genuinely physically attracted to him. She shook her head at the wonder of it. She was playing right into Jan's and the other women's hands.

The amazing thing was that Jonas had noticed her, as well—really noticed her. At least when Adam had complimented her, Jason hadn't told him that she was "only a substitute." A small smile tugged at the corners of her mouth. Maybe, just maybe, Jonas Lockwood didn't have a heart of ice, after all. Perhaps under that glacial exterior there was a warm, loving man. The thought was so incongruous with the mental picture she held of him that she shook her head to dispel the image. Without wasting further time inventing nonsensical fantasies about her employer, she finished styling her hair and changed clothes, then went downstairs to the restaurant.

Lunch passed without incident, as did the first series of meetings.

In bed that evening, Stephanie's thoughts spun. They'd called it an early night, but she wasn't able to sleep. The most beautiful city in the world lay at her doorstep, and she would be tied up in meetings for the entire visit. Sitting up, she wiped a hand across her face. She was undecided. They would only be in Paris another two nights. If this was to be her only opportunity, she was going to take it.

Dressing silently, she slipped the hotel key into her purse and carefully tiptoed across the carpet, letting herself out.

Since their hotel was in an older section of the city, she caught a taxi and instructed the friendly driver to take her to several points of interest. He escorted her through Les Halles, the mammoth central food market, which had once been located on the north of the river, but had been moved to Rungis, in the suburbs of Paris.

From there he drove her past Notre Dame cathedral, pointing out landmarks as he went. But she barely heard him. Her thoughts were focused on that moment in the hotel room earlier in the afternoon when Jonas had looked at her for perhaps the first time. Her hands grew clammy just thinking about it. At the time she'd been flippant. Now she was profoundly affected. Just remembering it caused her pulse to react. In those brief seconds he had seen her as a woman, and, just as importantly, she'd viewed him as a man. She was intensely attracted to him and had been for weeks, she just hadn't been ready to admit it.

The driver, chatting easily in French, pointed out the sights, but instead of seeing the magnificent beauty in the buildings that surrounded her, Stephanie's thoughts revolved around Jonas. She wondered about what he'd been like as a child, and what pain had snuffed out the joy in his life.

Straightening, she shook her head and said to him in French, "Please take me back to the hotel."

The driver gave her a funny look. *"Oui."*

Stephanie had hoped to see the Louvre, but it wouldn't have been open at this time of night, anyway. As it was, she didn't seem to be able to view any of the sights without including Jonas in what she saw. It was useless to pretend otherwise.

Back at the hotel, she gave the driver a generous tip and thanked him. The lobby was quiet, and the soft strains of someone playing the piano sounded in the distance. She briefly toyed with the idea of stopping in the lounge for a nightcap but quickly rejected the idea. She needed to get some sleep.

Being extra-cautious not to make any unnecessary noise, she silently slipped into the suite. She was halfway across the living room when a harsh voice ripped into her.

"Miss Coulter, I didn't bring you to Paris so you could sneak out in the middle of the night."

She reacted with a startled gasp, her hand flying to her breast.

"Just who were you meeting? Some young lover?" The words were spoken with a cutting edge, mocking and bitter.

"No. Of course not." She could barely make out Jonas's form in the shadows. He sat facing her, but his features were hidden by the darkness.

"Surely you don't expect me to believe that. I understand you spent a year in France. Undoubtedly you met several young men."

The words to tell him what to do with his nasty suspicions burned on the tip of her tongue. Instead, she shook her head and replied softly, "I don't know anyone in Paris. I couldn't sleep. It may sound foolish, but I decided that I might not get the opportunity to see the sights, so I—"

"You don't honestly expect me to believe you were out sightseeing?" The shadow began to move, and as her eyes adjusted to the darkness she noted that he was massaging his thigh.

Against her will, her heart constricted at the pain she knew his leg must be causing him. With everything that was in her, she yearned to ease that pain. She took a tentative step in his direction, claiming the chair across from him. In low, soft tones, she told him about the historic buildings she'd visited and the chatty taxicab driver who had given her a private tour of the older sections of Paris, along with a colorful account of his own ancestry.

She watched as the cynical quirk of his mouth gradually relaxed. "It's really an exceptionally lovely city," she finished.

"Holmes is attracted to you."

"Adam?" Stephanie couldn't believe what she was hearing and quickly dismissed the suggestion. "I'm sure you're mistaken."

"Do you find it so surprising?"

"Yes...n-no."

"It's only natural that he thinks you're lovely. As you said, you're in one of the most beautiful cities in the world. It's springtime. You're single, Holmes is single. What's there to discourage a little romance?"

"I hardly know the man."

"Does it matter?"

"Of course it does." She sighed and dropped her gaze, sorry now that she'd made the effort to turn aside angry words and be friendly. The man was impossible.

"You could do worse. Adam Holmes is a bright attorney with a secure future."

"If I were buying stock in the man, I might be interested. But we're talking about *people* here. I find him friendly and knowledgeable, but I have no romantic interest in him. I'm simply not attracted to him."

"Who *does* attract you?"

Stephanie swallowed uncomfortably as she battled back the instinctive response. Jonas attracted her. She was still shocked by the realization, but she wasn't willing to hand him that weapon. "I don't believe my private life is any of your affair," she informed him crisply.

"So there *is* someone." Impatience surged through his clipped response.

"I didn't say that." Bounding to her feet, she stalked over to the window and hugged her waist. "There's no use even trying to talk to you, is there?" Her voice revealed her distress. "We seem incapable of maintaining even a polite conversation."

"Does that disappoint you?"

She could feel his gaze as it ran over her; it seemed to caress her with its intensity—and to demand an answer.

"Yes," she admitted gently. "Very much. I feel there's so much locked up inside you that I don't understand."

"I'm not a puzzle waiting to be solved."

"In some ways you are."

He rubbed a hand over his face. "I can't see that this conversation will get us anywhere."

She couldn't, either. She was tired, and he was unreasonable and in pain. The best thing she could do now would be to leave the conversation for a more appropriate time. "Good night, Mr. Lockwood." She didn't wait for his acknowledgement before she headed for her room.

"Good night, Stephanie."

It wasn't until she had changed into her cotton pajamas that she realized that for the first time since they'd met, he'd used her first name. No longer was she a robot who responded to his clipped demands. Somehow, in some way, she had become a woman of flesh and blood. The realization was enough to send her spirits soaring. Hugging the extra pillow beside her, she drifted into a sound sleep, content with her world.

"Good morning," Adam greeted her early the following morning. From the looks of the table, he and Jonas had already been working for hours.

"Morning." She walked across the room and poured steaming coffee into a dainty cup, then held it to her mouth with both hands.

"I trust you slept well, Miss Coulter," Jonas said.

So they were back to that. "Thank you, *Mr. Lockwood*, I slept very well."

He glanced up momentarily, and she recognized the glint of amusement in his eyes. A brief smile moved across his mouth.

"Would you like a croissant?" Adam asked, preparing to lift the flaky pastry onto a china plate with a pair of metal tongs.

"No, thanks." Actually, she might have liked one, but she was afraid that something as simple as accepting a breakfast pastry would encourage him. She hadn't noticed it the day before, but the eagerness glinting in his gaze revealed the truth of Jonas's statement. Adam Holmes really was interested in her.

As it turned out, it was just as well that she hadn't accepted the croissant, because she barely had time to down the coffee before Jonas stood. "We have a lot of ground to cover today."

He limped to the door without his cane. She knew that he preferred not to use it and did so only when absolutely necessary. His leg had kept him up last night and would soon be aching again without the cane.

"In that case," she said, "you'll want your cane."

Jonas expelled his breath. "Miss Coulter, I require an executive assistant and a translator, not a mother."

"Your leg was bothering you yesterday." She knew she was on dangerously thin ice. Not once had she ever mentioned his limp before. "I see no reason to aggravate it further."

He didn't answer her, but she noted triumphantly that he reached for his cane before they left the suite.

What followed was a day she was not likely to forget. The first meeting that morning was a marathon exchange of proposals and counterproposals. They adjourned briefly for lunch, then were at it again before she had the opportunity to take more than a bite or two of her salad.

The afternoon was just as jam-packed. No sooner had she finished translating one statement than Jonas gave her another. Much of the conversation went completely over her head, but in the weeks since meeting him, she had gained valuable insight into her employer. She could see that he was tense, although she was certain no one else noticed it. For the meeting, he almost seemed to wear a mask that revealed none of his feelings or emotions. This, like most of his life, was business, with no room for fun and games. If she had accepted what she saw on the surface, he would have frozen her out completely. But she'd seen a rare glimpse of the man inside, and she'd been intrigued.

Though the afternoon session was both complicated and challenging, she noticed that he was cool to the point of being aloof, as though what they were discussing was of little consequence to him. She suspected that, like a gambler, he placed his money on the line for the pleasure of tossing the dice. He enjoyed the thrill, the excitement, and had poured his whole life into pursuing it.

Throughout the afternoon Adam drifted in and out of the room, returning with one document and then another.

It was early evening when the meeting came to an end. Jonas and his French counterpart stood and shook hands.

"We're breaking until morning," Jonas informed Adam outside the conference-room door. "Did you locate that report on the export tax I asked about earlier?"

"I have it with me," Adam responded, tapping the side of his briefcase.

"I'll want to look it over tonight."

For her part, Stephanie was exhausted and hungry. After no breakfast and virtually no lunch, her stomach was protesting strenuously.

Once they were back in the suite, she immediately slipped off her shoes. They were new, and pinched her heels. Sitting on the sofa, she crossed her legs and rubbed the tender portion of one foot, suspecting a blister.

On the other side of the room Jonas was drilling Adam about one thing or another. She couldn't have cared less. Then she noticed his gaze resting on her slender legs. When he realized she'd caught the direction of his glance, he turned his head. He looked tired, worn down. She wanted to suggest that he take this evening to rest, but after her comment that morning about his cane, she realized she would be pressing her luck. She was too weary to fight with him now.

"I'll get that statement for you as quickly as possible," Adam said, rising to his feet.

"Thanks."

The room seemed oddly quiet after Adam left.

"Miss Coulter, order a car."

She couldn't believe it. The man was a slave driver. Reaching for the phone, she contacted the front desk and asked that they have a car available. "How soon do you want it?" she asked, holding the receiver to her breast.

"Immediately."

She glared angrily at him. Not everyone was accustomed to his pace. She was tired, hungry and not in the most congenial mood.

"Will you be requiring my services?" She didn't bother to hide the resentment in her voice.

"Naturally, I'll need you to translate for me."

"Would you mind if I ate something first?" she asked as she reached for her shoes.

"Yes, I would."

Her gaze narrowed with frustration. "What is it with you? Maybe you can work all hours of the night and day, but others have limitations."

His mouth thinned, revealing his irritation; he picked up his cane. "Then stay here."

As much as she would have liked to do exactly that, she knew she couldn't. Reluctantly she followed him out of the suite. "Miss Coulter—" she mimicked his low voice sarcastically "—you've done a wonderful job today. Let me express my deepest appreciation. You deserve a break." She paused to eye him. The stone mask was locked tightly in place. "Why, thank you, Mr. Lockwood. Everyone needs a few words of encouragement now and then, and you seem to know just when I need them most. It's been a long grueling day, but those few words of appreciation seem to have made everything worthwhile."

"Are you through, Miss Coulter?" he asked sharply as they stepped into the elevator.

"Quite through." Her back was stiff and straight as they descended. She was tired, her feet ached, and she was hungry. For the last eleven hours she'd been at his beck and call. What more could he possibly expect from her now?

The driver was waiting outside the hotel when they approached. He held open the door, and she climbed inside. Jonas paused to speak to the driver, but what he said and whether the driver understood him didn't concern her at the moment. If he needed her to translate, he would tell her. "Telling" was something Jonas had no problem doing.

They'd gone only a few blocks when the driver pulled to the curb and parked. They were in front of an elegant restaurant. Tiny tables were set outside the door, and white-coated waiters with red cloths draped over their forearms stood in attendance, watching for the smallest hint of a request. Stephanie blinked twice. Exhausted and dispirited, she didn't know if she could bear another meeting now. And at a restaurant! Her stomach would growl through the entire affair.

"Are you coming, Miss Coulter?" Jonas said, climbing out of the car. "I did hear you say you were hungry, right?"

Stunned, she didn't move. "We're having dinner here?"

"Yes. That is, unless you have any objections?" He suddenly looked bored with the entire process.

"No… I'm starved."

"I believe you've already stated as much. Luckily I have a reservation—unless you'd prefer eating in the car?"

"I'm coming." This was almost too good to be true. Eagerly she made her way onto the pavement. As they walked into the plush interior, her gaze fell longingly on an empty table outside on the sidewalk.

Jonas surprised her by asking, "Would you prefer to dine outside?"

"Yes, I'd like that."

Jonas spoke to the maître d', who led them to the table

and politely held out Stephanie's chair for her, then handed each of them a menu. She was so hungry that she quickly scanned the contents. "Oh, I do love vichyssoise," she said aloud, biting her lower lip.

Before she knew what was happening Jonas had attracted the waiter's attention. "A bowl of vichyssoise for the lady."

"Jonas," she said, shocked. "Why did you do that?"

"From the way you were acting, I was afraid you were about to keel over from hunger."

"I am," she admitted, her gaze going up one side of the menu and down the other. "Everything looks wonderful."

"What would you like?"

"I can't decide between a huge spinach salad or a whole chicken."

The waiter returned, hands behind his back as he inquired courteously if they would like to place their orders. Jonas asked for the bouillabaisse, and raised questioning eyes to Stephanie.

"I'll have one of those," she said, pointing to the meal another waiter was delivering and indicating a huge salad that was piled high with fresh pink shrimp. "And one of those." Her gaze flew to the dessert cart, which was laden with a variety of scrumptious, calorie-laden goodies.

"Will that be all?" Jonas asked wryly.

"Oh, heavens, yes." She felt guilty enough already. "This is what you get for depriving me of nourishment," she joked. "I'm a grouch when I get too hungry."

"I hadn't noticed." One side of his mouth lifted in an aloofly mocking smile.

"I guess I owe you an apology for what I said earlier."

Her soup arrived, and she eagerly dipped her spoon into

it and tasted, closing her eyes at the heavenly flavor. "Oh, this is absolutely wonderful. Thank you, Jonas."

His eyes smiled into hers. "You're quite welcome."

"I really am sorry."

"My dear Stephanie, I've stopped counting the times you've let your mouth outdistance your mind."

She was so shocked that she stopped with her spoon poised halfway between the bowl and her mouth. Jonas joking? Jonas calling her *dear?* It was almost more than her numbed mind could assimilate.

No sooner had she finished the soup than her salad was delivered. The top was thick with shrimp. "I think I've died and gone to heaven."

"Then you're relatively easy to please. It was my understanding that women were more interested in jewels and other luxury items."

She eagerly stabbed her fork into a shrimp. "Personally, I prefer shrimp and lobster." She smiled. "I haven't eaten this well in months."

Jonas arched his eyebrows expressively. "So a man could win you over with cheesecake."

"Tonight he could." Unable to wait any longer, she ate the fat shrimp and closed her eyes at the scrumptious flavor. When she opened them, she discovered that Jonas was watching her. Tiny laugh lines fanned out from his eyes.

He was so handsome that she couldn't take her eyes from him. "Are you wooing me?" It seemed overwhelmingly important that she know where she stood with him.

"I will admit that you're the cheapest date I've had in a long time."

"Is this a date?"

"Think of it more as a token of appreciation for a job well done."

She pressed her hand dramatically to her forehead, and her bright blue eyes grew round with feigned shock. "Do my ears deceive me? Jonas Lockwood of Lockwood Industries has deigned to pay an employee a compliment? An employee who's a relatively young woman, at that—admittedly one with minor faults."

"I won't disagree with you there."

Despite herself, Stephanie laughed. "No, I don't suppose you will."

"You did very well today."

"Thank you." She felt inexplicably pleased.

"Where did you learn to speak French?"

He seemed eager to keep the conversation going, and she was just as eager to comply. For the first time since meeting the man, she didn't feel on guard around him.

"My grandmother was a French war bride, and she taught my mother the language as a child. Later, Mom majored in French at the University of Washington. I've been bilingual almost from the day I was born."

"You're from Washington State?"

"Colville. Ever hear of it?"

"I can't say that I have."

"Don't worry, most people haven't."

"I imagine you were the town's beauty queen."

"Not me. In fact, I was a tall, skinny kid with buckteeth and knobby knees most of my life. It wasn't until I was in my late teens and the braces came off that the boys started to notice me."

"I have trouble believing that."

"It's true." She reached for her purse, and took out her cell phone. "I carry this picture because people don't believe me." She brought it up and was about to show him when they were interrupted by the waiter, who was bringing a bottle of wine.

Jonas looked up and spoke briefly with the other man.

Stephanie's blue eyes widened with astonishment and surprise. The waiter nodded and stepped away.

"You speak French."

"Only a little."

"But very well."

"Thank you." He dipped his head, accepting her compliment.

A clenching sensation attacked her stomach. "You didn't really need me here at all, did you?"

Four

"I brought you along as a translator," Jonas answered simply.

Stephanie lowered her fork to her plate. Her thoughts were churning like water left to boil too long, bubbling and spitting out scalding suggestions she would have preferred to keep in her subconscious. He'd tricked her into accompanying him on this trip. The meal that had tasted like ambrosia only seconds before felt like a concrete block in the pit of her stomach. "You speak fluent French."

"My French is adequate," he countered, reaching for his wineglass.

"It's as good as my own."

"My linguistic abilities are not your business."

"But I don't understand. Why…?" She couldn't understand the man. One minute he was personable and considerate, and the next he became brusque and arrogant. The transformation was made with such ease that she hardly knew how to respond to him.

"That I required a translator is all you need to know."

Rather than argue with him further, she stabbed another plump shrimp. She ate it slowly, but for all the enjoyment it gave her she might as well have been chewing on rubber. "Letting the French company we're negotiating with believe you don't speak the language is all part of your strategy, isn't it?"

"Wine?" He lifted the long-necked green bottle of pinot noir and motioned to her with it.

"Jonas? Am I right?" she asked as he filled her glass.

He cocked his head to one side and nodded. "I can see you're learning."

She ate another shrimp and discovered that some of the flavor had returned. "You devil!"

"Stephanie, business is business."

"And what is this?" The wine was excellent, and she took another sip, studying him as she tilted the narrow glass to her lips.

He stiffened. "What do you mean?"

"Our dinner. Is it business or pleasure?"

The crow's-feet at the corners of Jonas's eyes fanned out as if he were smiling, yet his mouth revealed not a trace of amusement. "A little of both, I suspect."

"Then I'm honored. I would have assumed that you'd prefer to escort a much more *mature* woman to dinner." She felt the laughter slide up her throat and suppressed it with some difficulty. "Someone far less emotional than a *younger* woman."

"I believe it was you who commented that age has little to do with maturity."

"Touché." She raised her glass in salute and sipped her wine to toast his comeback. She felt light-headed and mellow, but she wasn't sure what was to blame: Jonas, her fatigue or the excellent wine.

She couldn't believe this was happening. The two of them together, enjoying each other's company, bantering like old friends, applauding each other's skill. As little as two hours ago, she would have thought it impossible to carry on a civil conversation with the man. She imagined that Jonas was about as relaxed as he ever allowed himself to be.

"I'll admit that the pleasure part comes from the fact that I knew you wouldn't be simpering at my feet," he commented, breaking into her thoughts.

"I never simper."

"You much prefer to challenge and bully."

"Bully? Me?" She laughed a little and shook her head. "I guess maybe I do at that, but just a bit." She didn't like admitting it, but he was right. She was the oldest of three girls, and did have a tendency to take matters into her own hands. "While we're on the subject of bullies, I don't suppose you've noticed the way *you* treat people?"

"We aren't discussing me," he said dryly.

"We most certainly are." She flattened her palms on either side of her plate and shook her head. "I've never known anyone who treats people the way you do. What I can't understand is how you command such loyalty."

He arched his eyebrows expressively, and his gaze swept her with mocking thoroughness.

She ignored him and continued. "It's more than just money. You pay well, but the benefits leave a lot to be desired." She felt obligated to mention that, since it had come up the other day and, she had to admit, the point was a good one.

"Is that a fact?"

"You're often unreasonable." She knew she was pressing her luck, but the wine had emboldened her.

"Perhaps others see it that way," he admitted reluctantly. "But only when the occasion calls for it."

For all the heed he paid her comments, they could have been discussing the traffic. "And I've yet to mention your outrageous temper."

"I wasn't aware that I had a temper."

Despite the fact he didn't seem to find their conversation the least bit amusing, Stephanie continued. "But by far, the very worst of your faults is your overactive imagination."

His gaze flew to hers and narrowed. "What makes you suggest something so absurd?"

She knew she'd trapped him, and she loved having the upper hand for the first time in their short acquaintance. "You actually believed I was meeting someone last night."

"With your own mouth you admitted as much."

She nearly choked on her wine, but she recovered and challenged his gaze with her own. "I most certainly did no such thing."

"You mentioned the taxi driver—"

"That's so farfetched, I can't believe you'd stoop that low."

"Perhaps, but you seemed to have enjoyed yourself. You sounded quite impressed by the sights you'd seen."

"If you want the truth, I hardly saw a thing. I was thinking about—" She stopped herself in the nick of time from admitting that her thoughts had been filled with him.

"Yes?" Jonas prompted.

"I was preoccupied with the meeting today. I was worried about how I'd do."

"Your French is superb. You needn't have been anxious, and you know it. What *did* occupy your thoughts? Or should I say who?"

Stephanie was saved from answering by the waiter, who reappeared to take their plates. She gave him a grateful smile and finished the last of her wine before the man returned with two steaming cups of coffee and her cheesecake.

A little while later Jonas asked for the bill, paused and looked at her. "Unless you'd like something more? Another dessert, perhaps?"

"No." She shook her head for emphasis and placed her hands over her stomach. After downing half of everything on the menu, she felt badly in need of exercise.

The sun had set, and the sky was darkening in shades of pink by the time they finished the last of their coffee.

"Shall we go?"

She nodded and stood. "Everything was wonderful. Thank you." The food *had* been marvelous—she freely admitted that—but it was this time with Jonas that had made the dinner so enjoyable. She didn't want the evening to end. For the first time since they'd begun working together, she felt at ease with him. She feared that once they arrived back at the hotel, everything would revert to the way it had been before. Jonas would immerse himself in the documents Adam was preparing for him, and everything would be business, business, business.

The maître d' was about to gesture for their waiting limousine when Stephanie placed her hand on Jonas's arm. "Would you mind if we walked a bit?"

"Not at all." He turned toward the maître d', who nodded and wished them a pleasant evening.

"I ate so much that I feel like a stuffed turkey at Thanksgiving. I'm sure a little exercise will help." She was conscious of his leg, but hoped that if it pained him, he would say something. His limp was barely noticeable as they strolled down the narrow sidewalk. "I see there's a park across the way."

"That sounds perfect."

They crossed the street and sauntered down the paved walkway that led them into the lush green lawns of a city park. Black wrought-iron fences bordered flower beds filled with bright red tulips and yellow crocuses. Row upon row of trees welcomed them, proudly displaying their buds with the promise of new life.

"I've always heard Paris in springtime couldn't be equaled," she said softly, musing that anyone happening upon them would think they were lovers. Paris in the spring was said to be a city meant for lovers. For tonight she would pretend—reality would crowd in on her soon enough.

They followed the walkway that led to the center of the park, where a tall fountain spilled water from the mouths of a ring of lions' heads.

"Shall we make a wish?" she asked, feeling happy and excited.

He snorted softly. "Why waste good money?"

"Don't be such a skeptic. It's traditional to throw a coin in a fountain, any fountain, and what better place than Paris for wishes to come true?" She opened her purse, digging for loose change. "Here, it's my treat." She handed him a dime, since she had only a few Euros with her.

"You don't honestly expect me to fall victim to such stupidity?"

"Humor me, Jonas." She noted the amusement in his blue eyes, and she ignored his tone, which sounded harsh and disapproving.

"All right." Without aim or apparent premeditation, he tossed the dime into the water with as much ceremony as if he were throwing something into the garbage.

"Good grief," she muttered beneath her breath. "I don't know of a single fairy in the entire universe who would honor such a wish."

"Why not?" he demanded.

"You obviously haven't given the matter much thought."

One corner of his mouth edged upward slightly. "I was humoring you, remember?"

"Did you even make a wish?"

He shrugged. "Not exactly."

"Well, no wonder." She shook her head dolefully and looked at him in mock disdain. "Try it again, and this time be a little more sincere."

His eyes revealed exactly what he thought of this exercise. Nonetheless, he reached inside his own pocket and took out a quarter.

Stephanie's hand stopped him. "That's too much."

"It's a big wish." This time his look was far more thoughtful as he took aim and sent the coin skipping over the surface of the water. The quarter made a small splash before sinking into the frothy depths.

She gave him a brilliant smile as she found another dime. "Okay, my turn." She turned her back to the fountain, rubbed the dime between her palms to warm it, closed her eyes and, with all the reverence due magical wish-granting fairies, flung it over her shoulder and into the fountain. "There," she said, satisfied.

"How long?" Jonas demanded.

"How long for what?"

"How long," he repeated with exasperation, "must one wait before the wish comes true?"

"It depends on what you wished for." She made it sound as though she had accumulated all the knowledge there was on the subject. "Certain wishes require a bit of manipulating by the powers that be. However, I'm only familiar with wishes made in American fountains. Things could be much different here. It could be that the wish fairies who guard this fountain work on a slower time scale than elsewhere."

"I see." It was clear from the frown that dented his brow that he didn't.

"Maybe you should just tell me what you wished for," she suggested, "and I can give you an estimate of the approximate time you'll have to wait for it to come true."

"It's my understanding that one must never reveal one's wish."

"That's not true anymore." She laughed, enjoying the inanity of their discussion. "Science has proved that theory to be inaccurate."

"Oh?"

"Yes, I'm surprised you didn't read about it in the papers. It was all over the news."

"I must have missed that." He reached for her hand, and they resumed their walk. "But if that's the case, then perhaps you'd be willing to share *your* wish with *me*."

Color instantly flooded her cheeks. She should have known he would turn the tables on her when she least expected it.

"Stephanie?"

It was completely absurd. With everything that was in her she'd wished that Jonas would take her in his arms and kiss her. It was silly and hopeless and, as he'd pointed out earlier, a waste of good money.

When she didn't respond immediately, he stopped and turned, standing directly in front of her so that he could look into her eyes.

She felt the color rise in her face.

"I would think that a self-proclaimed expert on the subject of fountains and wishes would have no qualms about revealing her own wish, especially after sharing that latest scientific newsflash." He placed his finger under her stubborn chin, elevating her gaze so that she couldn't avoid his.

"I…"

"You still haven't answered my question."

"I wasted the wish on something impractical," she blurted out. The whole park seemed to have gone quiet. A moment ago wind had ruffled the foliage around them and hissed through the branches, but now even the trees seemed to have paused, as though they, too, were interested in her reply. She swallowed uncomfortably, convinced that he could read her thoughts and was silently laughing at her.

"I fear I wasted my wish, as well," he informed her softly.

"You did?" Her eyes sought his for the first time.

He placed his hands on the gentle slopes of her shoulders and bent toward her. "I'm seldom impractical."

"I…know."

His mouth descended an inch closer to hers, so close that she could feel his warm breath fanning her face. An inch more and their lips would touch. Stephanie moistened her lips, realizing all at once how very much she wanted to taste his mouth on hers. Her breath froze in her lungs; even her heart felt as though it had stopped beating.

"Could your wish have been as impractical as mine?" There was an unmistakable uncertainty in his voice.

She levered her hands against his chest, flattening one palm over his heart. His heartbeat was strong and even. "Yes." The lone word was breathless and weak, barely audible.

His arms went around her, anchoring her against him. Gently, he laid his cheek alongside hers, rubbing the side of his face over her soft skin as though he feared her touch, yet craved it. She closed her eyes, savoring his nearness, his warmth and the vital feel of him. A thousand objections shot through her mind, but she refused to listen to even one. This was exactly what she'd wished for, fool that she was.

Jonas turned his head and nuzzled her ear, and she noticed that his breathing was shallow. His arms tightened around her, and he whispered her name, entreating her— for what, she was afraid to guess.

It was at the back of her mind that she should break free, but something much stronger than the force of her will kept her motionless. He was her employer, she reminded herself. They argued constantly, battling with each other both in and out of the office. Jonas Lockwood was an arrogant, domineering chauvinist. But all her arguments were burned away like deadwood in a forest fire as his lips moved to her hair. He kissed the top of her head, her cheek, her ear, and then moved back to her hair. He paused, holding her to him as though it were the most natural thing in the world for them to be wrapped in each other's arms.

"Tell me, Stephanie," he asked in a hoarse whisper. "Did you wish for the same thing I did?"

Their eyes met hungrily and locked. She nodded, unable to answer him with words.

He caught her closer and lowered his mouth to hers, finally claiming her lips in a greedy kiss that left her weak and clinging. She felt herself responding as her arms slid around his neck. Their lips clung, and his tongue sought and found hers. Against her will, she arched against him, seeking to lose herself in his arms for all time.

Abruptly they broke apart, both of them moving of their own accord. She was trembling inside and out. She dared not look at Jonas. Neither of them spoke. For a moment they didn't move, didn't breathe. The world that only seconds before had been silent now burst into a cacophony of sound.

Wind whistled through the trees. Car horns blared from a nearby street. An elderly couple could be heard arguing.

"Jonas, I..."

"Don't say anything."

She wouldn't have known what to say, anyway. She was as stunned as he was.

"It was the wine, and this silly wishing business," he said stiffly.

"Right."

"I told you wasting your money on wishes was foolish."

"Exactly," she agreed, though not very strenuously. Their wishes had come true; now they both wanted to complain.

She noticed on the way out of the park that he seemed to be keeping his distance from her. His steps were rushed. In order to keep up with him, she was forced into a half run. The instant they hit the main thoroughfare, he raised his hand and hailed the limo, which drove them directly back to the hotel.

"Well, how was Paris?" Jan asked the first day Stephanie was back at the office. They were sitting in the employee cafeteria. Jan had purchased the luncheon special, and Stephanie had brought a sandwich from home.

"Fine."

"Fine?"

"I was held captive in a stuffy room for most of the four days. This wasn't exactly a vacation, you know."

"How'd you get along with Mr. Lockwood?"

"Fine."

"Is that the only word you know?" Disgruntled, Jan tore open a small bag of potato chips and dumped them on her tray.

"I have an adequate vocabulary."

"Not today, you don't. Come on, Steph, you were with the man day and night for four days. Something must have happened."

The scene by the fountain, when Jonas had held her and kissed her, played back in Stephanie's mind in 3-D. If she were to close her eyes, she might be able to feel the pressure of his mouth on hers. She strenuously resisted the urge. "Nothing happened," she lied.

"Then why are you acting so strangely?"

"Am I?" Stephanie focused her attention on her friend, trying to look alert and intelligent, even though her thoughts were a thousand miles away in an obscure Paris park.

"Yes, very."

"What did you expect would happen?"

"I don't know, but the others thought you might have fallen in love with him."

"Oh, honestly, Jan, you're mistaking jet lag for love."

Disappointment clouded Jan's eyes. "This isn't going well."

"What isn't?"

"This romance. The girls and I had it all planned. We felt it would work out a whole lot easier than it is."

"How do you mean?"

"Well, in the books, the minute the hero and heroine are alone together for the first time, something usually happens."

"What do you mean, something happens?"

"You know, an intimate dinner for two, a shared smile, a kiss in the dark. Something!"

"We weren't exactly alone; Adam Holmes was with us." She avoided Jan's eyes as she carefully cracked a hard-boiled egg. If Jan could see her eyes, she would figure it all out. The egg took on new importance as she peeled the shell off piece by piece.

"At any rate," Jan continued, "we'd hoped that things might have taken off between you two."

"I'm sorry to disappoint you and the others, but the trip was a working arrangement, nothing else." Stephanie sprinkled salt and pepper on the egg.

"Well, I guess that's it, then."

"What do you mean?"

"If Mr. Lockwood was ever going to notice you, it would have been last week. You were constantly in each other's company, even if Adam Holmes was playing the part of legal chaperone. But if Mr. Lockwood isn't attracted to you by now, I doubt he ever will be."

"I couldn't agree more." Stephanie's heart contracted with a pang that felt strangely like disappointment. "Now can I get on with my life? I don't want to hear any more of your ridiculous romance ideas. Understand?"

"All right," Jan agreed, but she didn't look happy about it. "However, I wish you'd start reading romances. You'd understand what we're talking about and play your role a little better."

"Would you stop hounding me with those books? I'm not in the mood for romance."

"Okay, okay, but when you *are* ready, just say the word."

Stephanie took a look at her untouched egg, sighed and stuffed it in the sack to toss in the garbage, her appetite gone.

She couldn't decide how she felt about Jonas. Part of her wished the kiss had never happened. Those few minutes had made the remainder of the trip nearly intolerable. They had both taken pains to pretend nothing had happened, going out of their way to be cordial and polite, nothing less and certainly nothing more. It was as if Adam Holmes was their unexpected link with sanity. Neither Jonas nor Stephanie could do without him as they avoided any possibility of being trapped alone together. On the long flight home Jonas had worked out of his briefcase, while she and Adam played cards. For all the notice Jonas had given her, she could have been a piece of luggage. They'd separated at the airport, and she hadn't seen him since. It was just as well, she told herself. The incident at the fountain had been a moment out of time and was best forgotten.

"Steph?"

She shook her head to free her tangled thoughts. "I'm sorry, were you saying something?"

Jan gave her an odd look. "I was asking if you'd like to meet Jim's cousin, Mark. I thought we might double-date Saturday night. Dinner and a movie, maybe."

It took Stephanie a moment to remember who Jim was. "Sure, that sounds like fun." Anything was better than spending another restless weekend alone in her apartment.

"I knew Mark was interested, but I've held him off because I wanted to see how things developed between you and Mr. Lockwood."

Stephanie stared at her blankly and blinked twice, carefully measuring her words. She was saddened by the reality of what she had to say. "It isn't going to work between Jonas and me. Nothing's going to happen." The crazy part was that she was of two minds on the subject of the company president. He intrigued her. There wasn't a single man who interested her more. He was challenging, intelligent, pigheaded, stubborn and completely out of her league. Ah, well, she thought, sighing expressively, you won some and you lost some. And she'd lost Jonas without ever really having known him.

"Saturday at seven, then?"

"I'll look forward to it." She wasn't stretching the truth all that much. A date really did have to be better than staying home alone and moping.

"The three of us will pick you up at your apartment. Okay?"

"That sounds fine."

Jan groaned and laughed. "You're back to that word again."

Saturday evening, Stephanie washed and curled her hair, and spent extra time on her make-up. She dressed casually in slacks and a bulky knit sweater her mother had made for her last Christmas. The winter-wheat color reminded her of the rolling hills of grain outside her hometown.

The doorbell chimed, and she expelled her breath forcefully as she went to answer. She wasn't looking forward to this evening. All day her thoughts had drifted back to Jonas and their time in Paris, especially their stroll in the park. If she went out with anyone tonight, she wanted it to be with him. Wishful thinking, and not a fountain in sight. She wasn't especially eager to meet Jim's cousin, either. Jan had tried to build him up, but Stephanie knew from experience the pitfalls of blind dates. If she'd had her wits about her and been less concerned about revealing her attraction to Jonas, she would have declined the invitation. But it was too late now.

She needn't have worried about Mark, she quickly realized. He looked nice enough, although it came out immediately that he was newly divorced. Miserable, too, judging from the look in his eyes.

The vivacious Jan carried the conversation once the introductions were finished.

"Would anyone like some wine before we leave?" Stephanie asked. She'd set a tray with wineglasses on the coffee table, waiting for their arrival. "It's a light white wine."

"Sounds marvelous," Jan said, linking her fingers with Jim's. The two claimed the sofa and sat side by side. Mark took a chair, leaving its twin for Stephanie.

Still standing, she poured the wine. "What movie are we seeing?"

"There's a new foreign film out that sounds interesting," Jan said.

The doorbell chimed, and Stephanie got up to answer it. "I'm not expecting anyone," she said. "It's probably a neighbor looking for a cup of sugar or something."

She opened the door and stopped cold. It wasn't a neighbor who stood on the other side of her door. It was Jonas Lockwood.

Five

"Jonas!" Stephanie experienced a sense of joy so strong she nearly choked on it. Just when she'd given up any hope of seeing him again, he'd come to see her. But her joy quickly turned to regret as she heard the others talking behind her. "What are you doing here?" she whispered fiercely.

He stood stiffly on the other side of the door, his expression impossible to read. His grip on his cane tightened. "I came to see you. May I come in?"

"Yes...of course. I didn't mean to be rude." She stepped aside, still holding the doorknob. His timing couldn't have been worse, but she was so pleased to see him that she wouldn't have cared if he'd arrived unannounced on Christmas Eve.

"Mr. Lockwood, how nice to see you again," Jan said, tossing Stephanie a knowing look that was capable of translating entire foreign libraries.

Both Jim and Mark stood, and Stephanie made awkward introductions. "Jim, Mark, this is Mr. Lockwood."

"Jonas," he said, correcting her and offering them his hand.

"Would you care for a glass of wine?" Jan offered.

"Yes, of course," Stephanie hurried to add, her face filling with color at her lack of good manners. "Please stay and have some wine." Before he could answer, she walked into the kitchen for another glass, then came back, filled it and handed it to Jonas, who had claimed the chair next to Mark.

Resisting the urge to press her cool hands against her flaming cheeks, she took a seat on the sofa beside Jan, the three of them crowding together. The men were asking Jonas questions about the business as though it was the most interesting topic in the world. While they were occupied, Jan took the opportunity to jab Stephanie in the ribs with her elbow. "I thought you said he wasn't interested," she whispered under her breath.

"He isn't," Stephanie insisted. Glancing around, she wanted to groan with frustration. Although the small, one-bedroom apartment suited her nicely, she was intensely conscious that most of her furniture was secondhand and well-worn. She hadn't been the least bit ashamed to have Jan and her friends view her mix-and-match arrangement, but entertaining Jonas Lockwood was another matter entirely. Oh, for heaven's sake, what did she care? He hadn't stopped by to check out her china pattern.

"I can see that I've come at a bad time," Jonas said, standing. He set his glass aside, and Stephanie noted that he hadn't bothered to taste the wine.

She stood with him.

"We were about to leave for dinner," Jan explained apologetically. "But if you needed Steph for something at the office, we could change our plans."

"That won't be necessary." He shook hands with Jim and Mark again. "It was a pleasure meeting you both."

"I'll walk you to the door," Stephanie offered, locking her fingers together in front of her. He'd stopped in out of the blue, and she wasn't about to let him escape without knowing the reason for his impromptu visit.

Instead of stopping to ask him at her front door, she stepped into the hall with him. For a moment, neither spoke. She was trying to come up with a subtle way of mentioning that she'd only met Mark a few minutes earlier, that the blind date had been Jan's idea, and that she'd only accepted the offer because she didn't think that Jonas wanted to see her again. But she couldn't explain without sounding foolish.

"I apologize for not calling first," Jonas said finally.

"It…doesn't matter. I'm almost always home."

He cocked his brow as though he didn't quite believe her.

"It's true."

He glanced at his wristwatch. "I should be going."

"Jonas." Her hands were clenched so tightly that she was sure she'd cut off the blood supply to her fingers. "Why did you come?"

"It isn't important."

It was terribly important to her. "Is it something to do with work?"

"No."

"Then…why?"

"I believe there's someone in there waiting for you. It's not very polite of you to stand here with me, discussing my motives."

"What is this? Do you want to play twenty questions?" He frowned.

"All right, you obviously want me to guess the reason you stopped by. Fine. Since that's the way you want it, let's start with the basics. Is it animal, vegetable or mineral?"

"Ms. Coulter." He closed his eyes, seemingly frustrated by her tenacity.

"I'm not going back inside until you tell me why you're here."

"This is neither the time nor the place to discuss it." His gaze hardened.

The look was one she knew all too well. "It's common courtesy to tell someone why you stopped by."

"The only manners you need concern yourself with are your own toward your friends. I suggest that you join them. We can discuss this later."

"When?" She wasn't about to let him off as easily as that.

"Monday."

She didn't want to agree, but she could hear the others talking and knew they'd long since finished their wine. "All right. Monday."

His gaze rested on her for a long moment. "It would be far better if you forgot I was ever here."

"I'm not going to do that." How could she? She hadn't been so pleased to see anyone in months.

"I didn't think you would. Enjoy yourself tonight." He said it with such sincerity that she wanted to assure him that she would, even though she knew the entire evening was a waste.

"Goodbye, Jonas."

"Goodbye." He hung the end of his cane over his forearm and turned away from her.

Stephanie watched him go, biting into her lower lip to keep from calling him back. If there had been any decent way of doing so, she would have sent Jan, Jim and Mark on their way without her. Reluctantly, she went back inside her apartment.

As she had known it would be, the evening was time misspent. Mark's conversation consisted of an account of how misunderstood he was by his ex-wife and of how terribly he missed his children. Stephanie tried to appear sympathetic, but her thoughts were centered on Jonas. They wavered between quiet jubilation and heart-wrenching disappointment. More than once she had to resist the urge to tell Mark to be quiet and go back to his wife, since it was so obvious that he still loved her. A thousand times over she wished she'd never agreed to this blind date, and she silently vowed she wouldn't do it again, no matter how close the friend who arranged it. She hoped Jan appreciated what she was going through, but somehow she doubted it.

After the movie the four of them returned to Stephanie's apartment for coffee. Jan offered to help as an excuse to talk to her alone.

"Well, what do you think?"

"Mark's nice, but he's in love with his wife."

"Not about Mark. I'm talking about Mr. Lockwood," she said. "I knew it from the first. I knew he was hooked!"

"Oh, hardly. Mr. Lockwood has no feelings for me one way or the other." Stephanie filled the basket with coffee and slipped it into place above the glass pot with unnecessary force.

"Don't give me that," Jan countered sharply. "I saw the way you two looked at each other."

"I don't even know why he came." Stephanie busied herself opening and closing cupboards, and taking down four matching cups.

"Don't be such a dope. There's only one reason he showed up. He wanted to see you again. He's interested with a capital *I*." Jan crossed her arms and leaned against the kitchen counter. "He's so into you that he can't look at you without letting it show."

"You're exaggerating again." Stephanie prayed her friend was right, but she sincerely doubted it. Jonas Lockwood wasn't the kind of man to reveal his emotions as easily as that.

"I'm not exaggerating."

"Come on," Stephanie said, refusing to argue. "The guys are waiting."

"Just do me a favor."

"What now?" Stephanie asked, desperate to change the subject. It was bad enough that Jonas had dominated her thoughts all evening. Now Jan was bringing him up, as well.

"Just think about it. Jonas Lockwood wouldn't have stopped by here for any reason other than the fact that he wanted to see you."

Jan's logic was irrefutable, but Stephanie still wasn't sure she could believe it. "All right, I'll think about it, but for heaven's sake, don't tell anyone. The last thing I need is for the rest of your Gang of Four to find out about this."

"I won't breathe a word of it." But Jan's eyes were twinkling. "I'll give you some time to think things through. You're smart. You'll figure Lockwood out." She held the door open for Stephanie, who carried the tray with the four steaming cups of coffee into the living room.

After a half hour of strained conversation, mostly about Mark's ex-wife, Jan and the men departed. Stephanie sighed as she let them out the door. It was only eleven, but she hurriedly got ready for bed. Amazingly, for all her doubts and uncertainty regarding Jonas, she slept surprisingly well.

Sunday morning Jan was at Stephanie's front door, smiling broadly and carrying a large stack of romances under one arm.

"What are those for?" Stephanie asked, letting her friend into the apartment. She was still in her housecoat, fighting off a cold with orange juice and aspirin, and feeling guilty for being so lazy.

"Not what—who."

"All right. *Who* are those for?" Stephanie's sore throat had taken a lot of the fight out of her.

"You."

"Jan, I've told you repeatedly that I'm not interested. You can't force me to read them."

"No, but I thought you might be interested in a little research." Jan paused, noticing Stephanie's appearance for the first time. "What's the matter—you look sick."

"I'm just fighting off a cold." And maybe a touch of disappointment, too.

"Great, there's no better time to sit back and read."

"Jan…"

Her friend held up a hand to stop her. "I refuse to hear any arguments. I want you to sit down and read. If I have to, I'll stand over you until you do."

Muttering under her breath, Stephanie complied, sitting on the sofa with her back against the armrest and bringing her feet up so she could tuck them under a blanket. Jan picked up the book on the top of the pile, silently read the back cover and nodded knowingly. "You'll like this one. The circumstances are similar to what's happening between you and Mr. Lockwood."

Stephanie bolted to her feet. "Nothing's happening between me and Mr. Lockwood."

"You called him Jonas the other day," Jan said, ignoring Stephanie's bad mood. "The funny part is, until then I'd never thought of him other than as *Mr.* Lockwood."

To the contrary, Stephanie had almost always thought of him as Jonas, but she wasn't about to add ammunition to her friend's growing arsenal.

"But I don't think we need to worry about his name."

"Thank heaven for that much," Stephanie muttered, sitting back down.

"Promise me you'll read these?"

"I would never have taken you for such an unreasonable slave driver." Stephanie fought back a flash of rebellion and shook her head. "All right, I'll read one, but I won't like it."

"And I bet you a month's pay you'll end up loving them the way the rest of us do."

"I'm reserving judgment."

Jan left soon after Stephanie opened the cover of the first book. To be honest, she was curious what the other women saw in the novels that they read with such fervor. What was even more interesting was the fact that they did more than just read the books; the whole group talked about the characters as though they were living, breathing people. Stephanie had once heard Barbara comment that she wanted to punch out a certain hero, and the others had agreed wholeheartedly, as though it were an entirely possible option.

The next time Stephanie glanced at the clock it was afternoon and she'd finished the book, astonished at how well-written it was. All along she'd assumed that romance heroines were sappy, weak-willed women without a brain in their heads. From tidbits of information she'd heard among the others, she couldn't imagine anyone putting up with some of the things the heroines in the books did. But she was wrong. The heroines in the first romance she'd read and the one she reached for next were strong women with realistic problems. Although she might not have agreed completely with the way they handled their relationships with the heroes, she appreciated why they acted the way they did. With love, she realized, came tolerance, acceptance and understanding.

First thing on Monday morning Stephanie stopped at Jan's desk. She dutifully placed three romances in Jan's Out basket, willing to admit that she had misjudged her friend's favorite reading material.

"What's that for?"

"I read them."

"And?" Jan's eyes grew round.

"I loved them, just the way you said I would."

Laughing, Jan nodded, reached for her phone and punched in Maureen's extension. "She read the first three and she's hooked." Once she'd made her announcement, she replaced the receiver and sat back, folding her hands neatly on top of the desk and sighing. "I'm waiting."

Stephanie groaned and shook her head lightly. "I knew I wasn't going to get away this easily. You want to hear it, so...all right, all right—you told me so."

Jan laughed again. "You look especially nice today. Any reason?"

Stephanie considered a white lie but quickly changed her mind. Like the heroines in the romances, she was a mature woman, and if she happened to be attracted to a man, it wasn't a sin to admit as much. "I'll be talking to Jonas later, and I wanted to look my best."

"You'll keep me up to date, won't you?"

Stephanie secured the strap of her purse on her shoulder. "I don't know that there'll be anything to report. Our relationship isn't like those romances."

"Maybe not yet, but it will be," Jan said with the utmost confidence.

"I'm not half as convinced as you are. Just keep this under your hat. I don't want the others to know."

"My lips are sealed."

But Stephanie wondered if Jan was capable of keeping anything a secret. Her coworker was much too friendly, and much too eager to see something develop between Stephanie and Jonas to keep the news to herself.

The day went smoothly although Stephanie was constantly on edge, expecting to hear from Jonas. Each time her phone rang she felt certain it would be him, issuing a request to join him in his office. He didn't call, and by five o'clock she felt both disappointed and frustrated. He'd said he would talk to her on Monday, and she'd taken him at his word.

Jan, Toni, Maureen and Barbara sauntered in together at quitting time. "Well? What did he say?"

Stephanie glared at Jan, who quickly lowered her eyes. "I couldn't help it," she murmured, looking miserable. "Toni guessed, and I couldn't lie."

"You didn't have any problem promising me your lips were sealed."

"She had to tell us," Maureen insisted. "It was our right. We're the ones who got you into this."

Stephanie straightened the papers on her desk. "I'm not sure I can find it in my heart to thank you. Jonas Lockwood has been a thorn in my side from the moment we met."

"Perfect," Barbara announced.

"Enough of that," Toni said. "We want to know what he had to say today."

"Nothing." Stephanie tried unsuccessfully to hide the disappointment in her voice.

"Nothing!" the others echoed.

"I haven't seen him."

"Why not?"

"Good grief, how am I supposed to know?"

Toni paused, and pressed her forefinger to her temple. "I was thinking about what happened Saturday night, and in my opinion it wasn't necessarily such a bad thing that Jan's friend was there. It lets Mr. Lockwood know he's got competition."

"It might have been enough to scare him off, though," Barbara disagreed.

"Then he isn't worth his salt as a hero."

"Would you four stop!" Stephanie demanded, waving her arms for emphasis. She returned her attention to Jan. "Are they always like this?"

Jan shrugged. "It doesn't matter. What are you going to do?"

Stephanie had no idea. Jonas had said that he would talk to her on Monday, and there were still several hours left in the day. Maybe he intended to contact her at her apartment. No, she quickly dismissed the notion. He wouldn't be back; she'd seen it in his eyes.

"Steph?"

She looked up to notice that all four of her coworkers were studying her expectantly.

"I'm going up to his office," she said, the announcement shocking her as much as it did the others. The upper floor belonged to Jonas and was well guarded by his Martha Westheimer, who was reputed to have slain more than one persistent dragon.

Jan grinned. "Didn't I tell you she was heroine material?"

"The perfect choice," Maureen agreed.

The four of them followed Stephanie out of her office and to the elevator. Barbara pushed the button for her. Toni and Maureen stood behind her, rubbing her shoulders as though to prepare her for the coming confrontation. For a moment Stephanie felt as if she was getting ready for the heavyweight boxing championship of the world.

"Don't take any guff from Old Stone Face."

"Just remember to smile at Mr. Lockwood."

"And it wouldn't hurt to bat your lashes over those baby blues a time or two."

Armed with their advice, Stephanie entered the waiting elevator. Jan gave her the thumbs-up sign just before the heavy metal doors closed.

Now that she was alone, Stephanie felt herself losing her nerve. She sighed and leaned against the back of the elevator. The others had lent her confidence, but standing alone in the chilly, dimly lit elevator gave her cause to doubt. If there had been any way of disappearing from a moving elevator, she would have been tempted to try it.

The doors opened, and Martha Westheimer raised her eyes to frown at Stephanie's approach. A pair of glasses were delicately balanced at the end of the older woman's nose. She was near sixty, Stephanie guessed, tall and slender, with a narrow mouth. Just looking at the woman inspired fear.

"Do you have an appointment?" Martha asked stiffly, giving Stephanie a look that was not at all welcoming.

Stephanie stepped off the elevator and thrust back her shoulders, prepared for this first encounter. "Mr. Lockwood asked to see me." That was only a partial white lie.

"Your name, please?" With the eraser end of her pencil, Martha flipped through the appointment schedule.

"Stephanie Coulter."

"I don't see your name down here, Ms. Coulter."

"Then there must be some mistake."

There was challenge in Martha's dark brown eyes. "I don't make mistakes."

"Then I suggest you contact Mr. Lockwood."

"I'll do exactly that." The woman flipped on the intercom. "There's a Ms. Coulter here to see you. She claims she has an appointment." Her tone made it clear that she was certain Stephanie had lied.

"I said," Stephanie corrected her through clenched teeth, "that Mr. Lockwood had asked to see me." The hand clenching her purse tightened. "There's a difference."

The silence on the other end of the intercom stretched out uncomfortably, and Stephanie was convinced she was about to be dismissed.

"Mr. Lockwood?"

"Send her in, Miss Westheimer."

Stephanie flashed Jonas's guardian a brilliant smile of triumph as she waltzed past her desk. The older woman had to know that Stephanie had stepped in while she was ill, yet she gave no indication that she was aware who Stephanie was, or even that she was employed by Lockwood Industries.

Stephanie let herself into Jonas's office and was instantly met by a rush of memories. She liked this room, just as she respected the man who ruled from it.

He was busy writing, his head bowed, and didn't bother to acknowledge her presence. She stood awkwardly as she waited for him to finish, not enough at ease to take a seat without being asked.

When he'd finished, Jonas put the cap on his pen and set it aside before glancing in her direction. "Yes?"

His crisp tone made her all the more uncomfortable, but she pushed on. "You said you would talk to me on Monday."

"About?"

He was making this difficult, and she drew a deep breath before continuing. "About Saturday night. You told me we'd talk."

"I don't recall committing myself to that."

"Please, don't play games with me. You stopped by my apartment on Saturday, and I want to know why."

The lines around his mouth deepened, but he wasn't smiling. "I happened to be in the neighborhood."

"But…"

"Leave it at that, Ms. Coulter. It was a mistake, and one best forgotten."

"But I don't think it *was* a mistake." He was closing her out; she could see it by the way he sat, his back stiff with determination. His eyes looked past her as though he wanted to avoid seeing her.

The silence was broken by Jonas. "Sometimes it's better to leave things as they are. In my opinion, this is one of those times."

Her hands trembled slightly but she stood her ground. "I disagree."

His mouth twisted in a cynical smile. "Unfortunately, you have little say in the matter. Now, if you'll excuse me, I have several reports to read over."

It was clearly meant to be a dismissal, and she wavered between stalking out of the office and trying to forget him, and staying and admitting that she was attracted to him and that she would like to know him better. But for all the attention he was giving her now, she might as well have been a stack of signed papers on his desk. Out of sight, out of mind, she mused ruefully. Her pride told her that she had better things to do than allow Jonas Lockwood to poke holes in her fragile ego.

Finally her pride won, and she gave him a small, sad smile. "You don't need to be rude, Jonas. I get the message."

"Do you?" He focused his gaze on her.

"Thank you for that wonderful night in Paris. I'll always remember that—and you—fondly."

His hard blue eyes softened. "Stephanie, listen…"

He was interrupted by the phone. "I'm waiting for a call," he said, almost apologetically, as he reached for the receiver.

She turned to leave, but he stopped her as he reverted to French. She could tell that he was speaking to a government official regarding his negotiations with Lockwood Industries' French counterpart, but the conversation quickly became too technical for her to understand fully.

A few minutes later Jonas hung up the telephone. His eyes revealed his excitement.

"Congratulations are in order," he said, standing. "Our trip to France was a success. Our bid has been accepted."

"Congratulations," she whispered. His happiness was contagious; it filled the enormous room, encircling them both.

He walked around the front of the large rosewood desk, his eyes sparkling. "It seemed for a while that this deal could go either way."

Stephanie noticed that his limp was less pronounced now than at any time she'd seen him walk.

"Do you know what this means?" He walked to the other side of the room, as though he couldn't contain himself any longer.

She nodded eagerly, pretending she did know, when in actuality she was ignorant of nearly all the pertinent information.

He came back over to her and locked his hands on her shoulders. "I can't believe it's falling into place after all the problems we've encountered." His arms dropped to her waist and circled her. With a burst of infectious laughter, he lifted her off the plush carpet and swung her around.

Caught completely off guard, she gasped and placed her hands on his shoulders in an effort to maintain her balance. "I'm so happy for you."

As if suddenly aware that he was holding her, he relaxed his grip. Her feet found the floor, but her hands remained on his shoulders, and her eyes smiled warmly into his.

He tensed, and the exhilaration drained from him as his gaze locked with hers. His hand slid beneath her long hair, tilting her head to receive his kiss. She had no thought of objecting. Since that night in Paris, she'd longed for him to hold and kiss her again. But she hadn't admitted how *much* she'd wanted it until now. He kissed her a second time, and his mouth was hungry and demanding. His lips moved persuasively over hers, hot and possessive. She was equally hungry and eager for him. A slow fire burned through her, and she melted against him. "Oh, Jonas," she whispered longingly.

He brushed his lips over hers again, as though he couldn't get enough of the taste of her. She opened her mouth to him, drugged by the sensations he aroused.

His mouth ravaged the scented hollow of her throat and began a slow meandering trail to her ear. He paused, took a deep breath, and waited a moment longer before releasing her. "Forgive me." He brushed the wisps of hair from her temple. "That shouldn't have happened."

She felt like a fool. She'd savored the feel of his arms, lost herself in the taste of his kiss and the rush of sensations that flooded her, and he was apologizing.

"No apology necessary," she murmured stiffly. "Just don't let it happen again."

Jonas hesitated, as though he wanted to say something more but then decided against it. He turned sharply and stalked back to his desk.

Six

"Well?" Maureen was at Stephanie's desk early the following morning. "Don't keep me in suspense. What happened?"

"Nothing much." Stephanie kept her gaze lowered, doing her best not to reveal her emotions. She'd been depressed and out of sorts from the minute she left Jonas's office.

"'Nothing much'? What does that mean?"

"It means I don't want to talk about it."

"You had an argument?" Toni joined her friend. The two of them placed their hands on the edge of Stephanie's desk and leaned forward, as if what she had to say was a matter of national importance.

"I wish," Stephanie muttered, sighing heavily. "No, we didn't argue."

"But you don't want to talk about it?"

"Very perceptive, ladies." Stephanie searched for something to do and finally settled for inserting a pencil in the sharpener. Despite the loud grinding sound, neither Toni nor Maureen budged.

"I think we need to talk to the others," Toni said.

"You'll do no such thing," Stephanie insisted, her tone determined.

"Hey, come on, Steph, we're all in this together. We want to help. At least tell us what happened," Maureen said.

It was apparent to Stephanie that she wouldn't have a minute's peace until she confessed everything to her romance-loving friends. "Meet me at ten in the cafeteria," she told them. "I'll get it over with all at once, but only if you promise never to mention Jonas Lockwood's name to me again."

Toni and Maureen exchanged meaningful glances. "This doesn't sound good."

"It's my final offer." Replaying her humiliation was going to be bad enough; she didn't want it dragged out any more than necessary.

"All right, all right," Toni muttered. "We'll be there."

After that Stephanie's morning went smoothly. Her boss, George Potter, was on a two-day business trip to Seattle, but there was enough work to keep her occupied for another week if need be.

When she arrived in the cafeteria promptly at ten she found the four women sitting at the table closest to the window, eagerly awaiting her arrival. A fifth cup of coffee was on the table in front of an empty chair.

"From that frown you're wearing, I'd say the meeting with Mr. Lockwood didn't go very well," Jan commented, barely giving Stephanie time to take a seat.

"There are no adequate words to describe it," Stephanie said by way of confirmation, reaching for the coffee. "I'm sorry to be such a major disappointment to you all, but anything that might have happened between me and Jonas Lockwood is off."

"Why?"

"What happened?"

"I could have sworn he was hooked."

"To be honest," Stephanie said, striving to be as forthright as possible, "I think he may be attracted to me, but we're too different."

"That's what makes you so good together," Barbara countered.

"And I saw the way he looked at her," Jan inserted thoughtfully. "Now tell us what happened and let *us* figure out the next step."

Stephanie swallowed and shrugged. "If you must know, he kissed me."

"And you're complaining?"

"No, *he* was!"

"What?" All four of them looked at her as if she'd been working too much overtime.

"He kissed me, then immediately acted like he'd committed some terrible faux pas. The way he was looking at me, anyone seeing us would have assumed that *I'd* kissed *him* and he didn't like it in the least. He was angry and unreasonable, and worse, he insulted me with an apology."

"What did you say?"

"I told him never to let it happen again."

A chorus of moans and groans followed.

"You didn't!" Jan cried. "That was the worst thing you could have said."

"Well, it was his own fault," Stephanie flared. She'd been furious with him *and* with herself. She'd enjoyed his kisses—in fact, she'd wanted him to continue.

"Did you like it—the kiss, I mean?" Toni looked at her hopefully.

Stephanie pretended to find her black coffee enthralling. "Yes."

"How do you feel about Mr. Lockwood?"

"I… I don't know anymore."

"But if he'd asked you to dinner, you would have accepted?"

"Probably." She remembered the exhilaration in his eyes when he'd found out his bid had been accepted. He'd worked so hard, and given so much of himself to the business, that she'd experienced a sense of elation just watching him. She'd been happy for him and pleased to have played a small part in his triumph.

"Then you can't give up."

"It was Jonas who did that," Stephanie said sharply.

"But he hasn't. Don't you see?" Toni asked, and the others nodded in agreement.

Stephanie glanced around the table, thinking her co-workers must be kidding. "No. Not at all."

"She hasn't read enough romances yet," Jan said, defending her friend. "She doesn't understand."

"Mr. Lockwood is definitely attracted to you," Barbara claimed with all the seriousness of a clinical psychologist. "Otherwise he wouldn't have reacted to kissing you the way you described."

"I'd hate to see how he'd react if he *didn't* like me," Stephanie said sarcastically. "I'm sorry, but this is getting just too complicated to understand. I'll admit to being disappointed—he's not so bad once you get to know him. In fact, I might even have enjoyed the chance to fall in love with him." She admitted this at the expense of her own pride.

"It's hardly over yet," Maureen told her emphatically.

"Whose move is next?" Jan asked, looking around the table, seeking an answer from her peers.

"Mr. Lockwood's," Toni and Maureen said together, nodding in unison. "Definitely."

"Then I'm afraid we've got a long wait coming," Stephanie informed them, finishing her coffee. "A very long wait."

"We'll see."

That same afternoon Stephanie was on the computer at her desk when Jonas entered her office. He leaned heavily on his cane, waiting for her to notice him before he spoke.

She was aware of him the second he entered, but she finished the line she was typing before she turned her attention to him. Ignoring her pounding heart, she met his gaze squarely, refusing to give him the satisfaction of knowing the effect he had on her.

"Good afternoon, Mr. Lockwood," she said crisply. "Is there something I can do for you?"

"Miss Coulter." He paused and looked into Mr. Potter's office. "Is your boss available?"

Jonas had to know that he wasn't.

"Mr. Potter's in Seattle."

"Fine. Take a letter." He pulled up a chair and sat beside her desk.

She reached automatically for her steno pad, then paused. "Is Miss Westheimer ill again?"

"She was healthy the last time I looked."

"Then perhaps it would be better if she took your dictation." She raised her chin to a defiant angle, thinking as she did that her behavior would upset her friends. But she didn't care. She wouldn't let Jonas Lockwood boss her around, even at the cost of a good job. Her hold on the pencil was so tight that it was a miracle it didn't snap in half.

"Address the letter to Miss Stephanie Coulter."

"Me?"

"Dear Ms. Coulter," he continued, ignoring her. "In

thinking over the events of last evening, I am of the opinion that I owe you an apology."

As fast as her fingers could move the pencil, Stephanie transcribed his words. Not until her brain had assimilated the message did she pause. "I believe you already expressed your deep regret," she said stiffly. "You needn't have worried. I didn't take the kiss seriously."

"It was an impulse."

"Right." She felt her anger flare. "And, as you say, best forgotten." But she couldn't forget it, even though she wanted to banish it to the farthest reaches of her mind. He'd held and kissed her on two different occasions, and each time was engraved indelibly on her memory. She wondered if she would ever be the same again.

He scowled. "You're an attractive woman."

"I suppose I should thank you, but somehow that didn't sound like a compliment."

His frown deepened. "You could have any man you want."

She gave a self-deprecating laugh. "You clearly have an exaggerated opinion of my charms, Mr. Lockwood."

"I don't blame you for being offended that someone like me would kiss you."

"I wasn't offended." She was incensed that he'd even suggested such a thing. "If you want the truth, which you obviously do, I happened to find the whole experience rather pleasant."

"In Paris?"

"It was exactly what I wished for, and you know it." Even as she said it, she knew how true it was. Since leaving his office the night before, she'd been in a blue funk, cranky and unreasonable, and all because of him. As much as she'd disliked him those few days she'd spent filling in for Martha Westheimer, she admitted to liking him now. What she couldn't understand was why everything had changed. For days, angry sparks had flown every time they were in the same room. Sparks were still apparent, but now they set off an entirely different kind of response.

"What about my limp?"

"What about it?" Deliberately, she set the pencil aside.

"Does it trouble you?"

She noticed the way his hand had tightened around the handle of his cane. His knuckles were stark white, and some of her outrage dissipated. "Of course not. Why should it?"

"Some women would be repelled." He wouldn't look at her; his gaze rested on the filing cabinet on the opposite wall. "I want neither your sympathy nor your pity."

"That works out well, since you don't have either one." Her voice was crisp with impatience. She hated to believe that he had such a low opinion of her motives, but he gave her no choice but to think that.

"You could have your pick of any man in this company."

"Listen," she countered, her patience having long since evaporated. "It isn't like I've got a tribe of men seeking my company, and even if I did, what would it matter?"

"You're attractive, bright and witty."

"Such high praise. I don't know how I should deal with it, especially when it comes from you."

Jonas was still studying the filing cabinet. "I can see that our little talk has helped clear away some misconceptions," he said.

"I certainly hope so."

"Have a good day, Ms. Coulter."

"You, too, Mr. Lockwood."

Jonas had been gone for five minutes before Stephanie fully accepted the fact that he'd actually been in her office.

It took her another ten minutes to react. Her fingers were poised over the computer keyboard, ready to resume her task, when she realized she was shaking. She closed her eyes and savored the warm feelings that washed over her in waves. Then she felt chilled; nerves skirted up and down her spine. Jan and the others had been right about him. He was attracted to her, although he wore that stiff, businesslike facade like a heavy coat, not trusting her or the attraction they shared. He didn't have faith in her feelings for him, but she hoped that eventually he would realize they were genuine.

Unable to contain her excitement, she reached for her phone and dialed Jan's extension.

"Human Resources," Jan said when she answered.

"He was here."

"Who?"

"Guess," Stephanie said, laughing excitedly. "You were right. It was his move, and he made it."

"Mr. Lockwood?"

"Who else do you think I'm talking about?"

"I'll be right there."

Jan arrived a minute later, followed by Barbara, Toni and Maureen. "What did I tell you?" Jan said excitedly, slapping Barbara's open hand with her own.

"There isn't time for you to read more romances," Toni murmured, looking worried.

"The only thing she can do now is follow her instincts," Maureen said brightly. "He's interested. She's interested. Everything will follow its natural course."

"What do you mean 'natural course'?" Stephanie asked, concerned. This was beginning to sound a lot like kidney stones.

"Marriage." They said the word in unison, and looked

at her as though her elevator didn't go all the way to the top floor. "It's what we're all after."

"Marriage?" Stephanie repeated slowly. Everything was happening too fast for her to take in.

"You like him, right?" Toni challenged.

"Hey, wait a minute, you guys. Sure, I like Jonas Lockwood, but liking is a long way from love and marriage."

"You're perfect together." Maureen sounded incredulous that Stephanie could question her fate. The four romance-lovers had everything arranged, and her resistance obviously wasn't appreciated.

"Perfect together? Jonas and me?" Stephanie frowned. The two of them did more arguing than anything. They were barely beginning to come to an understanding.

"You have to plan your strategy carefully."

"My strategy?"

"Right." Barbara nodded.

"You'll need to make him believe that love and marriage are all his idea."

"Don't you think we could start by holding hands?"

"Very funny," Jan said, placing her fist on her hip.

"I feel it's more important to let this relationship take its own time." Stephanie looked up at the four women who were standing around her desk, arms crossed, staring disapprovingly down at her. "That is, if there's going to *be* a relationship."

Together, they all shook their heads. "Wrong."

"So tell us, what are you planning next?" Jan asked.

"Me?" Stephanie held her hand to her breast. "I'm not planning anything. Should I be?"

"Of course. Mr. Lockwood made his move, now it's your turn."

This romance business sounded a lot like playing chess, or perhaps tennis. "I...hadn't given it any thought."

"Well, don't worry, we'll figure out something. Are you doing anything after work?" Jan asked.

"Depositing my check and picking up the bookcase I've had on layaway."

"Well, for heaven's sake, what's more important?" Jan gave her an incredulous look.

"You want the truth?" Stephanie glanced around at her friends. It didn't matter if she was with them or not; they were going to plot her life to their own satisfaction. "I'm going with the bookcase. If you four come up with something brilliant, phone me."

Several pieces of polished wood lay across Stephanie's carpet, along with a bowl full of screws. The screwdriver was clenched between her teeth as she struggled with the instructions, turning them one way and then another. The phone rang, and she absently reached for it, forgetting about the screwdriver.

"Hebbloo."

"Stephanie?"

"Jonas?" Her heartbeat instantly quickened as she grabbed the screwdriver from between her lips. For one crazy second she actually wanted to tell him he couldn't contact her—it was her move!

"I hope this isn't a bad time."

"No...no, of course it isn't. I wasn't doing anything." She stared at the disembodied pieces of the bookcase scattered across her carpet and added, "Important."

"I know it's short notice, but I was wondering if you were free to join me for dinner."

"Dinner?" She knew she sounded amazingly like an

echo. She quickly toyed with the idea of contacting Jan before she agreed to do anything with Jonas, then just as quickly rejected that thought. Her coworkers were making her paranoid.

"If you have company or..."

"No, I'm alone." She picked up the instructions for assembling the bookcase and sighed. "Jonas, do you speak Danish?"

"Pardon?"

"How about Swedish?"

"No. Why?"

At that point she was so frustrated she wanted to cry. "It's not important."

"About dinner?"

"Yes, I'd love to go." Never mind that she had a pot roast in the oven, with small potatoes and fresh peas in the sink ready to be boiled.

"I'll pick you up in a few minutes, then."

"Great." She glanced down at her faded jeans, ten-year-old sweatshirt and purple Reeboks, and groaned. She picked up the receiver to phone Jan, decided she didn't have enough time and hurried into her room. The sweatshirt came off first and was flung to the farthest corner of her small bedroom. She found a soft pink silk blouse hanging in her closet and quickly slipped it on. Her fingers shook as she rushed to work the small pearl buttons.

She had the jeans down around her thighs when the doorbell chimed. She closed her eyes and prayed that it wasn't Jonas. It couldn't be! He'd only phoned a couple of minutes ago. She jumped, hauling her jeans back up to her waist, and ran to the door, yanking it open.

"Listen, I'm sorry if I sound rude, but I don't have the time to buy anything right now—" She stopped abruptly, wishing the earth would open up and swallow her. Her breath caught in her throat, and she closed her eyes momentarily. "Hello, Jonas."

"Did you know your pants are unzipped?"

She whirled around, sucked in her stomach and pulled up the zipper. "I didn't expect you so soon."

"Obviously. I called on my cell from across the street."

"Please come in. I'll only be a few minutes." If he so much as snickered, she swore, she would find a way to take revenge. Some form of justice fitting the crime, like a pot roast dumped over his head.

He glanced around at the pieces of wood strewn across her carpet. "You're building something?"

"A bookcase." She'd hoped to have that cleaned up before he arrived, but that had been her second concern. She'd wanted to be dressed first. He gave a soft cough that sounded suspiciously like a smothered laugh.

"Did you say something?" Her hands knotted at her sides, and she eyed the oven where the pot roast was cooking.

"I don't believe I've ever seen you flustered before." His look was amused, and his voice soft and gruff at the same time. "Not Stephanie Coulter, the woman who defies and challenges me at every turn."

"Try answering the door with your underwear showing. It has a humbling effect."

He chuckled, and the sound had a musical quality to it. Despite her embarrassment, she laughed, too, feeling completely at ease with him for the first time since Paris. "I'll only be a few minutes."

"Take your time."

She was halfway to her bedroom when she stopped, realizing that she'd forgotten her manners in her eagerness to escape. "Would you like something to drink while you wait?"

"No, thanks." He picked up the assembly instructions for the bookcase, which were on the end table by the phone. "Danish?" he asked, cocking both brows.

"I guess. It may be Swedish or Greek. I can't tell."

His gaze scanned the pieces on the floor. "Would you like a little help?"

"I'd like a lot of help." A wry smile curved her mouth. She'd spent the better part of two hours attempting to make sense of the diagrams and the foreign instructions.

"Do I detect a note of resignation in your voice, Ms. Coulter?"

"That's not resignation, it's out-and-out frustration, disillusionment, and more than a touch of anger."

"I'll see what I can do."

She started to leave, but when she saw him take off his suit jacket and reach for one long piece of shelving to join it to another, she paused. "That won't work." Soon she was kneeling on the floor opposite him. She began to feel like a nurse assisting a brain surgeon, handing him one part after another. In frustration, he paused to study the diagram, turning it upside down and around, just as she had done, but he still couldn't figure out which pieces linked together, either.

"Wait," Jonas said, shaking his head. "We've been doing this all wrong."

Stephanie, kneeling close to his side, groaned, then mumbled under her breath, "The man's a genius."

"If I was such a whiz, these bookcases would have books in them by now," he grumbled, his brow knit in a thoughtful frown. "Give me the screwdriver, would you?"

"Sure." She handed it to him.

He turned to thank her. Their eyes met, and they stared at each other for an endless moment. She blinked and looked away first. Never before had she been so aware of Jonas as a man. He looked different than any time she'd seen him in the office. Younger. Less worried. Almost boyishly handsome. He made no move to touch her, yet she felt a myriad of sensations shoot through her as though he had. He was so close that she could smell the spicy scent of his aftershave and feel the warmth of his hard, lean body chasing away the chill of her insecurities. She could feel his breath against her hair, and she welcomed it, swaying toward him.

She didn't know who moved first. It didn't matter. Before she was aware of anything, they were on their knees with their arms wrapped around each other. She closed her eyes and let the warm sensation of his touch thread through her limbs. His hands gripped her upper arms as he moved his mouth to hers. His kiss was tentative, exploring, as though he expected her to stop him. She couldn't. She'd been wanting him to hold and kiss her again from the moment he'd last released her and then apologized. His lips were warm as they covered hers. The tip of his tongue traced her lips, and she eagerly opened her mouth to his exploration.

Stephanie's fingers moved from his hard chest, and she slid her arms up and around his neck, flattening her torso to his. His hands were splayed across her back, drawing her as close as humanly possible. His kiss grew greedy, hungry and demanding.

She reveled in the feel of the hard muscles of his shoulders and the softness of the thick hair at the base of his neck. A delicious languor spread through her.

Jonas buried his face in the hollow of her throat and shuddered. "Stephanie?"

"Hmm." She felt warm and wonderful.

"I don't know what it is, but something smells like it's burning."

Her eyes flew open. She let out a small cry of alarm and jumped to her feet.

Seven

"Oh, Jonas, the roast!" She grabbed two pot holders and pulled open the oven to retrieve the pot roast. Black smoke filled the small kitchen, and Stephanie waved her hand to clear the air. "So much for that," she said, heaving an exasperated sigh.

"What is it?" He joined her, examining the charred piece of meat.

"What does it look like?" she said hotly, then stared at the crisp roast and slowly shook her head. "If you have any kindness left in your heart, you won't answer that."

Chuckling, he slipped his arm around her shoulders. "There are worse disasters."

"I imagine you're referring to an unassembled bookcase with instructions in a foreign language."

Amusement glinted in his blue eyes at the belligerent way her mouth thinned.

She couldn't help pouting. She was furious with herself for ruining a perfectly good piece of meat, and what was even worse was having to face the disgrace in front of Jonas.

"Come on," he prompted. "There's a fabulous Chinese

restaurant near here. The kitchen can air out while we're gone, and when we get back, I'll finish putting that bookcase together."

"All right," she agreed, and her mouth curved into a weak smile. He was right. The best thing she could do was to draw his attention away from her lack of culinary skill. If he continued to see her, at least she would know for certain that it wasn't her talent in the kitchen that had attracted him.

It was not until she had buckled the seat belt in Jonas's Mercedes that she realized she was still wearing her faded jeans and tennis shoes. "This restaurant isn't fancy, is it?" She placed her hand over the knee that showed white through the threadbare blue jeans.

His gaze followed hers. "Poor Stephanie." He chuckled. "You're having quite a night, aren't you?"

She folded her hands in her lap and crossed her legs. "It's an average night." Better than most. Worse than some. It wasn't every day that Jonas Lockwood took her in his arms and kissed her until her world spun out of its orbit. Just thinking about the way he'd held her produced a warm glow inside her until she was certain she must radiate with it.

"You do enjoy Chinese food?"

"Oh, yes."

"By the way, do you often wear purple tennis shoes?"

She glanced down at her feet and experienced a minor twinge of regret. "I bought them on sale—they were half price."

Jonas chuckled. "I think it was the color."

"I usually only wear them around the apartment," she said, only a little offended. "They work fine for *The Twenty-Minute Workout*."

"The what?"

"*The Twenty-Minute Workout*. It's on every morning at

six. Don't you ever watch it?" She wasn't sure the neighbor in the apartment below appreciated her jumping around the living room at such an ungodly hour, but Mrs. Humphrey had never complained.

"I take it you're referring to a televised exercise program."

"Yes. Have you heard of it?"

"No, I prefer my club."

"Oh, the joys of being rich." She said it with a sigh of feigned envy.

"Are you complaining about your salary?"

"Would it do any good?"

"No."

"That's what I thought." Her gaze slid to him, and again she marveled at the man at her side. The top buttons of his starched white shirt were unfastened, exposing bronze skin and dark curly hair. The long sleeves were rolled up, a sign of the eagerness with which he'd helped her with the bookcase. He stopped at a red light and seemed to feel her watching him. His gaze met hers, and she noted the fine lines that feathered out from the corners of his eyes. The grooves at the side of his mouth, which she had so often thought of as harsh, softened now as he smiled. Jonas Lockwood was a different man when he grinned. It transformed his entire face.

Stephanie was astonished how much his smile could affect her. Her pulse slowed, then started up again, sending the blood pulsing hotly through her veins. If given the least bit of encouragement, she would have impulsively eliminated the small space that separated them and pressed her mouth to his, revealing with a kiss how much being with him had stirred her heart.

She reluctantly dragged her gaze from his and glanced

down at her hands folded neatly in her lap. In that instant, as brief as it was, she'd recognized the truth. She was falling in love with Jonas Lockwood, and she was falling hard. Up to this point in their nonrelationship, she had considered him an intriguing challenge. Jan, Maureen and the others had piqued her interest in their domineering, arrogant employer. The trip to Paris, and their time at the fountain in the park, had added to her curiosity. She'd glimpsed the man buried deep beneath the gruff exterior and had been enthralled. Now she was caught, hook, line and sinker.

Long after they'd returned from dinner and the finished bookcase stood in the corner of her living room, Stephanie recalled the look they'd exchanged in the car on the way to the restaurant. Briefly she wondered if Jonas had recognized it for what it was. Certainly the evening had been altered because of that glance. Before that they had been teasing each other and joking, but from the moment they entered the restaurant, they had immersed themselves in serious conversation. He'd wanted to know everything about her. And she had talked for hours. She told him about growing up in Colville, and what living in the country had meant to a gawky young girl. When he asked how she happened to move to Minneapolis, she explained that her godparents lived nearby, and had encouraged her to move to the area. There were other relatives close by, as well, and clinching the deal was the fact that there were precious few job positions in the eastern part of Washington State.

It wasn't until their plates were cleared away and the waiter delivered two fortune cookies that she realized that while she'd been telling him her life story, he had revealed very little about himself. She felt guilty about dominating the conversation, but when she mentioned it, he brushed her concern aside, telling her there was plenty of time for her to get to know him better. For hours afterward she was on a natural high, exhilarated and happy. She enjoyed talking to him, and for the first time since Paris, they'd been at ease with each other.

When Stephanie arrived at work the following morning, there was a message on her desk from Jan. The note asked Stephanie to join her and the others in the cafeteria on their coffee break. All morning she toyed with the idea of telling her friends about the evening she'd spent with Jonas, but she finally decided against it. The night had been so special that she wanted to wrap the feelings around herself and keep them private.

At midmorning she found the four women gathered around the same table by the window that they'd occupied earlier in the week. Again her coffee was waiting for her.

"Morning."

"You're late," Jan scolded, glancing at her watch. "We've got a lot of ground to cover."

"We do?" Stephanie glanced around the table at her friends and wondered if the Geneva peace talks had held more somber, serious faces.

"It's your move with Mr. Lockwood," Maureen explained. "And we've been up half the night discussing the best way for you to approach him."

"I see." Stephanie took a sip of her coffee to hide an amused grin.

"Subtlety is the key," Barbara insisted. "It's imperative that he doesn't know that you've planned this next *chance* meeting."

"Would it be so wrong to let him know I'm interested?"

Stephanie let her gaze fall to the table so that her friends couldn't read her expression.

"That comes later," Toni told her. "This next step is the all-important one."

"I see." Stephanie didn't, but she doubted that her lack of understanding concerned her friends. "So what's my next move?"

"That's the problem—we can't decide," Jan explained. "We seem to be at a standstill."

"It's a toss-up between four different ideas."

One from each romantic, Stephanie reasoned.

"I thought you could wait until Old Stone Face has left her guard post for the day and then make up an excuse to go to his office. Any excuse would do—for that matter, I could give you one," Jan said eagerly. "You'd be on his turf, where he's most comfortable. Of course, you'd need to find a way to get close to him. You know, bend over the desk so your heads meet and your fingers accidentally brush against his. From there, everything will work out great."

"I don't like that idea," Maureen muttered, slowly shaking her head. "It's too obvious. Besides, Mr. Lockwood's too intelligent not to see through that ploy."

"George Potter is always taking one thing or another up to Jonas's office. I could volunteer to do it for him. I'm sure he wouldn't mind," Stephanie said, defending Jan's idea.

"Yes, but from everything I've read, it would be better if you force his hand."

"Force his hand? What do you mean?" Stephanie glanced at Maureen.

"Let him see you with another man."

"But that's already happened, with disastrous results," Jan argued. "Besides, where are we going to come up with another man?"

"My husband's brother is available."

"Ladies, please," Stephanie said, raising both hands to squelch that plan. "I've got to agree with any scheme you come up with, and that one is most definitely a *no*."

"Sympathy always works," Barbara said thoughtfully. "I've read lots of romances where the turning point in the relationship comes when either the hero or the heroine gets sick or is seriously hurt."

For a moment Stephanie actually believed her friends were about to suggest she came down with the mumps or chicken pox just so she could garner Jonas's sympathy.

"I've got a cousin who works for an orthopedic surgeon. He could put a cast on Stephanie's leg so Mr. Lockwood would think she had broken it." Again Barbara glanced around the table, gauging the others' reactions.

Stephanie could just see herself hobbling to and from work for weeks in a plaster cast up to her hip while she carried out a ridiculous charade. After all, she couldn't very well arrive one day later without the cast and announce to everyone that a miracle had occurred.

"No go." She nixed that plan before anyone else could endorse it and she ended up in a body cast without ever knowing how it happened. "What's wrong with me inviting him over to my apartment for dinner?"

"It's so obvious," Barbara groaned.

"And the rest of your ideas aren't?"

"Actually, something like that just might work," Jan said thoughtfully, chewing on the nail of her index finger. "It's not brilliant, but it has possibilities."

"There's only one problem," Stephanie informed her friends, remembering the charred pot roast from the night before. "I'm not much of a cook."

"That's not a problem. You could hire a chef to come in. Mr. Lockwood would never have to know."

"Isn't that a bit expensive?" Stephanie could visualize the balance in her checkbook rapidly reaching the point of no return.

"It's worth a try." Barbara rapidly discounted Stephanie's concern.

"What was your idea, Toni?" Everyone had revealed their schemes except the small brunette.

Toni shrugged. "Nothing great—I thought you might 'accidentally on purpose' meet Mr. Lockwood by the elevator sometime. You could strike up a casual conversation and let matters follow their natural course."

"But Steph could end up spending the entire day hanging around the elevator," Barbara said, her voice raised at what she considered an unreasonable plan.

"Not only that," Jan added, "but who's to say that the elevator will be empty? She'd look ridiculous if there were other people aboard."

Stephanie's gaze flew from one intent face to the other. "Actually, I like that idea best."

"What?" Three pairs of shocked eyes shot to Stephanie.

"Well, for heaven's sake! With the rest of your ideas, I'm either going to have to subject myself to Martha Westheimer's scrutiny, date Barbara's brother-in-law, sheath my body in plaster or deplete my checking account to hire a chef to cook for me. Toni's idea is the only one that makes any sense."

"But *you* suggested inviting him to dinner," Jan informed her.

Maureen folded her hands on the table top and studied Stephanie through narrowed eyes. "You know, it suddenly dawned on me that you're not fighting us anymore, Steph."

"No," she said and reached for her coffee, curving her fingers around the cup. She took a drink and when she set it back down, she noted that the others had all fallen silent.

"In fact, if you've noticed, she's even contributing her own ideas." Jan's look was approving.

"Could it be that you've developed feelings for Mr. Lockwood?" Barbara asked.

"It could be that I find the man a challenge."

"It's more than that," Toni said, pointing a finger at Stephanie. "I noticed when you first joined us this morning that there was something different about you."

So it shows, Stephanie mused to herself, a bit irritated.

"What do you feel for Mr. Lockwood?"

"I'm not completely sure yet," she admitted honestly. "He makes me so angry I could shake him."

"But…"

"But then, at other times, he looks at me and we share a smile, and I want to melt on the inside." Stephanie knew her eyes must have revealed her feelings, because the others grew quiet again.

"Could you see yourself married to him?" Maureen asked.

Stephanie didn't need to think twice about that. "Yes." They would argue and disagree and challenge each other— that was a given—but the loving between them would be exquisite.

The unexpected shout of joy that followed her announcement nearly knocked her out of her chair. "Good grief, be quiet," she said, her hand over her heart. "We're a long way from the altar."

"Not nearly as far as you think, honey," Barbara said with a wide, knowing grin. "Not nearly as far as you think."

Stephanie left the cafeteria a couple of minutes later.

In spite of everything, she had to struggle not to laugh. Her four romance-minded friends seemed to believe that a couple of dinners—one of which they knew nothing about—and a few stolen kisses in the moonlight practically constituted a proposal of marriage.

When she got back to her desk Stephanie placed her purse in the bottom drawer, sat down and turned on her computer, preparing to type a letter. She paused, her hands poised over the keyboard, trying to analyze her feelings for Jonas. The words on the screen blurred as she remembered his kisses. From the way he'd looked, he'd been as surprised as she was. The minute they'd met, she had disliked the man. He was so dictatorial and high-handed that he infuriated her. He enjoyed baiting her and challenging her. In some ways, Jonas Lockwood was the most difficult man she'd ever known. But at the same time, she suspected that the rewards of his love would be beyond any worldly treasure she could ever hope to accumulate.

At five that evening Stephanie cleared off the top of her desk, preparing to head home to her apartment. It had been so late by the time Jonas finished assembling the bookcase that she hadn't had the energy to fill it with the books that were propped against her bedroom wall. She'd learned as the evening progressed that he was an avid reader, and they'd had a lively discussion on their favorite authors. When he'd left her apartment, it had been close to midnight. She'd thanked him for dinner and his help, and had been mildly disappointed that he hadn't kissed her goodnight. Nor did he arrange for another meeting. At the time she had been in such a happy daze that she hadn't thought too much about it. Now she wondered how long it would be before she saw him again. She was a bit discouraged not to have heard from him yet. All day she'd been half expecting him to pop in unannounced and dictate another letter to her. The entire afternoon had felt strangely incomplete, and she realized that she'd been wanting to hear from him since the minute she arrived that morning.

On her way to the elevator, she spotted him talking to Donald Black, head of the accounting department. Her pulse quickened at the virile sight Jonas presented. He was tall and broad-shouldered, and—she freely admitted it—a handsome devil. Her heart swelled at the sight of him, and when his gaze happened to catch hers, she smiled warmly, revealing all the pleasure she felt at seeing him again.

Jonas didn't respond. If anything, he almost looked right through her, as if she were nothing more than a piece of furniture. If any emotion showed on his taut features, it was regret. She swallowed, feeling as if she had a pine cone lodged in her throat.

When he did happen to glance in her direction, she read the warning in his eyes. What happened outside the office was between them, but inside Lockwood Industries she was nothing more than George Potter's executive assistant, and she would do well to remember that.

Humiliated and insulted, she stiffened and looked past him as though he were a stranger, pretending she had neither the time nor the energy to play his infantile games. She thrust her shoulders back in a display of anger and pride, and held them so stiffly that her shoulder blades ached within seconds.

From the minute he had left her the night before, she had been happy and content. Now her spirits plummeted to the bottom floor at breakneck speed and landed with a sickening thud. She turned her gaze to the front of the elevator and refused to look at him another moment.

She heard the two men walking behind her, but she ignored them both.

"Good evening, Miss Coulter," Jonas said in passing.

"Good evening," she responded tightly, her tone professional and crisp.

The elevator arrived, and without another word, Stephanie joined the others in the five o'clock rush. Five minutes later she caught Metro bus #17, which dropped her off a block from her apartment.

Affronted by his attitude, chagrined at how much she had read into the simple evening they'd shared, and upset that she'd allowed Jan and her friends to talk her into believing Jonas Lockwood had a heart, Stephanie quickly changed clothes and decided to weed her miniature herb garden.

She hadn't been at it more than thirty minutes when the doorbell chimed. Glaring at her front door, she continued pulling up the weeds in the small redwood planters; then stared down at her garden gloves and realized she'd uprooted more basil than weeds.

She didn't need to answer the door to know it was Jonas who stood on the other side. When the doorbell rang sharply a second time, she impatiently set her trowel aside and stood up.

She muttered under her breath as she marched across the living room floor, and swore that if he commented on her purple tennis shoes one more time she would slam the door in his face. She jerked off a dirt-covered glove and pulled open the door.

"Hello, Stephanie."

"Mr. Lockwood," she responded tautly. "What an unpleasant surprise."

"May I come in?"

"No." She avoided his eyes. It took all her willpower not to close the door and be done with him. But she'd decided to play out this little charade. She might not come from a rich, powerful family like his, but she didn't lack pride. "As you can see, I'm busy," she finished.

"This will only take a minute."

"I'm surprised you're lowering yourself to come here," she said waspishly. "Your message this afternoon came through crystal clear."

"I'd like to explain that." Disregarding her unfriendly welcome and her unwillingness to allow him into her apartment, he stalked past her and into the living room.

"It seems I have no say in the matter. All right, since you're so keen to explain yourself, do so and then kindly leave."

"I honestly *would* like to explain—"

"Go ahead," she said. "But let me assure you, it isn't necessary."

Jonas leaned heavily on his cane as he walked to the center of the room. Stephanie stubbornly remained at the front door. She'd closed it but stood ready to yank it open the minute he finished.

He turned to face her and placed both hands on the curve of the polished oak cane, using it for support.

When long moments passed without him saying anything, she spoke into the heavy silence. "I realize the name Coulter may not cause a banker's heart to flutter, but it's a good name. My father's proud of it, and so am I."

"Stephanie, you misunderstood my intentions."

"I sincerely doubt that." Her voice trembled with the strength of her emotion. "I understood you perfectly."

His eyes were blue and probing as they swept her tightly controlled features. She wondered if a splattering of mud was smeared across her cheek but wouldn't give him the satisfaction of running her fingers over her face to find out. No doubt he would view that as a sign of weakness. She *was* weak, she realized, but only when he held her and kissed her, and she wouldn't allow that now.

"It wouldn't matter to me if your name was Getty or Buffet, or Gates, for that matter. Don't you understand that?"

"Obviously not," she returned stiffly. "You put me in my place this evening—and you did a good job of it, I might add. I'm a lowly assistant, and you're the big, mighty boss, and I shouldn't confuse the two. Since I'm not the mature woman you prefer, I would do well to bow low whenever your shadow passes near me. Isn't that what you meant to say?"

"No. I should have known you'd be unreasonable."

"Me? Unreasonable? That's a laugh. I've worked for Mr. Potter for nearly two years, and we've never exchanged a cross word. Two seconds in your company and I'm so angry I can hardly think."

"Would you stop with this lowly assistant bit? I wouldn't care if you were the first vice president," he said. "Anything that's between you and me has to stay out of the office!"

"Of course it does," she simpered. "It would do your reputation considerable harm if anyone knew you'd lowered yourself to actually date an employee."

"It's not me I'm thinking about."

"You could have fooled me."

"Stephanie, if you'd get off your high horse a minute, you'd see that it's good business. The fact is, I shouldn't even be seeing you now. I'm supposed to be at a meeting."

She jerked open the door. "Don't let me stop you." She recognized the flash of anger in his eyes and experienced a small sense of triumph.

He ran a hand over his face, wiping his expression clean as he fought for control of his considerable temper. "Don't you understand that I'm doing this for your own protection?"

"Forgive me for being dense, but quite frankly, I don't."

He continued as though she hadn't spoken. "Some no-good busybody is going to drag your name through the mud the minute they learn we're seeing each other. The next thing either of us knows, you'll be the subject of jealous, malicious gossip. You won't be able to walk into a room without people whispering your name."

Stephanie swallowed convulsively. "I hadn't thought of…that." Her friends were supportive, but they were only a tiny fraction of the staff at Lockwood Industries.

"A thousand times I told myself that seeing you would only lead to trouble." A dark, brooding look clouded his eyes. "Even now, I'm not convinced it's right for either of us."

She had to swallow down the words to argue with him, because being with him felt incredibly right to her.

"If you're seeking my apology for what happened earlier," he said in a gruff, low-pitched voice, "then you have it. It has never been my intention to offend you."

She swallowed tightly, and nodded, embarrassed. "*I owe you* an apology, as well." With her hands clasped in front of her, she took a step toward him. "You're right about the office, Jonas, only I was too much of an idiot to see it."

He smiled one of those rare, rich smiles of his, a smile that she was convinced could melt stone. "I'm pleased we cleared up this misunderstanding," he said, and glanced at his watch, frowning. "Now I really must be going."

"Thank you for coming." Knowing that he'd found it important to explain meant a great deal to her.

He walked to the door, then suddenly turned to her. "Do you sail?"

"Sure." She'd never been on a sailboat in her life. "At least, I think I can, given the chance."

"How about this weekend?"

"I'd like that very much."

"I'll call you later," he said on his way out the door. Then he muttered something about her not making bankers' hearts flutter but doing a mighty fine job with his own.

She closed the door after him and leaned against it, grinning with a warmth that beamed all the way from her heart.

Eight

A stiff breeze billowed the huge spinnaker, and the thirty-foot sailboat heeled sharply, shaving the waterline with a razor-sharp cut. Stephanie threw back her head and laughed into the wind. The pins holding her hair had long ago been discarded, and her blond tresses now unfurled behind her like a flag, waving in the crisp air. "Oh, Jonas, I love this."

His answering smile was warm. "Somehow I knew you'd be a natural on the water."

"This is so much fun." She crossed her arms over her breasts as though to hug the sense of exhilaration she felt.

"You've really never sailed before?"

"Never." She noted the way he steered the boat from the helm, his movements confident, sure. "Can I do that?"

"If you'd like."

She joined him and sat down at his side. "Okay, tell me what to do."

"Just head her into the wind."

"Okay." She placed both hands on the long narrow handle that controlled the rudder and watched as the boat turned sharply. Almost immediately the sails went slack, but one guiding touch from Jonas and they filled with wind again.

"This isn't as easy as it looks," she complained with a smile. The day was marvelous. There wasn't any other way to describe it.

Jonas had arrived at her apartment early that morning, bringing freshly squeezed orange juice, croissants still warm from the oven and two large cups of steaming coffee. She had always been a morning person, and apparently he was, as well.

She had prepared her own surprise by packing them a picnic lunch. Included in her basket were two small loaves of French bread, a bottle of white wine, a variety of cheeses and some fresh strawberries that had cost her more than she cared to think about. But one look at the plump, juicy fruit and she couldn't resist.

The journey into Duluth was pleasant, as Jonas spoke of his family and their home on Lake Superior. His mother lived there now, and he said they would be joining her later that afternoon.

"You're quiet all of a sudden," Jonas mentioned as he reached over to correct her steering once again. "Is anything troubling you?"

"How could anything possibly be wrong on a glorious day like this one?"

"You were frowning."

"I was?" Stephanie glanced out over the choppy water. There wasn't another boat in sight. It was as though she and Jonas alone faced the mighty power of this astonishing lake. "I was thinking about meeting your mother. I guess I'm nervous."

"Why?"

"Jonas, look at me. I could be confused with a fugitive

from justice in these old jeans. I only wish you'd said something earlier, so I could have brought a change of clothes along."

"Mother won't care."

Perhaps not, Stephanie mused, but *she* certainly did. If she was going to come face-to-face with Jonas's mother, she would have preferred to do it when she looked her best. Not now, with her hair in tangles and knots from the wind, and her face free of makeup and pink from a day in the sun. On the other hand, Mrs. Lockwood would be seeing her at her worst and would no doubt be pleasantly surprised if she met her again later. Her lazy smile grew and grew, and she glanced at Jonas.

His look was thoughtful. "Stephanie, I don't want you to fret about meeting my family."

"She must be an amazing woman."

"As a matter of fact she is, but you say that as if you know her, and that isn't possible."

Stephanie momentarily scanned the swirling green water in an effort to avoid meeting his intense gaze. "You're right. I could pass her on the street and not know who she is, but I'm sure she's a special person." The woman who'd born and raised Jonas would have to be.

Jonas placed his arm around her shoulder, and she leaned her head back against the solid cushion of his chest. Gently, he kissed the top of her head.

She turned so that her lips touched his throat where his shirt opened. His skin was warm, and she both felt and heard his answering sigh. His large hand was splayed against the back of her head, and he directed her mouth to his. She didn't need any more encouragement, and their mouths met in a gentle brushing of lips. She moved away from the helm and slipped her arms around his neck. He kissed her again, longer this time, much longer, but still he was infinitely gentle, as though he feared hurting her. He finally released her when the sails began to flap in the wind, but he did it with such reluctance that her heart sang.

"Are you hungry?" she asked, more for something to do than from any desire for lunch.

"Yes," he admitted hoarsely, but when she went toward the wicker picnic basket, he caught her hand, delaying her.

She raised questioning eyes to his. "Jonas?"

In a heartbeat, he gently pulled her back to him, his hand slipping around her waist. "It isn't food that tempts me." He kissed her again, his mouth moving on hers with an urgency as old as mankind itself. She threaded her fingers through his hair and held his head fast until she was so weak that she slumped against him.

"Jonas," she breathed

He brought her down so that they were sitting side by side. He put his arms around her and fused his mouth to hers. Again and again he kissed her, tasting, nipping at her lower lip, until she thought she would go mad with wanting him. Her hand crept up his hard chest and closed around the folds of his collar. The kiss was long and thorough. This day with Jonas was the sweetest she had ever known.

With his arms wrapped securely around her shoulders, she swayed with the gentle rocking of the boat, lulled by the peace that surrounded them. He had somehow lowered the sails without her even knowing it. He continued to hold her, staring out over the rolling water. Not for the first time she noticed that his eyes were incredibly blue. As though sensing her scrutiny, he gazed down at her. For a long moment they stared at each other, lost in a world that had been created just for them and for this moment.

Sometime later Jonas reached for the picnic basket. He

brought out a plump red strawberry, plucked the stem from the top and fed it to Stephanie. She bit into the pulp, and a thin line of juice ran down her chin. As she moved to wipe it away, his hand stopped hers. He bent his index finger, and with his knuckle rubbed the red juice aside. Then, very slowly, as though he couldn't resist, he lowered his mouth to hers. Their lips met and clung. His grip tightened as his tongue sought and found hers. When he lifted his mouth from her lips, he smiled gently. Moisture pooled in her eyes, and a tear slipped from the corner of her eye and rolled down her cheek.

A puzzled frown furrowed his brow. "You're crying."

"I know."

"Did I hurt you?"

"No."

"Then why?"

She turned her head into his shoulder, convinced he would laugh once he knew.

"Stephanie?"

"It was so beautiful. I always cry when I'm this happy." Feeling foolish, she rubbed her hands against her eyes. "It's a family curse. My mother cries every Christmas."

Jonas reached for the wine, opened it and poured them each a glass.

"Alcohol won't help," she said, sniffling, but she didn't refuse the glass Jonas offered her.

"Are there any other family curses I should know about?"

"I have a bit of a temper."

Jonas chuckled. "I've encountered that."

Laughing lightly, she straightened and took her first sip of wine. It felt cool and tasted sweet, reminding her that she was hungry. "Some cheese and bread?" she asked, looking at him.

He leaned forward to reach for it, and as he did, a look of pain shot across his face, widening his eyes. He sat back quickly.

"Jonas?" Concerned, she turned to him. "What is it?"

"It'll pass in a moment."

"What will pass?"

"The pain," he managed, his voice grating, stroking the length of his thigh in an effort to ease the agony. He closed his eyes and turned away from her.

She bent in front of him, nearly frantic. "Tell me what I can do."

"Nothing," he said through clenched teeth. "Go away."

"No," she said. "I won't... I couldn't." Because she didn't know what else to do, she put her hand on his, kneading the knotted flesh that had cramped so viciously. She could feel the muscles relax when the spasm passed.

"What happened? Did I do something?"

"No." He moved away from her, reaching for the ropes, preparing to raise the sails.

"Talk to me, for heaven's sake," she demanded, grabbing his forearm. "Don't close up on me now. I care about you, Jonas. I want to help!"

His hard gaze softened, and he tenderly cupped her cheek. Relieved, she turned her face into his palm and kissed it.

"Did I frighten you?" he asked her softly.

"Only because I didn't know what to do to help you." She sighed, feeling weak and emotionally drained. "Does that happen often?" The thought of him enduring such pain was intolerable.

"It happens often enough to make me appreciate my cane."

In spite of the circumstances, she bowed her head to hide a smile.

"You find that amusing?"

Her head shot up. "No, of course not. It's just that everyone in the office claims they know when your leg is hurting, because you're usually in a foul mood."

"They say that, do they?"

"It's true, isn't it?"

He shrugged. "To be honest, I hadn't given it much thought."

She reached inside the picnic basket for the two loaves of bread. She set them out, along with a plate of cheese, avoiding looking at Jonas as she asked him the question that had been on her mind since Paris. "How'd it happen?"

"My leg?" His gaze sharpened.

"You don't have to tell me if you'd rather not."

He hesitated, and when he finally spoke, she realized that telling her the story was an indication that he trusted her. "It happened several years ago, in a skiing accident. I was on the slopes with a…friend. There isn't much to say. She got in trouble, and when I went to help her, I fell."

"Down the slope?"

"No, off a cliff."

"Oh, Jonas." She felt sick at the thought of him being hurt. She closed her eyes to the mental image of him lying in some snow bank in agony, waiting for help to arrive.

"The doctors say I'm lucky to still have my leg. In the beginning I wished they had amputated it and been done with it. Now I'm more tolerant of the pain. I've learned to live with it." He grew silent, and Stephanie sensed that there was a great deal more to the story that he hadn't revealed, but she accepted what he had told her and didn't press him further.

"Thank you, Jonas," she said softly.

"For what?"

"For bringing me with you today. For relating what must be a difficult story for you to tell. For trusting me."

"No, Stephanie," he whispered, lifting her mouth to his. "Thank you."

Later that day, when Jonas pulled up to the large two-story brick mansion overlooking Lake Superior, Stephanie's breath caught at the sight of his magnificent family home. "Oh, Jonas," she said, awed. "It's beautiful." Imposing, as well, she thought, attempting to subdue her nervousness. Her hand went to her hair, and she ran her fingers through the tangled mass.

"You look fine," he told her.

She lowered her arm and rested her clenched hand in her lap. "Just you wait," she threatened. "I'm going to introduce you to my father. He'll be in mud-spattered coveralls, sitting on top of a tractor. You'll be in a thousand-dollar pin-striped suit, and you'll know what it feels like to be out of your element."

To her amazement, Jonas laughed. He parked the car at the front of the house, or perhaps the back—she couldn't actually tell which—and turned off the engine. "I look forward to meeting your family."

"You do?"

He climbed out of the car and came around to her side, opening her door for her. "One thing, though."

"Yes?"

"Don't introduce me to your mother at Christmas. I have a heck of a time dealing with crying women."

Stephanie got the giggles. They were probably a result of her nervousness, but once she started it was nearly impossible to stop. He laughed with her, and they were still laughing as, with his arm linked around her waist, he led her through the wide double doors of the house.

The minute they were inside her amusement vanished. The marble floor of the entryway had probably cost more than her family's farm in Colville. Marble that was probably imported from Italy. Maybe Greece. A large winding stairway angled off to the right, its polished mahogany balustrade gleaming in the sun.

"Jonas, is that you?" An elegantly dressed woman appeared. She was tall and regal-looking, with twinkling blue eyes that were the exact image of Jonas's. Her hair was completely gray, and she wore it in a neatly coiled French roll. She held her hands out to her son. He claimed them with his own and kissed her on the cheek.

"Mother."

They parted, and his mother paused to greet Stephanie. If she disapproved of Stephanie's attire, it wasn't revealed in the warmth of her smile. "You must be Stephanie."

For one crazy second Stephanie had the urge to curtsy. "Hello, Mrs. Lockwood." Even her voice sounded awed and a bit unnatural.

"Please call me Elizabeth."

"Thank you, I will."

"I can see you've had a full day on the lake." Elizabeth glanced at her son.

"It was marvelous," Stephanie confirmed.

"I hope you're hungry. Clara's been cooking all day, anticipating your arrival."

Jonas placed his hand along the back of Stephanie's neck and directed her into the largest room she had ever seen in a private home.

"Who's Clara?" she asked under her breath.

"The cook," he whispered. When his mother turned her back, he kissed Stephanie's cheek.

"Jonas," she hissed. "Don't do that!"

"Did you say something, Stephanie?" Elizabeth turned around questioningly.

"Actually...no," she stuttered, glowering hotly at Jonas, who coughed to disguise a laugh. "I didn't say anything."

"Would either of you care for a glass of wine before dinner?" Elizabeth asked, taking a seat on an elegant velvet sofa.

Stephanie claimed the matching chair across from her, and Jonas stood behind Stephanie.

"That would be fine, Mother," he said, answering for them both. "Would you like me to serve as bartender?"

"Please." Elizabeth folded her hands on her lap. "Jonas has spoken highly of you, Stephanie."

"He...has?" she sputtered.

"Yes. Is there something unusual about that?"

Jonas delivered a glass of wine to his mother before bringing Stephanie hers. He sat beside her on the arm of the chair and looped his arm around her shoulder.

"Clara will never forgive you if you don't say hello, Son," Elizabeth informed him. "While you do that, I'll show Stephanie my garden. It's lovely this time of year."

"I'd like that," Stephanie said, standing. She continued to hold her wine, although she had no intention of drinking it. All she needed was to get tipsy in front of Jonas's mother.

"I'll be back in a minute," he whispered as he left the room.

A small, awkward silence followed. Stephanie looked down at her soiled jeans and cringed inwardly. "I feel I should apologize for my attire," she began, following Jonas's mother out through French doors that led to a lush green garden. Roses were in bloom, and their sweet fragrance filled the air.

"Nonsense," Elizabeth countered. "You've been sailing. I didn't expect you to arrive in an evening gown."

"But I don't imagine you expected jeans and purple tennis shoes, either."

Elizabeth laughed; the sound was light and musical. "I believe I'm going to grow fond of you."

"I hope so." Stephanie studied her wine.

"Forgive me for being so blunt, but are you in love with my son?"

Stephanie raised her eyes to Jonas's mother's and nodded. "Yes."

Elizabeth placed her hand over her heart and sighed expressively. "I am so relieved to hear you say that."

"You are? Why?"

"Because *he* loves *you,* child."

Stephanie opened her mouth to argue, but Elizabeth stopped her.

"I don't know if he's admitted it to himself yet, but he will soon. A few minutes ago, when you came into the house, I heard Jonas laugh. It's been years since I've heard the sound of my son's laughter. Thank you for that."

"Really, I didn't do anything... I—"

"Please forgive me for interrupting, but we haven't much time."

Stephanie's heart shot to her throat. "Yes?"

"You must be patient with my son. He's been hurt, terribly hurt, and he is greatly in need of a woman's love. He probably hasn't told you about Gretchen. He loved her deeply, far more than the wretched woman deserved. She left him after the accident. She told him that she couldn't live with a cripple, even though it was she who had caused the accident with her carelessness."

Jonas's mother didn't need to say a word more for Stephanie to hate the fickle, faceless woman.

"That was nearly ten years ago, and he hasn't brought another woman to meet me until today. Knowing my son the way I do, I'm sure he'll battle what he feels for you. He's reluctant to trust again, so you must be patient and," she added, gently touching Stephanie's hand, "very strong. He deserves your love, and although he may be stubborn now and again, believe me, the woman my son loves will be the happiest woman alive. When Jonas loves again, I promise you it will be with all his heart and his soul."

Stephanie felt moisture gather in her eyes. "I don't know if I deserve someone as good as Jonas."

"Perhaps not," Elizabeth Lockwood said, her soft voice removing any harshness from her words. "But *he* deserves *you*." She glanced over her shoulder. "He's coming now, so smile, and please don't say anything about our conversation."

"I won't," Stephanie promised, blinking back tears.

"There you are," Jonas said as he joined his mother and Stephanie. "Did mother let you in on any family secrets?"

"Several, as a matter of fact," Elizabeth said with a small laugh.

"Clara wants me to tell you that dinner is ready any time you are."

"Wonderful," Elizabeth replied with a warm smile.

"She cooked my favorite dessert," Jonas said, sharing a secret smile with Stephanie. "Strawberry shortcake."

Stephanie could feel the heated color seep up her neck, invading her cheeks.

"I don't recall you being particularly fond of strawberries," Elizabeth commented as she led the way into the dining room.

"It's a recent addiction, Mother," Jonas said, reaching for Stephanie's hand and linking her fingers with his. He raised her knuckles to his mouth and lightly kissed them.

The meal was one Stephanie would long remember, but not because of the food, though it could have been served in a four-star restaurant. Jonas was a different person, chatting, joking, teasing. He insisted that Clara join them for coffee so Stephanie could meet her. Although Stephanie liked the rotund woman instantly, she could feel the older woman's distrust. But by the end of the evening all that had changed, and Stephanie knew she could count Clara as a friend.

When it came time to leave, Elizabeth hugged Stephanie and whispered softly in her ear, "Thank you, my dear, for giving me back my son. Remember what I said. Be patient."

"No. Thank *you*," Stephanie whispered back. They joined hands, and Stephanie nodded once. "I'll remember."

It was dark by the time they left Duluth, and Stephanie was physically drained from the long day. She yawned once and tried to disguise it. "I like your mother, Jonas."

"She seemed to be quite taken with you, too."

They talked a bit more, and she began to drop off, giving way to her fatigue. He woke her when they reached the outskirts of Minneapolis.

"I'm sorry to be such terrible company," she said, yawning.

"You're anything but," he said, contradicting her. He eased to a stop in front of her apartment building and parked the car, but he kept the engine running.

"Do you want to come in for coffee?" she asked.

"No, you're exhausted, and I have some work that I need to look over."

"Jonas, don't tell me you're going to work on a Saturday night." She glanced at her wristwatch, shocked to find that it was after eleven.

He chuckled, and leaned over to press his mouth lightly to hers. "No, but it was the best excuse I could come up with to refuse your invitation."

"Good, I was worried there for a minute. You work too hard." She yearned to tell him how much the day had meant to her, how much she'd enjoyed the time on the sailboat, and meeting his mother and Clara. But finding the right words was impossible. "Thank you for everything," she said when he helped her out of the car. "I can't remember a day I've enjoyed more."

"Me, either," he murmured, his gaze holding hers.

"We've got it!" Jan announced Monday morning, as she, Maureen, Toni and Barbara circled Stephanie's desk like warriors surrounding a wagon train.

"Got what?" Stephanie looked up blankly. She'd only arrived at the office a few minutes earlier and hadn't even turned on her computer. "What are you talking about?"

"Your next move with Mr. Lockwood."

"Oh, that," she returned with a sigh. She hadn't told her friends about the weekend sailing jaunt, but then she'd been keeping quite a few secrets from them lately.

"We've got it all worked out."

"Answer me this first," Stephanie said. "Will I need to wear a cast? Date someone's brother-in-law? Hire a French chef?"

"No."

"It's working out great. We've got a contact in the janitorial department."

"A what?"

"All you have to do," Maureen explained excitedly, "is get in the elevator alone with Mr. Lockwood."

"Yes?" Stephanie could feel the enthusiasm coming from her coworkers in waves. "What will that do?"

"That's where Mike from maintenance comes into the picture," Toni explained patiently.

"He'll flip the switch, and the two of you will be trapped alone together for hours."

"Isn't that a marvelous idea?" Barbara said.

"It works in all the best romances."

"It's a sure thing."

"You're game, aren't you, Steph?"

Nine

"No, I'm not game for your crazy schemes," Stephanie informed her friends primly. It wasn't that she objected to being alone with Jonas for hours on end—in fact, she would relish that—but to plot their meeting this way went against everything she hoped for in their relationship.

Jan, Maureen, Toni and Barbara exchanged an incredulous look.

"But it's perfect."

"Jonas and I don't need it," Stephanie said, knowing that the best way to appease her friends was with the truth.

"What do you mean, you don't need it?" Jan asked, her eyes narrowing with suspicion.

"You been holding out on us, girl?" Maureen barked, her hand on her hip.

"I do believe she has been," Barbara said before Stephanie had a chance to answer.

"Let's just say this," Stephanie said with a conspiratorial smile. "The romantic relationship between Mr. Lockwood and me is developing nicely."

"How nicely?" Jan wanted to know. "And put it into terms we understand."

"Like on a scale of one to ten," Barbara added.

"What's a ten?" Stephanie glanced up at her friends, uncertain.

"If you need to ask, we're in trouble."

"Right." Hot color blossomed in Stephanie's cheeks.

"If he phoned once or twice and showed up at your apartment—that's a four, a low four."

"But if you shared a couple of romantic evenings on the town, I'd call that a six."

"I'd say meeting his family is an eight," Toni murmured thoughtfully, her index finger pressed against her cheek. "Maybe a nine."

The four romantics paused expectantly, waiting for Stephanie to locate her relationship with Jonas on their makeshift scale. "Well?" Jan coaxed.

"An eight, then, maybe a nine," she admitted softly, waiting for her friends to break into shouts and cheers. Instead, she was greeted with a shocked, dubious silence.

"You're not teasing, are you?" Barbara murmured. "You really aren't joking?"

"No. Jonas introduced me to his mother this weekend. She's a wonderful woman."

"It's going to work," Maureen whispered in awe, her face revealing her surprise. "It's really going to work!"

"Speaking of work…" Stephanie said reluctantly, glancing at her watch. She was relieved not to be subjected to an endless list of questions from her coworkers, but she was so grateful to her romance-loving friends that she wanted them to share some of her happiness.

As though in a daze, Jan, Maureen, Toni and Barbara turned and walked away as if in a trance.

"Do you think the janitor will give us a refund?" Barbara asked no one in particular as they moved out the door.

"Who cares?" came the reply from the others.

Stephanie's boss, George Potter, arrived at the office a couple of minutes later, his first day back from Seattle. They exchanged a few pleasantries, and he handed her some notes from his briefcase. "If you get the chance, could you take these receipts to Donald Black?"

He said the name stiffly; Stephanie knew from experience that there was little love lost between the two men. She couldn't imagine her amiable boss disliking anyone, so she was quite certain he had a good reason for his animosity.

"I'll do it as soon as I finish this report," she said with a welcoming smile. There was so much to be happy about that she felt like humming love songs. She wondered briefly how Jonas's day was going, her thoughts wandering naturally to the man who just happened to be in sole possession of her heart.

The morning whizzed past. Stephanie was so close to finishing the report that she skipped her midmorning coffee break. Five minutes later, with the floor all but deserted and Mr. Potter in a meeting, she walked down the hallway to give the receipts to Donald Black.

"Good morning, Mr. Black," she said, knocking politely on his open door. "Mr. Potter asked me to bring these over."

"Put them over there," he said, indicating a table on the other side of the room.

Stephanie placed the envelope where he'd requested and turned to leave, but the middle-aged, potbellied man stood and blocked her way.

"You and Jonas Lockwood seem to be seeing a great deal of each other."

A plethora of possible answers crowded her mind. Jonas had mentioned that he would prefer to keep their personal relationship out of the office, but she wasn't in the habit of lying. Nor was it her custom to discuss her personal relationships with a stranger.

"We're…friends," she said, since apparently Jonas himself had mentioned her to the other man.

"I see." With slow, deliberate movements, Mr. Black placed his pencil on the edge of his desk. "How willing are you to be…friends with other Lockwood employees?"

She stiffened at the insulting way he uttered the word *friends*. "I'm not sure I understand the question."

"I'm quite certain you do."

She didn't know what game this middle-aged Don Juan was playing, but she had no intention of remaining in his office. "If you'll excuse me."

"As a matter of fact, I won't. We're having an important discussion here, and I'd consider it a desertion of your duties to this company and to me personally if you left."

She wasn't much into office gossip, but she was starting to understand why George Potter had no respect for Donald Black. As the head of the accounting department, Black had been through three assistants in the two years Stephanie had been employed by Lockwood Industries. From her own dismal experience with her former employers, she could guess the reason why he had trouble keeping decent employees.

"I'll desert my duties, then," she replied flippantly. She turned to go, but didn't make it to the door. He reached out and gripped her shoulder, spinning her around. She was so shocked that he would dare to touch her that she was momentarily speechless.

"Everyone in the company knows you're being generous with Lockwood. All I want is a share in the goods."

Still breathless with shock, she slapped his hand aside. "You sicken me."

"Give me time, honey, I promise to improve."

"I sincerely doubt that."

He drew her closer, obviously intent on kissing her, but she managed to evade him. With everything that was in her, she pushed against his chest with both hands and was astonished at the strength of the man.

Her eye happened to catch the clock, and she realized it would be another five minutes before anyone returned to the department. Crying out would do no good, since there wasn't anyone there to answer her plea for help.

"All I want is a little kiss," Mr. Black said coaxingly. "Just give me that and I'll let you go."

"I'd rather vomit!" she cried, kicking at him and missing. "You stupid—"

"Let her go."

The quietly spoken words evidenced such controlled anger that both Stephanie and her attacker froze. Black dropped his arms and released her.

With a strangled sob she turned aside and braced her hands against the edge of the desk, weak with relief. Her neatly coiled hair had fallen free of its restraining pins and hung in loose tendrils around her flushed face. It took her several deep breaths to regain her strength. She didn't know how or why Jonas was there, but she had never been so glad to see anyone.

"Clear out your desk, Black." The emotionless, frigid control in Jonas's voice sent a chill up her spine. She'd never heard a man sound more angry or more dangerous. Acid dripped from each syllable. An unspoken challenge hung over the room, almost as if Jonas was hoping for a physical confrontation.

"Hey, Jonas, you got the wrong idea here. Your lady

friend came on to me." Black raised both hands in an emotional plea of innocence.

Stephanie spun around, her eyes spitting fire.

"Is that true?" Jonas asked evenly.

"No!" she shouted, indignant and furious. "He grabbed me—"

"You didn't hear her crying out, did you?" Black shot back, interrupting Stephanie. "I swear, man, I'm not the kind of guy who has to force women. They come to me."

"I said clear out your desk." Jonas pointed the tip of his cane at the far door. "A check will be mailed to you tomorrow."

Donald Black gave Stephanie a murderous glare as he marched out of the office. "You'll regret this, Lockwood," he muttered on his way past Jonas.

Stephanie could see the coiled alertness drain from Jonas the minute Black was out of the room. "Did he hurt you?"

"No… I'm fine." She closed her eyes. She was too proud to allow a man like Donald Black to reduce her to tears.

Jonas's arm slipped around her, comforting and warm, chasing away the icy, numbing chill that had settled over her. "I'm fine," she whispered fiercely, burying her face in his shoulder. "Really," she insisted as she shuddered against him.

"Let's get out of here." He led her into the hallway and toward the elevator. She didn't recall anything of the ride to the top floor, but when the thick door glided open, Jonas called to Martha Westheimer.

"Bring me a strong cup of coffee, and add plenty of sugar."

"Jonas, really," Stephanie said, her voice wavering slightly. "I'm fine, and I'm certainly not in shock."

He ignored her, leading her into his office and sitting her

down in a heavy leather chair. He paced the area directly in front of her until the ever-efficient Martha appeared with the coffee, carefully handing it to Stephanie. The older woman gave her a sympathetic look that puzzled her. She couldn't understand why the other woman would regard her with such compassion, but then she remembered her hair, which was certainly evidence of a sort. She smiled back as Martha quietly left the room, softly closing the door behind her.

"I won't ever have you subjected to that kind of treatment again," Jonas seethed, still battling his rage.

She stared up at him blankly as he paced. He marched like a soldier doing sentry duty, going three or four feet, then swiftly making a sharp about-face. She realized his irritation wasn't directed at her.

"We're getting married," he announced forcefully.

Her immediate response was to take a sip of the syrupy coffee, convinced she'd misunderstood him.

"Well?" he barked.

"Would you mind repeating that? I'm certain I heard you wrong."

"I said we're getting married." He said it louder this time.

She blinked twice. "If I wasn't in shock before, I am now. You can't possibly mean that, Jonas."

"My name will protect you."

"But, Jonas—"

"Will you or won't you be my wife?" he demanded.

"Stop shouting at me!" she cried, jumping to her feet. The coffee nearly sloshed over the edges of the cup, and she set it down before she ended up spilling it all over the front of her dress.

"Anything could have happened down there," he continued. "If I hadn't arrived when I did..." He left the rest to her imagination.

She went still, her gaze studying this man she loved. "Isn't marriage a little drastic?"

"Not in these circumstances." He looked at her as though she were the one being unreasonable.

"Jonas, do you love me?" She asked the question softly, almost fearing his response.

"I'd hardly be willing to make you my wife if I didn't."

"I see."

He hesitated, looking uneasy. "How do you feel about me?"

"Oh, Jonas, do you really need to ask?" Her gaze softened, and her heart melted at the pride and doubt she read in his hard expression. He was more vulnerable now than at any time since she'd begun working for him. "I've been in love with you from the moment we stood in front of the fountain in Paris—only it took me a while to realize it."

His eyes looked deeply into hers, and when he spoke, the burning anger had been replaced by tenderness. "Stephanie, I love you. I never expected to fall so hard, and certainly not for a woman who is so proud and forthright. But it's happened, and I'll thank God every day of my life if you'll agree to marry me."

"Oh, Jonas." She battled back the tidal wave of emotion that threatened to engulf her. Then she sniffled and turned around, desperately seeking a tissue.

He handed her one and paused to cup her face in his hands, smiling at her gently, lovingly. "We're going to have a wonderful life together," he said as he lowered his mouth to hers. His kiss was tender and sweet. The wonder of being in his arms, knowing he loved her, made her knees grow weak.

She locked her arms around his neck as his mouth meandered over her lips to her ear. "You're a crazy woman."

"Crazy about you," she admitted, loving the feel of him rubbing against her, knowing that their lovemaking would be exquisite.

"A man attacks you and you're a fireball. I ask you to marry me, and you burst into tears."

"I'm happy."

"You will, won't you?"

"Marry you? Oh, Jonas, yes. A thousand times yes."

"Do you want children?"

"A dozen, at least," she said with a happy laugh. Fresh tears misted her eyes at the thought of their raising a family together.

"A dozen?" He cocked his brows and grinned sheepishly. "I'm willing, but you may change your mind after three or four." Still holding her, he flipped the switch to the intercom. "Miss Westheimer?"

"Yes," came the tinny-sounding reply.

"Contact Mr. Potter and tell him that Miss Coulter won't be in for the remainder of the day."

"Jonas," Stephanie whispered. "I told you, Black didn't hurt me. I'm fine, really."

He ignored her, but his grip on her shoulder tightened. "And cancel my appointments for today, as well."

"Yes, of course," Martha said, but the reluctance in her voice was evident even to Stephanie.

"Is that a problem, Miss Westheimer?"

"Adam Holmes is scheduled for four-thirty, and he'll be leaving town this evening."

Jonas closed his eyes and sighed with frustration. "All right, I'll make a point of being back before four-thirty, then."

When he'd finished speaking, he released the switch and turned Stephanie into his arms. "We have some shopping to do."

"Shopping?" For some reason her mind flashed to the grocery store. She hadn't eaten breakfast and had hoped to pick up something on her coffee break, but she'd been so involved working on the report for Mr. Potter that her plan had fallen by the wayside.

"Shopping for a ring. A diamond, preferably, and so large anyone looking at it will know how special you are and how much I love you."

"Jonas," she said slowly, measuring her words carefully, "a plain gold band would do as long as I'm marrying you."

"I can afford a whole lot more, and I have every intention of indulging you from this minute to the end of our lives."

She swallowed her objections. She loved Jonas, and not for the material wealth he could give her. She remembered Elizabeth Lockwood's words. His mother had told her that when Jonas admitted that he loved her, he would make her the happiest woman alive. For now he equated bringing her joy with adorning her with riches. And diamonds *were* wonderful, but her happiness came from being loved by Jonas and nothing more. It wouldn't matter to her if he made sandwiches at the corner deli; she loved the man. In time he would learn that her happiness was linked to his. He was all she would ever need to be content and whole.

His look grew sober and thoughtful. "What do you think about making Potter a vice president?"

Stephanie was both stunned and thrilled. She was surprised and complimented that he had asked her opinion. "George Potter is a wonderful choice."

"Then consider it done," Jonas said with a decisive nod. "Now that I'm going to be a married man, I don't want to spend nearly so much time at the office. Not when I have more important matters to concern myself with."

"Right," she said with a wide grin, thinking of all the years they would have to build a life together. She could see them thirty-five years from now, teaching their grandchildren to sail. "Jonas," she said suddenly, remembering her own happy childhood. "I want you to meet my parents and my sisters."

"We can fly out next week," he answered matter-of-factly.

"When do you want to have the wedding?" she asked. He was moving so fast he was making her head spin.

"Is next month too soon?"

"Oh, Jonas," she said, wrapping her arms around his neck and hugging him fiercely. "I wonder if it will be soon enough."

From that point the afternoon took on the feel of a circus ride. Their first stop was the jewelers, where Jonas bought a lovely diamond solitaire. When he slipped it on her finger, she felt emotion tighten her chest. She bit into her lower lip to keep her feelings at bay, not wanting to embarrass either of them with a display of tears. From the jewelers, Jonas drove to an exclusive French restaurant in memory of their trip to Paris. They dined on veal, sipped champagne and shared secret glances with eyes full of love.

At four, he glanced irritably at his watch. "I may be tied up with Holmes for several hours, and then I've got a dinner engagement."

"Not with another woman, I hope," she teased.

He looked startled for a moment. "There will never be another woman for me, Stephanie. Never."

"Jonas, I was only joking."

"You need never doubt me on this. All my life I've been

intensely loyal. I'm sure my mother can give you several examples from my boyhood, if you want to hear them."

"Jonas, please, I didn't mean to imply…"

"I know, love." He paused to caress the side of her face tenderly. "I knew I was falling in love with you, too, you know—perhaps even as early as Paris—but I fought it. I thought I was in love once before, and I was thoroughly disgusted with myself, given how things turned out. But this morning, when I saw Black pawing at you—I've never experienced such overwhelming rage. I knew in that moment that the feelings I hold for you could be nothing less than love."

She found his hand and squeezed it gently.

His blue eyes darkened by several shades, and she realized that had they been anywhere other than a restaurant, he would have taken her in his arms and kissed her until she begged him to stop.

From the restaurant they drove back to the office. She was about to burst with happiness, and if she didn't share it with Jan and the others soon, she was convinced she would start screaming that Jonas Lockwood loved her from the top floor for all of Minneapolis to hear.

Her first stop after they parted at the elevator was Human Resources. Jan looked up from her desk and blinked.

"Hey, where were you at lunchtime? I have a feeling you were trying to avoid questions. You can't do this to us, Steph. We're all dying to find out what's happening."

"I wasn't avoiding anyone."

Jan looked at her more intently. "You've got that saucy grin again. Would you care to tell me the reason you look like a contented cat with feathers in his mouth?"

In response, Stephanie held out her left hand. The large diamond solitaire sparkled in the artificial light.

Jan gasped, and her eyes shot to Stephanie's. "Mr. Lockwood?"

"Who else would it be?"

Jan's hand flew to her breast. "I think I'm going into cardiac arrest. You did it! You actually did it!" Even as she spoke, she was reaching for the phone.

"Tell the others to meet us at that place you took me to that night. The drinks are on me this time," Stephanie said happily. "I owe all of you at least that."

An hour later the five of them were gathered around a table, sipping wine and munching on an assortment of appetizers,.

"How did you get him to propose?" Barbara wanted to know.

"I didn't do anything. I was more surprised than any of you."

Jan refilled Stephanie's glass, and they all raised their drinks in a silent salute to their illustrious boss.

"To years and years of happiness," Maureen said.

"And romance," Stephanie added, a believer now. She recalled the first time she'd met with her coworkers and how they'd claimed to have recognized her as the perfect match for Jonas. At the time she had been shocked, even appalled. She wouldn't have given the man a free bus ticket. Now, at the very mention of his name her knees turned to butter, she was so much in love with him. Truly head over heels in love, for the first time in her life.

"Who guessed today?" Toni asked.

"No one," Jan answered.

"Today? What are you talking about?" Stephanie glanced around the table at her friends. True, they'd all had their share of wine—and she'd had a bit more than her share, since she'd also had champagne at lunch with

Jonas. But until this moment, everything her friends said had made perfect sense.

"Have you decided on a date for the wedding yet?"

Stephanie noticed how intense their faces became as they awaited her reply. "I'm not answering your question until you answer mine," she said, crossing her arms stubbornly. "What's all this about guessing the day?"

"The marriage pool."

"The what?" Stephanie cried.

"You know, like a football pool, only we had a bet going on when Lockwood was going to pop the question."

Stephanie took another swallow of her wine. "I can't believe I'm hearing this."

"A lot of people bet that you wouldn't be able to carry this off. They lost out big time." Jan and Maureen slapped hands high above the table.

"Money?"

"Three hundred dollars is riding on your wedding date."

Stephanie placed her elbows on the table and cradled her head in her hands. "So that's how Black heard about me and Jonas," she mumbled under her breath.

"Say, do you know what happened to him today?" Jan asked.

"How would I know?" Stephanie didn't look her friend in the eye. She hoped that by asking the question she could avoid lying outright.

"I got a call from Old Stone Face shortly after I returned from break this morning. She told me that Donald Black had been terminated, and to arrange for his check to be mailed to him at his home."

"How unusual," Stephanie commented, struggling not to reveal any of her involvement with the situation.

"I don't know anyone who's sorry to see him go," Maureen added. "He was a real—"

"We know what he was," Toni inserted quickly.

"So what else has been going on today?" Stephanie tried to steer the conversation away from the unpleasant subject of Donald Black.

"You mean other than you and Mr. Lockwood getting engaged, and Donald Black biting the dust? I'd say that was enough to make it one crazy Monday."

"Can you imagine what Tuesday's going to be like?" Maureen asked.

From there the five of them went to dinner at a Mexican restaurant, and by the time Stephanie got home it was close to nine o'clock. She hoped Jonas hadn't tried to get in touch with her and felt a little guilty for staying out so late. As it was, her head was swimming, so she took a quick shower and hurried to bed.

The following morning she was at her desk bright and early, hoping Jonas would stop in on his way up to his floor. She didn't know how she was going to be able to work when all she could think about was how much she loved him and how eager she was to share his life.

Before George Potter arrived, Stephanie received a call from Jan. "Can you come to my office?"

"Sure, what's up? You don't sound right."

"Just get here."

Stephanie couldn't think of a reason why her friend should sound so upset, and she hurried to her office. She took one look at Jan's red eyes and grew worried. Her friend reached for a tissue and loudly blew her nose.

"What's wrong?" Stephanie asked, taking a chair. She'd never seen Jan cry.

"Mr. Lockwood contacted me first thing this morning."

"Jonas?"

"You've been terminated."

Alarm filled Stephanie for an instant, but then she sighed and offered Jan a reassuring grin. "Of course I have. Jonas and I are getting married. I can't very well continue to work here." They hadn't talked about it specifically, but she was sure that was it.

"I don't think so," Jan said. She reached for another tissue, blinking back fresh tears.

"You're not making any sense. What did he say?"

"He said..." Jan paused to wipe her eyes. "He said to mail you your check just the way I was instructed to do with Mr. Black, and...and he asked that you give me the engagement ring. He doesn't want you on Lockwood property again. He was clear as glass on that subject."

Stephanie felt as though someone had kicked her in the stomach. For a moment she couldn't breathe. Her heart constricted with an intolerable pain.

"Steph, did you hear me?"

She nodded numbly. "Why?" The word came from deep within her throat, low and guttural.

"He...he didn't say, but he was serious, Steph. Very serious. I've never heard him more angry. You'd better give me the ring."

Ten

Stephanie's right hand covered the large diamond engagement ring protectively. "I don't understand. That doesn't make any sense."

"He was very precise when he contacted me."

Pacing the carpet in front of Jan's desk, Stephanie folded her arms around her waist and pondered her friend's words. "Call Barbara, Toni and Maureen, and ask them to get here right away."

"What?"

"Just do it," Stephanie snapped, impatient now. "And tell them to hurry."

Momentarily dumbfounded, Jan hesitated, then reached for the phone. A few minutes later their co-workers rushed into the office.

"What is it?" Maureen, the first to arrive, asked breathlessly.

Toni followed on her heels. "Hey, what's so important?"

Barbara came in last, paused, glanced around and said, "All right, I'm here, what's the big deal?"

Jan gestured toward Stephanie. "You called them here, you explain."

"Apparently," Stephanie began, swallowing past the thickening in her throat, "Jonas wants to call off the engagement."

"What?" All three newcomers cried out simultaneously in disbelief.

Barbara recovered first. "What happened?"

"I...don't know," Stephanie admitted honestly, her stomach churning as she considered the incredible situation. "I arrived at the office this morning, and Jan contacted me. She told me I had been terminated by Lockwood Industries, and I was to return the engagement ring to her."

Barbara, Toni and Maureen turned accusing eyes on Jan.

"Hey," Jan said. "It wasn't *my* fault. I'm as shocked as the rest of you."

Stephanie twisted the diamond around and around on her finger, almost believing that she would prefer to lose the appendage than surrender the ring that had been a token of Jonas's love. "You four are the self-proclaimed experts on romance. You're the ones who convinced me that Jonas and I were meant for each other. I need your advice now more than ever." Stephanie spoke quietly, doing her best to keep the emotion from her voice. "What can I do now?"

"Did he give any reason?"

"None," Jan answered. "But he was so angry...worse than I can ever remember hearing him."

"Can you think of anything?" Maureen turned to Stephanie, her brow creased in a frown that revealed the depth of her bafflement.

"Nothing. Absolutely nothing." She turned her palms to them in a gesture indicating her own confusion. Unless Donald Black had somehow convinced Jonas that she hadn't been speaking the truth...but that wasn't possible, she decided. Jonas knew her better than that. At least she prayed he did.

"Are you going to give him back the ring?" Toni asked quietly, her voice dejected and unhappy.

"I...don't know yet."

"It's obvious he doesn't want to face you," Jan said, her expression thoughtful.

"Probably because he's afraid of what would happen."

"But I would never hurt him," Stephanie returned, appalled at the suggestion that she would do anything to cause him pain.

"Not physically, silly," Barbara explained with a long sigh. "It's obvious that he loves you—that isn't going to change overnight—so breaking off the engagement is bound to be emotionally painful."

"Maybe even impossible, if he's forced to face you."

"Then that's exactly what's going to happen." For the first time Stephanie thought she could see a glimmer of hope. She wouldn't make things easy for Jonas. "I'm not going to hand over this ring without an explanation."

"You shouldn't," Maureen stated emphatically.

"He isn't going to let you leave," Toni said.

"He isn't?" Stephanie wasn't nearly as convinced as her friends.

"Oh, he might let you get as far as the door—"

"Maybe even the elevator," Jan interrupted.

"But he'll come for you once he realizes you really mean to leave."

"He'll stop me?" Stephanie was doubtful.

"Oh, yes, the hero always rejects the heroine, and then at the very last second he realizes that he couldn't possibly live without her."

"He may even quietly plead with you and say 'Don't go'

in a tormented voice. You'd be crazy to walk away from him then."

"It's like that in all the best romances," Maureen said, nodding sharply.

"But Jonas hasn't read any romances." Stephanie wanted desperately to believe that what her friends said was true, but she was afraid to count on it. Jonas was too proud. Too stubborn. Too Jonas.

"He's enough of a hero to know when he's turning away from the best thing that's ever happened to him. He loves you."

Barbara's words were the cool voice of reason cutting through the fog of doubt that clouded Stephanie's troubled mind. Even Elizabeth Lockwood had told her how much Jonas needed her love. She couldn't doubt his mother.

"He must love you, or he wouldn't have asked you to marry him." Toni was equally convincing.

"So the next move is mine, right?" Stephanie glanced around at her friends' intent expressions.

"Most definitely."

The four followed Stephanie out of Jan's office, moving in single file like troops marching into battle. Down the hallway they paraded, finally coming to a halt in front of the elevator. Jan pushed the button for Stephanie, while the others offered words of encouragement.

"Fight for him," Barbara advised her. "If he's going to do this to you, then don't make it easy on him."

"Right," Toni concurred. "Let him know what he's missing."

"Good luck," Jan said as Stephanie walked into the elevator. Just before the thick steel doors glided shut her friends gave her the thumbs-up sign.

All the confidence Stephanie had felt when she stepped

into the elevator deserted her the minute she faced Martha Westheimer. The woman barely looked in her direction. It was apparent the dragon was prepared for this confrontation.

For a full, intolerable minute Stephanie stood in front of the dragon's desk while Martha ignored her.

"Excuse me, please," Stephanie said in a strong, controlled tone. "I'm here to see Mr. Lockwood."

"He's in a meeting."

"I don't believe that."

"It is not my concern what you believe. Mr. Lockwood has no desire to see you."

"Now *that* I believe."

For the first time since Stephanie had known her, Martha Westheimer smiled. Well, almost smiled, Stephanie corrected herself. She wasn't completely convinced that the woman was capable of feeling amusement, much less revealing it.

"I'd like to help you, but…"

"I'll simply tell him you weren't able to stop me."

"Mr. Lockwood would know better," Martha said quietly. "If I can persevere against pesky attorneys and keep persistent salesmen at bay, one female employee is a piece of cake."

But Stephanie could see that Martha was weakening, which was in itself a sight to behold. She held her ground but didn't speak.

"He's in a rare mood," Martha whispered under her breath. "I don't remember ever seeing him quite like this."

"Is it his leg?"

"I beg your pardon?" The horn-rimmed glasses that balanced so precariously at the tip of the woman's nose threatened to slide off. Martha rescued them in the nick of time. "I don't understand your question."

"Jonas is often irritable when his leg is hurting him."

"No, it's not his leg, Ms. Coulter. It's you. First thing this morning, I asked about you. When Mr. Lockwood brought you up to his office yesterday it was apparent there'd been some trouble. You were shaking like a frightened rabbit and...well, the minute I said your name this morning, he nearly bit my head off. He said if I cared about my job I was to forget I'd ever met you. I've been with Mr. Lockwood for a good number of years, and I have never seen him like he was this morning. From the looks of it, I'd say he didn't go home last night."

A sense of urgency filled Stephanie. "It's imperative that I talk to him."

"I have my instructions, but quite honestly, Ms. Coulter, I don't believe I can go through—"

"Ms. Westheimer." Jonas's voice boomed over the intercom, startling both women. "Just how much longer am I to be kept waiting for the Westinghouse file?"

Stephanie's heart pounded frantically at the cold, hard sound of Jonas's voice. She'd thought she'd seen him in every mood imaginable. He could be unreasonable and flippant, but she had never known him to be deliberately cruel. Judging from the edge in his voice, she didn't doubt he was capable of anything today.

"Right away, sir," Martha answered quickly. She raised her head and whispered to Stephanie, "It would be better if you came back another day...perhaps tomorrow, when he's had a chance to mull things over."

"No," Stephanie countered, and shook her head for emphasis. "It's now or never." Squaring her shoulders, she picked up the file he'd requested from the corner of Martha's desk. "I'll take this to him."

Martha half rose from her chair, indecision etched on her pointed features. "I…can't let you do that."

"You can and you will," Stephanie told her firmly.

Slumping back into her chair, Martha shook her head slowly and shut her eyes. "I hope I'm doing the right thing."

With her hand on the knob of the door that led to Jonas's office, Stephanie hesitated for a second, then pushed open the door. With quick firm steps, she marched across the plush carpeting and placed the file on his desk. He was busy writing and didn't glance in her direction.

"I believe you asked for this," she said softly.

His head flew up so fast that for a moment she wondered if he'd given himself whiplash.

"Get out!"

The harsh words cut through her, but she refused to give in to the pain. "Not until you tell me what's going on. Jan Michaels gave me the most ridiculous message this morning. If you want to end our engagement, I have the right to know why."

He pointed viciously at the door. "I've had a change of heart. Leave the ring with Ms. Westheimer and get out of my sight."

She winced at the cold, merciless way he looked at her. "It's not that simple, Jonas," she said quietly, fighting back her anger and pain. "I have a right to know what happened. This doesn't make any sense. One afternoon you love me enough to ask me to share your life, and the following morning you despise me."

Jonas lowered his gaze, and it looked for a minute as though he was going to snap the pen he was holding in half. His hands clenched and unclenched.

"Does it have anything to do with Donald Black?"

His eyes shot to hers and narrowed. "No, but perhaps I was hasty in firing the man."

She decided to let that comment slide. "Then what possible explanation could there be?"

He rose slowly from his chair and braced his hands on the side of the desk, leaning forward. His eyes were as blue as a glacier and just as cold. "An interesting thing happened on my way out of the office yesterday afternoon. I heard howls of laughter coming from a group of male employees. By pure chance I happened to overhear that Stephanie Coulter had managed to pull off the feat of the century. A mere executive assistant had won the heart of the company president. Apparently some money was riding on just how quickly you could make a fool of me."

Stephanie blanched. "Jonas, I…"

"I didn't believe it at first," he went on, his voice as sharp as a new razor blade. "At least not until I saw the betting sheet posted on the bulletin board. You did amazingly well. The odds weren't in your favor. Several of the women seemed to have underestimated you. But I noticed the men were quick to trust your many charms. But only three hundred dollars? Really, Stephanie, you sold yourself cheap." His eyes narrowed as he mentioned the money.

"I didn't have anything to do with the marriage pool."

"Not according to what I overheard. You've been in on this little setup from the beginning. You and half the office were plotting my downfall as if I was some puppet on a string. Tricking me into falling in love with you was all part of the plan, wasn't it?"

"I—"

"Don't bother to deny it. At least have the decency to own up to the truth."

"I never had any intention of falling in love with you," she admitted.

"I suppose not. All you wanted—all anyone wanted—was to see me make a fool of myself."

Stephanie inhaled sharply. "You want the truth, then fine, I'll tell you everything."

Jonas reclaimed his chair and reached for his pen. "I have no desire to hear it."

He started writing, ignoring her, but she refused to walk away from him now. He had to understand that it had never been a game with her. She'd fallen into her coworkers' plan as an unwilling victim.

"Several weeks ago, a few of the women from the office approached me. It was right after I'd worked for you when Ms. Westheimer was ill." She waited for some response, but when he didn't give her any, she continued undaunted. "They believed…that you worked so hard and demanded so much of everyone else because you needed a wife and family to fill your time. They thought you and I would be perfect together."

He snickered.

She did her best to ignore his derision. "Anyway, I laughed at them and told them it was a crazy idea. I didn't want any part of it."

"Obviously something changed your mind."

"Yes, something did!" she cried. "Paris. I met the real Jonas Lockwood at a fountain in a French park, and I knew then that I'd never be the same. For just a fleeting instant I glimpsed the man beneath that thick facade and discovered how much I could come to love him."

"More's the pity."

"I had no intention of falling in love with you. It just… happened. Even now, I don't regret it, I can't. I love you,

Jonas Lockwood. I apologize that their game got carried to that extent, but please believe me, I didn't have anything to do with the marriage pool. I didn't even know anything about it until yesterday." She paused, her chest heaving with the tension that coiled her insides like a finely tuned violin. "I'd never do anything to hurt you. Never."

He dropped his gaze again. "Okay, you've had your say, and I've listened. It's what you wanted. Now kindly do as I request and leave the ring with Ms. Westheimer. Whatever was between us, and I sincerely doubt it was love, is over."

She felt as though she'd been hit physically. Tears burned in her eyes, but she refused to give in to the emotion. "You put this ring on my finger," she said softly, slowly. "If you want it off, you'll have to remove it yourself." She held her hand out to him and waited.

Although he refused to look at her, she could sense his indecision. "If it isn't love between us, I don't know what it is," she added softly.

"I saw you last night," he said, in a voice so low that the words were barely audible. "You came out of some lounge, laughing and joking with a group of women, and I knew it was a victory celebration. You'd achieved the impossible. You'd brought me to my knees."

"Not that...never that." She didn't know how to explain that she'd simply been happy and had wanted to share her joy with her friends. Words would only condemn her now.

"Keep the diamond," he said finally. "You've earned it."

"Jonas, please—"

"Either you leave quietly, or I'll call security and have you thrown out." His tone left little doubt that the threat was real.

Stunned almost to the point of numbness, she turned away from him. Tears blinded her as she headed for the door. Her hand was on the knob when she paused, not daring to look at him. "Did you say something?" she asked hopefully.

"No."

She nodded and, leaving the door open, moved into the foyer and to the elevator. Something came over her then. A sensation so strong and so powerful that she could barely contain it. With a burst of magnetic energy she whirled around and stormed back into his office, stopping at his desk. "Well?" she cried, her hands on her hips. "Aren't you going to stop me?"

Jonas glanced up and snarled. "What are you talking about?"

"They said you'd stop me."

"Who?"

"The others. They said if you really loved me...if anything between us was real, that you wouldn't be such an idiot as to let me leave." She'd improvised a bit, but that had been the gist of their message.

"I can assure you that after yesterday I have no feelings for you. None. At this point, my only intention regarding you is to sever our relationship and be done with you once and for all."

"You fool," she said, swallowing a hysterical sob. "If your pride is worth so much to you, then fine—so be it. If you want your ring back, then here it is." She paused long enough to slip it off her finger and place it on his desk. "It's over now, and all the trust and promise that went with it: the love, the joy, the laughter, the home, the family." She sucked in her breath at the unexpected pain that gripped her heart. "Our children would have been so special."

Jonas's mouth went taut, but he said nothing.

"It may surprise you to know that you're not the only

one with an abundance of pride." Although she said each word as clearly as possible, the tears rained down her face. She turned and pointed to the elevator. "It's going to tear my heart out to walk out that door, but I'm going to do it. From here on, you'll live your life and I'll live mine, and we'll probably never meet again. But I love you, Jonas, I'll always love you. Not now, and probably not soon, but someday you'll regret this. My love will haunt you, Jonas, all the way to your grave."

"I suggest if you're going to leave you do it quickly," he said tonelessly, "before security arrives."

"Stop trying to hurt me more," she said, her voice cracking. "Isn't this humiliation enough?"

Again he refused to answer her.

"Goodbye, Jonas," she said softly, her voice trembling violently. She turned and walked away from him, telling herself over and over again not to look back. It wasn't until she was in the elevator that she realized she was speaking out loud.

As the elevator carried her to the bottom floor, she felt as though she were descending into the depths of hell. She paused in the washroom to wipe the tears from her face and repair the damage to her makeup. Unable to face anyone at the moment, she took the bus directly home and contacted Jan from there.

"What happened?" Jan demanded. "Everyone's dying to know."

"The engagement is off," Stephanie announced, doing her utmost to keep her voice from cracking. "I'm going to call my parents. I'm letting go of the apartment and flying home at the end of the week. The sooner I leave Minneapolis the better."

"Steph, don't do anything foolish. It'll work out."

"It's not going to resolve itself," Stephanie said, pressing her fist against her forehead. "Jonas made that very clear, and I refuse to remain in this city any longer." Not when there was a chance she would run into him again. She could bear anything but that.

"I feel terrible," Jan mumbled, "Really terrible—I was the one who got you into this."

"I got myself into it, and no one else. I love him, Jan, and a part of me always will."

"Are you crying?"

"No." Stephanie tried to smile, but the effort was a miserable failure. "The tears are gone now. I'm not saying I didn't cry—believe me, this morning it was Waterworks International around here. But my crying jag is over. I'll recover in time. That's the best thing about being a Coulter—we bounce back."

Jan sighed with a hint of envy. "I can't believe you—you're so strong. If this were to happen to me and Jim, I'd come unglued."

Family was the sticking agent that would hold Stephanie together. Her parents would help her get through this ordeal. Now, more than at any time since she'd left home, she felt the need for their comforting love and all that was familiar. The wheat farm, the old two-story farmhouse with the wide front porch. The half-mile-long driveway with rolling fields of grain on either side. Home. Family. Love.

"Is there anything I can do for you?" Jan wanted to know.

"Nothing. If…if I don't see you before Saturday, say goodbye to everyone for me. I'll miss you all."

"Oh, Steph, I hate to see it come to this."

"I do, too, but it's for the best."

* * *

For four days Stephanie tried to pick up the pieces of her life. She packed her bags, sold what furniture she could and gave the rest to charity. None of it was worth much, since she'd bought most of it secondhand. The bookcase was the most difficult to part with, and in the end she disassembled it and packed the long boards with the rest of the things she was having trucked to Colville. The expense of doing so was worth more than three similar sets of bookshelves, but it was all that she would have to remember Jonas by, and even though she was doing everything humanly possible to purge him from her life, she wanted to hang on to the bookcase and the memory of that night together.

Late Friday afternoon, her suitcases resting in the barren apartment, she waited for Jan to pick her up and drive her to a hotel close to the airport. She half expected Maureen, Toni and Barbara to arrive with Jan, and she mentally braced herself for the drain on her emotions. Goodbyes were always difficult.

When the doorbell chimed, she took a deep breath and attempted to smile brightly.

"Hello, Stephanie." A vital, handsome Jonas stood in the doorway.

"Jonas." Her fingers clutched the door handle so tightly that she thought the knob would break off. All week she'd been praying for a miracle, but finally she had given up hope. Jonas was too proud, and she knew it.

"May I come in?"

She blinked twice and stepped aside. "As you can see, I can't offer you a seat," she said, leaning against the closed door.

He stepped into the middle of the bare room and whirled around sharply. "You're leaving?"

"I'm expecting my ride in a few minutes—I thought you were Jan."

"I see."

"You wanted something?" She tried to keep the eagerness from her voice. In her dreams, he'd had her in his arms by now.

"I've come to offer you your job back."

Her hopeful expectations died a cruel death. "No, thank you."

"Why not?"

"Surely you know the reason, Jonas."

He hesitated, ambled to the other side of the room and glanced out the window to the street below. "You're a good executive assistant."

She held her ground. "Then I shouldn't have a problem finding work in Washington."

"I'll double your salary," he said, not bothering to turn around.

She was incredulous. She could see the expression on his face; he looked weary and defeated. "Jonas, why are you really here?" she asked in a soft whisper.

He smiled then, a sad smile that didn't reach his eyes. "I'm afraid I have a mutiny on my hands."

"A what?"

"Five of my top female employees are threatening to quit their jobs."

"Five?"

"Perhaps more."

"I… I don't understand."

"For that matter, I'm having a problem comprehending it myself." He wiped a hand over his face. "This afternoon Martha Westheimer, and four others I barely know, walked into my office."

"Martha Westheimer?" Every bad thought she'd ever entertained about Jonas's executive assistant vanished in a flood of surprise and pleasure.

"Was she in on this from the beginning?" His gaze captured Stephanie's but quickly released it.

"No...just Jan, Barbara, Toni and Maureen."

His mouth formed a half smile. "They accused me of not being hero material."

"They didn't mean anything by it—they're still upset."

"I take it that being rejected as a hero makes me the lowest of the low?" He cocked his thick brows questioningly.

"Something like that." Despite the seriousness of the conversation, she was forced to disguise a smile. "This whole thing started because Jan and the others thought I was heroine material—but they were mistaken about me, as well. I did everything wrong."

"How's that?" He turned and leaned against the windowsill, studying her.

She shrugged, lowered her gaze and rubbed the palms of her hands together nervously. "You kissed me once in your office, and I told you never to let it happen again. I was forever saying and doing the worst possible thing."

"But I did kiss you again."

This was a subject she wanted to avoid. "What else did they say?"

"Just that if I let you go I would be making the biggest mistake of my life, and that they refused to stand idly by and let it happen."

"What did they suggest you do?"

"They said if I didn't do something to prevent you from leaving they were handing in their resignations effective that minute."

Looking at him was impossible; it hurt far too much.

"So that's why you offered me my old job back—you were seeking a compromise?"

"No," he said harshly. "I figured if you agreed to that, then there would be hope of you agreeing to more."

"More?"

"The ring's in my pocket, Stephanie." He brought it out and handed it to her. "It's yours."

The diamond felt warm in her palm, as though he'd been holding on to it. She raised her eyes to his, not understanding. "Jonas," she whispered past the tight knot that formed in her throat. "I can't accept this ring."

He went pale. "Why not?"

"For the same reason I refuse to go back to Lockwood Industries."

"I love you, Stephanie."

"But not enough to truly want me as your wife," she said accusingly, feeling more wretched than the day he'd fired her. "Don't worry about Jan and the others. I'll explain everything. You needn't worry about them quitting. That's the reason you're here, isn't it?"

"No," he said huskily, then paused and seemed to regain control of his emotions. "I don't want you to leave. I thought about what you said, and you're right. If you go, everything I've ever dreamed about will disappear with you. I have my pride, Stephanie, but it's been cold comfort the last few days."

"Oh, Jonas, don't tease me, I don't think I could bear it—are you saying you *want* me for your wife?"

"Yes." He raised his eyes toward heaven as if to plead for patience. "What did you think I meant?"

"I don't know. That they'd blackmailed you into proposing again, I guess."

He reached for her, drawing her soft body to his and inhaling the fresh sunshine scent of her hair. "I've been half out of my mind the last few days. To be honest, I was glad Ms. Westheimer and the others came. It gave me the excuse I needed to contact you. Right after you left it dawned on me that I'd been an idiot. I'd overreacted to that stupid marriage pool. Why should any of that silliness matter to me when I've got you?" He pressed his mouth hungrily down on hers.

Stephanie melted against him and sniffled loudly. "I love you so much."

"I know." He rubbed his chin against the top of her head. "I think we fooled the odds makers this time."

"How's that?"

"Odds were three to one that we'd get back together again."

"Three to one?"

"You know what else?"

"No," she said with a watery smile.

"There are other odds floating around the office. They say you'll be pregnant by the end of the year."

"That soon?" She wound her arms around his neck and moved her body against his, telling him without words her eagerness to experience all that marriage had to offer them.

"I say they're way off," he growled in her ear. "It shouldn't take nearly that long."

* * * * *

RAINY DAY KISSES

Prologue

"Is it true, Michelle?" Jolyn Johnson rolled her chair from her cubicle across the aisle and nearly caught the wheel on a drooping length of plastic holly. The marketing department had won the Christmas decoration contest for the third year in a row.

Michelle Davidson glanced away from her computer screen and immediately noticed her neighbor's inquisitive expression. It certainly hadn't taken long for the rumors to start. She realized, of course, that it was unusual for a high school senior to be accepted as an intern at a major company like Windy Day Toys, one of the most prestigious toy manufacturers in the country. She'd be working here during the Christmas and summer breaks—and she'd actually be getting paid!

Michelle had connections—*good* connections. She'd been a bit naive, perhaps, to assume she could keep her relationship to Uncle Nate under wraps. Still, she'd hoped that with the Christmas season in full swing, her fellow workers would be too preoccupied with the holidays to pay any attention to her. Apparently that wasn't the case.

"Whatever you heard is probably true," she answered, doing her best to look busy.

"Then you *are* related to Mr. Townsend?" Jolyn's eyes grew large.

"I'm his niece."

"Really?" the other girl said in awe. "Wow."

"I'm the one who introduced my aunt Susannah to my uncle Nate." If the fact that Michelle was related to the company owner and CEO impressed Jolyn, then this piece of information should send her over the moon.

"You've got to be kidding! When was that? I thought the Townsends have been married for years and years. I heard they have three children!"

"Tessa, Junior and Emma Jane." When she left the office this afternoon, Michelle would be heading over to her aunt and uncle's home on Lake Washington to babysit. She didn't think it would be good form to mention that, however. She figured interns for Windy Day Toys didn't usually babysit on the side.

"*You* were responsible for introducing your aunt and uncle?" Jolyn repeated, sounding even more incredulous. "When?" she asked again.

"I was young at the time," Michelle answered evasively.

"You must have been."

Michelle grinned and gave in to Jolyn's obvious curiosity. Might as well tell the truth, which was bound to emerge anyway. "I think that might be why Uncle Nate agreed to let me intern here." He loved to tease her about her—admittedly inadvertent—role as matchmaker, but Michelle knew he was grateful. So was her aunt Susannah.

Michelle planned to major in marketing when she enrolled in college next September, and doing an internship this winter and during the summer holidays was the perfect opportunity to find out whether she liked the job. It was only her second day, but already Michelle could see that she was going to love it.

A couple of the other workers had apparently been listening in on the conversation and rolled their chairs toward her cubicle, as well. "You can't stop the story there," Karen said.

Originally Michelle had hoped to avoid this kind of attention, but she accepted that it was inevitable. "When my aunt was almost thirty, she was absolutely sure she'd never marry or have a family."

"Susannah Townsend?"

This news astonished the small gathering, as Michelle had guessed it would. Besides working with Nate, her mother and aunt had started their own company, Motherhood, Inc., about ten years ago and they'd done incredibly well. It seemed that everything the Townsend name touched turned to gold.

"I know it sounds crazy, considering everything that's happened since."

"Exactly," Jolyn murmured.

"Aunt Susannah's a great mother. But," Michelle added, "at one time, she couldn't even figure out how to change a diaper." Little did the others know that the diaper Susannah had such difficulty changing had been Michelle's.

"This is a joke, right?"

"I swear it's true. Hardly anyone knows the whole story."

"What really happened?" the third woman, whom Michelle didn't know, asked.

Michelle shrugged. "Actually, I happened."

"What do you mean?"

"My mother was desperate for a babysitter and asked her sister, my aunt Susannah, to look after me."

"How old were you?"

"About nine months," she admitted.

"So how did everything turn out the way it did?" Jolyn asked.

"I'd love to hear, too," Karen said, and the third woman nodded vigorously.

Michelle leaned back in her chair. "Make yourselves comfortable, my friends, because I have a story to tell," she began dramatically. "A story in which I play a crucial part."

The three women scooted their chairs closer.

"It all started seventeen years ago…"

One

Susannah Simmons blamed her sister, Emily, for this. As far as she was concerned, her weekend was going to be the nightmare on Western Avenue. Emily, a nineties version of the "earth mother," had asked Susannah, the dedicated career woman, to babysit nine-month-old Michelle.

"Emily, I don't think so." Susannah had balked when her sister first phoned. What did she, a twenty-eight-year-old business executive, know about babies? The answer was simple—not much.

"I'm desperate."

Her sister must have been to ask her. Everyone knew what Susannah was like around babies—not only Michelle, but infants in general. She just wasn't the motherly type. Interest rates, negotiations, troubleshooting, staff motivation, these were her strong points. Not formula, teething and diapers.

It was nothing short of astonishing that the same two parents could have produced such completely different daughters. Emily baked her own oat-bran muffins, subscribed to *Organic Gardening* and hung her wash to dry on a clothesline—even in winter.

Susannah, on the other hand, wasn't the least bit domestic and had no intention of ever cultivating the trait. She was too busy with her career to let such tedious tasks disrupt her corporate lifestyle. She was currently a director in charge of marketing for H&J Lima, the nation's largest sporting goods company. The position occupied almost every minute of her time.

Susannah Simmons was a woman on the rise. Her name appeared regularly in trade journals as an up-and-coming achiever. None of that mattered to Emily, however, who needed a babysitter.

"You know I wouldn't ask you if it wasn't an emergency," Emily had pleaded.

Susannah felt herself weakening. Emily was, after all, her younger sister. "Surely, there's got to be someone better qualified."

Emily had hesitated, then tearfully blurted, "I don't know what I'll do if you won't take Michelle." She began to sob pitifully. "Robert's left me."

"What?" If Emily hadn't gained her full attention earlier, she did now. If her sister was an earth mother, then her brother-in-law, Robert Davidson, was Abraham Lincoln, as solid and upright as a thirty-foot oak. "I don't believe it."

"It's true," Emily wailed. "He…he claims I give Michelle all my attention and that I never have enough energy left to be a decent wife." She paused to draw in a quavery breath. "I know he's right…but being a good mother demands so much time and effort."

"I thought Robert wanted six children."

"He does…or did." Emily's sobbing began anew.

"Oh, Emily, it can't be that bad," Susannah had murmured in a soothing voice, thinking as fast as she could.

"I'm sure you misunderstood Robert. He loves you and Michelle, and I'm positive he has no intention of leaving you."

"He does," Emily went on to explain between hiccuping sobs. "He asked me to find someone to look after Michelle for a while. He says we have to have some time to ourselves, or our marriage is dead."

That sounded pretty drastic to Susannah.

"I swear to you, Susannah, I've called everyone who's ever babysat Michelle before, but no one's available. No one—not even for one night. When I told Robert I hadn't found a sitter, he got so angry...and that's not like Robert."

Susannah agreed. The man was the salt of the earth. Not once in the five years she'd known him could she recall him even raising his voice.

"He told me that if I didn't take this weekend trip to San Francisco with him he was going alone. I *tried* to find someone to watch Michelle," Emily said. "I honestly tried, but there's no one else, and now Robert's home and he's loading up the car and, Susannah, he's serious. He's going to leave without me and from the amount of luggage he's taking, I don't think he plans to come back."

The tale of woe barely skimmed the surface of Susannah's mind. The key word that planted itself in fertile ground was *weekend*. "I thought you said you only needed me for one night?" she asked.

At that point, Susannah should've realized she wasn't much brighter than a brainless mouse, innocently nibbling away at the cheese in a steel trap.

Emily sniffled once more, probably for effect, Susannah mused darkly.

"We'll be flying back to Seattle early Sunday afternoon. Robert's got some business in San Francisco Saturday morning, but the rest of the weekend is free...and it's been such a long time since we've been alone."

"Two days and two nights," Susannah said slowly, mentally tabulating the hours.

"Oh, please, Susannah, my whole marriage is at stake. You've always been such a good big sister. I know I don't deserve anyone as good as you."

Silently Susannah agreed.

"Somehow I'll find a way to repay you," Emily continued.

Susannah closed her eyes. Her sister's idea of repaying her was usually freshly baked zucchini bread shortly after Susannah announced she was watching her weight.

"Susannah, please!"

It was then that Susannah had caved in to the pressure. "All right. Go ahead and bring Michelle over."

Somewhere in the distance, she could've sworn she heard the echo of a mousetrap slamming shut.

By the time Emily and Robert had deposited their offspring at Susannah's condominium, her head was swimming with instructions. After planting a kiss on her daughter's rosy cheek, Emily handed the clinging Michelle to a reluctant Susannah.

That was when the nightmare began in earnest.

As soon as her sister left, Susannah could feel herself tense up. Even as a teenager, she hadn't done a lot of babysitting; it wasn't that she didn't like children, but kids didn't seem to take to her.

Holding the squalling infant on her hip, Susannah paced while her mind buzzed with everything she was supposed to remember. She knew what to do in case of diaper rash, colic and several other minor emergencies, but Emily hadn't said one word about how to keep Michelle from crying.

"Shhh," Susannah cooed, jiggling her niece against her hip. She swore the child had a cry that could've been heard a block away.

After the first five minutes, her calm cool composure began to crack under the pressure. She could be in real trouble here. The tenant agreement she'd signed specifically stated "no children."

"Hello, Michelle, remember me?" Susannah asked, doing everything she could think of to quiet the baby. Didn't the kid need to breathe? "I'm your auntie Susannah, the business executive."

Her niece wasn't impressed. Pausing only a few seconds to gulp for air, Michelle increased her volume and glared at the door as if she expected her mother to miraculously appear if she cried long and hard enough.

"Trust me, kid, if I knew a magic trick that'd bring your mother back, I'd use it now."

Ten minutes. Emily had been gone a total of ten minutes. Susannah was seriously considering giving the state Children's Protective Services a call and claiming that a stranger had abandoned a baby on her doorstep.

"Mommy will be home soon," Susannah murmured wistfully.

Michelle screamed louder. Susannah started to worry about her stemware. The kid's voice could shatter glass.

More tortured minutes passed, each one an eternity. Susannah was desperate enough to sing. Not knowing any appropriate lullabies, she began with a couple of ditties from her childhood, but quickly exhausted those. Michelle didn't seem to appreciate them anyway. Since Susannah didn't keep up with the current top twenty, the best she could do was an old Christmas favorite. Somehow singing "Jingle Bells" in the middle of September didn't feel right.

"Michelle," Susannah pleaded, willing to stand on her head if it would keep the baby from wailing, "your mommy will be back, I assure you."

Michelle apparently didn't believe her.

"How about if I buy municipal bonds and put them in your name?" Susannah tried next. "Tax-free bonds, Michelle! This is an offer you shouldn't refuse. All you need to do is stop crying. Oh, please stop crying."

Michelle wasn't interested.

"All right," Susannah cried, growing desperate. "I'll sign over my Microsoft stock. That's my final offer, so you'd better grab it while I'm in a generous mood."

Michelle answered by gripping Susannah's collar with both of her chubby fists and burying her wet face in a once spotless white silk blouse.

"You're a tough nut to crack, Michelle Margaret Davidson," Susannah muttered, gently patting her niece's back as she paced. "You want blood, don't you, kid? You aren't going to be satisfied with anything less."

A half hour after Emily had left, Susannah was ready to resort to tears herself. She'd started singing again, returning to her repertoire of Christmas songs. "You'd better watch out,/ you'd better not cry,/ Aunt Susannah's here telling you why...."

She was just getting into the lyrics when someone knocked heavily on her door.

Like a thief caught in the act, Susannah whirled around, fully expecting the caller to be the building superintendent. No doubt there'd been complaints and he'd come to confront her.

Expelling a weary sigh, Susannah realized she was defenseless. The only option she had was to throw herself on his mercy. She squared her shoulders and walked across the lush carpet, prepared to do exactly that.

Only it wasn't necessary. The building superintendent wasn't the person standing on the other side of her door. It was her new neighbor, wearing a baseball cap and a faded T-shirt, and looking more than a little disgruntled.

"The crying and the baby I can take," he said, crossing his arms and relaxing against the door frame, "but your singing has got to go."

"Very funny," she grumbled.

"The kid's obviously distressed."

Susannah glared at him. "Nothing gets past you, does it?"

"Do something."

"I'm trying." Apparently Michelle didn't like this stranger any more than Susannah did because she buried her face in Susannah's collar and rubbed it vigorously back and forth. That at least helped muffle her cries, but there was no telling what it would do to white silk. "I offered her my Microsoft stock and it didn't do any good," Susannah explained. "I was even willing to throw in my municipal bonds."

"You offered her stocks and bonds, but did you suggest dinner?"

"Dinner?" Susannah echoed. She hadn't thought of that. Emily claimed she'd fed Michelle, but Susannah vaguely remembered something about a bottle.

"The poor thing's probably starving."

"I think she's supposed to have a bottle," Susannah said. She turned and glanced at the assorted bags Emily and Robert had deposited in her condominium, along with the necessary baby furniture. From the number of things stacked on the floor, it must seem as if she'd been granted permanent guardianship. "There's got to be one in all this para-phernalia."

"I'll find it—you keep the kid quiet."

Susannah nearly laughed out loud. If she was able to keep Michelle quiet, he wouldn't be here in the first place. She imagined she could convince CIA agents to hand over top-secret documents more easily than she could silence one distressed nine-month-old infant.

Without waiting for an invitation, her neighbor moved into the living room. He picked up one of the three over-night bags and rooted through that. He hesitated when he pulled out a stack of freshly laundered diapers, and glanced at Susannah. "I didn't know anyone used cloth diapers any-more."

"My sister doesn't believe in anything disposable."

"Smart woman."

Susannah made no comment, and within a few seconds noted that he'd come across a plastic bottle. He removed the protective cap and handed the bottle to Susannah, who looked at it and blinked. "Shouldn't the milk be heated?"

"It's room temperature, and frankly, at this point I don't think the kid's going to care."

He was right. The instant Susannah placed the rubber nipple in her niece's mouth, Michelle grasped the bottle with both hands and sucked at it greedily.

For the first time since her mother had left, Michelle stopped crying. The silence was pure bliss. Susannah's tension eased, and she released a sigh that went all the way through her body.

"You might want to sit down," he suggested next.

Susannah did, and with Michelle cradled awkwardly in her arms, leaned against the back of the sofa, trying not to jostle her charge.

"That's better, isn't it?" Her neighbor pushed the baseball cap farther back on his head, looking pleased with himself.

"Much better." Susannah smiled shyly up at him. They hadn't actually met, but she'd certainly noticed her new neighbor. As far as looks went, he was downright handsome. She supposed most women would find his mischievous blue eyes and dark good looks appealing. He was tanned, but she'd have wagered a month's pay that his bronzed features weren't the result of any machine. He obviously spent a great deal of time outdoors, which led her to the conclusion that he didn't work. At least not in an office. And frankly, she doubted he was employed outside of one, either. The clothes he wore and the sporadic hours he kept had led her to speculate about him earlier. If he had money, which apparently he did or else he wouldn't be living in this complex, then he'd inherited it.

"I think it's time I introduced myself," he said conversationally, sitting on the ottoman across from her. "I'm Nate Townsend."

"Susannah Simmons," she said. "I apologize for all the racket. My niece and I are just getting acquainted and— oh, boy—it's going to be a long weekend, so bear with us."

"You're babysitting for the weekend?"

"Two days and two nights." It sounded like a whole lifetime to Susannah. "My sister and her husband are off on a second honeymoon. Normally my parents would watch Michelle and love doing it, but they're visiting friends in Florida."

"It was kind of you to offer."

Susannah thought it best to correct this impression. "Trust me, I didn't volunteer. In case you hadn't noticed, I'm not very maternal."

"You've got to support her back a little more," he said, watching Michelle.

Susannah tried, but it felt awkward to hold on to her niece *and* the bottle.

"You're doing fine."

"Sure," Susannah muttered. She felt like someone with two left feet who'd been unexpectedly ushered onto center stage and told to perform the lead in *Swan Lake*.

"Relax, will you?" Nate encouraged.

"I told you already I'm not into this motherhood business," she snapped. "If you think you can do better, you feed her."

"You're doing great. Don't worry about it."

She wasn't doing great at all, and she knew it, but this was as good as she got.

"When's the last time you had anything to eat?" he asked.

"I beg your pardon?"

"You sound hungry to me."

"Well, I'm not," Susannah said irritably.

"I think you are, but don't worry, I'll take care of that." He walked boldly into her kitchen and paused in front of the refrigerator. "Your mood will improve once you have something in your stomach."

Shifting Michelle higher, Susannah stood and followed him. "You can't just walk in here and—"

"I'll say I can't," he murmured, his head inside her fridge. "Do you realize there's nothing in here except an open box of baking soda and a jar full of pickle juice?"

"I eat out a lot," Susannah said defensively.

"I can see that."

Michelle had finished the bottle and made a slurping sound that prompted Susannah to remove the nipple from her mouth. The baby's eyes were closed. Little wonder, Susannah thought. She was probably exhausted. Certainly Susannah was, and it was barely seven on Friday evening. The weekend was just beginning.

Setting the empty bottle on the kitchen counter, Susannah awkwardly lifted Michelle onto her shoulder and patted her back until she produced a tiny burp. Feeling a real sense of accomplishment, Susannah smiled proudly.

Nate chuckled and when Susannah glanced in his direction, she discovered him watching her, his grin warm and appraising. "You're going to be fine."

Flustered, Susannah lowered her gaze. She always disliked it when a man looked at her that way, examining her features and forming a judgment about her by the size of her nose, or the direction in which her eyebrows grew. Most men seemed to believe they'd been granted a rare gift of insight and could determine a woman's entire character just by looking at her face. Unfortunately, Susannah's was too austere by conventional standards to be classified as beautiful. Her eyes were deep-set and dark, her cheekbones high. Her nose came almost straight from her forehead and together with her full mouth made her look like a classic Greek sculpture. Not pretty, she thought. Interesting perhaps.

It was during Susannah's beleaguered self-evaluation that Michelle stirred and started jabbering cheerfully, reaching one hand toward a strand of Susannah's dark hair.

Without her realizing it, her chignon had come undone. Michelle had somehow managed to loosen the pins and now the long dark tresses fell haphazardly over Susannah's shoulder. If there was one thing Susannah was meticulous about, and actually there were several, it was her appearance. She must look a rare sight, in an expensive business suit with a stained white blouse and her hair tumbling over her shoulder.

"Actually I've been waiting for an opportunity to introduce myself," Nate said, leaning against the counter. "But after the first couple of times we saw each other, our paths didn't seem to cross again."

"I've been working a lot of overtime lately." If the truth be known, Susannah almost always put in extra hours. Often she brought work home with her. She was dedicated, committed and hardworking. Her neighbor, however, didn't seem to possess any of those qualities. She strongly suspected that everything in life had come much too easily for Nate Townsend. She'd never seen him without his baseball cap or his T-shirt. Somehow she doubted he even owned a suit. And if he did, it probably wouldn't look right on him. Nate Townsend was definitely a football-jersey type of guy.

He seemed likable—friendly and outgoing—but from what she'd seen, he lacked ambition. Apparently there'd never been anything he'd wanted badly enough to really strive for.

"I'm glad we had the chance to introduce ourselves," Susannah added, walking back into the living room and toward her front door. "I appreciate the help, but as you said, Michelle and I are going to be fine."

"It didn't sound that way when I arrived."

"I was just getting my feet wet," she returned, defending herself, "and why are you arguing with me? You're the one who said I was doing all right."

"I lied."

"Why would you do that?"

Nate shrugged nonchalantly. "I thought a little self-confidence would do you good, so I offered it."

Susannah glared at him, resenting his attitude. So much

for the nice-guy-who-lives-next-door image she'd had of him. "I don't need any favors from you."

"You may not," he agreed, "but unfortunately Michelle does. The poor kid was starving and you didn't so much as suspect."

"I would've figured it out."

Nate gave her a look that seemed to cast doubt on her intelligence, and Susannah frowned right back. She opened the door with far more force than necessary and flipped her hair over her shoulder with flair a Paris model would have envied. "Thanks for stopping in," she said stiffly, "but as you can see everything's under control."

"If you say so." He grinned at her and without another word was gone.

Susannah banged the door shut with her hip, feeling a rush of satisfaction as she did so. She knew this was petty, but her neighbor had annoyed her in more ways than one.

Soon afterward Susannah heard the soft strains of an Italian opera drifting from Nate's condominium. At least she thought it was Italian, which was unfortunate because that made her think of spaghetti and how hungry she actually was.

"Okay, Michelle," she said, smiling down on her niece. "It's time to feed your auntie." Without too much trouble, Susannah assembled the high chair and set her niece in that while she scanned the contents of her freezer.

The best she could come up with was a frozen Mexican entrée. She gazed at the picture on the front of the package, shook her head and tossed it back inside the freezer.

Michelle seemed to approve and vigorously slapped the tray on her high chair.

Crossing her arms and leaning against the freezer door, Susannah paused. "Did you hear what he said?" she asked, still irate. "I guess he was right, but he didn't have to be so superior about it."

Michelle slapped her hands in approval once again. The music was muted by the thick walls, and wanting to hear a little more, Susannah cracked open the sliding glass door to her balcony, which was separated from Nate's by a concrete partition. It bestowed privacy, but didn't muffle the beautiful voices raised in triumphant song.

Susannah opened the glass door completely and stepped outside. The evening was cool, but pleasantly so. The sun had just started to set and had cast a wash of golden shadows over the picturesque waterfront.

"Michelle," she muttered when she came back in, "he's cooking something that smells like lasagna or spaghetti." Her stomach growled and she returned to the freezer, taking out the same Mexican entrée she'd rejected earlier. It didn't seem any more appetizing than it had the first time.

A faint scent of garlic wafted into her kitchen. Susannah turned her classic Greek nose in that direction, then followed the aroma to the open door like a puppet drawn there by a string. She sniffed loudly and turned eagerly back to her niece. "It's definitely Italian, and it smells divine."

Michelle pounded the tray again.

"It's garlic bread," Susannah announced and whirled around to face her niece, who clearly wasn't impressed. But then, thought Susannah, she wouldn't be. She'd eaten.

Under normal conditions, Susannah would've reached for her jacket and headed to Mama Mataloni's, a fabulous Italian restaurant within easy walking distance. Unfortunately Mama Mataloni's didn't deliver.

Against her better judgment, Susannah stuck the frozen entrée into her microwave and set the timer. When there was another knock on her door, she stiffened and looked at Michelle as if the nine-month-old would sit up and tell Susannah who'd come by *this* time.

It was Nate again, holding a plate of spaghetti and a glass of red wine. "Did you fix yourself something to eat?" he asked.

For the life of her Susannah couldn't tear her gaze away from the oversize plate, heaped high with steaming pasta smothered in a thick red sauce. Nothing had ever looked— or smelled—more appetizing. The fresh Parmesan cheese he'd grated over the top had melted onto the rich sauce. A generous slice of garlic bread was balanced on the side.

"I, ah, was just heating up a…microwave dinner." She pointed behind her toward the kitchen as if that would explain what she was trying to say. Her tongue seemed to be stuck to the roof of her mouth.

"I shouldn't have acted like such a know-it-all earlier," he said, pushing the plate toward her. "I'm bringing you a peace offering."

"This…is for me?" She raised her eyes from the plate, wondering if he knew how hungry she felt and was toying with her.

He handed her the meal and the wine. "The sauce has been simmering most of the afternoon. I like to pretend I'm a bit of a gourmet chef. Every once in a while I get creative in the kitchen."

"How…nice." She conjured up a picture of Nate standing in his kitchen stirring sauce while the rest of the world struggled to make a living. Her attitude wasn't at all gracious and she mentally apologized. Without further ado, she marched into her kitchen, reached for a fork and plopped herself down at the table. She might as well eat this feast while it was hot!

One sample told her everything she needed to know.

"This is great." She took another bite, pointed her fork in his direction and rolled her eyes. "Marvelous. Wonderful."

Nate pulled a bread stick out of his shirt pocket and gave it to Michelle. "Here's looking at you, kid."

As Michelle chewed contentedly on the bread stick, Nate pulled out a chair and sat across from Susannah, who was too busy enjoying her dinner to notice anything out of the ordinary until Nate's eyes narrowed.

"What's wrong?" Susannah asked. She wiped her mouth with a napkin and sampled the wine.

"I smell something."

Judging by his expression, whatever it was apparently wasn't pleasant. "It might be the microwave dinner," she suggested hopefully, already knowing better.

"I'm afraid not."

Susannah carefully set the fork beside her plate as uneasiness settled over her.

"It seems," Nate said, covering his nose with one hand, "that someone needs to change Michelle's diaper."

Two

Holding a freshly diapered Michelle on her hip, Susannah rushed out of the bathroom into the narrow hallway and gasped for breath.

"Are you all right?" Nate asked, his brow creased with a concerned frown.

She nodded and sagged against the wall, feeling lightheaded. Once she'd dragged several clean breaths through her lungs, she straightened and even managed a weak smile.

"That wasn't so bad now, was it?"

Susannah glared at him. "I should've been wearing an oxygen mask."

Nate's responding chuckle did little to improve her mood.

"In light of what I just experienced," she muttered, "I can't understand why the population continues to grow." To be on the safe side, she opened the hall linen closet and took out a large can of disinfectant spray. Sticking her arm inside the bathroom, she gave a generous squirt.

"While you were busy I assembled the crib," Nate told her, still revealing far too much amusement to suit Susannah. "Where would you like me to put it?"

"The living room will be fine." His action had been thoughtful, but Susannah wasn't accustomed to depending on others, so when she thanked him, the words were forced.

Susannah followed him into the living room and found the bed ready. She laid Michelle down on her stomach and covered her with a hand-knit blanket. The baby settled down immediately, without fussing.

Nate walked toward the door. "You're sure everything's okay?" he said softly.

"Positive." Susannah wasn't, but Michelle was her niece and their problems weren't his. Nate had done more than enough already. "Thanks for dinner."

"Anytime." He paused at the door and turned back. "I left my phone number on the kitchen counter. Call if you need me."

"Thanks."

He favored her with a grin on his way out the door, and Susannah stood a few moments after he'd left the apartment, thinking about him. Her feelings were decidedly mixed.

She began sorting through the various bags her sister had brought, depositing the jars of baby food in the cupboard and putting the bottles of formula in the fridge. As Nate had pointed out, there was plenty of room—all she had to do was scoot the empty pickle jar aside.

She supposed she should toss the jar in the garbage, but one of the guys from the office had talked about making pickled eggs. It sounded so simple—all she had to do was peel a few hard-boiled eggs and keep them refrigerated in the jar for a week or so. Susannah had been meaning to try it ever since. But she was afraid that when the mood struck her, she wouldn't have any pickle juice around, so she'd decided to keep it on hand.

Once she'd finished in the kitchen, Susannah soaked in a hot bath, leaving the door ajar in case Michelle woke and needed her. She felt far more relaxed afterward.

Walking back into the living room on the tips of her toes, she brought out her briefcase and removed a file. She glanced down at her sleeping niece and gently patted her back. The little girl looked so angelic, so content.

Suddenly a powerful yearning stirred within Susannah. She felt real affection for Michelle, but the feeling was more than that. This time alone with her niece had evoked a longing buried deep in Susannah's heart, a longing she'd never taken the time to fully examine. And with it came an aching restless sensation that she promptly submerged.

When Susannah had chosen a career in business, she'd realized she was giving up the part of herself that hungered for a husband and children. There was nothing that said she couldn't marry, couldn't raise a child, but she knew herself too well. From the time she was in high school it had been painfully apparent that she was completely inadequate in the domestic arena. Especially when she compared herself to Emily, who seemed to have been born with a dust rag in one hand and a cookbook in the other.

Susannah had never regretted the decision she'd made to dedicate herself to her career, but then she was more fortunate than some. She had Emily, who was determined to supply her with numerous nieces and nephews. For Susannah, Michelle and the little ones who were sure to follow would have to be enough.

Reminding herself that she was comfortable with her choices, Susannah quietly stepped away from the crib. For the next hour, she sat on her bed reading the details of the proposed marketing program the department had sent her.

The full presentation was scheduled for Monday morning and she wanted to be informed and prepared.

When she finished reading the report, she tiptoed back to her desk, situated in the far corner of the living room, and replaced the file in her briefcase.

Once more she paused to check on her niece. Feeling just a little cocky, she returned to the bedroom convinced this babysitting business wasn't going to be so bad after all.

Susannah changed her mind at one-thirty when a piercing wail startled her out of a sound sleep. Not knowing how long Michelle had been at it, Susannah nearly fell out of bed in her rush to reach her niece.

"Michelle," she cried, stumbling blindly across the floor, her arms stretched out in front of her. "I'm coming.... There's no need to panic."

Michelle disagreed vehemently.

Turning on a light only made matters worse. Squinting to protect her eyes from the glare, Susannah groped her way to the crib, then let out a cry herself when she stubbed her toe on the leg of the coffee table.

Michelle was standing, holding on to the bars and looking as if she didn't have a friend in the world.

"What's the matter, sweetheart?" Susannah asked softly, lifting the baby into her arms.

A wet bottom told part of the story. And the poor kid had probably woken and, finding herself in a strange place, felt scared. Susannah couldn't blame her.

"All right, we'll try this diapering business again."

Susannah spread a thick towel on the bathroom counter, then gently placed Michelle on it. She was halfway through the changing process when the phone rang. Straightening, Susannah glanced around her, wondering what she should do. She couldn't leave Michelle, and picking her up and carrying her into the kitchen would be difficult. Whoever was calling at this time of night should know better! If it was important they could leave a message on her answering machine.

But after three rings, the phone stopped, followed almost immediately by a firm knock at her door.

Hauling Michelle, newly diapered, Susannah squinted and checked the peephole to discover a disgruntled Nate on the other side.

"Nate," she said in surprise as she opened the door. She couldn't even guess what he wanted. And she wasn't too keen about letting him into her apartment at this hour.

He stood just inside the condo, barefoot and dressed in a red plaid housecoat. His hair was mussed, which made Susannah wonder about her own disheveled appearance. She suspected she looked like someone who'd walked out of a swamp.

"Is Michelle all right?" he barked, despite the evidence before him. Not waiting for a reply, he continued in an accusing tone, "You didn't answer the phone."

"I couldn't. I was changing her diaper."

Nate hesitated, then studied her closely. "In that case, are *you* all right?"

She nodded and managed to raise one hand. It was difficult when her arms were occupied with a baby. "I lived to tell about it."

"Good. What happened? Why was Michelle crying?"

"I'm not sure. Maybe when she woke up and didn't recognize her surroundings, she suffered an anxiety attack."

"And, from the look of us, caused a couple more."

Susannah would rather he hadn't mentioned that. Her long, tangled hair spilled over her shoulders and she, too, was barefoot. She'd been so anxious to get to Michelle that she hadn't bothered to reach for her slippers or her robe.

Michelle, it seemed, was pleased with all the unexpected attention, and when she leaned toward Nate, arms outstretched, Susannah marveled at how fickle an infant could be. After all, she was the one who'd fed and diapered her. Not Nate.

"It's my male charm," he explained delightedly.

"More likely, it's your red housecoat."

Whatever it was, Michelle went into his arms as if he were a long-lost friend. Susannah excused herself to retrieve her robe from the foot of her bed. By the time she got back, Nate was sitting on the sofa with his feet stretched out, supported by Susannah's mahogany coffee table.

"Make yourself at home," she muttered. Her mood wasn't always the best when she'd been abruptly wakened from a sound sleep.

He glanced up at her and grinned. "No need to be testy."

"Yes, there is," she said, but destroyed what remained of her argument by yawning loudly. Covering her mouth with the back of her hand, she slumped down on the chair across from him and flipped her hair away from her face.

His gaze followed the action. "You should wear your hair down more often."

She glared at him. "I always wear my hair up."

"I noticed. And frankly, it's much more flattering down."

"Oh, for heaven's sake," she cried, "are you going to tell me how to dress next?"

"I might."

He said it with such a charming smile that any sting there might have been in his statement was diluted.

"You don't have to stick with business suits every day, do you? Try jeans sometime. With a T-shirt."

She opened her mouth to argue with him, then decided not to bother. The arrogance he displayed seemed to be characteristic of handsome men in general, she'd noted. Because a man happened to possess lean good looks and could smile beguilingly, he figured he had the right to say anything he pleased to a woman—to comment on how she styled her hair, how she chose to dress or anything else. These were things he wouldn't dream of discussing if he were talking to another man.

"You aren't going to argue?"

"No," she said, and for emphasis shook her head.

That stopped him short. He paused and blinked, then sent her another of his captivating smiles. "I find that refreshing."

"I'm gratified to hear there's something about me you approve of." There were probably plenty of other things that didn't please him. Given any encouragement, he'd probably be glad to list them for her.

Sweet little traitor that she was, Michelle had curled up in Nate's arms, utterly content just to sit there and study his handsome face, which no doubt had fascinated numerous other females before her. The least Michelle could do was show some signs of going back to sleep so Susannah could return her to the crib and usher Nate out the door.

"I shouldn't have said what I did about your hair and clothes."

"Hey," she returned flippantly, "you don't need to worry about hurting my feelings. I'm strong. I've got a lot of emotional fortitude."

"Strong," he repeated. "You make yourself sound like an all-weather tire."

"I've had to be tougher than that."

His face relaxed into a look of sympathy. "Why?"

"I work with men just like you every day."

"Men just like me?"

"It's true. For the past seven years, I've found myself up against the old double standard, but I've learned to keep my cool."

He frowned as if he didn't understand what she was talking about. Susannah felt it was her obligation to tell him. Apparently Nate had never been involved in office politics. "Let me give you a few examples. If a male coworker has a cluttered desk, then everyone assumes he's a hard worker. If my desk is a mess, it's a sign of disorganization."

Nate looked as if he wanted to argue with her, but Susannah was just warming to her subject and she forged ahead before he had a chance to speak. "If a man in an office marries, it's good for the company because he'll settle down and become a more productive employee. If a woman marries, it's almost the kiss of death because management figures she'll get pregnant and quit. If a man leaves because he's been offered a better job, everyone's pleased for him because he's taking advantage of an excellent career opportunity. But if the same position is offered to a woman and she takes it, then upper management shrugs and claims women aren't dependable."

When she'd finished there was a short pause. "You have very definite feelings on the subject," he said at last.

"If you were a woman, you would, too."

His nod of agreement was a long time coming. "You're right, I probably would."

Michelle seemed to find the toes of her sleeper fascinating and was examining them closely. Personally, Susannah didn't know how anyone could be so wide-awake at this ungodly hour.

"If you turn down the lights, she might get the hint," Nate said, doing a poor job of smothering a yawn.

"You're beat," said Susannah. "There's no need for you to stay. I'll take her." She held out her arms to Michelle, who whimpered and clung all the more tightly to Nate. Susannah's feelings of inadequacy were reinforced.

"Don't worry about me. I'm comfortable like this," Nate told her.

"But..." She could feel the warmth invading her cheeks. She lowered her eyes, regretting her outburst of a few minutes ago. She'd been standing on her soapbox again. "Listen, I'm sorry about what I said. What goes on at the office has nothing to do with our being neighbors."

"Then we're even."

"Even?"

"I shouldn't have commented on your hair and clothes." He hesitated long enough to envelop her in his smile. "Friends?"

Despite the intolerable hour, Susannah found herself smiling back. "Friends."

Michelle seemed to concur because she cooed loudly, kicking her feet.

Susannah stood and turned the lamp down to its lowest setting, then reached for Michelle's blanket, covering the baby. Feeling slightly chilled herself, she fetched the brightly colored afghan at the foot of the sofa, which Emily had crocheted for her last Christmas.

The muted light created an intimate atmosphere, and suddenly self-conscious, Susannah suggested, "Maybe I'll sing to her. That should help her go to sleep."

"If anyone sings, it'll be me," he said much too quickly.

Susannah's pride was a little dented, but remembering

her limited repertoire of songs, she gestured toward him and said, "All right, Frank Sinatra, have a go."

To Susannah's surprise, Nate's singing voice was soothing and melodious. Even more surprisingly, he knew exactly the right kind of songs. Not lullabies, but easy-listening songs, the kind she'd heard for years on the radio. She felt her own eyes drifting closed and battled to stay awake. His voice dropped to a mere whisper that felt like a warm caress. Much too warm. And cozy, as if the three of them belonged together, which was ridiculous since she'd only just met Nate. He was her neighbor and nothing more. There hadn't been time for them to get to know each other, and Michelle was her *niece,* not her daughter.

But the domestic fantasy continued, no matter how hard she tried to dispel it. She couldn't stop thinking about what it would be like to share her life with a husband and children—and she could barely manage to keep her eyes open for more than a second or two. Perhaps if she rested them for a moment…

The next thing Susannah knew, her neck ached. She reached up to secure her pillow, then realized she didn't have one. Instead of being in bed, she was curled up in the chair, her head resting uncomfortably against the arm. Slowly, reluctantly, she opened her eyes and discovered Nate across from her, head tilted back, sleeping soundly. Michelle was resting peacefully in his arms.

It took Susannah a minute or so to orient herself. When she saw the sun breaking across the sky and spilling through her large windows, she closed her eyes again. It was morning. Morning! Nate had spent the night at her place.

Flustered, Susannah twisted her body into an upright position and rubbed the sleep from her face, wondering what she should do. Waking Nate was probably not the best idea. He was bound to be as unnerved as she was to discover he'd fallen asleep in her living room. To complicate matters, the afghan she'd covered herself with had somehow become twisted around her hips and legs. Muttering under her breath, Susannah yanked it about in an effort to stand.

Her activity disturbed Nate's restful slumber. He stirred, glanced in her direction and froze for what seemed the longest moment of Susannah's life. Then he blinked several times and glared at her as though he hoped she'd vanish into thin air.

Standing now, Susannah did her best to appear dignified, which was nearly impossible with the comforter still twisted around her.

"Where am I?" Nate asked dazedly.

"Ah...my place."

His eyes drifted shut. "I was afraid of that." The mournful look that came over Nate's face would have been comical under other circumstances. Only neither of them was laughing.

"I, ah, must've fallen asleep," she said, breaking the embarrassed silence. She took pains to fold the afghan, and held it against her stomach like a shield.

"Me, too, apparently," Nate muttered.

Michelle woke and struggled into a sitting position. She looked around her and evidently didn't like what she saw, either. Her lower lip started to tremble.

"Michelle, it's okay," Susannah said quickly, hoping to ward off the scream she feared was coming. "You're staying with Auntie Susannah this weekend, remember?"

"I think she might be wet," Nate offered when Michelle began to whimper softly. He let out a muffled curse and hastily lifted the nine-month-old from his lap. "I'm positive she's wet. Here, take her."

Susannah reached for her niece and a dry diaper in one smooth movement, but it didn't help. Michelle was intent on letting them both know, in no uncertain terms, that she didn't like her schedule altered. Nor did she appreciate waking up in a stranger's arms. She conveyed her displeasure in loud boisterous cries.

"I think she might be hungry, too," Nate suggested, trying to brush the dampness from his housecoat.

"Brilliant observation," Susannah said sarcastically on her way to the bathroom, Michelle in her arms.

"My, my, you certainly get testy in the mornings," he said.

"I need coffee."

"Fine. I'll make us both a cup while I'm heating a bottle for Michelle."

"She's supposed to eat her cereal first," Susannah shouted. At least that was what Emily had insisted when she'd outlined her daughter's schedule.

"I'm sure she doesn't care. She's hungry."

"All right, all right," Susannah yelled from the bathroom. "Heat her bottle first if you want."

Yelling was a mistake, she soon discovered. Michelle clearly wasn't any keener on mornings than Susannah was. Punching the air with her stubby legs, her niece made diapering a nearly impossible task. Susannah grew more frustrated by the minute. Finally her hair, falling forward over her shoulders, caught Michelle's attention. She grasped it, pausing to gulp in a huge breath.

"Do you want me to get that?" she heard Nate shout.

"Get what?"

Apparently it wasn't important because he didn't answer her. But a moment later he was standing at the bathroom door.

"It's for you," he said.

"What's for me?"

"The phone."

The word bounced around in her mind like a ricocheting bullet. "Did...did they say who it was?" she asked, her voice high-pitched and wobbly. No doubt it was someone from the office and she'd be the subject of gossip for months.

"Someone named Emily."

"Emily," she repeated. That was even worse. Her sister was sure to be full of awkward questions.

"Hi," Susannah said as casually as possible into the receiver.

"Who answered the phone?" her sister demanded without preamble.

"My neighbor. Nate Townsend. He, ah, lives next door." That awkward explanation astonished even her. Worse, Susannah had been ready to blurt out that Nate had spent the night, but she'd stopped herself just in time.

"I haven't met him, have I?"

"My neighbor? No, you haven't."

"He sounds cute."

"Listen, if you're phoning about Michelle," Susannah hurried to add, anxious to end the conversation, "there's no need for concern. Everything's under control." That was a slight exaggeration, but what Emily didn't know couldn't worry her.

"Is that Michelle I hear crying in the background?" Emily asked.

"Yes. She just woke up and she's a little hungry." Nate was holding the baby and pacing the kitchen, waiting impatiently for Susannah to get off the phone.

"My poor baby," Emily moaned. "Tell me when you met your neighbor. I don't remember you ever mentioning anyone named Nate."

"He's been helping me out," Susannah said quickly. Wanting to change the subject, she asked, "How are you and Robert?"

Her sister sighed audibly. "Robert was so right. We needed this weekend alone. I feel a thousand times better and so does he. Every married couple should get away for a few days like this—but then everyone doesn't have a sister as generous as you to fill in on such short notice."

"Good, good," Susannah said, hardly aware of what she was supposed to think was so fantastic. "Uh-oh," she said, growing desperate. "The bottle's warm. I hate to cut you off, but I've got to take care of Michelle. I'm sure you understand."

"Of course."

"I'll see you tomorrow afternoon, then. What time's your flight landing?"

"One-fifteen. We'll drive straight to your place and pick up Michelle."

"Okay, I'll expect you sometime around two." Another day with Michelle. She could manage for another twenty-four hours, couldn't she? What could possibly go wrong in that small amount of time?

Losing patience, Nate took the bottle and Michelle and returned to the living room. Susannah watched through the doorway as he turned on her television and plopped himself down as if he'd been doing it for years. His concentration moved from the TV long enough to place the rubber nipple in Michelle's eager mouth.

Her niece began greedily sucking, too hungry to care who was feeding her. Good heavens, Susannah thought,

Michelle had spent the night in his arms. A little thing like letting this man feed her paled in comparison.

Emily was still chatting, telling her sister how romantic her first night in San Francisco had been. But Susannah barely heard. Her gaze settled on Nate, who looked rumpled, crumpled and utterly content, sitting in her living room, holding an infant in his arms.

That sight affected Susannah as few ever had, and she was powerless to explain its impact on her senses. She'd dated a reasonable number of men—debonair, rich, sophisticated ones. But the feeling she had now, this attraction, had taken her completely by surprise. Over the years, Susannah had always been careful to guard her heart. It hadn't been difficult, since she'd never met anyone who truly appealed to her. Yet this disheveled, disgruntled male, who sat in her living room feeding her infant niece with enviable expertise, attracted her more profoundly than anyone she'd ever met. It wasn't the least bit logical. Nothing could ever develop between them—they were as different as…as gelatin and concrete. The last thing she wanted was to become involved in a serious relationship. With some effort, she forced her eyes away from the homey scene.

When at last she was able to hang up the phone, Susannah moved into the living room, feeling weary. She brushed the tangled curls from her face, wondering if she should take Michelle from Nate so he could return to his own apartment. No doubt her niece would resist and humiliate her once more.

"Your sister isn't flying with Puget Air, is she?" he asked, frowning. His gaze remained on the television screen.

"Yes, why?"

Nate's mouth thinned. "You…we're in trouble here. Big

trouble. According to the news, maintenance workers for
Puget Air are going on strike. By six tonight, every plane
they own will be grounded."

Three

"If this is a joke," Susannah told him angrily, "it's in poor taste."

"Would I kid about this?" Nate asked mildly.

Susannah slumped down on the edge of the sofa and gave a ragged sigh. This couldn't be happening, it just couldn't. "I'd better call Emily." She assumed her sister was blissfully unaware of the strike.

Susannah was back a few minutes later.

"Well?" Nate demanded. "What did she say?"

"Oh, she knew all along," Susannah replied disparagingly, "but she didn't want to say anything because she was afraid I'd worry."

"How exactly docs shc intend to get home?"

"Apparently they booked seats on another airline on the off chance something like this might happen."

"That was smart."

"My brother-in-law's like that. I'm not to give the matter another thought," she said, quoting Emily. "My sister will be back Sunday afternoon as promised." If the Fates so decreed—and Susannah said a fervent prayer that they would.

But the Fates had other plans.

* * *

Sunday morning, there were bags under Susannah's eyes. She was mentally and physically exhausted, and convinced anew that motherhood was definitely not for her. Two nights into the ordeal, Susannah had noticed that the emotional stirring for a husband and children came to her only when Michelle was sleeping or eating. And with good reason.

Nate arrived around nine bearing gifts. He brought freshly baked cinnamon rolls still warm from the oven. He stood in her doorway, tall and lean, with a smile bright enough to dazzle the most dedicated career woman. Once more, Susannah was shocked by her overwhelming reaction to him. Her heart leaped to her throat, and she immediately wished she'd taken time to dress in something better than her faded housecoat.

"You look terrible."

"Thanks," she said, bouncing Michelle on her hip.

"I take it you had a bad night."

"Michelle was fussing. She didn't seem the least bit interested in sleeping." She wiped a hand over her face.

"I wish you'd called me," Nate said, taking her by the elbow and leading her into the kitchen. He actually looked guilty because he'd had a peaceful night's rest. Ridiculous, Susannah thought.

"Call you? Whatever for?" she asked. "So you could have paced with her, too?" As it was, Nate had spent a good part of Saturday in and out of her apartment helping her. Spending a second night with them was above and beyond the call of duty. "Did I tell you," Susannah said, yawning, "Michelle's got a new tooth coming in—I felt it myself." Deposited in the high chair, Michelle was content for the moment.

Nate nodded and glanced at his watch. "When does your sister's flight get in?"

"One-fifteen." No sooner had the words left her lips than the phone rang. Susannah's and Nate's eyes met, and as it rang a second time she wondered how a telephone could sound so much like a death knell. Even before she answered it, Susannah knew it would be what she most dreaded hearing.

"Well?" Nate asked when she'd finished the call.

Covering her face with both hands, Susannah sagged against the wall.

"Say something."

Slowly she lowered her hands. "Help."

"Help?"

"Yes," she cried, struggling to keep her voice from cracking. "All Puget Air flights are grounded just the way the news reported, and the other airline Robert and Emily made reservations with is overbooked. The earliest flight they can get is tomorrow morning."

"I see."

"Obviously you don't!" she cried. "Tomorrow is Monday and I've got to be at work!"

"Call in sick."

"I can't do that," she snapped, angry with him for even suggesting such a thing. "My marketing group is giving their presentation and I've got to be there."

"Why?"

She frowned at him. It was futile to expect someone like Nate to understand something as important as a sales presentation. Nate didn't seem to have a job; he didn't worry about a career. For that matter, he couldn't possibly grasp that a woman holding a management position had to strive twice as hard to prove herself.

"I'm not trying to be cute, Susannah," he said with infuriating calm. "I honestly want to know why that meeting is so important."

"Because it is. I don't expect you to appreciate this, so just accept the fact that I *have* to be there."

Nate cocked his head and idly rubbed the side of his jaw. "First, answer me something. Five years from now, will this meeting make a difference in your life?"

"I don't know." She pressed two fingers to the bridge of her nose. She'd had less than three hours' sleep, and Nate was asking impossible questions. Michelle, bless her devilish little heart, had fallen asleep in her high chair. Why shouldn't she? Susannah reasoned. She'd spent the entire night fussing, and was exhausted now. By the time Susannah had discovered the new tooth, she felt as if she'd grown it herself.

"If I were you, I wouldn't sweat it," Nate said with that same nonchalant attitude. "If you aren't there to hear their presentation, your marketing group will give it Tuesday morning."

"In other words," she muttered, "you're saying I don't have a thing to worry about."

"Exactly."

Nate Townsend knew next to nothing about surviving in the corporate world, and he'd obviously been protected from life's harsher realities. It was all too obvious to Susannah that he was a man with a baseball-cap mentality. He couldn't be expected to fully comprehend her dilemma.

"So," he said now, "what are you going to do?"

Susannah wasn't sure. Briefly, she closed her eyes in an effort to concentrate. *Impose discipline,* she said to herself. *Stay calm.* That was crucial. *Think slowly and analyze your objectives.* For every problem there was a solution.

"Susannah?"

She glanced at him; she'd almost forgotten he was there. "I'll cancel my early-morning appointments and go in for the presentation," she stated matter-of-factly.

"What about Michelle? Are you going to hire a sitter?"

A babysitter hired by the babysitter. A novel thought, perhaps even viable, but Susannah didn't know anyone who sat with babies.

Then she made her decision. She would take Michelle to work with her.

And that was exactly what she did.

As she knew it would, Susannah's arrival at H&J Lima caused quite a stir. At precisely ten the following morning, she stepped off the elevator. Her black leather briefcase was clutched in one hand and Michelle was pressed against her hip with the other. Head held high, Susannah marched across the hardwood floor, past the long rows of doorless cubicles and shelves of foot-thick file binders. Several employees moved away from their desks to view her progress. A low rumble of hushed whispers followed her.

"Good morning, Ms. Brooks," Susannah said crisply as she walked into her office, the diaper bag draped over her shoulder like an ammunition pouch.

"Ms. Simmons."

Susannah noted that her assistant—to her credit—didn't so much as bat an eye. The woman was well trained; to all outward appearances, Susannah regularly arrived at the office with a nine-month-old infant attached to her hip.

Depositing the diaper bag on the floor, Susannah took her place behind a six-foot-wide walnut desk. Content for the moment, Michelle sat on her lap, gleefully viewing her aunt's domain.

"Would you like some coffee?" Ms. Brooks asked.

"Yes, please."

Her assistant paused. "Will your, ah..."

"This is my niece, Michelle, Ms. Brooks."

The woman nodded. "Will Michelle require anything to drink?"

"No, but thanks anyway. Is there anything urgent in the mail?"

"Nothing that can't wait. I canceled your eight- and nine-o'clock appointments," her assistant went on to explain. "When I spoke to Mr. Adams, he asked if you could join him for drinks tomorrow night at six."

"That'll be fine." The old lecher would love to do all their business outside the office. On this occasion, she'd agree to his terms, since she'd been the one to cancel their appointment, but she wouldn't be so willing a second time. She'd never much cared for Andrew Adams, who was over-weight, balding and a general nuisance.

"Will you be needing me for anything else?" Ms. Brooks asked when she delivered the coffee.

"Nothing. Thank you."

As she should have predicted, the meeting was an un-mitigated disaster. The presentation took twenty-two min-utes, and in that brief time Michelle managed to dismantle Susannah's Cross pen, unfasten her blouse and pull her hair free from her carefully styled French twist. The baby clapped her hands at various inappropriate points and made loud noises. At the low point of the meeting, Susannah had been forced to leave her seat and dive under the conference table to retrieve her niece, who was cheerfully crawling over everyone's feet.

By the time she got home, Susannah felt like climb-ing back into bed and staying there. It was the type of day that made her crave something chocolate and excessively sweet. But there weren't enough chocolate chip cookies in the world to see her through another morning like that one.

To Susannah's surprise, Nate met her in the foyer outside the elevator. She took one look at him and resisted the urge to burst into tears.

"I take it things didn't go well."

"How'd you guess?" she asked sarcastically.

"It might be the fact you're wearing your hair down when I specifically remember you left wearing it up. Or it could be that your blouse is buttoned wrong and there's a gaping hole in the middle." His smile was mischievous. "I wondered if you were the type to wear a lacy bra. Now I know."

Susannah groaned and slapped a hand over her front. He could have spared her that comment.

"Here, kiddo," he said, taking Michelle out of Susannah's arms. "It looks like we need to give your poor aunt a break."

Turning her back, Susannah refastened her blouse and then brought out her key. Her once orderly, immaculate apartment looked as if a cyclone had gone through it. Blankets and baby toys were scattered from one end of the living room to the other. She'd slept on the couch in order to be close to Michelle, and her pillow and blankets were still there, along with her blue suit jacket, which she'd been forced to change when Michelle had tossed a spoonful of plums on the sleeve.

"What happened here?" Nate asked, looking in astonishment at the scene before him.

"Three days and three nights with Michelle and you need to ask?"

"Sit down," he said gently. "I'll get you a cup of coffee." Susannah did as he suggested, too grateful to argue with him.

Nate stopped just inside the kitchen. "What's this purple stuff all over the walls?"

"Plums," Susannah informed him. "I discovered the hard way that Michelle hates plums."

The scene in the kitchen was a good example of how her morning had gone. It had taken Susannah the better part of three hours to get herself and Michelle ready for the excursion to the office. And that was just the beginning.

"What I need is a double martini," she told Nate when he carried in two cups of coffee.

"It's not even noon."

"I know," she said, slowly lowering herself to the sofa. "Can you imagine what I'd need if it was two o'clock?"

Chuckling, Nate handed her the steaming cup. Michelle was sitting on the carpet, content to play with the very toys she'd vehemently rejected that morning.

Nate unexpectedly sat down next to her and looped his arm over her shoulder. She tensed, but if he noticed, he chose to ignore it. He stretched his legs out on the coffee table and relaxed.

Susannah felt her tension mount. The memory of the meeting with marketing was enough to elevate her blood pressure, but when she analyzed the reasons for this anxiety, she discovered it came from being so close to Nate. It wasn't that Susannah objected to his touch; in reality, quite the opposite was true. They'd spent three days in close quarters, and contrary to everything she'd theorized about her neighbor, she'd come to appreciate his happy-go-lucky approach to life. But it was diametrically opposed to her own, and the fact that she could be so attracted to him was something of a shock.

"Do you want to talk about marketing's presentation?"

She released her breath. "No, I think this morning is best

forgotten by everyone involved. You were right, I should have postponed the meeting."

Nate sipped his coffee and said, "It's one of those live-and-learn situations."

Pulling herself to a standing position at the coffee table, Michelle cheerfully edged her way around until she was stopped by Nate's outstretched legs. Then she surprised them both by reaching out one arm and granting him a smile that would have melted concrete.

"Oh, look," Susannah said proudly, "you can see her new tooth!"

"Where?" Lifting the baby onto his lap, Nate peered inside her mouth. Susannah was trying to show him where to look when someone, presumably her sister, rang impatiently from the lobby.

Susannah opened her door a minute later, and Emily flew in as if she'd sprouted wings. "My baby!" she cried. "Mommy missed you so-o-o much."

Not half as much as I missed you, Emily, she mused, watching the happy reunion.

Robert followed on his wife's heels, obviously pleased. The weekend away had apparently done them both good. Never mind that it had nearly destroyed Susannah's peace of mind *and* her career.

"You must be Nate," Emily said, claiming the seat beside Susannah's neighbor. "My sister couldn't say enough about you."

"Coffee anyone?" Susannah piped up eagerly, rubbing her palms together. The last thing she needed was her sister applying her matchmaking techniques to her and Nate. Emily strongly believed it was unnatural for Susannah to live the way she did. A career was fine, but choosing to forgo the personal satisfaction of a husband and family was beyond her sister's comprehension. Being fulfilled in that role herself, Emily assumed that Susannah was missing an essential part of life.

"Nothing for me," Robert answered.

"I'll bet you're eager to pack everything up and head home," Susannah said hopefully. Her eye happened to catch Nate's, and it was obvious that he was struggling not to laugh at her less-than-subtle attempt to usher her sister and family on their way.

"Susannah's right," Robert announced, glancing around the room. It was clear he'd never seen his orderly, efficient sister-in-law's home in such a state of disarray.

"But I've hardly had a chance to talk to Nate," Emily protested. "And I was looking forward to getting to know him better."

"I'll be around," Nate said lightly.

His gaze settled on Susannah, and the look he gave her made her insides quiver. For the first time she realized how much she wanted this man to kiss her. Susannah wasn't the type of person who looked at a handsome male and wondered how his mouth would feel on hers. She was convinced this current phenomenon had a lot to do with sheer exhaustion, but whatever the cause she found her eyes riveted to his.

Emily suddenly noticed what was happening. "Yes, I think you may be right, Robert," she said, and her voice contained more than a hint of amusement. "I'll pack Michelle's things."

Susannah's cheeks were pink with embarrassment by the time she tore her gaze away from Nate's. "By the way, did you know Michelle has an aversion to plums?"

"I can't say I did," Emily said, busily throwing her daughter's things together.

Nate helped disassemble the crib and the high chair, and it seemed no more than a few minutes had passed before Susannah's condo was once more her own. She stood in the middle of the living room savoring the silence. It was pure bliss.

"They're off," she said when she saw that Nate had stayed behind.

"Like a herd of turtles."

Susannah had heard that saying from the time she was a kid. She didn't find it particularly funny anymore, but she shared a smile with him.

"I have my life back now," she sighed. It would probably take her a month to recover, though.

"Your life is your own," Nate agreed, watching her closely.

Susannah would've liked to attribute the tears that flooded her eyes to his close scrutiny, but she knew better. With her arms cradling her middle, she walked over to the window, which looked out over Elliott Bay. A green-and-white ferry glided peacefully over the darker green waters. Rain tapped gently against the window, and the sky, a deep oyster-gray, promised drizzle for most of the afternoon.

Hoping Nate wouldn't notice, she wiped the tears from her face and drew in a deep calming breath.

"Susannah?"

"I... I was just looking at the Sound. It's so lovely in the fall." She could hear him approach her from behind, and when he placed his hands on her shoulders it was all she could do to keep from leaning against him.

"You're crying."

She nodded, sniffling because it was impossible to hold it inside any longer.

"It's not like you to cry, is it? What's wrong?"

"I don't know..." she said and hiccuped on a sob. "I can't believe I'm doing this. I love that little kid...we were just beginning to understand each other...and...dear heaven, I'm glad Emily came back when...she did." Before Susannah could recognize how much she was missing without a husband and family.

Nate ran his hands down her arms in the softest of caresses.

He didn't say anything for a long time, and Susannah was convinced she was making an absolute idiot of herself. Nate was right; it wasn't like her to dissolve into tears. This unexpected outburst must've been a result of the trauma she'd experienced that morning in her office, or the fact that she hadn't had a decent night's sleep in what felt like a month and, yes, she'd admit it, of meeting Nate.

Without saying another word, Nate turned her around and lifted her chin with his finger, raising her eyes to his. His look was so tender, so caring, that Susannah sniffled again. Her shoulders shook and she wiped her nose.

He brushed away the hair that clung to the sides of her damp face. His fingertips slid over each of her features as though he were a blind man trying to memorize her face. Susannah was mesmerized, unable to pull away. Slowly, as if denying himself the pleasure for as long as he could, he lowered his mouth.

When his lips settled on hers, Susannah released a barely audible sigh. She'd wondered earlier what it would be like when Nate kissed her. Now she knew. His kiss was soft and warm. Velvet smooth and infinitely gentle, and yet it was undeniably exciting.

As if one kiss wasn't enough, he kissed her again. This time it was Nate who sighed. Then he dropped his hands and stepped back.

Startled by his abrupt action, Susannah swayed slightly. Nate's arms righted her. Apparently he'd come to his senses at the same time she had. For a brief moment they'd decided to ignore their differences. The only thing they had in common was the fact that they lived in the same building, she reminded herself. Their values and expectations were worlds apart.

"Are you all right?" he asked, frowning.

She blinked, trying to find a way to disguise that she wasn't. Everything had happened much too fast; her heart was galloping like a runaway horse. She'd never been so attracted to a man in her life. "Of course I'm all right," she said with strained bravado. "Are you?"

He didn't answer for a moment. Instead, he shoved his hands in his pants pocket and moved away from her, looking annoyed.

"Nate?" she whispered.

He paused, scowling in her direction. Rubbing his hand across his brow, he twisted the ever-present baseball cap until it faced backward. "I think we should try that again."

Susannah wasn't sure what he meant until he reached for her. His first few kisses had been gentle, but this one was meant to take charge of her senses. His mouth slid over hers until she felt the starch go out of her knees. In an effort to maintain her balance, she gripped his shoulders, and although she fought it, she quickly surrendered to the swirling excitement. Nate's kiss was debilitating. She couldn't breathe, couldn't think, couldn't move.

Nate groaned, then his hands shifted to the back of her head. He slanted his mouth over hers. At length he released a jagged breath and buried his face in the soft curve of her neck. "What about now?"

"You're a good kisser."

"That's not what I meant, Susannah. You feel it, too, don't you? You must! There's enough electricity between us to light up a city block."

"No," she lied, and swallowed tightly. "It was nice as far as kisses go—"

"Nice!"

"Very nice," she amended, hoping to appease him, "but that's about it."

Nate didn't say anything for a long minute, a painfully long minute. Then, scowling at her again, he turned and walked out of the apartment.

Trembling, Susannah watched him go. His kiss had touched a chord within her, notes that had been long-silent, and now she feared the music would forever mark her soul. But she couldn't let him know that. They had nothing in common. They were too mismatched.

Now that she was seated in the plush cocktail lounge with her associate, Andrew Adams, Susannah regretted having agreed to meet him after hours. It was apparent from the moment she stepped into the dimly lit room that he had more on his mind than business. Despite the fact that Adams was balding and overweight, he would have been attractive enough if he hadn't seen himself as some kind of modern-day Adonis. Although Susannah struggled to maintain a businesslike calm, it was becoming increasingly difficult, and she wondered how much longer her good intentions would hold.

"There are some figures I meant to show you," Adams said, holding the stem of his martini glass with both hands and studying Susannah with undisguised admiration. "Unfortunately I left them at my apartment. Why don't we conclude our talk there?"

Susannah made a point of looking at her watch and frowning, hoping he'd get the hint. Something told her differently. "I'm afraid I won't have the time," she said. It was almost seven and she'd already spent an hour with him.

"My place is only a few blocks from here," he coaxed.

His look was much too suggestive, and Susannah was growing wearier by the minute. As far as she could see, this entire evening had been a waste of time.

The only thing that interested her was returning to her own place and talking to Nate. He'd been on her mind all day and she was eager to see him again. The truth was, she felt downright nervous after their last meeting, and wondered how they'd react to each other now. Nate had left her so abruptly, and she hadn't talked to him since.

"John Hammer and I are good friends," Adams claimed, pulling his chair closer to her own. "I don't know if you're aware of that."

He didn't even bother to veil his threat—or his bribe, whichever it was. Susannah worked directly under John Hammer, who would have the final say on the appointment of a new vice president. Susannah and two others were in the running for the position. And Susannah wanted it. Badly. She could achieve her five-year goal if she got it, and in the process make H&J Lima history—by being the first female vice president.

"If you're such good friends with Mr. Hammer," she said, "then I suggest you give those figures to him directly, since he'll need to review them anyway."

"No, that wouldn't work," he countered sharply. "If you come with me it'll only take a few minutes. We'd be in and out of my place in, say, half an hour at the most."

Susannah's immediate reaction to situations such as this was a healthy dose of outrage, but she managed to control her temper. "If your apartment is so convenient, then I'll wait here while you go back for those sheets." As she spoke, a couple walked past the tiny table where she was seated with Andrew Adams. Susannah didn't pay much attention to the man, who wore a gray suit, but the blonde with him was striking. Susannah followed the woman with her eyes and envied the graceful way she moved.

"It would be easier if you came with me, don't you think?"

"No," she answered bluntly, and lowered her gaze to her glass of white wine. It was then that she felt an odd sensation prickle down her spine. Someone was staring at her; she could feel it as surely as if she were being physically touched. Looking around, Susannah was astonished to discover Nate sitting two tables away. The striking blonde was seated next to him and obviously enjoying his company. She laughed softly and the sound was like a melody, light and breezy.

Susannah's breath caught in her chest, trapped there until the pain reminded her it was time to breathe again. When she did, she reached for her wineglass and succeeded in spilling some of the contents.

Nate's gaze centered on her and then moved to her companion. His mouth thinned and his eyes, which had been so warm and tender a day earlier, now looked hard. Almost scornful.

Susannah wasn't exactly thrilled herself. Nate was dating a beauty queen while she was stuck with Donald Duck.

Four

Susannah vented her anger by pacing the living room carpet. Men! Who needed them?

Not her. Definitely not her! Nate Townsend could take his rainy day kisses and stuff them in his baseball cap for all she cared. Only he hadn't been wearing it for Miss Universe. Oh no, with the other woman, he was dressed like someone out of *Gentlemen's Quarterly*. Susannah, on the other hand, rated worn football jerseys or faded T-shirts.

Susannah hadn't been home more than five minutes when there was a knock at her door. She whirled around. Checking the peephole, she discovered that her caller was Nate. She pulled back, wondering what she should do. He was the last person she wanted to see. He'd made a fool of her… Well, that wasn't strictly true. He'd only made her *feel* like a fool.

"Susannah," he said, knocking impatiently a second time. "I know you're in there."

"Go away."

Her shout was followed by a short pause. "Fine. Have it your way."

Changing her mind, she turned the lock and yanked

open the door. She glared at him with all the fury she could muster—which just then was considerable.

Nate glared right back. "Who was that guy?" he asked with infuriating calm.

She was tempted to inform Nate that it wasn't any of his business. But she decided that would be churlish.

"Andrew Adams," she answered and quickly followed her response with a demand of her own. "Who was that woman?"

"Sylvia Potter."

For the longest moment, neither spoke.

"That was all I wanted to know," Nate finally said.

"Me, too," she returned stiffly.

Nate retreated two steps, and like precision clockwork Susannah shut the door. "Sylvia Potter," she echoed in a low-pitched voice filled with disdain. "Well, Sylvia Potter, you're welcome to him."

It took another fifteen minutes for the outrage to work its way through her system, but once she'd watched a portion of the evening news and read her mail, she was reasonably calm.

When Susannah really thought about it, what did she have to be so furious about? Nate Townsend didn't mean anything to her. How could he? Until a week ago, she hadn't even known his name.

Okay, so he'd kissed her a couple of times, and sure, there'd been electricity, but that was all. Electricity did not constitute a lifetime commitment. If Nate Townsend chose to date every voluptuous blonde between Seattle and New York it shouldn't matter to her.

But it did. And that infuriated Susannah more than anything. She didn't *want* to care about Nate. Her career goals were set. She had drive, determination and a positive mental attitude. But she didn't have Nate.

Jutting out her lower lip, she expelled her breath forcefully, ruffling the dark wisps of hair against her forehead. Maybe it was her hair color—perhaps Nate preferred blondes. He obviously did, otherwise he wouldn't be trying to impress Sylvia Potter.

Refusing to entertain any more thoughts of her neighbor, Susannah decided to fix herself dinner. An inspection of the freezer revealed a pitifully old chicken patty. Removing it from the cardboard box, Susannah took one look at it and promptly tossed it into the garbage.

Out of the corner of her eye she caught a movement on her balcony. She turned and saw a sleek Siamese cat walking casually along the railing as if he were strolling across a city park.

Although she remained outwardly calm, Susannah's heart lunged to her throat. Her condo was eight floors up. One wrong move and that cat would be history. Walking carefully to her sliding glass door, Susannah eased it open and called, "Here, kitty, kitty, kitty."

The cat accepted her invitation and jumped down from the railing. With his tail pointing skyward, he walked directly into her apartment and headed straight for the garbage pail, where he stopped.

"I bet you're hungry, aren't you?" she asked softly. She retrieved the chicken patty and stuck it in her microwave. While she stood waiting for it to cook, the cat, with his striking blue eyes and dark brown markings, wove around her legs, purring madly.

She'd just finished cutting the patty into bite-size pieces and putting it on a plate when someone pounded at her door. Wiping her fingers clean, she moved into the living room.

"Do you have my cat?" Nate demanded when she opened the door. He'd changed from his suit into jeans and a bright blue T-shirt.

"I don't know," she fibbed. "Describe it."

"Susannah, this isn't the time for silly games. Chocolate Chip is a valuable animal."

"Chocolate Chip," she repeated with a soft snicker, crossing her arms and leaning against the doorjamb. "Obviously you didn't read the fine print in the tenant's agreement, because it specifically states in section 12, paragraph 13, that no pets are allowed." Actually she didn't have a clue what section or what paragraph that clause was in, but she wanted him to think she did.

"If you don't tattle on me, then I won't tattle on you."

"I don't have any pets."

"No, you had a baby."

"But only for three days," she said. Talk about nitpicking people! He was flagrantly disregarding the rules and had the nerve to throw a minor infraction in her face.

"The cat belongs to my sister. He'll be with me for less than a week. Now, is Chocolate Chip here, or do I go into cardiac arrest?"

"He's here."

Nate visibly relaxed. "Thank God. My sister dotes on that silly feline. She flew up from San Francisco and left him with me before she left for Hawaii." As if he'd heard his name mentioned, Chocolate Chip casually strolled across the carpet and paused at Nate's feet.

Nate bent down to retrieve his sister's cat, scolding him with a harsh look.

"I suggest you keep your balcony door closed," she told him, striving for a flippant air.

"Thanks, I will." Chocolate Chip was tucked under his

arm as Nate's gaze casually caught Susannah's. "You might be interested to know that Sylvia Potter's my sister." He turned and walked out her door.

"'Sylvia Potter's my sister,'" Susannah mimicked. It wasn't until she'd closed and locked her door that she recognized the import of what he'd said. "His sister," she repeated. "Did he really say that?"

Susannah was at his door before she stopped to judge the wisdom of her actions. When Nate answered her furious knock, she stared up at him, her eyes confused. "What was that you just said?"

"I said Sylvia Potter's my sister."

"I was afraid of that." Her thoughts were tumbling over one another like marbles in a bag. She'd imagined...she'd assumed....

"Who's Andrew Adams?"

"My brother?" she offered, wondering if he'd believe her. Nate shook his head. "Try again."

"An associate from H&J Lima," she said, then hurried to explain. "When I canceled my appointment with him Monday morning, he suggested we get together for a drink to discuss business this evening. It sounded innocent enough at the time, but I should've realized it was a mistake. Adams is a known sleazeball."

An appealing smile touched the edges of Nate's mouth. "I wish I'd had a camera when you first saw me in that cocktail lounge. I thought your eyes were going to fall out of your face."

"It was your sister—she intimidated me," Susannah admitted. "She's lovely."

"So are you."

The man had obviously been standing out in the sun too long, Susannah decided. Compared to Sylvia, who was tall, blonde and had curves in all the right places, Susannah felt about as pretty as a professional wrestler.

"I'm flattered that you think so." Susannah wasn't comfortable with praise. She was much too levelheaded to let flattery affect her. When men paid her compliments, she smiled and thanked them, but she treated their words like water running off a slick surface.

Except with Nate. Everything was different with him. She seemed to be accumulating a large stack of exceptions because of Nate. As far as Susannah could see, he had no ambition, and if she'd met him anyplace other than her building, she probably wouldn't have given him a second thought. Instead she couldn't stop thinking about him. She knew better than to allow her heart to be distracted this way, and yet she couldn't seem to stop herself.

"Do you want to come in?" Nate asked and stepped aside. A bleeping sound drew Susannah's attention to a five-foot-high television screen across the room. She'd apparently interrupted Nate in the middle of an action-packed video game. A video game!

"No," she answered quickly. "I wouldn't want to interrupt you. Besides I was…just about to make myself some dinner."

"You cook?"

His astonishment—no, shock—was unflattering, to say the least.

"Of course I do."

"I'm glad to hear it, because I seem to recall that you owe me a meal."

"I—"

"And since we seem to have gotten off on the wrong foot tonight, a nice quiet dinner in front of the fireplace sounds like exactly what we need."

Susannah's thoughts were zooming at the speed of light. Nate was inviting himself to dinner—one she was supposed to whip up herself! Why did she so glibly announce that she could cook? Everything she'd ever attempted in the kitchen had been a disaster. Other than toast. Toast was her specialty. Her mind whirled with all the different ways she could serve it. Buttered? With honey? Jam? Cheese? The list was endless.

"You fix dinner and I'll bring over the wine," Nate said in a low seductive voice. "It's time we sat down together and talked. Deal?"

"I, ah, I've got some papers I have to read over tonight."

"No problem. I'll make it a point to leave early so you can finish whatever you need to."

His eyes held hers for a long moment, and despite everything Susannah knew about Nate, she still wanted time alone with him. She had some papers to review and he had to get back to his video game. A relationship like theirs was not meant to be. However, before she was even aware of what she was doing, Susannah nodded.

"Good. I'll give you an hour. Is that enough time?"

Once more, like a remote-controlled robot, she nodded.

Nate smiled and leaned forward to lightly brush his lips over hers. "I'll see you in an hour then."

He put his hand at her lower back and guided her out the door. For a few seconds she did nothing more than stand in the hallway, wondering how she was going to get herself out of this one. She reviewed her options and discovered there was only one.

The Western Avenue Deli.

Precisely an hour later, Susannah was ready. A tossed green salad rested in the middle of the table in a crystal bowl, which had been a gift when she graduated from college. Her aunt Gerty had given it to her. Susannah loved her aunt dearly, but the poor soul had her and Emily confused. Emily would have treasured the fancy bowl. As it happened, this was the first occasion Susannah had even used it and now that she looked at it, she thought the bowl might have been meant for punch. Maybe Nate wouldn't notice. The Stroganoff was simmering in a pan and the noodles were in a foil-covered dish, keeping warm in the oven.

Susannah drew in a deep breath, then frantically waved her hands over the simmering food to disperse the scent around the condo before she opened her door.

"Hi," Nate said. He held a bottle of wine.

His eyes were so blue, it was like looking into a clear, deep lake. When she spoke, her voice trembled slightly. "Hi. Dinner's just about ready."

He sniffed the air appreciatively. "Will red wine do?"

"It's perfect," she told him, stepping aside so he could come in.

"Shall I open it now?"

"Please." She led him into the kitchen.

He cocked an eyebrow. "It looks like you've been busy."

For good measure, Susannah had stacked a few pots and pans in the sink and set out an array of spices on the counter. In addition, she'd laid out several books. None of them had anything to do with cooking—she didn't own any cookbooks—but they looked impressive.

"I hope you like Stroganoff," she said cheerfully.

"It's one of my favorites."

Susannah swallowed and nodded. She'd never been very good at deception, but then she'd rarely put her pride on the line the way she had this evening.

While she dished up the Stroganoff, Nate expertly opened the wine and poured them each a glass. When everything was ready, they sat across the table from each other.

After one taste of the buttered noodles and the rich sauce, Nate said, "This is delicious."

Susannah kept her eyes lowered. "Thanks. My mother has a recipe that's been handed down for years." It was a half-truth that was stretched about as far it could go without snapping back and hitting her in the face. Yes, her mother did have a favorite family recipe, but it was for Christmas candies.

"The salad's excellent, too. What's in the dressing?"

This was the moment Susannah had dreaded. "Ah..." Her mind faltered before she could remember exactly what usually went into salad dressings. "Oil!" she cried, as if black gold had just been discovered in her living room.

"Vinegar?"

"Yes," she agreed eagerly. "Lots of that."

Planting his elbows on the table, he smiled at her. "Spices?"

"Oh, yes, those, too."

His mouth was quivering when he took a sip of wine.

Subterfuge had never been Susannah's strong suit. If Nate hadn't started asking her these difficult questions, she might've been able to pull off the ruse. But he obviously knew, and there wasn't any reason to continue it.

"Nate," she said, after fortifying herself with a sip of wine, "I... I didn't exactly cook this meal myself."

"The Western Avenue Deli?"

She nodded, feeling wretched.

"An excellent choice."

"H-how'd you know?" Something inside her demanded further abuse. Anyone else would have dropped the matter right then.

"You mean other than the fact that you've got enough pots and pans in your sink to have fed a small army? By the way, what could you possibly have used the broiler pan for?"

"I…was hoping you'd think I'd warmed the dinner rolls on it."

"I see." He was doing an admirable job of not laughing outright, and Susannah supposed she should be grateful for that much.

After taking a bite of his—unwarmed—roll, he asked, "Where'd you get all the spices?"

"They were a Christmas gift from Emily one year. She continues to hold out hope that a miracle will happen and I'll suddenly discover I've missed my calling in life and decide to chain myself to the stove."

Nate grinned. "For future reference, I can't see how you'd need poultry seasoning or curry powder for stroganoff."

"Oh." She should've quit when she was ahead. "So…you knew right from the first?"

Nate nodded. "I'm afraid so, but I'm flattered by all the trouble you went to."

"I suppose it won't do any more harm to admit that I'm a total loss in the kitchen. I'd rather analyze a profit-and-loss statement any day than attempt to bake a batch of cookies."

Nate reached for a second dinner roll. "If you ever do, my favorite are chocolate chip."

Perhaps he was the one who'd named his sister's cat, she mused. Or maybe chocolate chip cookies were popular with his whole family. "I'll remember that." An outlet for Rainy Day Cookies had recently opened on the waterfront and they were the best money could buy.

Nate helped her clear the table once they'd finished.

While she rinsed the plates and put them in the dishwasher, Nate built a fire. He was seated on the floor in front of the fireplace waiting for her when she entered the room.

"More wine?" he asked, holding up the bottle.

"Please." Inching her straight skirt slightly higher, Susannah carefully lowered herself to the carpet beside him. Nate grinned and reached for the nearby lamp, turning it to the lowest setting. Shadows from the fire flickered across the opposite wall. The atmosphere was warm and cozy.

"All right," he said softly, close to her ear. "Ask away."

Susannah frowned, not sure what he meant.

"You've been dying of curiosity about me from the moment we met. I'm simply giving you the opportunity to ask me anything you want."

Susannah gulped her wine. If he could read her so easily, then she had no place in the business world. Yes, she was full of questions about him and had been trying to find a subtle way to bring some of them into the conversation.

"First, however," he said, "let me do this."

Before she knew what was happening, Nate had pressed her down onto the carpet and was kissing her. Kissing her deeply, drugging her senses with a mastery that was just short of arrogant. He'd caught her unprepared, and before she could raise any defenses, she was captured in a dizzying wave of sensation.

When he lifted his head, Susannah stared up at him, breathless and amazed at her own ready response. Before she could react, Nate slid one hand behind her. He unpinned her hair, then ran his fingers through it.

"I've been wanting to do that all night," he murmured.

Still she couldn't speak. He'd kissed and held her, but it didn't seem to affect his power of speech, while she felt completely flustered and perplexed.

"Yes, well," she managed to mutter, scrambling to a sitting position. "I...forget what we were talking about."

Nate moved behind her and pulled her against his chest, wrapping his arms around her and nibbling on the side of her neck. "I believe you were about to ask me something."

"Yes...you're right, I was... Nate, do you work?"

"No."

Delicious shivers were racing up and down her spine. His teeth found her earlobe and he sucked on it gently, causing her insides to quake in seismic proportions.

"Why not?" she asked, her voice trembling.

"I quit."

"But why?"

"I was working too hard. I wasn't enjoying myself anymore."

"Oh."

His mouth had progressed down the gentle slope of her neck to her shoulder, and she closed her eyes to the warring emotions churning inside her. Part of her longed to surrender to the thrill of his touch, yet she hungered to learn all she could about this unconventional man.

Nate altered his position so he was in front of her again. His mouth began exploring her face with soft kisses that fell like gentle raindrops over her eyes, nose, cheeks and lips.

"Anything else you want to know?" he asked, pausing.

Unable to do more than shake her head, Susannah sighed and reluctantly unwound her arms from around his neck.

"Do you want more wine?" he asked.

"No...thank you." It demanded all the fortitude she possessed not to ask him to keep kissing her.

"Okay," he said, making himself comfortable. He raised his knees and wrapped his arms around them. "My turn."

"Your turn?"

"Yes," he said with a lazy grin that did wicked things to her equilibrium. "I have a few questions for you."

Susannah found it difficult to center her attention on anything other than the fact that Nate was sitting a few inches away from her and could lean over and kiss her again at any moment.

"You don't object?"

"No," she said, gesturing with her hand.

"Okay, tell me about yourself."

Susannah shrugged. For the life of her, she couldn't think of a single thing that would impress him. She'd worked hard, climbing the corporate ladder, inching her way toward her long-range goals.

"I'm up for promotion," she began. "I started working for H&J Lima five years ago. I chose this company, although the pay was less than I'd been offered by two others."

"Why?"

"There's opportunity with them. I looked at the chain of command and saw room for steady advancement. Being a woman is both an asset and a detriment, if you know what I mean. I had to prove myself, but I was also aware of being the token woman on the staff."

"You mean you were hired because you were female?"

"Exactly. But I swallowed my pride and set about proving I could handle anything asked of me, and I have."

Nate looked proud of her.

"Five years ago, I decided I wanted to be the vice president in charge of marketing," she said, her voice gaining strength and conviction. "It was a significant goal, because I'd be the first woman to hold a position that high within the company."

"And?"

"And I'll find out in the next few weeks if I'm going to

get it. I'll derive a great deal of satisfaction from knowing I earned it. I won't be their token female in upper management anymore."

"What's the competition like?"

Susannah slowly expelled her breath. "Stiff. Damn stiff. There are two men in the running, and both have been with the company as long as me, in one case longer. Both are older, bright and dedicated."

"You're bright and dedicated, too."

"That may not be enough," she murmured. Now that her dream was within reach, she yearned for it even more. She could feel Nate's eyes studying her.

"This promotion means a lot to you, doesn't it?"

"Yes. It's everything. From the moment I was hired, I've striven toward this very thing. And it's happening faster than I dared hope."

Nate was silent for a moment. He put another log on the fire, and although she hadn't asked for it, he replenished her wine.

"Have you ever stopped to think what would happen if you achieved your dreams and then discovered you weren't happy?"

"How could I not be happy?" she asked. She honestly didn't understand. For years she'd worked toward obtaining this vice presidency. Of course she was going to be happy! She'd be thrilled, elated, jubilant.

Nate's eyes narrowed. "Aren't you worried about there being a void in your life?"

Oh, no, he was beginning to sound like Emily. "No," she said flatly. "How could there be? Now before you start, I know what you're going to say, so please don't. Save your breath. Emily has argued with me about this from the time I graduated from college."

Nate looked genuinely puzzled. "Argued with you about what?"

"Getting married and having a family. But the roles of wife and mother just aren't for me. They never have been and they never will be."

"I see."

Susannah was convinced he didn't. "If I were a man, would everyone be pushing me to marry?"

Nate chuckled and his eyes rested on her for a tantalizing moment. "Trust me, Susannah, no one's going to mistake you for a man."

She grinned and lowered her gaze. "It's the nose, isn't it?"

"The nose?"

"Yes." She turned sideways and held her chin at a lofty angle so he could view her classic profile. "I think it's my best feature." The wine had obviously gone to her head. But that was all right because she felt warm and comfortable and Nate was sitting beside her. Rarely had she been more content.

"Actually I wasn't thinking about your nose at all. I was remembering that first night with Michelle."

"You mean when we both fell asleep in the living room?"

Nate nodded and reached for her shoulder, his eyes trapping hers. "It was the only time in my life I can remember having one woman in my arms and wanting another."

Five

"I've decided not to see him again," Susannah announced.

"I beg your pardon?" Ms. Brooks stopped in her tracks and looked at her boss.

Unnerved, Susannah made busywork at her desk. "I'm sorry, I didn't realize I'd spoken out loud."

Her assistant brought a cup of coffee to her desk and hesitated. "How late did you end up staying last night?"

"Not long," Susannah lied. It had, in fact, been past ten when she left the building.

"And the night before?" Ms. Brooks pressed.

"Not so late," Susannah fibbed again.

Eleanor Brooks walked quietly out of the room, but not before she gave Susannah a stern look that said she didn't believe her for one moment.

As soon as the door closed, Susannah pressed the tips of her fingers to her forehead and exhaled a slow steady breath. Dear heaven, Nate Townsend had her so twisted up inside she was talking to the walls.

Nate hadn't left her condo until almost eleven the night he'd come for dinner, and by that time he'd kissed her nearly senseless. Three days had passed and Susannah could still taste and feel his mouth on hers. The scent of his aftershave lingered in her living room to the point that she looked for him whenever she entered the room.

The man didn't even hold down a job. Oh, he'd had one, but he'd quit and it was obvious, to her at least, that he wasn't in any hurry to get another. He'd held her and kissed her and patiently listened to her dreams. But he hadn't shared any of his own. He had no ambition, and no urge to better himself.

And Susannah was falling head over heels for him.

Through the years, she had assumed she was immune to falling in love. She was too sensible for that, too practical, too career-oriented. Not once did she suspect she'd fall so hard for someone like Nate. Nate, with his no-need-to-rush attitude and tomorrow-will-take-care-of-itself lifestyle.

Aware of what was happening to her, Susannah had done the only thing she could—gone into hiding. For three days she'd managed to avoid Nate. He'd left a couple of messages on her answering machine, which she'd ignored. If he confronted her, she had a perfect excuse. She was working. And it was true: she spent much of her time holed up in the office. She headed out early in the morning and arrived home late at night. The extra hours she was putting in served two distinct purposes. they showed her employer that she was dedicated, and they kept her from having to deal with Nate.

Her intercom buzzed, pulling Susannah from her thoughts. She reached over and hit the speaker button. "Yes?"

"Mr. Townsend is on the phone."

Susannah squeezed her eyes shut and her throat muscles tightened. "Take a message, please," she said, her voice little more than a husky whisper.

"He insists on speaking to you."

"Tell him I'm in a meeting and…unavailable."

It wasn't like Susannah to lie, and Eleanor Brooks knew it. She finally asked, "Is this the man you plan never to see again?"

The abruptness of her question caught Susannah off guard. "Yes…"

"I assumed as much. I'll tell him you're not available."

"Thank you." Susannah's hand was trembling as she released the intercom button. She hadn't dreamed Nate would call her at the office.

By eleven, a feeling of normalcy had returned. Susannah was gathering her notes for an executive meeting with the finance committee when her assistant came in. "Mr. Franklin phoned and canceled his afternoon appointment."

Susannah glanced up. "Did he want to reschedule?"

"Friday at ten."

She nodded. "That'll be fine." It was on the tip of her tongue to ask how Nate had responded earlier when told she was unavailable, but she resisted the temptation.

"Mr. Townsend left a message. I wrote it out for you."

Her assistant knew her too well, it seemed. "Leave it on my desk."

"You might want to read it," the older woman urged.

"I will. Later."

Halfway through the meeting, Susannah wished she'd followed her assistant's advice. Impatience filled her. She wanted this finance meeting over so she could hurry back to her desk and read the message from Nate. Figures flew overhead—important ones with a bearing on the outcome of the marketing strategy she and her department had planned. Yet, again and again, Susannah found her thoughts drifting to Nate.

That wasn't typical for her. When the meeting ended, she was furious with herself. She walked briskly back to her office, her low heels making staccato taps against the polished hardwood floor.

"Ms. Brooks," she said, as she went into the outer office. "Could you—"

Susannah stopped dead in her tracks. The last person she'd expected to see was Nate. He was sitting on the corner of her assistant's desk, wearing a Mariners T-shirt, faded jeans and a baseball cap. He tossed a baseball in the air and deftly caught it in his mitt.

Eleanor Brooks looked both unsettled and inordinately pleased. No doubt Nate had used some of his considerable male charm on the gray-haired grandmother.

"It's about time," Nate said, grinning devilishly. He leaped off the desk. "I was afraid we were going to be late for the game."

"Game?" Susannah repeated. "What game?"

Nate held out his right hand to show her his baseball mitt and ball—just in case she hadn't noticed them. "The Mariners are playing, and I've got two of the best seats in the place reserved for you and me."

Susannah's heart sank to the pit of her stomach. It was just like Nate to assume she could take off in the middle of the day on some lark. He obviously had no understanding of what being a responsible employee meant. It was bad enough that he'd dominated her thoughts during an important meeting, but suggesting they escape for an afternoon was too much.

"You don't honestly expect me to leave, do you?"

"Yes."

"I can't. I won't."

"Why not?"

"I'm working," she said, deciding that was sufficient explanation.

"You've been at the office every night this week. You need a break. Come on, Susannah, let your hair down long enough to have a good time. It isn't going to hurt. I promise."

He was so casual about the whole thing, as if obligation and duty were of little significance. It proved more than anything that he didn't grasp the concept of hard work being its own reward.

"It *will* hurt," she insisted.

"Okay," he said forcefully. "What's so important this afternoon?" To answer his own question, he walked around her assistant's desk. Then he leaned forward and flipped open the pages of her appointment schedule.

"Mr. Franklin canceled his three-o'clock appointment," Ms. Brooks reminded her primly. "And you skipped lunch because of the finance meeting."

Susannah frowned at the older woman, wondering what exactly Nate had said or done that had turned her into a traitor on such short acquaintance.

"I have more important things to do," Susannah told them both stiffly.

"Not according to your appointment schedule," Nate said confidently. "As far as I can see, you haven't got an excuse in the world not to attend that baseball game with me."

Susannah wasn't going to stand there and argue with him. Instead she marched into her office and dutifully sat down at her desk.

To her chagrin both Nate and Ms. Brooks followed her inside. It was all Susannah could do not to bury her face in her hands and demand that they leave.

"Susannah," Nate coaxed gently, "you need a break.

Tomorrow you'll come back rejuvenated and refreshed. If you spend too much time at the office, you'll begin to lose perspective. An afternoon away will do you good."

Her assistant seemed about to comment, but Susannah stopped her with a scalding look. Before she could say anything to Nate, someone else entered her office.

"Susannah, I was just checking over these figures and I—" John Hammer stopped midsentence when he noticed the other two people in her office.

If there'd been an open window handy, Susannah would gladly have hurled herself through it. The company director smiled benignly, however, looking slightly embarrassed at having interrupted her. Now, it seemed, he was awaiting an introduction.

"John, this is Nate Townsend...my neighbor."

Ever the gentleman, John stepped forward and extended his hand. If he thought it a bit odd to find a man in Susannah's office dressed in jeans and a T-shirt, he didn't show it.

"Nate Townsend," he repeated, pumping his hand. "It's a pleasure, a real pleasure."

"Thank you," Nate said. "I'm here to pick up Susannah. We're going to a Mariners game this afternoon."

John removed the glasses from the end of his nose, and nodded thoughtfully. "An excellent idea."

"No, I really don't think I'll go. I mean..." She stopped when it became obvious that no one was paying any attention to her protests.

"Nate's absolutely right," John said, setting the file on her desk. "You've been putting in a lot of extra hours lately. Take the afternoon off. Enjoy yourself."

"But—"

"Susannah, are you actually going to argue with your boss?" Nate prompted.

Her jaw sagged. "I…guess not."

"Good. Good." John looked as pleased as if he'd made the suggestion himself. He was smiling at Nate and nodding as if the two were longtime friends.

Her expression more than a little smug, Eleanor Brooks returned to her own office.

Nate glanced at his watch. "We'd better go now or we'll miss the opening pitch."

With heavy reluctance, Susannah scooped up her purse. She'd done everything within her power to avoid Nate, yet through no fault of her own, she was spending the afternoon in his company. They didn't get a chance to speak until they reached the elevator, but once the door glided shut, Susannah tried again. "I can't go to a baseball game dressed like this."

"You look fine to me."

"But I've got a business suit on."

"Hey, don't sweat the small stuff." His hand clasped hers and when the elevator door opened on the bottom floor, he led her out of the building. Once outside, he quickened his pace as he headed toward the stadium.

"I want you to know I don't appreciate this one bit," she said, forced to half run to keep pace with his long-legged stride.

"If you're going to complain, wait until we're inside and settled. As I recall, you get testy on an empty stomach." His smile could have caused a nuclear meltdown, but she was determined not to let it influence her. Nate had a lot of nerve to come bursting into her office, and as soon as she could catch her breath, she'd tell him so.

"Don't worry, I'm going to feed you," he promised as they waited at a red light.

His words did nothing to reassure her. Heaven only knew

what John Hammer thought—although she had to admit that her employer's reaction had baffled her. John was as hardworking and dedicated as Susannah herself. It wasn't like him to fall in with Nate's offbeat idea of attending a ball game in the middle of the afternoon. In fact, it almost seemed as if John knew Nate, or had heard of him. Hardly ever had she seen her employer show such enthusiasm when introduced to anyone.

The man at the gate took their tickets and Nate directed her to a pair of seats right behind home plate. Never having attended a professional baseball game before, Susannah didn't realize how good these seats were—until Nate pointed it out.

She'd no sooner sat down in her place than he leaped to his feet and raised his right hand, glove and all. Susannah slouched as low as she could in the uncomfortable seat. The next thing she knew, a bag of peanuts whizzed past her ear.

"Hey!" she cried, and jerked around.

"Don't panic," Nate said, chuckling. "I'm just playing catch with the vendor." Seconds after the words left his mouth he expertly caught another bag.

"Here." Nate handed her both bags. "The hot dog guy will be by in a minute."

Susannah had no intention of sitting still while food was being tossed about. "I'm getting out of here. If you want to play ball, go on the field."

Once more Nate laughed, the sound husky and rich. "If you're going to balk at every little thing, I know a good way to settle you down."

"Do you think I'm a complete idiot? First you drag me away from my office, then you insist on throwing food around like some schoolboy. I can't even begin to guess what's going to happen next and—"

She didn't get any further, although her outrage was mounting with every breath she drew. Before she could guess his intention, Nate planted his hands on her shoulders, pulled her against him and gave her one of his dynamite-packed kisses.

Completely unnerved, she numbly lowered herself back into her seat and closed her eyes, her pulse roaring in her ears.

A little later, Nate was pressing a fat hot dog into her lifeless hands. "I had them put everything on it," he said.

A glance at the overstuffed bun informed her that "everything" included pickles, mustard, ketchup, onions and sauerkraut and one or two other items she wasn't sure she could identify.

"Now eat it before I'm obliged to kiss you again."

His warning was all the incentive she needed. Several minutes had passed since he'd last kissed her and she was still so bemused she could hardly think. On cue, she lifted the hot dog to her mouth, prepared for the worst. But to her surprise, it didn't taste half bad. In fact, it was downright palatable. When she'd polished it off, she started on the peanuts, which were still warm from the roaster. Warm and salty, and excellent.

Another vendor strolled past and Nate bought them each a cold drink.

The first inning was over by the time Susannah finished eating. Nate reached for her hand. "Feel better?" His eyes were fervent and completely focused on her.

One look certainly had an effect on Susannah. Whenever her eyes met his she felt as though she was caught in a whirlpool and about to be sucked under. She'd tried to resist the pull, but it had been impossible.

"Susannah?" he asked. "Are you okay?"

She managed to nod. After a moment she said, "I still feel kind of foolish...."

"Why?"

"Come on, Nate. I'm the only person here in a business suit."

"I can fix that."

"Oh?" Susannah had her doubts. What did he plan to do? Undress her?

He gave her another of his knowing smiles and casually excused himself. Puzzled, Susannah watched as he made his way toward the concession stand. Then he was back—with a Mariners T-shirt in one hand, a baseball cap in the other.

Removing her suit jacket, Susannah slipped the T-shirt over her head. When she'd done that, Nate set the baseball cap on her head, adjusting it so the bill dipped low over her forehead.

"There," he said, satisfied. "You look like one of the home team now."

"Thanks." She smoothed the T-shirt over her straight skirt and wondered how peculiar she looked. Funny, but it didn't seem to matter. She was having a good time with Nate, and it felt wonderful to laugh and enjoy life.

"You're welcome."

They both settled back in their seats to give their full attention to the game. The Seattle Mariners were down by one run at the bottom of the fifth inning.

Susannah didn't know all that much about baseball, but the crowd was lending vociferous support to the home team and she loved the atmosphere, which crackled with excitement, as if everyone was waiting for something splendid to happen.

"You've been avoiding me," Nate said halfway through the sixth inning. "I want to know why."

She couldn't very well tell him the truth, but lying seemed equally unattractive. Pretending to concentrate on the game, Susannah shrugged, hoping he'd accept that as explanation enough.

"Susannah?"

She should've known he'd force the issue. "Because I don't like what happens when you kiss me," she blurted out.

"What happens?" he echoed. "The first time we kissed, you nearly dealt my ego a fatal blow. As I recall, you claimed it was a pleasant experience. I believe you described it as 'nice,' and said that was about it."

Susannah kicked at the litter on the cement floor with the toes of her pumps, her eyes downcast. "Yes, I do remember saying something along those lines."

"You lied?"

He didn't need to drill her to prove his point. "All right," she admitted, "I lied. But you knew that all along. You must have, otherwise…"

"Otherwise what?"

"You wouldn't be kissing me every time you want to coerce me into doing something I don't want to do."

Crow's-feet fanned out beside his eyes as he grinned, making him look naughty and angelic at once.

"You knew all along," she repeated, "so don't give me that injured-ego routine!"

"There's electricity between us, Susannah, and it's about time you recognized that. I did, from the very first."

"Sure. But there's a big difference between standing next to an electrical outlet and fooling around with a high-voltage wire. I prefer to play it safe."

"Not me." He ran a knuckle down the side of her face.

Circling her chin, his finger rested on her lips, which parted softly. "No," he said in a hushed voice, studying her. "I always did prefer to live dangerously."

"I've noticed." Nerve endings tingled at his touch, and Susannah held her breath until he removed his hand. Only then did she breathe normally again.

The cheering crowd alerted her to the fact that something important had taken place on the field. Glad to have her attention diverted from Nate, she watched as a Mariner rounded the bases for a home run. Pleased, she clapped politely, her enthusiasm far more restrained than that of the spectators around her.

That changed, however, at the bottom of the ninth. The bases were loaded and Susannah sat on the edge of her seat as the designated hitter approached home plate.

The fans chanted, "Grand slam, grand slam!" and Susannah soon joined in. The pitcher tossed a fastball, and unable to watch, she squeezed her eyes shut. But the sound of the wood hitting the ball was unmistakable. Susannah opened her eyes and jumped to her feet as the ball flew into left field and over the wall. The crowd went wild, and after doing an impulsive jig, Susannah threw her arms around Nate's neck and hugged him.

Nate appeared equally excited, and when Susannah had her feet back on the ground, he raised his fingers to his mouth and let loose a piercing whistle.

She was laughing and cheering and even went so far as to cup her hands over her mouth and boisterously yell her approval. It was then that she noticed Nate watching her. His eyes were wide with feigned shock, as if he couldn't believe the refined and businesslike Susannah Simmons would lower herself to such uninhibited behavior.

His apparent censure instantly cooled her reactions, and

she returned to her seat and demurely folded her hands and crossed her ankles, embarrassed now by her response to something as mindless as a baseball game. When she dared to glance in Nate's direction, she discovered him watching her intently.

"Nate," she whispered, disconcerted by his attention. The game was over and the people around them had started to leave their seats. Susannah could feel the color in her cheeks. "Why are you looking at me like that?"

"You amaze me."

More likely, she'd disgraced herself in his eyes by her wild display. She was mortified.

"You're going to be all right, Susannah Simmons," he said cryptically. "We both are."

"Susannah, I didn't expect to find you home on a Saturday," Emily said as she stepped inside her sister's apartment. "Michelle and I are going to the Pike Place Market this morning and decided to drop by and see you first. You don't mind, do you?"

"No. Of course not. Come in." Susannah brushed the disheveled hair from her face. "What time is it anyway?"

"Eight-thirty."

"That late, huh?"

Emily chuckled. "I forgot. You like to sleep in on the weekends, don't you?"

"Don't worry about it," she said on the tail end of a yawn. "I'll put on a pot of coffee and be myself in no time."

Emily and Michelle followed her into the kitchen. Once the coffee was brewing, Susannah took the chair across from her sister. Michelle gleefully waved her arms, and despite the early hour, Susannah found herself smiling at her niece's enthusiasm for life. She held out her arms to the baby and was pleasantly surprised when Michelle came happily into them.

"She remembers you," Emily said.

"Of course she does," Susannah said as she nuzzled her niece's neck. "We had some great times, didn't we, kiddo? Especially when it came to feeding you plums."

Emily chuckled. "I don't think I'll ever be able to thank you enough for keeping Michelle that weekend. It was just what Robert and I needed."

"Don't mention it." Susannah dismissed Emily's appreciation with a weak gesture of her hand. She was the one who'd profited from that zany weekend. It might've been several more weeks before she met Nate if it hadn't been for Michelle.

Emily sighed. "I've been trying to get hold of you, but you're never home."

"Why didn't you leave a message?"

Emily shook her head and her long braid swung back and forth. "You know I hate doing that. I get all tongue-tied and I can't seem to talk. You might phone *me* sometime, you know."

Over the past couple of weeks, Susannah had considered it, but she'd been avoiding her sister because she knew that the minute she called, Emily was going to ply her with questions about Nate.

"Have you been working late every night?" Emily asked.

Susannah dropped her gaze. "Not exactly."

"Then you must've been out with Nate Townsend." Emily didn't give her time to respond, but immediately started jabbering away. "I don't mind telling you, Susannah, both Robert and I were impressed with your new neighbor. He was wonderful with Michelle, and from the way he was looking at you, I think he's interested. Now, please don't tell me to keep my nose out of this. You're twenty-eight, for heaven's sake, and that biological clock is ticking away. If you're ever going to settle down and get serious about a man, the time is now. And personally, I don't think you'll find anyone better than Nate. Why, he's…"

She paused to breathe, giving Susannah the chance she'd been waiting for. "Coffee?"

Emily blinked, then nodded. "You didn't listen to a word I said, did you?"

"I listened."

"But you didn't *hear* a single word."

"Sure I did," Susannah countered. "You're saying I'd be a fool not to put a ring through Nate Townsend's nose. You want me to marry him before I lose my last chance at motherhood."

"Exactly," Emily said, looking pleased that she'd conveyed her message so effectively.

Michelle squirmed and Susannah set her on the floor to crawl around and explore.

"Well?" Emily pressed. "What do you think?"

"About marrying Nate? It would never work," she said calmly, as though they were discussing something as mundane as stock options, "for more reasons than you realize. But to satisfy your curiosity I'll list a few. First and foremost I've got a career and he doesn't, and furthermore—"

"Nate's unemployed?" her sister gasped. "But how can he not work? I mean, this is an expensive complex. Didn't you tell me the condominium next to yours is nearly twice as large? How can he afford to live there if he doesn't have a job?"

"I have no idea."

Susannah forgot about Nate for the moment as her eyes

followed Michelle, astonished by how much she'd missed her. She stood and got two cups from the cupboard.

"That's not decaffeinated, is it?" Emily asked.

"No."

"Then don't bother pouring me a cup. I gave up caffeine years ago."

"Right." Susannah should have remembered. Michelle crawled across the kitchen floor toward her and, using Susannah's nightgown for leverage, pulled herself into a standing position. She smiled proudly at her achievement.

"Listen," Susannah said impulsively, leaning over to pick up her niece. "Why don't you leave Michelle with me? We'll take this morning to become reacquainted and you can do your shopping without having to worry about her."

There was a shocked silence. "Susannah?" Emily said. "Did I hear you correctly? I thought I just heard you volunteer to babysit."

Six

The morning was bright and sunny, and unable to resist, Susannah opened the sliding glass door and let the salty breeze off Elliott Bay blow into her apartment. Sitting on the kitchen floor with a saucepan and a wooden spoon, Michelle proceeded to demonstrate her musical talents by pounding out a loud enthusiastic beat.

When the phone rang, Susannah knew it was Nate.

"Good morning," she said, pushing her hair behind her ears. She hadn't pinned it up when she got dressed, knowing Nate preferred it down, and she didn't try to fool herself with excuses for leaving it that way.

"Morning," he breathed into the phone. "Do you have a drummer visiting?"

"No, a special friend. I think she'd like to say hello. Wait a minute." Susannah put down the receiver and lifted Michelle from the floor. Holding the baby on her hip, she pressed the telephone receiver to the side of Michelle's face. Practically on cue, the child spouted an excited flow of gibberish.

"I think she said good-morning," Susannah explained.

"Michelle?"

"How many other babies would pay me a visit?"

"How many Simmons girls are there?"

"Only Emily and me," she answered with a soft laugh, "but trust me, the two of us were enough for any one set of parents to handle."

Nate's responding chuckle was warm and seductive. "Are you in the mood for more company?"

"Sure. If you bring the Danish, I'll provide the coffee."

"You've got yourself a deal."

It wasn't until several minutes had passed that Susannah realized how little resistance she'd been putting up lately when it came to Nate. Since the baseball game, she'd given up trying to avoid him; she simply didn't have the heart for it, although deep down, she knew anything beyond friendship was impossible. Yet despite her misgivings, after that one afternoon with him she'd come away feeling exhilarated. Being with Nate was like recapturing a part of her youth that had somehow escaped her. But even though seeing him was fun, it wasn't meant to last, and Susannah reminded herself of that every time they were together. Nate Townsend was like an unexpected burst of sunshine on an overcast day, but soon the rain would come, the way it always did. Susannah wasn't going to be fooled into believing there could ever be anything permanent between them.

When Nate arrived, the reunion was complete. He lifted Michelle high in the air and Susannah smiled at the little girl's squeals of delight.

"Where's Emily?" he wanted to know.

"Shopping. She won't be more than an hour or so."

With Michelle in one arm, Nate moved into the kitchen, where Susannah was dishing up the pastries and pouring coffee. "She's grown, hasn't she?" she said.

"Is that another new tooth?" he asked, peering inside the baby's mouth.

"It might be," Susannah replied, taking a look herself.

Nate slipped his free arm around her shoulder and smiled at her. "Your hair's down," he murmured, his smile caressing her upturned face.

She nodded, not knowing how else to respond, although a dozen plausible excuses raced through her mind. But none of them would have been true.

"For me?"

Once more, she answered him with a slight nod.

"Thank you," he whispered, his face so close to her own that his words were like a kiss.

Susannah leaned into him, pressing herself against his solid length. When he kissed her, she could hardly stop herself from melting into his arms.

Michelle thought it was great fun to have two adults for company. She wove her fingers into Susannah's hair and yanked until Susannah was forced to pull away from Nate.

Smiling, Nate disengaged the baby's hand from her aunt's hair and kissed Susannah again. "Hmm," he said when he lifted his head. "You taste better than any sweet roll ever could."

Unnerved, and suddenly feeling shy, Susannah busied herself setting the pastries on the table.

"Do you have plans for today?" he asked, taking a chair, Michelle gurgling happily on his lap.

Michelle was content for now, but from experience Susannah knew she'd want to be back on the floor soon. "I... I was planning to go to the office for an hour or so."

"I don't think so," Nate said flatly.

"You don't?"

"I'm taking you out." He surveyed her navy blue slacks

and the winter-white sweater she wore. "I don't suppose you have any jeans."

Susannah nodded. She knew she did, somewhere, but it was years since she'd worn them. As long ago as college, and maybe even her last year of high school. "I don't know if they'll fit, though."

"Go try them on."

"Why? What are you planning? Knowing you, I could end up on top of Mount Rainier looking over a crevasse, with no idea how I got there."

"We're going to fly a kite today," he said casually, as if it was something they'd done several times.

Susannah thought she'd misunderstood him. Nate obviously loved this kind of surprise. First a baseball game in the middle of a workday, and now kites?

"You heard me right. Now go find your jeans."

"But...kites...that's for kids. Frankly, Nate," she said, her voice gaining conviction, "I don't happen to have one hidden away in a closet. Besides, isn't that something parents do with their children?"

"No, it's for everyone. Adults have been known to have fun, too. Don't worry about a thing. I built a huge one and it's ready for testing."

"A kite?" she repeated, holding in the desire to laugh outright. She'd been in grade school when she'd last attempted anything so...so juvenile.

By the time Susannah had rummaged in her closet and found an old pair of jeans, Emily had returned for Michelle. Nate let her sister inside, but the bedroom door was cracked open, and Susannah could hear the conversation. She held her breath, first because her hips were a tiny bit wider than the last time she'd worn her jeans, and also because Susannah could never be sure what her sister was going to say. Or do.

It'd be just like Emily to start telling Nate how suitable Susannah would be as a wife. That thought was sobering and for a moment Susannah stopped wriggling into her pants.

"Nate," she heard her sister say, "it's so good of you to help with Michelle." In her excitement, her voice was a full octave higher than usual.

"No problem. Susannah will be out in a minute—she's putting on a pair of jeans. We're going to Gas Works Park to fly a kite."

There was a short pause. "Susannah wearing jeans and flying a kite? You mean she's actually going with you?"

"Of course I am. Don't look so shocked," Susannah said, walking into the room. "How did the shopping go?"

Emily couldn't seem to close her mouth. She stared at her sister to the point of embarrassment, then swung her gaze to Nate and back to Susannah again.

Susannah realized she must look different, wearing jeans and with her hair down, but it certainly didn't warrant this openmouthed gawking.

"Emily?" Susannah waved her hand in front of her sister's face in an effort to bring her back to earth.

"Oh…the shopping went just fine. I was able to get the fresh herbs I wanted. Basil and thyme and…some others." As though in a daze, Emily lifted the home-sewn bag draped over her arm as evidence of her successful trip to the market.

"Good," Susannah said enthusiastically, wanting to smooth over her sister's outrageous reaction. "Michelle wasn't a bit of trouble. If you need me to watch her again, just say so."

Her sister's eyes grew wider. She swallowed and nodded. "Thanks. I'll remember that."

The sky was as blue as Nate's eyes, Susannah thought,
sitting with her knees tucked under her chin on the lush
green grass of Gas Works Park. The wind whipped Nate's
box kite back and forth as he scrambled from one hill to
the next, letting the brisk breeze carry the multicolored
crate in several directions. As it was late September, Susannah didn't expect many more glorious Indian summer
days like this one.

She closed her eyes and soaked up the sun. Her spirits
raced with the kites that abounded in the popular park. She
felt like tossing back her head and laughing triumphantly,
for no other reason than that it felt good to be alive.

"I'm beat," Nate said, dropping down on the grass beside her. He lay on his back, arms and legs spread-eagle.

"Where's the kite?"

"I gave it to one of the kids who didn't have one."

Susannah smiled. That sounded exactly like something
Nate would do. He'd spent hours designing and construct-
ing the box kite, and yet he'd impulsively given it away
without a second thought.

"Actually I begged the kid to take it, before I keeled over
from exhaustion," he amended. "Don't let anyone tell you
otherwise. Flying a kite is hard work."

Work was a subject Susannah stringently avoided with
Nate. From the first he'd been completely open with her.
Open and honest. She was confident that if she quizzed
him about his profession or lack of one, he'd answer her
truthfully.

Susannah had decided that what she didn't know about
him couldn't upset her. Nate apparently had plenty of

money. He certainly didn't seem troubled by financial difficulties. But it was his attitude that worried her. He seemed to see life as a grand adventure; he leaped from one interest to another without rhyme or reason. Nothing appeared to be more important or vital than the moment.

"You're frowning," he said. He slipped a hand around her neck and pulled her down until her face was within inches of his own. "Aren't you having fun?"

She nodded, unable to deny the obvious.

"Then what's the problem?"

"Nothing."

He hesitated and the edges of his mouth lifted sensuously. "It's a good thing you didn't become an attorney," he said with a roguish grin. "You'd never be able to fool a jury."

Susannah was astonished that Nate knew she'd once seriously considered going into law.

He grinned at her. "Emily told me you'd thought about entering law school."

Susannah blinked a couple of times, then smiled, too. She was determined not to ruin this magnificent afternoon with her concerns.

"Kiss me, Susannah," he whispered. The humor had left his face and his gaze searched hers.

Her breath caught. She lifted her eyes and quickly glanced around. The park was crowded and children were everywhere.

"No," he said, cradling the sides of her face. "No fair peeking. I want you to kiss me no matter how many spectators there are."

"But—"

"If you don't kiss me, I'll simply have to kiss you. And, honey, if I do, watch out because—"

Not allowing him to finish, she lowered her mouth and gently skimmed her lips over his. Even that small sample was enough to send the blood racing through her veins. Whatever magic quality this man had should be bottled and sold over the counter. Susannah knew she'd be the first one in line to buy it.

"Are you always this stingy?" he asked when she raised her head.

"In public, yes."

His eyes were smiling and Susannah swore she could have drowned in his look. He exhaled, then bounded to his feet with an energy she had to envy.

"I'm starved," he announced, reaching out for her. Susannah placed her hand in his and he pulled her to her feet. "But I hope you realize," he whispered close to her ear, wrapping his arm around her waist, "my appetite isn't for food. I'm crazy about you, Susannah Simmons. Eventually we're going to have to do something about that."

"I hope I'm not too early," Susannah said as she entered her sister's home on Capitol Hill. When Emily had called to invite her to Sunday dinner, she hadn't bothered to disguise her intentions. Emily was dying to grill Susannah about her budding relationship with Nate Townsend. A week ago, Susannah would've found an excuse to get out of tonight's dinner. But after spending an entire Saturday with Nate, she was so confused that she was willing to talk this out with her sister, who seemed so much more competent in dealing with male/female relationships.

"Your timing's perfect," Emily said, coming out of the kitchen to greet her. She wore a full-length skirt with a bib apron, and her long hair was woven into a single braid that fell halfway down her back.

"Here." Susannah handed her sister a bottle of chardonnay, hoping it was appropriate for the meal.

"How thoughtful," Emily murmured, leading her back into the kitchen. The house was an older one, built in the early forties, with a large family kitchen. The red linoleum countertop was crowded with freshly canned tomatoes. Boxes of jars were stacked on the floor, along with a wicker basket filled with sun-dried diapers. A rope of garlic dangled above the sink and a row of potted plants lined the windowsill.

"Whatever you're serving smells wonderful."

"It's lentil soup."

Emily opened the oven and pulled out the rack, wadding up the skirt of her apron to protect her fingers. "I made a fresh apple pie. Naturally I used organically grown apples so you don't need to worry."

"Oh, good." That hadn't been a major concern of Susannah's.

"Where's Michelle?" Father and daughter were conspicuously absent.

Emily turned around, looking mildly guilty, and Susannah realized that her sister had gone to some lengths to provide time alone with her. No doubt she was anxious to wring out as much information about Nate as possible. Not that Susannah had a lot to tell.

"How was your day in the park?"

Susannah took a seat on the stool and made herself comfortable for the coming inquisition. "Great. I really enjoyed it."

"You like Nate, don't you?"

Like was the understatement of the year. Contrary to every ounce of sense she possessed, Susannah was falling in love with her neighbor. It wasn't what she wanted, but she hadn't been able to stop herself.

"Yes, I like him," she answered after a significant pause.

Emily seemed thrilled by her admission. "I thought as much," she said, nodding profoundly. She pushed a stool next to Susannah and sat down. Emily's hands were rarely idle, and true to form, she reached for her crocheting.

"I'm waiting," Susannah said, growing impatient.

"For what?"

"For the lecture."

Emily cracked a knowing smile. "I was gathering my thoughts. You were always the one who could evaluate things so well. I always had trouble with that and you aced every paper."

"School reports have very little to do with real life," Susannah reminded her. How much simpler it would be if she could just look up everything she needed to know about dealing with Nate.

"I knew that, but I wasn't sure you did."

Perhaps Susannah hadn't until she'd met Nate. "Emily," she said, her stomach tightening, "I need to ask you something...important. How did you know you loved Robert? What was it that told you the two of you were meant to share your lives?" Susannah understood that she was practically laying her cards faceup on the table, but she was past the point of subtlety. She wanted hard facts.

Her sister smiled and tugged at her ball of yarn before she responded. "I don't think you're going to like my answer," she murmured, frowning slightly. "It was the first time Robert kissed me."

Susannah nearly toppled from her perch on the stool, remembering her experience with Nate. "What happened?"

"We'd gone for a nature walk in the rain forest over on

the Olympic Peninsula and had stopped to rest. Robert helped me remove my backpack, then he looked into my eyes and leaned over and kissed me." She sighed softly at the memory. "I don't think he intended to do it because he looked so shocked afterward."

"Then what?"

"Robert took off his own backpack and asked if I minded that he'd kissed me. Naturally I told him I rather liked it, and he sat down next to me and did it again—only this time it wasn't a peck on the lips but a full-blown kiss." Emily's shoulders sagged a little in a sigh. "The moment his lips touched mine I couldn't think, I couldn't breathe, I couldn't even move. When he finished I was trembling so much I thought something might be physically wrong with me."

"So would you say you felt...electricity?"

"Exactly."

"And you never had that with any of the other men you dated?"

"Never."

Susannah wiped a hand down her face. "You're right," she whispered. "I don't like your answer."

Emily paused in her crocheting to glance at her. "Nate kissed you and you felt something?"

Susannah nodded. "I was nearly electrocuted."

"Oh, Susannah, you poor thing!" She patted her sister's hand. "You don't know what to do, do you?"

"No," she admitted, feeling wretched.

"You never expected to fall in love, did you?"

Slowly Susannah shook her head. And it couldn't be happening at a worse time. The promotion was going to be announced within the next week, and the entire direction of her life could be altered if she became involved with Nate. She didn't even know if that was what either of them wanted. Susannah felt mystified by everything going on in her life, which until a few short weeks ago had been so straightforward and uncluttered.

"Are you thinking of marriage?" Emily asked outright.

"Marriage," Susannah echoed weakly. It seemed the natural conclusion when two people were falling in love. She was willing to acknowledge her feelings, but she wasn't completely confident Nate felt the same things she did. Nor was she positive that he was ready to move into something as permanent as a lifelong commitment. She knew *she* wasn't, and the very thought of all this was enough to throw her into a tizzy.

"I don't…know about marriage," Susannah said. "We haven't discussed anything like that." The fact was, they hadn't even talked about dating regularly.

"Trust me, if you leave it to Nate the subject of marriage will never come up. Men never want to talk about getting married. The topic is left totally up to us women."

"Oh, come on—"

"No, it's true. From the time Eve slipped Adam the apple, we've been stuck with the burden of taming men, and it's never more difficult than when it comes to convincing one he should take a wife."

"But surely Robert wanted to get married?"

"Don't be silly. Robert's like every other man alive. I had to convince him this was what he wanted. Subtlety is the key, Susannah. In other words, I chased Robert until he caught me." She stopped working her crochet hook to laugh at her own wit.

From the first day she met her brother-in-law, Susannah had assumed he'd taken one look at her sister and dropped to his knees to propose. It had always seemed obvious to

Susannah that they were meant for each other, far more obvious than it was that Nate was right for her.

"I don't know, Emily," she said with a deep sigh. "Everything's so confused in my mind. How could I possibly be so attracted to this man? It doesn't make any sense! Do you know what we did yesterday afternoon when we'd finished at the park?" She didn't wait for a response. "Nate brought over his Nintendo game and Super Mario Brothers cartridge, and we played video games. Me! I can't believe it even now. It was a pure waste of time."

"Did you have fun?"

That was a question Susannah wanted to avoid. She'd laughed until her stomach hurt. They'd challenged each other to see who could achieve the higher score, and then had done everything possible to sabotage each other.

Nate had discovered a sensitive area behind her ear and taken to kissing her there just when she was about to outscore him. Fair was fair, however, and Susannah soon discovered that Nate had his own area of vulnerability. Without a qualm, she'd used it against him, effectively disrupting his game. Soon they both forgot Nintendo and became far more interested in learning about each other.

"We had fun" was all Susannah was willing to admit.

"What about the kite flying?"

Her sister didn't know when to quit. "Then, too," she said reluctantly. "And at the baseball game Thursday, as well."

"He took you to a Mariners game...on Thursday? But they played in the middle of the afternoon. Did you actually leave the office?"

Susannah nodded, without explaining the details of how Nate had practically kidnapped her. "Back to you and Robert," she said, trying to change the subject.

"You want to know how I convinced him he wanted to get married? It wasn't really that difficult."

For Emily it wouldn't have been, but for Susannah it would be another story entirely. The biggest problem was that she wasn't sure she *wanted* Nate to be convinced. However, she should probably learn these things for future reference. She'd listen to what her sister had to say and make up her mind later.

"Remember that old adage—the way to a man's heart is through his stomach? It's true. Men equate food with comfort and love—that's a well-known fact."

"Then I'm in trouble," Susannah said flatly. Good grief, she thought, Nate could cook far better than she could any day of the week. She couldn't attract him with her cooking. All she had in the way of looks was her classic profile. Painful as it was to accept, men simply weren't attracted to her.

"Now don't overreact. Just because you can't whip up a five-course meal doesn't mean your life is over before it even begins."

"My married life is. I can't put together soup and a sandwich and you know it."

"Susannah, I wish you'd stop demeaning yourself. You're bright and pretty, and Nate would be the luckiest man in the world if he were to marry you."

Now that they were actually discussing marriage, Susannah was having mixed feelings. "I...don't know if Nate's the marrying kind," she muttered. "For that matter, I don't know if I am."

Emily ignored that. "I'll start you out on something simple and we'll work our way up."

"I don't understand."

"Cookies," Emily explained. "There isn't a man alive who doesn't appreciate homemade cookies. There's something magical about them—really," she added when Susannah cast her a doubtful glance. "Cookies create an aura of domestic bliss—it sounds crazy, but it's true. A man can't resist a woman who bakes him cookies. They remind him of home and mother and a fire crackling in the fireplace." Emily paused and sighed. "Now, it's also true that men have been fighting this feeling since the beginning of time."

"What feeling?"

Emily rolled her eyes. "Domestic contentment. It's exactly what they need and want, but they fight it."

Susannah mulled over her sister's words. "Now that you mention it, Nate did say chocolate chip's his favorite."

"See what I mean?"

Susannah couldn't believe she was pursuing this subject with her sister. Okay, so she and Nate had shared some good times. But lots of people had good times together. She was also willing to admit there was a certain amount of chemistry between them. But that wasn't any reason to run to the nearest altar.

For the past few minutes, she'd been trying to sensibly discuss this situation between Nate and her with her sister, and before she even knew how it'd happened, Emily had her talking about weddings and chocolate chip cookies. At this rate Emily would have her married and pregnant by the end of the week.

"So how did dinner with your sister go?" Nate asked her later that same night. He'd been on the Seattle waterfront earlier in the day and had brought her back a polished glass paperweight made of ash from the Mount St. Helens volcano.

"Dinner was fine," she said quickly, perhaps too quickly. "Emily and I had a nice talk."

Nate put his arms around her, trapping her against the kitchen counter. "I missed you."

Swallowing tensely, she murmured, "I missed you, too."

He threaded his fingers through the length of her hair, pulling it away from her face and holding it there. "You wore it down again today," he whispered against her neck.

"Yes… Emily says she likes it better that way, too." Talking shouldn't be this difficult, but every time Nate touched her it was. Susannah's knees had the consistency of pudding and her resolve was just as weak. After analyzing her talk with Emily, Susannah had decided to let the situation between her and Nate cool for a while. Things were happening much too quickly. She wasn't ready, and she doubted Nate was, either.

When he kissed her lightly at the hollow of her throat, it was all she could do to remain in an upright position. As she braced her hands against his chest, she began to push him gently away. But when his lips traveled up the side of her neck, blazing a trail of moist kisses, she was lost. His mouth grazed the line of her jaw, slowly edging its way toward her lips, prolonging the inevitable until Susannah thought she'd dissolve at his feet.

When he finally kissed her mouth, they both sighed, caught in a swelling tide of longing. His mouth moved hungrily over hers. Then he tugged at her lower lip with his teeth, creating a whole new wave of sensation.

By the time Nate went back to his own apartment, Susannah was shaking from the inside out. She'd walked all the way to the kitchen before she was conscious of her intent. She stared at the phone for a long moment. Calling

Emily demanded every ounce of courage she had. With a deep calming breath, she punched out her sister's number.

"Emily," she said when her sister answered on the second ring, "do you have a recipe for chocolate chip cookies?"

Seven

The recipe for chocolate chip cookies was safely tucked away in a kitchen drawer. The impulse to bake them had passed quickly and reason had returned.

Monday morning, back at the office, Susannah realized how close she'd come to the edge of insanity. The vice presidency was almost within her grasp, and she'd worked too long and too hard to let this promotion slip through her fingers simply because she felt a little weak in the knees when Nate Townsend kissed her. To even contemplate anything beyond friendship was like...like amputating her right hand because she had a sliver in her index finger. She'd been overreacting, which was understandable, since she'd never experienced such a strong attraction to a man before.

"There's a call for you on line one," Ms. Brooks told her. She paused, then added dryly, "It sounds like that nice young man who stopped by last week."

Nate. Squaring her shoulders—and her resolve—Susannah picked up the phone. "This is Susannah Simmons."

"Good morning, beautiful."

"Hello, Nate," she said stiffly. "What can I do for you?"

He chuckled. "That's a leading question if there ever was one. Trust me, honey, you don't want to know."

"Nate," she breathed, briefly closing her eyes. "Please. I'm busy. What do you want?"

"Other than your body?"

Hot color leaped into her cheeks and she gave a distressed gasp. "We'd better put an end to this conversation—"

"All right, all right, I'm sorry. I just woke up and I was lying here thinking how nice it would be if we could escape for the day. Could I tempt you with a drive to the ocean? We could dig for clams, build a sand castle, and then make a fire and sing our favorite camp songs."

"As a matter of interest, I've been up for several hours. And since you've obviously forgotten, I do have a job—an important one. At least it's important to me. Now exactly what is the purpose of this call, other than to embarrass me?"

"Lunch."

"I can't today. I've got an appointment."

"Okay." He sighed, clearly frustrated. "How about dinner, just you and me?"

"I'm working late and was planning on sending out for something. Thanks, anyway."

"Susannah," he said in a burst of impatience, "are we going to go through this again? You should've figured out by now that avoiding me won't change anything."

Perhaps not, she reasoned, but it would certainly help. "Listen, Nate, I really am busy. Perhaps we should continue this conversation another time."

"Like next year—I know you. You'd be willing to bury your head in the sand for the next fifteen years if I didn't come and prod you along. I swear, I've never met a more stubborn woman."

"Goodbye, Nate."

"Susannah," he persisted, "what about dinner? Come on, change your mind. We have a lot to talk about."

"No. I wasn't lying—I do have to work late. The fact is, I can't go outside and play today—or tonight."

"Ouch," Nate cried. "That hurt."

"Perhaps it hit too close to home."

A short silence followed. "Maybe it did," he murmured thoughtfully. "But before we hang up, I do want to know when I can see you again."

Susannah leaned forward and stretched her arm across the desk to her calendar, flipping the pages until she found a blank space. "How about lunch on Thursday?"

"All right," he said, "I'll see you Thursday at noon."

For a long moment after they'd hung up, Susannah kept her hand on the receiver. As crazy as it seemed, spending the afternoon with Nate at the beach sounded far too appealing. The way he made her think and feel was almost frightening. The man was putting her whole career in jeopardy. Something had to be done, only Susannah wasn't sure what.

An hour later, Ms. Brooks tapped on her door and walked inside, carrying a huge bouquet of red roses. "These just arrived."

"For me?" Surely there was some mistake. No one had ever sent her flowers. There'd never been any reason. There wasn't now.

"The card has your name on it," her assistant informed her. She handed the small white envelope to Susannah.

Not until Eleanor had left the room did Susannah read the card. The roses were from Nate, who wrote that he was sorry for having disturbed her earlier. She was right, he told her, now wasn't the time to go outside and play. He'd signed it with his love. Closing her eyes, Susannah held the card to her breast and fought down a swelling surge of emotion. The least he could do was stop being so damn wonderful. Then everything would be easier.

As it turned out, Susannah finished work relatively early that evening and returned home a little after seven. Her apartment was dark and empty—but it was that way every night and she didn't understand why it should matter to her now. Yet it did.

It was when she stood outside Nate's door and knocked that she realized how impulsive her behavior had become since she'd met him. She was doing everything in her power to avoid him, and yet she couldn't stay away.

"Susannah," he said when he opened the door. "This is a pleasant surprise."

She laced her fingers together. "I... I just wanted you to know how much I appreciated the roses. They're lovely and the gesture was so thoughtful."

"Come in," he said, stepping inside. "I'll put on some coffee."

"No, thanks. I've got to get back, but I wanted to thank you for the flowers...and to apologize if I sounded wasp-ish on the phone. Monday mornings aren't exactly my best time."

Grinning, he leaned against the doorjamb and crossed his arms over his broad chest. "Actually, I'm the one who owed you an apology. I should never have phoned you this morning. I was being selfish. You do have an important job and these are anxious days for you. Didn't you tell me you'd hear about that promotion within the next week or two?"

Susannah nodded.

"You might find this hard to believe, but I don't want to say or do anything to take that away from you. You're a dedicated, hardworking employee and you deserve to be the first female vice president of H&J Lima."

His confidence in her was reassuring, but it confused her, too. From everything she'd witnessed about Nate, she could only conclude that he didn't appreciate hard work and its rewards.

"If I do get the promotion," she said, watching him closely, "things will change between you and me. I... I won't have a lot of free time for a while."

"Does that mean you won't be able to go outside and play as often?" he asked, his mouth curving into a sensuous smile. He was taunting her with the words she'd used earlier that day.

"Exactly."

"I can accept that. Just..." He hesitated.

"What?" Nate was frowning and that wasn't like him. He wore a saucy grin as often as he donned a baseball cap. "Tell me," she demanded.

"I want you to do everything possible to achieve your dreams, Susannah, but there are plenty of pitfalls along the way."

Now it was her turn to frown. She wasn't sure she understood what he was talking about.

"All I'm saying," he elaborated, "is that you shouldn't lose sight of who you are because this vice presidency means so much to you. And most important, count the cost." With that he stepped forward, gazed hungrily into her eyes and kissed her lightly on the lips. Then he stepped back reluctantly.

For a second Susannah teetered, then she moved forward into his arms as if that was the most natural place in the world for her to be. Even now, she didn't entirely understand what he meant, but she couldn't mistake the tenderness she heard in his voice. Once her head had cleared and she wasn't wrapped up in this incredible longing he created every time he touched her, she'd mull over his words.

Susannah woke around midnight, and rolling over, adjusted her pillow. The illuminated dial on her clock radio told her she'd only been sleeping for a couple of hours. She yawned, wondering what had woken her out of a sound peaceful slumber. Closing her eyes, she tucked the blankets more securely over her shoulders, determined to sleep. She tried visualizing herself accepting the promotion to vice president. Naturally, there'd be a nice write-up about her in the evening paper and possibly a short piece in a business journal or two.

Susannah's eyes drifted open as she recalled Nate's words reminding her not to forget who she was. Who *was* she? A list of possible replies skipped easily through her mind. She was Susannah Simmons, future vice president in charge of marketing for the largest sporting-goods store in the country. She was a daughter, a sister, an aunt… And then it hit her. *She was a woman.* That was what Nate had been trying to tell her. It was the same message Emily had tried to get across to her on Sunday. From the time Susannah had set her goals, she'd dedicated her life to her career and pushed aside every feminine part of herself. Now was the time for her to deal with that aspect of her life.

It was the following evening after work. Susannah was leaning against the kitchen counter, struggling to remove the heavy food mixer from its reinforced cardboard box. Emily's recipe for chocolate chip cookies made three dozen.

After her trip to the grocery, plus a jaunt to the hardware store for the mixer, cookie sheets and measuring utensils, these cookies were costing her $4.72 apiece.

Price be damned. She was setting out to prove something important—although she wasn't sure exactly what. She would've preferred to dismiss all her sister's talk about cookies being equated with warmth and love as a philosophy left over from an earlier generation. Susannah didn't actually believe Emily's theory, but she wanted to give it a try. Susannah didn't know why she was doing this anymore. All she knew was that she had this urge to bake chocolate chip cookies.

Emily had eagerly given her the recipe, and Susannah had read it carefully. Just how difficult could baking cookies be?

Not very, she determined twenty minutes later when everything was laid out on her extended counter. Pushing up the sleeves of her shirt, she turned on the radio to keep her company. Next she tied the arms of an old shirt around her waist, using that as an apron. Emily always seemed to wear one when she worked in the kitchen and if her sister did, then it must be the thing to do.

The automatic mixer was blending the butter and white sugar nicely and, feeling extraordinarily proud of herself, Susannah cracked the eggs on the edge of the bowl with a decided flair.

"Damn," she cried when half the shell fell into the swirling blades. She glared at it a moment, watching helplessly as the beater broke the fragile shell into a thousand bits. Shrugging, she figured a little extra protein—or was it calcium?—wasn't going to hurt anyone. Finally she turned off the mixer and stirred in the flour, then the chocolate chips.

The oven was preheated exactly as the recipe required

when Susannah slipped the shiny new cookie sheet inside. She closed the oven door with a swing of her hip and set the timer for twelve minutes.

Sampling a blob of dough from the end of her finger, she had to admit it was tasty. At least as good as Emily's. But Susannah considered it best not to let anyone know her secret ingredient was eggshell.

With a sense of genuine satisfaction, she poured herself a cup of coffee and sat down at the table with the evening paper.

A few minutes later she smelled smoke. Suspiciously sniffing the air, she set the paper aside. It couldn't possibly be her cookies—they'd been in the oven less than five minutes. To be on the safe side, however, she reached for a towel and opened the oven door.

She was immediately assaulted by billowing waves of smoke, followed by flames that licked out at her. Gasping in horror, she dropped the towel and gave a piercing scream. "Fire! Fire!"

The smoke alarm blared, and she thought she'd never heard anything louder in her life. Like a madwoman, Susannah raced for the door, throwing it open in an effort to allow the smoke to escape. Then she ran back to the table and hurled her coffee straight into the belly of the oven. Coughing hoarsely, she slammed the door shut.

"Susannah!" Breathless, Nate burst into her condominium.

"I started a fire," she shouted above the deafening din of the smoke alarm. Her voice still sounded raspy.

"Where?" Nate circled her table several times, looking frantically for the source of her panic.

"In the oven." Standing aside, she covered her face with her hands, not wanting to look.

A few minutes later, Nate took her in his arms. The smoke alarm was off. Two blackened sheets of charred cookies were angled into the sink. "Are you all right?"

Somehow she managed a nod.

"You didn't burn yourself?"

She didn't have so much as a blister and told him so.

Gently he brushed the hair away from her face, and expelled his breath, apparently to ease his tension. "Okay, how did the fire get started?"

"I don't know," she said dismally. "I... I did everything the recipe said, but when I put the cookies in the oven they...they caught on fire." Her voice quavered as she spoke.

"The cookies weren't responsible for the fire," he corrected her. "The cookie sheets were the culprits. They must've been new—it seems, ah, you forgot to remove the paper covering."

"Oh," she whispered. Her shoulders were shaking with the effort to repress her sobs.

"Susannah, there's no reason to cry. It was a reasonable mistake. Here, sit down." Gently he lowered her onto the kitchen chair and knelt in front of her, taking her hands in his and rubbing them. "It isn't the biggest disaster in the world."

"I know that," she wailed, unable to stop herself. "You don't understand. It was sort of a test...."

"A test?"

"Yes. Emily claims men love cookies...and I was baking them for you." She didn't go on to add that Emily also claimed that men loved the women who baked those cookies. "I can't cook... I started a fire...and I dropped part of the eggshell in the batter and...and left it.... I wasn't going to tell anyone."

Her confession must have shocked Nate because he stood up and left the room. Burying her face in her hands, Susannah endeavored to regain her composure and was doing an admirable job of it when Nate returned, holding a box of tissue.

Effortlessly lifting her into his arms, he pulled out the chair and sat down, holding her securely on his lap. "Okay, Betty Crocker, explain yourself."

She wiped her face dry with the tissue, feeling rather silly at the way she was reacting. So she'd burned a couple of cookie sheets and ruined a batch of chocolate chip cookies. Big deal, she told herself with as much bravado as she could muster. "Explain what?"

"The comment about men loving cookies. Were you trying to prove something to me?"

"Actually it was Emily I wanted to set straight," she whispered.

"You said you were baking them for my benefit."

"I was. Yesterday you said I shouldn't forget who I was, I should find myself, and… I think this sudden urge to bake was my response to that." Susannah suspected she wasn't making much sense. "Believe me, after today, I know I'm never going to be worth a damn in the kitchen."

"I don't remember suggesting you 'find yourself' in the kitchen," Nate said, looking confused.

"Actually that part was Emily's idea," she admitted. "She's the one who gave me the recipe. My sister seems to believe a woman can coerce a man into giving up his heart and soul if she can bake chocolate chip cookies."

"And you want my heart and soul?"

"Of course not! Don't be ridiculous."

He hesitated for a moment and seemed to be considering her words. "Would it come as a surprise if I said I wanted yours?"

Susannah barely heard him; she wasn't in the mood to talk about heart and soul right now. She'd just shown how worthless she was in the kitchen. Her lack in that area hadn't particularly troubled her—until now. She'd made a genuine effort and fallen flat on her face. Not only that, having Nate witness her defeat had badly dented her pride. "When I was born something must've been missing from my genes," she murmured thoughtfully. "Obviously. I can't cook, and I don't sew, and I can hardly tell one end of a knitting needle from the other. I can't do any of the things that…normal people associate with the female gender."

"Susannah." He said her name on a disgruntled sigh. "Did you hear what I just said?"

She shook her head. She understood the situation perfectly. Some women had it and others didn't. Unfortunately, she was in the latter group.

"I was telling you something important. But I can see you're going to force me to say it without words." Cupping her face, Nate directed her mouth to his. But he didn't only kiss her. The hot moist tip of his tongue traced the sensitive line of her lips until she shivered with a whole new realm of unexplored sensations. All her disheartened thoughts dissolved instantly. She forgot to think, to breathe, to do anything but tremble in his arms. The fire in her oven was nothing compared to the one Nate had started in her body. Without conscious volition, she wrapped her arms around his neck and slanted her mouth over his, surrendering to the hot currents of excitement he'd created. She opened herself to him, granting him anything he wanted. His tongue found hers, and Susannah whimpered at the shock of pleasure she received. Her response was innocent and abandoned, unskilled and unknowing, yet eager.

"There," he whispered, supporting his forehead against hers, while he drew in deep breaths. His husky voice was unsteady.

He seemed to think their kiss was enough to prove everything. Susannah slowly opened her eyes. She took a steadying breath herself, one that made her tremble all the way to her toes. If she was going to say anything, it would be to whisper his name repeatedly and ask why he was doing this and then plead with him never to stop.

He threaded his fingers through her hair and kissed her again with a mastery that caused her to cling to him as if he were a life raft in a stormy sea. Unable to keep still, Susannah ran her palms along his neck and onto his shoulders and down the length of his arms. He must have liked her touch because he groaned and deepened the kiss even more.

"Unfortunately I don't think you're ready to hear it yet," he said.

"Hear what?" she asked, when she could find her voice.

"What I was telling you."

She puckered her brow. "What was that?"

"Forget the cookies. You're more than enough woman for any man."

She blinked, not understanding him. She barely understood herself.

"I never meant for you to test who you are. All I suggested was that you take care not to lose sight of your own personality. Goals are all well and good, even necessary, but you should always calculate the cost."

"Oh." Her mind was still too hazy to properly assimilate his meaning.

"Are you going to be all right?" he asked, as he grazed

her cheek with his fingertips. He kissed Susannah's eyelids, closing them.

All she could do was nod.

"John Hammer would like to see you right away," Ms. Brooks told Susannah when she walked into her office Thursday morning.

Susannah's heart flew into her throat and stayed there for an uncomfortable moment. This was it. The day for which she'd been waiting five long years.

"Did he say what he wanted?" she asked, making an effort to appear at least outwardly calm.

"No," Ms. Brooks replied. "He just asked me to tell you he wanted to talk to you at your convenience."

Susannah slumped into her high-backed office chair. She propped her elbows on the desk and hid her face in her hands, trying to put some order to her muddled thoughts. "At my convenience," she repeated in a ragged whisper. "I didn't get the promotion. I just know it."

"Susannah," her assistant said sternly, calling her by her first name—something she rarely did. "I think you might be jumping to conclusions."

Susannah glared at her, annoyed by the woman's obtuseness. "If he planned to appoint me vice president, he would've called me into his office late in the afternoon. That's how it's done. Then he'd go through this long spiel about me being a loyal employee and what an asset I am to the company and all that stuff. Wanting to talk to me *now* means... Well, you know what it means."

"I can't say I do," Ms. Brooks said primly. "My suggestion is that you pull yourself together and get over to Mr. Hammer's office before he changes his mind."

Susannah got to her feet and stiffened her spine. But

no matter how hard she tried she couldn't seem to stop shaking.

"I'll be waiting here when you get back," Ms. Brooks told her on her way out the door. She smiled then, an encouraging gesture that softened her austere features. "Break a leg, kid."

"I probably will, whatever happens," she muttered. If she didn't get this promotion, she was afraid she'd fall apart. Assuming a calm manner, she decided not to worry until she knew for sure.

John Hammer stood when she was announced. Susannah walked into his office, and the first thing she noticed was that the two men who were her competition hadn't been called. The company president smiled benignly and motioned toward a chair. Susannah sat on the edge of the cushion, doing her best to disguise how nervous she was.

A smile eased over her boss's face. "Good morning, Susannah…"

True to her word, Susannah's assistant was waiting for her when she strolled back to her office.

"Well?"

Eleanor Brooks followed her to her desk and watched as Susannah carefully sat down.

"What happened?" she demanded a second time. "Don't just sit there. Talk!"

Susannah's gaze slowly moved from the phone to her assistant. Then she started to chuckle. The laughter came from deep within her and she had to cover her mouth with her palms. When she could talk, she wiped the tears from the corners of her eyes.

"The first thing he did was ask me if I wanted to trade offices while mine was being repainted."

"What?"

Susannah thought Ms. Brooks's expression probably reflected her own when Mr. Hammer had asked that question. "That was my reaction, too," Susannah exclaimed. "I didn't understand what he meant. Then he said he was going to have my office redone, because he felt it was only right that the vice president in charge of marketing have a brand-new office."

"You got the promotion?" Eleanor Brooks clapped her hands in sheer delight, then pressed them over her lips.

"I got it," Susannah breathed, squeezing her eyes shut. "I actually got it."

"Congratulations."

"Thank you, thank you." Already she was reaching for the phone. She had to tell Nate. Only a few days before, he'd said she should go after her dreams, and now everything was neatly falling into place.

There was no answer at his apartment and, dejected, she replaced the receiver. But the need to talk to him consumed her, and she tried again every half hour until she thought she'd go crazy.

At noon, she was absorbed in her work when Ms. Brooks announced that her luncheon date had arrived.

"Send him in," Susannah said automatically, irritated that her concentration had been broken.

Nate strolled casually into her office and plopped himself down in the chair opposite her desk.

"Nate," she cried, leaping to her feet. "I've been trying to get hold of you all morning. What are you doing here?"

"We're going out to lunch, remember?"

Eight

"Nate!" Susannah ran around her desk until she stood directly in front of him. "John Hammer called me into his office this morning," she explained breathlessly. "I got the promotion! You're looking at the vice president in charge of marketing for H&J Lima."

For a moment Nate said nothing. Then he slowly repeated, "You got the promotion?"

"Yes," she told him. "I got it." In her enthusiasm, Susannah nodded several times, with a vigor that almost dislocated her neck. She was smiling so hard, her face ached.

Throwing back his head, Nate let out a shout that must have shaken the ceiling tile. Then he locked his arms around her waist, picked her up and swung her around, all the while howling with delight.

Susannah laughed with him. She'd never experienced joy more profoundly. The promotion hadn't seemed real to her until she'd shared it with Nate. The first person she'd thought to tell had been him. He'd become the very center of her world, and it was time to admit she was in love with him.

Nate had stopped whirling her around, but he continued to clasp her middle so that her face was elevated above his own.

Breathless with happiness, Susannah smiled down on him and on impulse buried her fingers in his hair. She couldn't resist him, not now, when she was filled with such exhilaration. Her mouth was trembling when she kissed him. She made a soft throaty sound of discovery and pleasure. Her gaze fell to the sensual lines of his mouth, and she remembered how she'd felt when he'd held and reassured her after the cookie disaster. She lowered her lips once more, lightly rocking her head back and forth, creating a friction that was so hot, she thought she'd catch fire.

In an unhurried movement, Nate lowered her to the ground and slid his arms around her. "Susannah," he moaned, kissing the corner of her mouth with exquisite care.

With a shudder, she opened her mouth to him. She wanted him to kiss her the way he had in the past. Deep, slow, moist, kisses that made her forget to breathe. She yearned for the taste and scent of him. This was the happiest moment of her life, and only a small part of it could be attributed to the promotion. Everything else was Nate and the growing love she felt for him each time they were together.

Someone coughed nervously in the background, and Nate broke off the kiss and glanced past her to the open door.

"Ms. Simmons," her assistant said, smiling broadly.

"Yes?" Breaking away from Nate, Susannah smoothed the hair at the sides of her head and struggled to replace her business facade.

"I'll be leaving now. Ms. Andrews will be answering your calls."

"Thank you, Ms. Brooks," Nate muttered, but there was little appreciation in his tone.

Susannah chastised him with a look. "We'll… I'll be leaving directly for my lunch appointment."

"I'll tell Ms. Andrews."

"This afternoon, I'd like you to call a meeting of my staff," Susannah said, "and I'll announce the promotion."

Eleanor Brooks nodded, but her smiling eyes landed heavily on Nate. "I believe everyone's already guessed from the…commotion that came from here a few minutes ago."

"I see." Susannah couldn't help smiling, too.

"There isn't an employee here who isn't happy about your news."

"I can think of two," Susannah said under her breath, considering the men she'd been competing against. Nate squeezed her hand, and she knew he'd heard her sardonic remark.

Her assistant closed the door on her way out, and the minute she did, Nate reached for Susannah to bring her back into the shelter of his arms. "Where were we?"

"About to leave for lunch, as I recall."

Nate frowned. "That's not the way I remember it."

Susannah laughed and hugged him tightly. "We both forgot ourselves for a while there." She broke away again and reached for her purse, hooking the long strap over her shoulder. "Are you ready?"

"Anytime you are." But the eager look in his eyes told her he was talking about something other than lunch.

Susannah could feel the color working its way up her neck and suffusing her face. "Nate," she whispered, "behave yourself. Please."

"I'm doing the best I can under the circumstances," he

whispered back, his eyes filled with mischief. "In case you haven't figured it out yet, I'm crazy about you, woman."

"I… I'm pretty keen on you myself."

"Good." He tucked his arm around her waist and led her out of the office and down the long hallway to the elevator. Susannah was sure she could feel the stares of her staff, but for the first time, she didn't care what image she projected. Everything was right in her world, and she'd never been happier.

Nate chose the restaurant, Il Bistro, which was one of the best in town. The atmosphere was festive, and playing the role of gentleman to the hilt, Nate wouldn't allow her to even look at the menu, insisting that he'd order for her.

"Nate," she said once the waiter had left the table, "I want to pay for this. It's a business lunch."

His thick brows arched upward. "And how are you going to rationalize *that* when your boss questions you about it, my dear?" He wiggled his eyebrows suggestively.

"There's a reason I agreed to go to lunch with you— other than celebrating my promotion, which I didn't even know about until this morning." As she'd explained to Nate earlier, her life was going to change with this promotion. New responsibility would result in a further commitment of time and energy to the company, and could drastically alter her relationship with Nate. If anything, she wanted them to grow closer, not apart. This advancement had the potential to make or break them, and Susannah was looking for a way to keep them together. She thought she'd found it.

"A reason?" Nate questioned.

They were interrupted by the waiter as he produced a bottle of expensive French wine for their inspection. He removed the cork and poured a sample into Nate's glass to taste. When Nate nodded in approval, the waiter filled their glasses and discreetly retreated.

"Now, you were saying?" Nate continued, studying her. His mouth quirked up at the edges.

Gathering her resolve, Susannah reached across the table and took Nate's hand. "You've always been open and honest with me. I want you to know how much I value that. When I asked you if you had a job, you told me you'd had one until recently and that you'd quit." She waited for him to elaborate on his circumstances, but he didn't, so she went on. "It's obvious you don't need the money, but there's something else that's obvious, too."

Nate removed his fingers from hers and twirled the stem of the wineglass between his open palms. "What's that?"

"You lack purpose."

His eyes rose to meet hers and his brow creased in query.

"You have no direction," she said. "Over the past several weeks, I've watched you flit from one interest to another. First it was baseball, then it was video games and kite flying, and tomorrow, no doubt, it'll be something completely different."

"Traveling," he concluded for her. "I was thinking of doing some serious sightseeing. I have a hankering to stroll the byways of Hong Kong."

"Hong Kong," she repeated, gesturing with one hand. "That's exactly what I mean." Her heart slowed to a sluggish beat at the thought of his being gone for any length of time. She'd become accustomed to having Nate nearby, to sharing bits and pieces of her day with him. Not only had she fallen in love with Nate Townsend, he'd quickly become her best friend.

"Do you think traveling is wrong?" he asked.

"Not wrong," she returned swiftly. "But what are you

going to do once you've run out of ways to entertain yourself and places to travel? What are you going to do when you've spent all your money?"

"I'll face that when the time comes."

"I see." She lowered her gaze, wondering if she was only making matters worse. There wasn't much she could say to counter his don't-worry attitude.

"Susannah, you make it sound like the end of the world. Trust me, wealth isn't all that great. If I run out of money, fine. If I don't, that's all right, too."

"I see," she murmured miserably.

"Why are you so worried?" he asked in a gentle voice.

"It's because I care about you, I guess." She paused to take a deep breath. "We may live in the same building, but our worlds are totally opposite. My future is charted, right down to the day I retire. I know what I want and how to get there."

"I thought I did once, too, but then I learned how unimportant it all was."

"It doesn't have to be like that," she told him, her voice filled with determination. "Listen, there's something important I'm going to propose, but I don't want you to answer me now. I want you to give yourself time to think about it. Promise me you'll at least do that."

"Are you suggesting we get married?" he teased.

"No." Flustered, she smoothed out the linen napkin in her lap, her fingers lingering there to disguise her nervousness. "I'm offering you a job."

"You're doing what?" He half rose out of his seat.

Embarrassed, Susannah glanced nervously around and noted that several people had stopped eating and were gazing in their direction. "Don't look so aghast. A job would make a lot of difference in your attitude toward life."

"And exactly what position are you offering me?" Now that the surprise had worn off, he appeared amused.

"I don't know yet. We'd have to figure something out. But I'm sure there'd be a position that would fit your qualifications."

The humor drained from his eyes, and for a long moment Nate said nothing. "You think a job would give me purpose?"

"I believe so." In her view, it would help him look beyond today and toward the future. Employment would give Nate a reason to get out of bed in the morning, instead of sleeping in until nine or ten every day.

"Susannah—"

"Before you say anything," she interrupted, holding up her hand, "I want you to think it over seriously. Don't say anything until you've had a chance to consider my offer."

His eyes were more serious than she could ever remember seeing them—other than just before he kissed her. His look was almost brooding.

Their meal arrived, and the lamb was as delicious as Nate had promised. He was unusually quiet during the remainder of the meal, but that didn't alarm her. He was reflecting on her job offer, which was exactly what she wanted. She hoped he'd come to the right decision. Loving him the way she did, she longed to make his world as right as her own.

Despite Nate's protests, Susannah paid for their lunch. He walked her back to her office, standing with her on the sidewalk while they exchanged a few words of farewell. Susannah kissed him on the cheek and asked once more that he consider her offer.

"I will," he promised, running his finger lightly down the side of her face.

He left her then, and Susannah watched as he walked away, letting her gaze linger on him for several minutes.

"Any messages?" she asked Dorothy Andrews, who was sitting in her assistant's place.

"One," Dorothy said, without looking up. "Emily—she didn't leave her full name. She said she'd catch you later."

"Thanks." Susannah went into her office and, sitting down at her desk, punched out her sister's telephone number.

"Emily, this is Susannah. You phoned?"

"I know I probably shouldn't have called you at the office, but you never seem to be home and I had something important to ask you," her sister said, talking so fast she ran her words together.

"What's that?" Already Susannah was reaching for a file, intending to read while her sister spoke. It sometimes took Emily several minutes to get around to the reason for any call.

Her sister hesitated. "I've got a bunch of zucchini left from my garden, and I was wondering if you wanted some."

"About as much as I want a migraine headache." After her disaster with the chocolate chip cookies, Susannah planned to never so much as read a recipe again.

"The zucchini are excellent," Emily prompted, as if that would be enough to induce Susannah into agreeing to take a truckload.

Her sister hadn't phoned her to ask about zucchini; Susannah would have staked her promotion on it. That was merely a lead-in for some other request, and no doubt Susannah would have to play a guessing game. Mentally, she scanned a list of possible favors and decided to jump in with both feet.

"Zucchini are out, but I wouldn't mind looking after Michelle again, if you need me to."

"Oh, Susannah, would you? I mean, it'd work out so well if you could take her two weeks from this Saturday."

"All night?" As much as she loved her niece, another overnight stretch was more than Susannah wanted to contemplate. Still, Nate would probably be more than willing to lend a hand. No doubt she'd need it.

"Oh, no, not for the night, just for dinner. Robert's boss is taking us out to eat, and it wouldn't be appropriate if we brought Michelle along. Robert got a big promotion."

"Congratulate him for me, okay?"

"I'm so proud of him," Emily said. "I think he must be the best accountant in Seattle."

Susannah toyed with the idea of letting her sister in on her own big news, but she didn't want to take anything away from her brother-in-law. She could tell them both in two weeks when they dropped off Michelle.

"I'll be happy to keep Michelle for you," Susannah said, and discovered, as she marked the date on her calendar, how much she actually meant that. She might be a disaster waiting to happen in the kitchen, but she didn't do half badly with her niece. The time might yet come when she'd consider having a child of her own—not now, of course, but sometime in the future. "All right, I've got you down for the seventeenth."

"Susannah, I can't tell you how much this means to me," Emily said.

When Susannah arrived home that evening she was tipsy. The staff meeting that afternoon had gone wonderfully well. After five, she'd been taken out for a drink by her two top aides, to celebrate. Several others from her section had unexpectedly dropped by the cocktail lounge and insisted on buying her drinks, too. By seven, Susannah was flushed and excited, and from experience, she knew it was time to call it quits and phone for a taxi.

Dinner probably would have cut the effects of the alcohol, but she was more interested in getting home. After a nice hot bath, she'd fix herself some toast and be done with it.

She hadn't been back more than half an hour when her phone rang. Dressed in her robe and sipping tea in the kitchen, she grabbed the receiver.

"Susannah, it's Nate. Can I come over?"

Glancing down at her robe and fuzzy slippers, she decided it wouldn't take her long to change.

"Give me five minutes."

"All right."

Dressed in slacks and a sweater, she opened the door at his knock. "Hi," she said cheerfully, aware that her mouth had probably formed a crooked grin despite her efforts to smile naturally.

Nate barely looked at her. His hands were thrust deep in his pockets, and his expression was disgruntled as he marched into her apartment. He didn't take a seat but paced the carpet in front of her fireplace. Obviously something was going on.

She sat on the edge of the sofa, watching him, feeling more than a little reckless and exhilarated from her promotion and the celebration afterward. She was amused, too, at Nate's peculiar agitation.

"I suppose you want to talk to me about the job offer," she said, surprised by how controlled her voice sounded.

He paused, splayed his fingers through his thick hair and nodded. "That's exactly what I want to talk about."

"Don't," she said, smiling up at him.

His forehead puckered in a frown. "Why not?"

"Because I'd like you to give long and careful consideration to the proposal."

"I need to explain something to you first."

Susannah wasn't listening. There were far more important things she had to tell him. "You're personable, bright and attractive," she began enthusiastically. "You could be anything you wanted, Nate. Anything."

"Susannah…"

She waved a finger at him and shook her head. "There's something else you should know."

"What?" he demanded.

"I'm in love with you." Her glorious confession was followed by a loud yawn. Unnerved, she covered her mouth with the tips of her fingers. "Oops, sorry."

Nate's eyes narrowed suspiciously. "Have you been drinking?"

She pressed her thumb and index finger together and held them up for his inspection. "Just a little, but I'm more happy than anything else."

"Susannah!" He dragged her name out into the sigh. "I can't believe you."

"Why not? Do you want me to shout it to all of Seattle? Because I will. Watch!" She waltzed into the kitchen and jerked open the sliding glass door.

Actually, some of the alcohol had worn off, but she experienced this irrepressible urge to tell Nate how much she'd come to care for him. They'd skirted around the subject long enough. He didn't seem to want to admit it, but she did, especially now, fortified as she was with her good fortune. This day had been one of the most fantastic of her life. After years of hard work, everything was falling into place, and she'd found the most wonderful man in the world to love—even if he *was* misguided.

The wind whipped against her on the balcony, and the multicolored lights from the waterfront below resembled those on a Christmas tree. Standing at the railing, she cupped her hands around her mouth and shouted, "I love Nate Townsend!" Satisfied, she whirled to face him and opened her arms as wide as she could. "See? I announced it to the world."

He joined her outside and slid his arms around her and closed his eyes. Susannah had expected him to show at least *some* emotion.

"You don't look very happy about it," she challenged.

"You're not yourself," he said as he released her.

"Then who am I?" Fists digging into her hips, she glared up at him, her eyes defiant. "I feel like me. I bet you think I'm drunk, but I'm not."

He didn't reply. Instead he threw an arm over her shoulder and urged her into the kitchen. Then, quickly and efficiently, he started to make coffee.

"I gave up caffeine," she muttered.

"When was this? You had regular coffee today at lunch," he said.

"Just now." She giggled. "Come on, Nate," she cried, bending forward and snapping her fingers. "Loosen up."

"I'm more concerned about sobering *you* up."

"You could kiss me."

"I could," he agreed, "but I'm not going to."

"Why not?" She pouted, disappointed by his refusal.

"Because if I do, I may not be able to stop."

Sighing, she closed her eyes. "That's the most romantic thing you've ever said to me."

Nate rubbed his face and leaned against the kitchen counter. "Have you had anything to eat since lunch?"

"One stuffed mushroom, a water chestnut wrapped in a slice of bacon and a piece of celery filled with cheese."

"But no dinner?"

"I was going to make myself some toast, but I wasn't hungry."

"After a stuffed mushroom, a celery stick and a water chestnut? I can see why not."

"Are you trying to be cute with me? Oh, just a minute, there was something I was supposed to ask you." She pulled herself up short and covered one eye, while she tugged at her memory for the date her sister had mentioned. "Are you doing anything on the seventeenth?"

"The seventeenth? Why?"

"Michelle's coming over to visit her auntie Susannah and I know she'll want to see you, too."

Nate looked even more disturbed, but he hadn't seemed particularly pleased about anything from the moment he'd arrived.

"I've got something else that night."

"Oh, well, I'll make do. I have before." She stopped abruptly. "No, I guess I haven't, but Michelle and I'll be just fine, I think…"

The coffee had finished dripping into the glass pot. Nate poured a cup and, scowling, handed it to her.

"Oh, Nate, what's wrong with you? You've been cranky since you got here. We should be kissing by now and all you seem to do is ignore me."

"Drink your coffee."

He stood over her until she'd taken the first sip. She grimaced at the heat. "You know what I drank tonight? I've never had them before and they tasted so good. Shanghai Slungs."

"They're called Singapore Slings."

"Oh." Maybe she was more confused than she thought.

"Come on, drink up, Tokyo Rose."

Obediently Susannah did as he said. The whole time she was sipping her coffee, she was watching Nate, who moved restlessly about her kitchen, as if unable to stand still. He was disturbed about something, and she wished she knew what.

"Done," she announced when she'd finished her coffee, pleased with herself and this minor accomplishment. "Nate," she said, growing concerned, "do you love me?"

He turned around to face her, his eyes serious. "So much I can't believe it myself."

"Oh, good," she said with an expressive sigh. "I was beginning to wonder."

"Where are your aspirin?" He was searching through her cupboards, opening and closing the ones closest to the sink.

"My aspirin? Did telling me how you feel give you a headache?"

"No." He answered her with a gentle smile. "I want to have it ready for you in the morning because you're going to need it."

Her love for him increased tenfold. "You are so thoughtful!"

"Take two tablets when you wake up. That should help." He crouched in front of her and took both her hands in his. "I'm leaving tomorrow and I won't be back for a couple of days. I'll call you, all right?"

"You're going away to think about my job offer, aren't you? That's a good idea—when you come back you can tell me your decision." She was forced to stop in order to yawn, a huge jaw-breaking yawn that depleted her strength. "I think I should go to bed, don't you?"

The next thing Susannah knew, her alarm was buzzing angrily. With the noise came a piercing pain that shot straight through her temple. She groped for the clock, turned it off and sighed with relief. Sitting up in bed proved to be equally overwhelming and she groaned.

When she'd managed to maneuver herself into the kitchen, she saw the aspirin bottle and remembered that Nate had insisted on setting it out the night before.

"Bless that man," she said aloud and winced at the sound of her own voice.

By the time she arrived at the office, she was operating on only three cylinders. Eleanor Brooks didn't seem to be any better off than Susannah was. They took one look at each other and smiled knowingly.

"Your coffee's ready," her assistant informed her.

"Did you have a cup yourself?"

"Yes."

"Anything in the mail?"

"Nothing that can't wait. Mr. Hammer was in earlier. He told me to give you this magazine and said you'd be as impressed as he was." Susannah glanced at the six-year-old issue of *Business Monthly,* a trade magazine that was highly respected in the industry.

"It's several years old," Susannah noted, wondering why her employer would want her to read it now.

"Mr. Hammer said there was a special feature in there about your friend."

"My friend?" Susannah didn't understand.

"Your friend," Eleanor Brooks repeated. "The one with the sexy eyes—Nathaniel Townsend."

Nine

Susannah waited until Eleanor had left the office before opening the magazine. The article on Nathaniel Townsend was the lead feature. The picture showed a much younger Nate standing in front of a shopping-mall outlet for Rainy Day Cookies, the most successful cookie chain in the country. He was holding a huge chocolate chip cookie.

Rainy Day Cookies were Susannah's absolute favorite. There were several varieties, but the chocolate chip ones were fantastic.

Two paragraphs into the article, Susannah thought she was going to be physically ill. She stopped reading and closed her eyes to the waves of nausea that lapped against her. Pressing a hand to her stomach, she resolutely focused her attention on the article, storing away the details of Nate's phenomenal success in her numb mind.

He had started his cookie company in his mother's kitchen while still in college. His specialty was chocolate chip cookies, and they were so popular, he soon found himself caught up in a roller-coaster ride that had led him straight to the top of the corporate world. By age twenty-eight, Nate Townsend was a multimillionaire.

Now that she thought about it, an article she'd read six or seven months ago in the same publication had said the company was recently sold for an undisclosed sum, which several experts had estimated to be a figure so staggering Susannah had gasped out loud.

Bracing her elbows on the desk, Susannah took several calming breaths. She'd made a complete idiot of herself over Nate, and worse, he had let her. She suspected this humiliation would stay with her for the rest of her life.

To think she'd baked the cookie king of the world chocolate chip cookies, and in the process nearly set her kitchen on fire. But that degradation couldn't compare to yesterday's little pep talk when she'd spoken to him about drive, ambition and purpose, before—dear heaven, it was too much—she'd offered him a job. How he must have laughed at that.

Eleanor Brooks brought in the mail and laid it on the corner of Susannah's desk. Susannah looked up at her and knew then and there that she wasn't going to be able to cope with the business of the day.

"I'm going home."

"I beg your pardon?"

"If anyone needs me, tell them I'm home sick."

"But…"

Susannah knew she'd shocked her assistant. In all the years she'd been employed by H&J Lima, Susannah had never used a single day of her sick leave. There'd been a couple of times she probably *should* have stayed home, but she'd insisted on working anyway.

"I'll see you Monday morning," she said on her way out the door.

"I hope you're feeling better then."

"I'm sure I will be." She needed some time alone to lick

her wounds and gather the scattered pieces of her pride. To think that only a few hours earlier she'd drunkenly declared her undying love to Nate Townsend!

That was the worst of it.

When Susannah walked into her apartment she felt as if she was stumbling into a bomb shelter. For the moment she was hidden from the world outside. Eventually she'd have to go back and face it, but for now she was safe.

She picked up the afghan her sister had crocheted for her, wrapped it around her shoulders and sat staring sightlessly into space.

What an idiot she'd been! What a fool! Closing her eyes, she leaned her head against the back of the sofa and drew in several deep breaths, releasing the anger and hurt before it fermented into bitterness. She refused to dwell on the might-have-beens and the if-onlys, opting instead for a more positive approach. *Next time,* she would know enough not to involve her heart. *Next time,* she'd take care not to make such a fool of herself.

It astonished her when she awoke an hour later to realize she'd fallen asleep. Tucking the blanket more securely around her, she analyzed her situation.

Things weren't so bad. She'd achieved her primary goal and was vice president in charge of marketing. The first female in the company's long history to hold such a distinguished position, she reminded herself. Her life was good. If on occasion she felt the yearning for a family of her own, there was always Emily, who was more than willing to share. Heaving a sigh, Susannah told herself that she lacked for nothing. She was respected, hardworking and healthy. Yes, life was good.

Her head ached and her stomach didn't feel much better, but at noon, Susannah heated some chicken noodle soup and forced that down. She was putting the bowl in the dishwasher when the telephone rang. Ms. Brooks was the only one who knew she was home, and her assistant would call her only if it was important. Susannah answered the phone just as she would in her office.

"Susannah Simmons."

"Susannah, it's Nate."

She managed to swallow a gasp. "Hello, Nate," she said as evenly as possible. "What can I do for you."

"I called the office and your assistant said you'd gone home sick."

"Yes. I guess I had more to drink last night than I realized. I had one doozy of a hangover when I woke up this morning." But she didn't add how her malady had worsened once she read the article about him.

"Did you find the aspirin on the kitchen counter?"

"Yes. Now that I think about it, you were by last night, weren't you?" She was thinking fast, wanting to cover her tracks. "I suppose I made a fool of myself," she said, instilling a lightness in her tone. "I didn't say anything to embarrass you—or me, did I?"

He chuckled softly. "You don't remember?"

She did, but she wasn't going to admit it. "Some of it, but most of the evening's kind of fuzzy."

"Once I'm back in Seattle I'll help you recall every single word." His voice was low, seductive and filled with promise.

That was one guarantee, however, that Susannah had no intention of accepting.

"I...probably made a complete idiot of myself," she mumbled. "If I were you, I'd forget anything I said. Obviously, I can't be held responsible for it."

"Susannah, Susannah, Susannah," Nate said gently. "Let's take this one step at a time."

"I...think we should talk about it later, I really do...because it's all too obvious I wasn't myself." Tears pooled at the corners of her eyes. Furious at this display of emotion, she wiped them aside with the back of her hand.

"You're feeling okay now?"

"Yes...no. I was about to lie down."

"Then I'll let you," Nate said. "I'll be back Sunday. My flight should arrive early afternoon. I'd like us to have dinner together."

"Sure," she said, without thinking, willing to agree to just about anything in order to end this conversation. She was still too raw, still bleeding. By Sunday, she'd be able to handle the situation far more effectively. By Sunday, she could disguise her pain.

"I'll see you around five, then."

"Sunday," she echoed, feeling like a robot programmed to do exactly as its master requested. She had no intention of having dinner with Nate, none whatsoever. He'd find out why soon enough.

The only way Susannah made it through Saturday was by working. She went to her office and sorted through the mail Ms. Brooks had left on her desk. News of her promotion was to be announced in the Sunday business section of the *Seattle Times,* but apparently word had already leaked out, probably through her boss; there was a speaking invitation in the mail, for a luncheon at a conference of local salespeople who had achieved a high level of success. The request was an honor and Susannah sent a note of acceptance to the organizer. She considered it high praise to have been asked. The date of the conference was the seventeenth, which was only two weeks away, so she spent a good part of the morning making notes for her speech.

On Sunday, Susannah woke feeling sluggish and out of sorts. She recognized the source of her discomfort almost instantly. This afternoon, she would confront Nate. For the past two days, she'd gone over in her mind exactly what she planned to say, how she'd act.

Nate arrived at four-thirty. She answered his knock, dressed in navy blue slacks and a cream shell-knit sweater. Her hair was neatly rolled into a chignon.

"Susannah." His gaze was hungry as he stepped across the threshold and reached for her.

It was too late to hide her reaction by the time she realized he intended to kiss her. He swept her into his arms and eagerly pressed his mouth over hers. Despite everything that he'd failed to tell her, Susannah felt an immediate excitement she couldn't disguise.

Nate slipped his fingers into her hair, removing the pins that held it in place, while he leisurely moved his mouth over hers.

"Two days have never seemed so long," he breathed, then nibbled on her lower lip.

Regaining her composure, she broke away, her shoulders heaving. "Would you like some coffee?"

"No. The only thing I want is you."

She started to walk away from him, but Nate caught her, hauling her back into the warm shelter of his arms. He linked his hands at the small of her back and gazed down at her, his eyes soft and caressing. Gradually, his expression altered.

"Is everything all right?" he asked.

"Yes…and no," she admitted dryly. "I happened upon

an article in an old issue of *Business Monthly*. Does that tell you anything?"

He hesitated, and for a moment Susannah wondered if he was going to say anything or not.

"So you know?"

"That you're the world's cookie king, or once were—yes, I know."

His eyes narrowed slightly. "Are you angry?"

She sighed. A good deal depended on her delivery, and although she'd practiced her response several times, it was more difficult than she'd expected. She was determined, however, to remain calm and casual.

"I'm more embarrassed than amused," she said. "I wish you'd said something before I made such a fool of myself."

"Susannah, you have every right to be upset." He let her go and rubbed the back of his neck as he began to walk back and forth between the living room and kitchen. "It isn't like it was a deep dark secret. I sold the business almost six months ago, and I was taking a sabbatical—hell, I needed one. I'd driven myself as far as I could. My doctor thinks I was on the verge of a complete physical collapse. When I met you, I was just coming out of it, learning how to enjoy life again. The last thing I wanted to do was sit down and talk about the past thirteen years. I'd put Rainy Day Cookies behind me, and I was trying to build a new life."

Susannah crossed her arms. "Did you ever intend to tell me?"

"Yes!" he said vehemently. "Thursday. You were so sweet to have offered me a job and I knew I had to say something then, but you were…"

"Tipsy," she finished for him.

"All right, tipsy. You have to understand why I didn't. The timing was all wrong."

"You must have got a good laugh from the cookie disaster," she said, surprised at how steady her voice remained. Her poise didn't even slip, and she was proud of herself.

The edges of his mouth quivered, and it was apparent that he was struggling not to laugh.

"Go ahead," she said, waving her hand dramatically. "I suppose those charred cookies and the smoldering cookie sheets were pretty comical. I don't blame you. I'd probably be in hysterics if the situation were reversed."

"It isn't that. The fact that you made those cookies was one of the sweetest things anyone's ever done for me. I want you to know I was deeply touched."

"I didn't do it for you," she said, struggling to keep the anger out of her voice. "It was a trial by fire—" Hearing what she'd said, Susannah closed her eyes.

"Susannah—"

"You must've got a real kick out of that little pep talk I gave you the other day, too. Imagine *me* talking to *you* about drive, motivation and goals."

"That touched me, too," he insisted.

"Right on the funny bone, I'll bet." She faked a laugh herself just to prove what a good sport she was. Still, she wasn't exactly keen on being the brunt of a joke.

Nate paused, then gestured at her. "I suppose it looks bad considered from your point of view."

"Looks bad," she echoed, with a short hysterical laugh. "That's one way of putting it!"

Nate strode from one end of the room to the other. If he didn't stop soon, he was going to wear a path in the carpet.

"Are you willing to put this misunderstanding behind us, Susannah, or are you going to hold it against me? Are you willing to ruin what we have over a mistake?"

"I don't know yet." Actually she did, but she didn't want

him to accuse her of making snap decisions. It would be so easy for Nate to talk his way out of this. But Susannah had been humiliated. How could she possibly trust him now? He'd thought nothing of hiding an important portion of his life from her.

"How long will it be before you come to a conclusion about us?"

"I don't know that, either."

"I guess dinner is out?"

She nodded, her face muscles so tight, they ached.

"Okay, think everything through. I trust you to be completely fair and unbiased. All I want you to do is ask yourself one thing. If the situation were reversed, how would you have handled it?"

"All right." She'd grant him that much, although she already knew what she would have done—and it wasn't keep up a charade the way he had.

"There's something else I want you to think about," he said when she held open the door for him.

"What?" Susannah was frantic to get him out of her home. The longer he stayed, the more difficult it was to remain angry with him.

"This." He kissed her then and it was the type of kiss that drove to the very depths of her soul. His mouth on hers was hot, the kiss deep and moist and so filled with longing that her knees almost buckled. Tiny sounds interrupted the moment, and Susannah realized she was the one making them.

When Nate released her, she backed away and nearly stumbled. Breathing hard, she leaned against the door frame and heaved in giant gulps of oxygen.

Satisfied, Nate smiled infuriatingly. "Admit it, Susannah," he whispered and ran his index finger over her collarbone. "We were meant for each other."

"I... I'm not willing to admit anything."

His expression looked forlorn. It was no doubt calculated to evoke sympathy, but it wouldn't work. Susannah wouldn't be fooled a second time.

"You'll phone me?" he pressed.

"Yes." When the moon was in the seventh house, which should be somewhere around the time the government balanced the budget. Perhaps a decade from now.

For two days, Susannah's life returned to a more normal routine. She went in to the office early and worked late, doing everything she could to avoid Nate, although she was sure he'd wait patiently for some signal from her. After all, he, too, had his pride; she was counting on that.

When she arrived home on Wednesday, there was a folded note taped to her door. Susannah stared at it for several thundering heartbeats, then finally reached for it.

She waited until she'd put her dinner in the microwave before she read it. Her heart was pounding painfully hard as she opened the sheet and saw three words: "Call me. Please."

Susannah gave a short hysterical laugh. Ha! Nate Townsend could tumble into a vat of melted chocolate chips before she'd call him again. Guaranteed he'd say or do something that would remind her of what a fool she'd been! And yet... Damn, but it was hard to stay angry with him!

When the phone rang she was still ambivalent. Jumping back, she glared at it before answering.

"Hello," she said cautiously, quaveringly.

"Susannah? Is that you?"

"Oh, hi, Emily."

"Good grief, you scared me. I thought you were sick. You sounded so weak."

"No. No, I'm fine."

"I hadn't talked to you in a while and I was wondering how you were doing."

"Fine," she repeated.

"Susannah!" Her sister's tone made her name sound like a warning. "I know you well enough to realize something's wrong. I also know it probably has to do with Nate. You haven't mentioned him the last few times we've talked, but before you seemed to be overflowing with things you wanted to say about him."

"I'm not seeing much of Nate these days."

"Why not?"

"Well, being a multimillionaire keeps him busy."

Emily paused to gulp in a breath, then gasped, "I think there must be a problem with the phone. I thought you just said—"

"Ever been to Rainy Day Cookies?"

"Of course. Hasn't everyone?"

"Have you made the connection yet?"

"You mean Nate…"

"…is Mr. Chocolate Chip himself."

"But that's marvelous! That's wonderful. Why, he's famous… I mean his cookies are. To think that the man who developed Rainy Day Cookies actually helped Robert carry out Michelle's crib. I can't wait until he hears this."

"Personally, I wasn't all that impressed." It was difficult to act indifferent when her sister was bubbling over with such enthusiasm. Emily usually only got excited about something organic.

"When did you find out?" Emily asked, her voice almost accusing, as if Susannah had been holding out on her.

"Last Friday. John Hammer gave me a magazine that

had an article about Nate in it. The issue was a few years old, but the article told me everything Nate should have."

A brief sound of exclamation followed. "So you just found out?"

"Right."

"And you're angry with him?"

"Good heavens, no. Why should I be?" Susannah was afraid Emily wouldn't appreciate the sarcasm.

"He probably planned on telling you," Emily argued, defending Nate. "I don't know him all that well, but he seemed straightforward enough to me. I'm sure he intended to explain the situation when the time was right."

"Perhaps," Susannah said, but as far as she was concerned, that consolation was too little, too late. "Listen, I've got something in the microwave, so I've got to scoot." The excuse was feeble, but Susannah didn't want to continue discussing Nate. "Oh, before I forget," she added quickly. "I've got a speaking engagement on the seventeenth, but I'll be finished before five-thirty so you can count on me watching Michelle."

"Great. Listen, if you want to talk, I'm always here. I mean that. What are sisters for if not to talk?"

"Thanks, I'll remember that."

Once she replaced the receiver, Susannah was left to deal, once more, with Nate's three-word note. By all rights, she should crumple it up and toss it in the garbage. She did, feeling a small—very small—sense of satisfaction.

Out of sight, out of mind, or so the old adage went. Only this time it wasn't working. Whenever she turned around, the sight of the telephone seemed to pull at her.

Her dinner was ready, but as she gazed down at the unappetizing entrée, she considered throwing it out and going to the Western Avenue Deli for a pastrami on rye instead.

That would serve two purposes; first, it would take her away from the phone, which seemed to be luring her to its side; and second, she'd at least have a decent meal.

Having made her decision, she was already in the living room when there was a knock at the door. Susannah groaned, knowing even before she answered it that her visitor had to be Nate.

"You didn't call," he snapped the minute she opened the door.

He stormed inside without waiting for an invitation, looking irritated but in control. "Just how long were you planning to keep me waiting? It's obvious you're going to make me pay for the error of my ways, which to a certain point I can understand. But we've gone well past that point. So what are you waiting for? An apology? Okay—I'm sorry."

"Ah—"

"You have every reason to be upset, but what do you want? Blood? Enough is enough. I'm crazy about you, Susannah, and you feel the same about me, so don't try to fool me with this indifference routine, because I can see right through it. Let's put this foolishness behind us and get back on track."

"Why?" she demanded.

"Why what?"

"Why did you wait to tell me? Why couldn't you have said something sooner?"

He gave her a frown that suggested they were rehashing old news, then started his usual pacing. "Because I wanted to put Rainy Day Cookies out of my mind. I'd made the business my entire world." He stopped and whirled to face her. "I recognized a kindred spirit in you. Your entire life is wrapped up in some sporting-goods company—"

"Not just *some* sporting-goods company," she returned, indignant. "H&J Lima is the largest in the country."

"Forgive me, Susannah, but that doesn't really impress me. What about your *life?* Your whole world revolves around how far you can climb up the corporate ladder. Let me tell you that once you're at the top, the view isn't all that great. You forget what it means to appreciate the simple things in life. I did."

"Are you telling me to stop and smell the flowers? Well, I've got news for you, Nate Townsend. I like my life just the way it is. I consider it insulting that you think you can casually walk into my world and my career and tell me I'm headed down the road to destruction, because I'll tell you right now—" she paused to take a deep breath "—I don't appreciate it."

Nate's expression tightened. "I'm not talking about flowers, Susannah. I want you to look out this window at Puget Sound and see the lovely view with ferryboats and snow-capped mountains. Life, abundant life, is more than that. It's meaningful relationships. Connecting with other people. Friends. Fun. We'd both lost sight of that. It happened to me first, and I can see you going in the same direction."

"That's fine for you, but I—"

"You need the same things I do. We need each other."

"Correction," she said heatedly. "As I told you, I like my life just the way it is, thank you. And why shouldn't I? My five-year goals have been achieved, and there are more in the making. I can go straight to the top with this company, and that's exactly what I want. As for needing relationships, you're wrong about that, too. I got along fine before I met you, and the same will be true when you're out of my life."

The room went so still that for a second Susannah was convinced Nate had stopped breathing.

"*When* I'm out of your life," he echoed. "I see. So you've made your decision."

"Yes," she said, holding her head high. "It was fun while it lasted, but if I had to choose between you and the vice presidency, the decision wouldn't be difficult at all. I'm sure you'll encounter some other young woman who needs to be saved from herself and her goals. As far as I can see, from your perspective our relationship was more of a rescue mission. Now that you know how the cookie crumbles—the pun's intended—perhaps you'll leave me to my sorry lot."

"Susannah, would you listen to me?"

"No." She held up her hand for effect. "I'll try to be happy," she said, a heavy note of mockery in her voice.

For a moment, Nate said nothing. "You're making a mistake, but that's something you're going to have to learn on your own."

"I suppose you're planning on being around to pick up the pieces when I fall apart?"

His blue eyes bored into hers. "I might be, but then again, I might not."

"Well, you needn't worry, because either way, you've got a long wait."

Ten

"Ms. Simmons, Mr. Hammer, it's an honor to meet you."

"Thank you," Susannah said, smiling politely at the young man who'd been sent to greet her and her boss. The Seattle Convention Center was filled to capacity. The moment Susannah realized her audience was going to be so large, her stomach was attacked by a bad case of nerves. Not the most pleasant conditions under which to be eating lunch.

"If you'll come this way, I'll show you to the head table."

Susannah and John Hammer followed the young executive toward the front of the crowded room. There were several other people already seated on the stage. Susannah recognized the mayor and a couple of city councillors, along with the King County executive and two prominent local businessmen.

She was assigned the chair to the right of the podium. John was assigned the place beside her. After shaking hands with the conference coordinator, she greeted the others and took her seat. Almost immediately, the caterers started serving lunch, which consisted of an elegantly prepared salad tossed with a raspberry vinaigrette, wild rice and broiled fresh salmon with a teriyaki glaze.

She didn't think she could manage even a bite while sitting in front of so many people. Glancing out over the sea of unfamiliar faces, she forced herself to remain calm and collected. She was, after all, one of the featured speakers for the afternoon, and she'd come well prepared.

There was a slight commotion to her right, but the podium blocked her view.

"Hi, gorgeous. No one told me you were going to be here."

Nate. Susannah nearly swallowed her forkful of salmon whole. It stuck in her throat and she would've choked had she not reached for her water and hurriedly gulped some down.

Twisting around in her chair, she came eye to eye with him. "Hello, Nate," she said as nonchalantly as she could. Her smile was firmly in place.

"I thought Nate Townsend might be here," John whispered, looking pleased with himself.

"I see you've taken to following me around now," Nate taunted as he took his seat, two chairs down from John's.

Susannah ignored his comment and both men, studiously returning to her salmon, hoping to suggest that her meal was far more appealing than their conversation.

"Have you missed me?"

It was ten agonizing days since she'd last seen Nate. Avoiding him hadn't been easy. He'd made sure of that. The first night she'd come home to an Italian opera played just loud enough to be heard through her kitchen wall. The sound of the music was accompanied by the tangy scent of his homemade spaghetti sauce. The aroma of simmering tomatoes and herbs mingled with the pungent scent of hot garlic and butter.

Evidently Nate assumed the way to *her* heart was

through her stomach. She'd nearly succumbed then, but her conviction was strong and she'd hurried to a favorite Italian restaurant to alleviate her sudden craving for pasta.

By the weekend, Susannah could've sworn Nate had whipped up every recipe in an entire cookbook, each one more enticing than the last. Susannah had never eaten as many restaurant meals as she had in the past week.

When Nate realized she couldn't be bought so easily with fine food, wine and song, he'd tried another tactic, this one less subtle.

A single red rose was waiting outside her door when she arrived home from the office. There wasn't any note with it, just a perfect fresh flower. She picked it up and against her better judgment took it inside with her, inhaling the delicate scent. The only person who could have left it was Nate. Then, in a flurry of righteousness, she'd taken the rose and put it back where she found it. Five minutes later, she jerked open her door and to her dismay discovered the flower was still there, looking forlorn and dejected.

Deciding to send him her own less than subtle message, Susannah dropped the rose outside Nate's door. She hoped he'd understand once and for all that she refused to be bought!

Nate, however, wasn't dissuaded. The rose was followed the next evening by a small box of luscious chocolates. This time Susannah didn't even bring them inside, but marched them directly to Nate's door.

"No," she said now, forcing her thoughts back to the present and the conference. She surveyed the crowded, noisy room. "I haven't missed you in the least."

"You haven't?" He looked dashed. "But I thought you were trying to make it up to me. Why else would you leave those gifts outside my door?"

For just a second her heart thumped wildly. Then she gave him a fiery glare and diligently resumed her meal, making sure she downed every bite. If she didn't, Nate would think she was lovesick for want of him.

Her boss tilted his head toward her, obviously pleased with himself. "I thought it would be a nice surprise for you to be speaking with Nate. Fact is, I arranged it myself."

"How thoughtful," Susannah murmured.

"You have missed me, haven't you?" Nate asked again, balancing on two legs of his chair in an effort to see her.

Okay, she was willing to admit she'd been a bit lonely, but that was to be expected. For several weeks, Nate had filled every spare moment of her time with silliness like baseball games and kite flying. But she'd lived a perfectly fine life before she met him, and now she'd gone back to that same serene lifestyle without a qualm. Her world was wonderful. Complete. She didn't need him to make her a whole person. Nate was going to a lot of trouble to force her to admit she was miserable without him. She wasn't about to do that.

"I miss you," he said, batting his baby blues at her. "The least you could do is concede that you're as lonely and miserable as me."

"But I'm not," she answered sweetly, silently acknowledging the lie. "I have a fantastic job and a promising career. What else could I want?"

"Children?"

She leaned forward and spoke across the people between them. "Michelle and I have loads of fun together, and when we get bored with each other, she goes home to her mother. In my opinion that's the perfect way to enjoy a child."

The first speaker approached the podium, and Susannah's attention was diverted to him. He was five minutes into his greeting when Susannah felt something hit her arm. She darted a glance at Nate, who was holding up a white linen napkin. *"What about a husband?"* was inked across the polished cloth.

Groaning, Susannah prayed no one else had seen his note, especially her boss. She rolled her eyes and emphatically shook her head. It was then that she noticed how everyone was applauding and looking in her direction. She blinked, not understanding, until she realized that she'd just been introduced and they were waiting for her to stand up and give her talk.

Scraping back her chair, she stood abruptly and approached the podium, not daring to look at Nate. The man was infuriating! A lesser woman would have dumped the contents of her water glass over his smug head. Instead of venting her irritation, she drew in a deep calming breath and gazed out over her audience. That was a mistake. There were so many faces, and they all had their eyes trained on her.

Her talk had been carefully planned and memorized. But to be on the safe side, she'd brought the typed sheets with her. She had three key points she intended to share, and had illustrated each one with several anecdotes. Suddenly her mind was blank. It took all her courage not to bolt and run from the stage.

"Go get 'em, Susannah," Nate mouthed, smiling up at her.

His eyes were so full of encouragement and faith that the paralysis started to leave her. Although she'd memorized her speech, she stared down at the written version. The instant she read the first sentence she knew she was going to be fine.

For the next twenty minutes she spoke about the importance of indelibly marking a goal on one's mind and how to minimize difficulties and maximize strengths. She closed by explaining the significance of building a mental ladder to one's dreams. She talked about using determination, discipline, dedication and demeanor as the rungs of this ladder to success.

Despite Nate's earlier efforts to undermine her dignity and poise, she was pleased by the way her speech was received. Many of her listeners nodded at key points in her talk, and Susannah knew she was reaching them. When she came to the end, she felt good, satisfied with her speech and with herself.

As she turned to go back to her seat, her gaze caught Nate's. He was smiling as he applauded, and the gleam in his eyes was unmistakably one of respect and admiration. The warm, caressing look he sent her nearly tripped her heart into overdrive. Yet he'd maddened her with his senseless questions, distracted her, teased and taunted her with his craziness and then written a note on a napkin. But when she finished her speech, the first person she'd looked at, whether consciously or unconsciously, was Nate.

Once Susannah was seated, she saw that her hands were trembling. But she couldn't be sure if it was a release from the tension that had gripped her when she first started to speak, or the result of Nate's tender look.

Nate was introduced next, and he walked casually to the podium. It would serve him right, Susannah thought, if she started writing messages on her napkin and holding them up for him to read while he gave his talk. She was immediately shocked by the childishness of the idea. Five minutes with Nate seemed to reduce her mentality to that of a ten-year-old.

With a great deal of ceremony, or so it seemed to Susannah, Nate retrieved his notes from inside his suit jacket. It was all she could do to keep from laughing out loud when she saw that everything he planned to say had been jotted on the back of a single index card. So this was how seriously he'd taken that afternoon's address. It looked as if he'd scribbled a couple of notes while she was delivering her speech. He hadn't given his lecture a second thought until five minutes before he was supposed to stand at the podium.

But Nate proved her wrong, as seemed to be his habit. The minute he opened his mouth, he had the audience in the palm of his hand. Rarely had she heard a more dynamic speaker. His strong voice carried to the farthest corners of the huge hall, and although he used the microphone, Susannah doubted he really needed it.

Nate told of his own beginnings, of how his father had died the year he was to enter college, so that the funds he'd expected to further his education were no longer available. It was the lowest point of his life and out of it had come his biggest success. Then he explained that his mother's chocolate chip cookies had always been everyone's favorite. Because of his father's untimely death, she'd taken a job in a local factory, and Nate, eager to find a way to attend university in the fall, had started baking the cookies and selling them to tourists for fifty cents each.

Halfway through the summer he'd made more than enough money to see him through his first year of school. Soon a handful of local delis had contacted him, wanting to include his cookies as part of their menus. These requests were followed by others from restaurants and hotels.

Nate went to school that first year and took every business course available to him. By the end of the following summer, he had set up a kitchen with his mother's help and opened his own business, which thrived despite his mistakes. The rest was history. By the time he graduated from college, Nate was already a millionaire and his mother was able to retire comfortably. To his credit, he'd resisted the temptation to abandon his education. It had served him well since, and he was glad he'd stuck with it, even though everyone around him seemed to be saying he knew more, from personal experience, than most of the authors of the textbooks did. A fact he was quick to dispute.

Susannah was enthralled. She'd assumed Nate would be telling this audience what he'd been beating her over the head with from the moment they'd met—that the drive to succeed was all well and good, but worthless if in the process one forgot to enjoy life. However, if that thought was on Nate's mind, he didn't voice it. Susannah suspected he'd reserved that philosophy for her and her alone.

When he returned to his seat, the applause was thunderous. The first thing he did was look at Susannah, who smiled softly, as touched by his story as the rest of the audience was. Not once had he patted himself on the back, or taken credit for the phenomenal success of Rainy Day Cookies. Susannah would almost have preferred it if his talk had been a boring rambling account of his prosperous career. She didn't want to feel so much admiration for him. It would be easier to get Nate out of her life and her mind if she didn't.

The luncheon ended a few minutes later. Gathering up her things, Susannah hoped to make a speedy escape. She should've known Nate wouldn't allow that. Several people had hurried up to the podium to talk to him, but he excused himself and moved to her side.

"Susannah, could we talk for a minute?"

She made a show of glancing at her watch, then at her boss. "I have another appointment," she said stiffly. She secured the strap of her purse over her shoulder and offered him what she hoped was a regretful smile.

"Your speech was wonderful."

"Thank you. So was yours," she said, then mentioned the one thing that had troubled her. "You never told me about your father's death."

"I've never told you I love you, either, but I do."

His words, so casual, so calm and serene, were like a blow to her solar plexus. Susannah felt the tears form in her eyes and tried to blink them back. "I... I wish you hadn't said that."

"The way I feel about you isn't going to change."

"I...really have to go," she said, turning anxiously toward John Hammer. All she wanted to do was escape with her heart intact.

"Mr. Townsend," a woman bellowed from the audience. "You're going to be at the auction tonight, aren't you?"

Nate's gaze slid reluctantly from Susannah to the well-dressed woman on the floor. "I'll be there," he called back.

"I'll be looking for you," she said and laughed girlishly.

Susannah decided the other woman's laugh resembled the sound an unwell rooster would make. She was tempted to ask Nate exactly what kind of auction he planned to attend where he expected to run into someone who yelled questions across a crowded room. But she ignored the urge, which was just as well.

"Goodbye, Nate," she said, moving away.

"Goodbye, my love." It wasn't until she was walking out of the Convention Center that Susannah realized how final his farewell had sounded.

It was what she wanted, wasn't it? As far as she was concerned, Nate had proved he wasn't trustworthy; he had an infuriating habit of keeping secrets. So now that he wasn't going to see her again, there was absolutely no reason for her to complain. At least that was what Susannah told herself as she headed home, making a short side trip to the Seattle waterfront.

Within a couple of hours, Emily and Robert would be dropping off Michelle before they went to dinner with Robert's employer. Once the baby was with her, Susannah reminded herself, she wouldn't have a chance to worry about Nate or anyone else.

By the time Emily arrived with her family, Susannah was in a rare mood. She felt light-headed and witty, as though she'd downed something alcoholic, but the strongest thing she'd had all day was coffee.

"Hi," she said cheerfully, opening the door. Michelle looked at her with large round eyes and grabbed for her mother's collar.

"Sweetheart, this is your auntie Susannah, remember?"

"Emily, the only thing she remembers is that every time you bring her here, you leave," Robert said, carrying in the diaper bag and a sack full of blankets and toys.

"Hello, Robert," Susannah murmured, kissing him on the cheek. The action surprised her as much as it did her brother-in-law. "I understand congratulations are in order."

"For you, too."

"Yes, well, it wasn't that big a deal," she said, playing down her own success.

"Not according to the article in the paper."

"Oh," Emily said, whirling around. "Speaking of the paper, I read Nate's name today."

"Yes…we were both speakers at a conference this afternoon."

Emily seemed impressed, but Susannah couldn't be sure if it was because of her or Nate.

"That wasn't what I read about him," Emily continued, focusing her attention on removing the jacket from Michelle's arms. The child wasn't being cooperative. "Nate's involved in the auction."

"Da-da!" Michelle cried once her arms were free.

Robert looked on proudly. "She finally learned my name. Michelle's first and only word," he added, beaming. "Da-da loves his baby, yes, he does."

It was so unusual to hear Robert using baby talk that for an instant, Susannah didn't catch what her sister was saying. "What was that?"

"I'm trying to tell you about the auction," Emily said again, as if that should explain everything. At Susannah's puzzled look, she added, "His name was in an article about the auction to benefit the Children's Home Society."

The lightbulb that clicked on inside Susannah's head was powerful enough to search the night sky. "Not the *bachelor* auction?" Her question was little more than a husky murmur. No wonder the woman who'd shouted to Nate at the luncheon had been so brazen! She was going to bid on him.

Slowly, hardly conscious of what she was doing, Susannah lowered herself onto the sofa next to her sister.

"He didn't tell you?"

"No, but then why should he? We're nothing more than neighbors."

"Susannah!"

Her sister had the annoying ability to turn Susannah's name into an entire statement just by the way she said it.

"Honey," Robert said, studying his watch, "it's quarter to seven. We'd better leave now if we're going to be at the restaurant on time. I don't want to keep my boss waiting."

Emily's glance at Susannah promised a long talk later.

At least Susannah had several hours during which to come up with a way of warding off her sister's questions.

"Have a good time, you two," Susannah said lightheartedly, guiding them toward the door, "and don't worry about a thing."

"Bye, Michelle," Emily said as she waved from the doorway.

"Tell Mommy goodbye." Since the baby didn't seem too inclined to do so, Susannah held up the chubby hand and waved it for her.

As soon as Emily and Robert had left, Michelle started whimpering softly. Susannah took one look at her niece and her spirits plummeted. Who was she trying to fool? Herself? She'd been miserable and lonely from the moment she'd rejected Nate. Michelle sniffled, and Susannah felt like crying right along with her.

So the notorious Nate Townsend had done it again—he hadn't even bothered to mention the bachelor auction. Obviously he'd agreed to this event weeks in advance and it had never even occurred to him to tell her. Oh, sure, he swore undying love to her, but he was willing to let some strange woman buy him. Men, she was quickly learning, were not to be trusted.

The more Susannah thought back to their previous conversations, the angrier she became. When she'd asked Nate about helping her out with Michelle, he'd casually said he had "something else" this evening. He sure did. Auctioning off his body to the highest bidder!

"I told him I didn't want to see him again," Susannah announced to her niece, her fervor causing her to raise her voice. "That man was trouble from the night we met. You were with me at the time, remember? Don't we wish we'd known then what we know now?"

Michelle's shoulders began to shake, with the effort to either cry or keep from crying. Susannah didn't know which.

"He has this habit of hiding things from me—important information. But I'm telling you right now that I'm completely over that man. Any woman who wants him tonight can have him, because I'm not interested."

Michelle buried her face against Susannah's neck.

"I know exactly how you feel, kid," she said, stalking the carpet in front of the large picture window. She stared out at the lights and sounds of the city at night. "It's like you've lost your best friend, right?"

"Da-da."

"He's with your mommy. I thought Nate was my friend once," she said sadly to the baby. "But I learned the hard way what he really is—nothing earth-shattering, don't misunderstand me. But he let me make a complete idiot of myself. And…and he doesn't trust me enough to tell me anything important."

Michelle looked at Susannah wide-eyed, apparently enthralled with her speech. In an effort to keep the baby appeased, she continued chattering. "I hope he feels like a fool on the auction block tonight," she said as she imagined him standing in front of an auditorium full of screaming women. She slowly released a sigh, knowing that with his good looks, Nate would probably bring in top money. In past auctions, several of the men had gone for thousands of dollars. All for an evening in the company of one of Seattle's eligible bachelors.

"So much for love and devotion," she muttered. Michelle watched her solemnly, and Susannah felt it was her duty as the baby's aunt to give her some free advice. "Men aren't all they're cracked up to be. You'd be wise to figure that out now."

Michelle gurgled cheerfully, obviously in full agreement. "I for one don't need a man. I'm totally happy living on my own. I've got a job, a really good job, and a few close friends—mostly people I work with—and of course your mother." Michelle raised her hand to Susannah's face and rubbed her cheek where a tear had streaked a moist trail.

"I know what you're thinking," Susannah added, although it was unnecessary to explain all that to anyone so young. "If I'm so happy, then why am I crying? Darned if I know. The problem is I can't help loving him and that's what makes this so difficult. Then he had to go and write that note on a napkin." She brought her fingers to her mouth, trying to calm herself. "He asked me if I was willing to live my life without a husband...on a napkin he asked me that. Can you imagine what the caterers are going to think when they read it? And we were sitting at the head table, no less."

"Da-da."

"He asked about that, too," Susannah said, sniffling as she spoke. She was silent a moment and when she began again her voice trembled slightly. "I never thought I'd want children, but then I didn't realize how much I could love a little one like you." Holding the baby against her breast, Susannah closed her eyes to the pain that clawed at her. "I'm so mad at that man."

Fascinated by Susannah's hair, Michelle reached up and tugged it free from the confining pins.

"I wore it up this afternoon to be contrary—and to prove to myself that I'm my own woman. Then he was there and the whole time I was speaking I wished I'd left it down— just because Nate prefers it that way. Oh, honestly, Michelle, I think I may be ready to go off the deep end here. Any advice you'd care to give me?"

"Da-da."

"That's what I thought you'd say." Forcing in a deep breath, Susannah tried to control the tears that sprang to her eyes. She hadn't expected to cry.

"I really believed that once I was promoted to vice president everything would be so wonderful and, well, it *has* been good, but I feel...empty inside. Oh, Michelle, I don't know if I can explain it. The nights are so long and there are only so many hours I can work without thinking about getting home and the possibility of seeing Nate. I... I seem to have lost my drive. Here I was talking to all these people today about determination and drive and discipline, and none of it seemed real. Then...then on the way home I was walking along the waterfront and I saw an old college friend. She's married and has a baby a little older than you and she looked so happy." She paused long enough to rub the back of her hand under her nose. "I told her all about my big promotion and Sally seemed genuinely happy for me, but I felt this giant hole inside."

"Da-da."

"Michelle, can't you learn another word? Please. How about Auntie? It's not so difficult. Say it after me. Auntie."

"Da-da."

"Nate's probably going to meet some gorgeous blonde and fall madly in love with her. She'll bid thousands of dollars for him and he'll be so impressed he won't even mind when she—" Susannah stopped, her mind whirling. "You won't believe what I was thinking," she said to Michelle, who was studying her curiously. "It's completely crazy, but...perhaps not."

Michelle waved her arms and actually seemed interested in hearing about this insane idea that had popped into Susannah's head. It was impossible. Absurd. But then she'd made a fool of herself over Nate so many times that once more certainly wasn't going to hurt.

It took several minutes to get Michelle back into her coat. Susannah would've sworn the thing had more arms than an octopus.

After glancing at the balance in her checkbook, she grabbed her savings-account records and, carrying Michelle, headed to the parking garage. She'd been saving up to pay cash for a new car, but bidding for Nate was more important.

The parking lot outside the theater where the bachelor auction was being held was full, and Susannah had a terrible time finding a place to leave her car. Once she was inside the main entrance, the doorman was hesitant to let her into the auditorium, since Michelle was with her and neither one of them had a ticket.

"Ma'am, I'm sorry, I can't let you in there without a ticket and a bidding number—besides I don't think married women are allowed."

"I'll buy one and this is my niece. Now, either you let me in there or…or you'll… I'll… I don't know what I'll do. Please," she begged. "This is a matter of life and death." Okay, so that was a slight exaggeration.

While the doorman conferred with his supervisor, Susannah looked through the swinging doors that led into the theater. She watched as several women raised their hands, and leaped enthusiastically to their feet to show their numbers. A television crew was there taping the proceedings, as well.

Susannah was impatiently bouncing Michelle on her hip when the doorman returned.

"Ma'am, I'm sorry, but my supervisor says the tickets are sold out."

Susannah was about to argue with him when she heard the master of ceremonies call out Nate's name. A fervent murmur rose from the crowd.

Desperate times demanded desperate measures, and instead of demurely going back outside, Susannah rushed to the swinging doors, shoved them open and hurried down the narrow aisle.

As soon as the doorman saw what she'd done, he ran after her, shouting, "Stop that woman!"

The master of ceremonies ceased speaking, and a hush fell over the room as every head in the place turned toward Susannah, who was clutching Michelle protectively to her chest. She'd made it halfway down the center aisle before the doorman caught up with her. Susannah cast a wretched pleading glance at Nate, who had shielded his eyes from the glare of the lights and was staring at her.

Michelle cooed and with her pudgy hand, pointed toward Nate.

"Da-da! Da-da!" she cried, and her voice echoed loudly in the auditorium.

Eleven

An immediate uproar rose from the theater full of women. Nothing Susannah did could distract Michelle from pointing toward Nate and calling him Da-da. For his part, Nate appeared to be taking all the commotion in his stride. He walked over to the master of ceremonies, whom Susannah recognized as Cliff Dolittle, a local television personality, and whispered something in his ear.

"What seems to be the problem?" Cliff asked the doorman.

"This lady doesn't have a ticket or a bidding number," he shouted back. He clutched Susannah's upper arm and didn't look any too pleased with this unexpected turn of events.

"I may not have a number, but I've got $6,010.12 I'd like to bid for this man," she shouted.

Her announcement was again followed by a hubbub of whispering voices, which rolled over the theater like a wave crashing onto the shore. That six thousand was the balance in Susannah's savings account, plus all the cash she had with her.

A noise from the back of the room distracted her, and that was when she realized the television crew had the cameras rolling. Every single detail of this debacle was being documented.

"I have a bid of $6,010.12," Cliff Dolittle announced, sounding a little shocked. "Going once, going twice—" he paused and scanned the female audience "—sold to the lady who gate-crashed this auction. The one with the baby in her arms."

The doorman released Susannah and reluctantly directed her to where she was supposed to pay. It seemed that everyone was watching her and whispering. Several of the women were bold enough to shout bits of advice to her.

A man with a camera balanced on his shoulder hurried toward her. Loving the attention, Michelle pointed her finger at the lens and cried "Da-da" once more for all the people who would soon be viewing this disaster at home.

"Susannah, what are you doing here?" Nate whispered, joining her when she'd reached the teller's booth.

"You know what really irritates me about this?" she said, her face bright with embarrassment. "I probably could've had you for three thousand, only I panicked and offered every penny I have. Me, the marketing wizard. I'll never be able to hold my head up again."

"You're not making any sense."

"And you are? One moment you're saying you love me and the next you're on the auction block, parading around for a bunch of women."

"That comes to $6,025.12," the white-haired woman in the teller's booth told her.

"I only bid $6,010.12," Susannah protested.

"The extra money is the price of the ticket. You weren't supposed to bid without one."

"I see."

Unzipping her purse and withdrawing her checkbook while balancing Michelle on her hip proved to be difficult.

"Here, I'll take her." Nate reached for Michelle, who surprised them both by protesting loudly.

"What have you been telling her about me?" Nate teased.

"The truth." With considerable ceremony, Susannah wrote out the check and ripped it from her book. Reluctantly she slid it across the counter to the woman collecting the fees.

"I'll write you a receipt."

"Thank you," Susannah said absently. "By the way, what exactly am I getting for my hard-earned money?"

"One evening with this young man."

"One evening," Susannah repeated grimly. "If we go out to dinner does he pay or do I?"

"I do," Nate answered for her.

"It's a good thing, because I don't have any money left."

"Have you eaten?"

"No, and I'm starved."

"Me, too," he told her, smiling sheepishly, but the look in his eyes said he wasn't talking about snacking on crêpes suzette. "I can't believe you did this."

"I can't, either," she said, shaking her head in wonder. "I'm still reeling with the shock." Later, she'd probably start trembling and not be able to stop. Never in her life had she done anything so bold. Love apparently did things like that to a woman. Before she met Nate she'd been a sound, logical, dedicated businesswoman. Six weeks later, she was smelling orange blossoms and thinking about weddings and babies—all because she was head over heels in love!

"Come on, let's get out of here," Nate said, tucking his arm around her waist and leading her toward the theater doors.

Susannah nodded. The doorman seemed relieved that she was leaving his domain.

"Susannah," Nate said, once they were in the parking lot. He turned and placed his hands on her shoulders, then closed his eyes as if gathering his thoughts. "You were the last person I expected to see tonight."

"Obviously," she returned stiffly. "When we're married, I'm going to have to insist that you keep me informed of your schedule."

Nate's head snapped up. "When we're married?"

"You don't honestly believe I just spent six thousand dollars for one dinner in some fancy restaurant, did you?"

"But—"

"And there'll be children, as well. I figure that two are about all I can handle, but we'll play that by ear."

For the first time since she'd met him, Nate Townsend seemed speechless. His mouth made several movements in an attempt to talk, but nothing came out.

"I suppose you're wondering how I plan to manage my career," she said, before he could ask the question. "I'm not sure what I'm going to do yet. Since I'm looking at the good side of thirty, I suppose we could delay having children for a few more years."

"I'm thirty-three. I want a family soon."

Nate's voice didn't sound at all like it normally did, and Susannah peered at him carefully, wondering if the shock had been too much for him. It had been for her! And she was going to end up on the eleven-o'clock news. "Fine, we'll plan on starting our family right away," she agreed. "But before we do any more talking about babies, I need to ask you something important. Are you willing to change messy diapers?"

A smile played at the edges of his mouth as he nodded.

"Good." Susannah looked at Michelle, who'd laid her head against her aunt's shoulder and closed her eyes. Apparently the events of the evening had tired her out.

"What about dinner?" Nate asked, tenderly brushing the silky hair from the baby's brow. "I don't think Michelle's going to last much longer."

"Don't worry about it. I'll buy something on the way home." She paused, then gestured weakly with her hand. "Forget that. I… I don't have any money left."

Nate grinned widely. "I'll pick up some takeout and meet you back at your place in half an hour."

Susannah smiled her appreciation. "Thanks."

"No," Nate whispered, his eyes locked with hers. "Thank *you*."

He kissed her then, slipping his hand behind her neck and tilting her face up to meet his. His touch was so potent Susannah thought her heart would beat itself right out of her chest.

"Nate." Her eyes remained shut when his name parted her lips.

"Hmm?"

"I really do love you."

"Yes, I know. I love you, too. I knew it the night you bought the Stroganoff from the Western Avenue Deli and tried to make me think you'd whipped it up yourself."

She opened her eyes and raised them to his. "But I didn't even realize it then. We barely knew each other."

He kissed the tip of her nose. "I was aware from the first time we met that my life was never going to be the same."

His romantic words stirred her heart and she wiped a tear from the corner of her eye. "I… I'd better take Michelle home," she said, and sniffled.

Nate's thumb stroked the moisture from her cheek before he kissed her again. "I won't be long," he promised.

He wasn't. Susannah had no sooner got Michelle home and into her sleeper when there was a light knock at the door.

Hurriedly, she tiptoed across the carpet and opened it. She brought her finger to her lips as she let Nate inside.

"I got Chinese."

She nodded. "Great."

She paused on her way into the kitchen and showed him Michelle, who was sleeping soundly on the end of the sofa. Susannah had taken the opposite cushion and braced it against the side so there wasn't any chance she could fall off.

"You're going to be a good mother," he whispered, kissing her forehead.

It was silly to get all misty-eyed over Nate's saying that, but she did. She succeeded in disguising her emotion by walking into the kitchen and getting two plates from the cupboard. Opening the silverware drawer, she took out forks.

Nate set the large white sack on the table and lifted out five wire-handled boxes. "Garlic chicken, panfried noodles, ginger beef and two large egg rolls. Do you think that'll be enough?"

"Were you planning on feeding the Seventh Infantry?" she teased.

"You said you were hungry." He opened all the boxes but one.

Susannah filled her plate and sat next to Nate, propping her feet on the chair opposite hers. The food was delicious, and after the first few mouthfuls she decided if Nate could eat with chopsticks she should try it, too. Her efforts had a humbling effect on her.

Watching her artless movements, Nate laughed, then leaned over and kissed the corner of her mouth.

"What's in there?" she asked pointing a chopstick at the fifth box.

He shrugged. "I forget."

Curious, Susannah picked up the container and opened it. Her breath lodged in her throat as she raised her eyes to Nate's. "It's a black velvet box."

"Oh, yes, now that you mention it I remember the chef saying something about black velvet being the special of the month." He went on expertly delivering food to his mouth with the chopsticks.

Susannah continued to stare at the velvet box as if it would leap out and open itself. It was the size of a ring box.

Nate waved a chopstick in her direction. "You might as well take it out and see what's inside."

Wordlessly she did as he suggested. Once the box was free, she set the carton aside and lifted the lid. She gasped when she saw the size of the diamond. For one wild moment she couldn't breathe.

"I picked it up when I was in San Francisco," Nate told her, with no more emotion than if he'd been discussing the weather.

The solitary diamond held her gaze as effectively as a magnet. "It's the most beautiful ring I've ever seen."

"Me, too. I took one look at it and told the jeweler to wrap it up."

He acted so casual, seeming far more interested in eating his ginger beef and noodles than talking about anything as mundane as an engagement ring.

"I suppose I should tell you that while I was in San Francisco, I made an offer for the Cougars. They're a professional baseball team, in case you don't know."

"The baseball team? You're going to own a professional baseball team?" Any news he hit her with, it seemed, was going to be big.

He nodded. "I haven't heard back yet, but if that doesn't work out, I might be able to interest the owner of the New York Wolves in selling."

He made it all sound as if he were buying a car instead of something that cost millions of dollars.

"But whatever happens, we'll make Seattle our home."

Susannah nodded, although she wasn't sure why.

"Here." He set his plate aside and took the ring box from her limp hand. "I suppose the thing to do would be to place this on your finger."

Once again, Susannah nodded. Her meal was sitting like a ton of lead in the pit of her stomach. From habit, she held out her right hand. He grinned and reached for her left one.

"I had to guess the size," he said, deftly removing the diamond from its lush bed. "I had the jeweler make it a size five, because your fingers are dainty." The ring slipped on easily, the fit perfect.

Susannah couldn't stop staring at it. Never in all her life had she dreamed she'd ever have anything so beautiful. "I...don't dare go near the water with this," she whispered, looking down at her hand. Lowering her eyes helped cover her sudden welling up of tears. The catch in her voice was telltale enough.

"Not go near the water...why?"

"If I accidentally fell in," she said, managing a light laugh, "I'd sink from the weight of the diamond."

"Is it too big?"

Quickly she shook her head. "It's perfect."

Catching her unawares, Nate pressed his mouth to her trembling lips, kissing what breath she had completely away. "I planned to ask you to marry me the night I came back from the trip. We were going out for dinner, remember?"

Susannah nodded. That had been shortly after she'd read the article in *Business Monthly* about Nate. The day it felt as though her whole world was rocking beneath her feet.

"I know we talked briefly about your career, but I have something else I need to tell you."

Susannah nodded, because commenting at this point was becoming increasingly impossible.

"What would it take to lure you away from H&J Lima?"

The diamond on her ring finger seemed incentive enough, but she wasn't going to let him know that quite yet. "Why?"

"Because I'm starting a kite company. Actually, it's going to be a nationwide franchise. I've got plans to open ten stores in strategic cities around the country to see how it flies." He stopped to laugh at his pun. "But from the testing we're doing, this is going to be big. However—" he drew in a deep breath "—I'm lacking one important member of my team. I need a marketing expert, and was wondering if you'd like to apply for the job."

"I suppose," she said, deciding to play his game. "But I'd want top salary, generous bonuses, a four-day week, a health and retirement plan and adequate maternity leave."

"The job's yours."

"I don't know, Nate, there could be problems," she said, cocking her head to one side, implying that she was already having second thoughts. "People are going to talk."

"Why?"

"Because I intend to sleep with the boss. And some old fuddy-duddy's bound to think that's how I got the job."

"Let them." He laughed, reaching for her and pulling her into his lap. "Have I told you I'm crazy about you?"

Smiling into his eyes, she nodded. "There's one thing I want cleared up before we go any further, Nate Townsend. No more secrets. Understand?"

"I promise." He spit on the end of his fingertips and used the same fingers to cross his heart. "I used to do that when I was a kid. It meant I was serious."

"Well," Susannah murmured, "since you seem to be in a pledging mood, there are a few other items I'd like to have you swear to."

"Such as?"

"Such as…" she whispered, and lowered her mouth to a scant inch above his. Whatever thoughts had been in her mind scattered like autumn leaves in a brisk wind. Her tongue outlined his lips, teasing and taunting him as he'd taught her to do.

"Susannah…"

Whatever he meant to say was interrupted by the door. Susannah lifted her head. It took a moment to clear her muddled thoughts before she realized it must be her sister and brother-in-law returning from their celebration dinner with Robert's boss.

She tried to move from Nate's lap, but he groaned in protest and tightened his arms around her. "Whoever it is will go away," he said close to her ear.

"Nate—"

"Go back to doing what you were just doing and forget whoever's at the door."

"It's Emily and Robert."

Nate moaned and released her.

Susannah had no sooner unlocked the door than Emily flew in as though she were being pursued by a banshee.

She marched into the living room and stopped suddenly. Robert followed her, looking nearly as frenzied as his wife. Sane sensible Robert!

"What's wrong?" Susannah asked, her heart leaping with concern.

"You're asking *us* that?" Robert flared.

"Now, Robert," Emily said, gently placing her hand on her husband's forearm. "There's no need to be so angry. Stay calm."

"Me? Angry?" he cried, facing his wife. "In the middle of our after-dinner drink you let out a shriek that scared me out of ten years of my life and now you're telling me not to be angry?"

"Emily," Susannah tried again, "what's wrong?"

"Where's Nate?" Robert shouted. One corner of her brother-in-law's mouth curved down in a snarl. He raised his clenched fist. "I'd like ten minutes alone with that man. Give me ten minutes."

"Robert!" Emily and Susannah cried simultaneously.

"Did someone say my name?" Nate asked, as he strolled out of the kitchen.

Emily threw herself in front of her husband, patting his heaving chest with her hands. "Now, honey, settle down. There's no need to get so upset."

Susannah was completely confused. She'd never heard her brother-in-law raise his voice before. Whatever had happened had clearly unsettled him to the point of violence.

"He's not getting away with this," Robert shouted, straining against his wife's restricting hands.

"Away with what?" Nate said with a calm that seemed to inflame Robert even more.

"Taking my daughter away from me!"

"What?" Susannah cried. It astonished her that Michelle

could be sleeping through all this commotion. But fortunately the baby seemed oblivious to what was happening.

"You'd better start at the beginning," Susannah said, leading everyone into the kitchen. "There's obviously been some kind of misunderstanding. Now sit down and I'll put on some decaffeinated coffee and we can sort this out in a reasonable manner."

Her brother-in-law pulled out a chair and put his elbows on the table, supporting his head in his hands.

"Why don't you start?" Susannah said, looking at her sister.

"Well," Emily began, taking in a deep breath, "as I told you, we were having dinner with Robert's boss and—"

"They know all that," Robert interrupted. "Tell them about the part when we were having a drink in the cocktail lounge."

"Yes," Emily said, heaving a great sigh. "That does seem to be where the problem started, doesn't it?"

Susannah shared a look with Nate, wondering if he was as lost as she was. Neither Emily nor Robert was making any sense.

"Go on," Susannah encouraged.

"As I explained, we were all sitting in the cocktail lounge having a drink. There was a television set in the corner of the room. I hadn't been paying much attention to it, but I looked up and I saw you and Michelle on the screen."

"Then she gave a scream that was loud enough to curdle a Bloody Mary," Robert explained. "I got everyone to be quiet while the announcer came on. He said you'd taken *my daughter* to this…this bachelor auction. They showed Michelle pointing her finger at Nate and calling him Da-da."

"That was when Robert let out a fierce yell," Emily said.

"Oh, no." Susannah slumped into a chair, wanting to

find a hole to crawl into and hibernate for the next ten years. Maybe by then Seattle would have forgotten how she'd disgraced herself.

"Did they say anything else?" Nate wanted to know, doing a poor job of disguising his amusement.

"Only that the details would follow at eleven."

"I demand an explanation!" Robert said, frowning at Nate.

"It's all very simple," Susannah rushed to explain. "See... Nate's wearing a suit that's very similar to yours. Same shade of brown. From the distance, Michelle obviously mistook him for you."

"She did?" Robert muttered.

"Of course," Susannah went on. "Besides, Da-da is the only word she can say...." Her voice trailed off.

"Michelle knows who her daddy is," Nate said matter-of-factly. "You don't need to worry that—"

"Susannah," Emily broke in, "when did you get that diamond? It looks like an engagement ring."

"It is," Nate said, reaching to the middle of the table for the last egg roll. He looked at Susannah. "You don't mind, do you?"

"No. Go ahead."

"What channel was it?" Nate asked between bites.

Emily told him.

"Must be a slow news day," Susannah mumbled.

"Gee, Susannah," said Emily, "I always thought if you were going to make the television news it would be because of some big business deal. I never dreamed it would be over a man. Are you going to tell me what happened?"

"Someday," she said, expelling her breath. She'd never dreamed it would be over a man, either, but this one was special. More than special.

"Well, since we're going to be brothers-in-law I guess I can forget about this unfortunate incident," Robert said generously, having regained his composure.

"Good. I'd like to be friends," Nate said, holding out his hand for Robert to shake.

"You're going to be married?" Emily asked her sister.

Susannah exchanged a happy smile with Nate and nodded.

"When?"

"Soon," Nate answered for her. His eyes told her the sooner the better.

She felt the heat crawl into her face, but she was as eager as Nate to get to the altar.

"Not only has Susannah agreed to be my wife, she's also decided to take on the position of marketing director for Windy Day Kites."

"You're leaving H&J Lima?" Robert asked, as if he couldn't believe his ears.

"Had to," she said. She moved to Nate's side, wrapped her arms around his waist and smiled up at him. "The owner made me an offer I couldn't refuse."

Nate's smile felt like a summer's day. Susannah closed her eyes, basking in the warmth of this man who'd taught her about love and laughter and rainy day kisses.

Epilogue

Michelle Davidson arrived at her aunt and uncle's waterfront home just before six. Although she'd been to the house countless times, its beauty never failed to impress her. The place was even lovelier at Christmas, illuminated by string upon string of sparkling lights. The figures on the lawn—the reindeer and St. Nick and everything else—were downright magical.

Michelle's favorite was the young boy running with his kite flying high above his head. Her uncle's kites were what had launched Windy Day Toys all those years ago. Michelle didn't have any memory of those early days, of course. She'd been much too young.

Her aunt Susannah had worked with Uncle Nate for seven years. In that time, the company had gone from one successful venture to another. The first major success had been with kites, and then there was a series of outdoor games, geared toward getting kids outside instead of sitting in front of a TV or a computer screen. Buried Treasure came next and then a game called Bugs that caught national attention.

In the meantime Aunt Susannah had three children in

quick succession and became a stay-at-home mother for a while. Despite her initial doubts, she'd loved it. Michelle's own mother had three children in addition to her, all born within a few months of their Townsend cousins. When her youngest sibling, Glory, entered kindergarten, Michelle's mother and Aunt Susannah had formed Motherhood, Inc.

The two sisters had introduced a series of baby products that were environmentally friendly, starting with cloth diapers and organic baby food. They'd recognized the desire of young mothers all across the country for alternatives to disposable diapers and ways to feed their babies wholesome food.

"Michelle! Michelle!"

Ten-year-old Junior was out the door and racing toward her even before Michelle had made it up the driveway. Eight-year-old Emma Jane was directly behind him. Tessa, who was twelve, was far too aloof, too cool, to show any excitement over Michelle's visit. That was all right, because Michelle knew exactly how Tessa felt. Michelle had hated it when her parents had insisted on hiring a sitter, so she couldn't very well blame Tessa now.

"Michelle." Aunt Susannah waited for her by the entrance. "I really appreciate your doing this," she said. Two large evergreen wreaths decorated the front doors, and a fifteen-foot-high Christmas tree dominated the entry, with gifts stacked all around.

Her aunt finished fastening an earring. "How'd it go at the office today?"

"People heard that we're related," Michelle confessed.

Junior and Emma Jane sat down beneath the massive Christmas tree and began sorting through the gifts—obviously an activity they indulged in often.

"I suppose everyone was likely to find out sooner or

later," Aunt Susannah said, turning toward the stairs. "Nate, hurry up or we're going to be late for dinner."

"I ended up telling everyone that it was because of me that you met Uncle Nate."

At that, Tessa came out of the library. "You were?"

"It's true," Michelle said, accustomed to looks of astonishment after her coworkers' reactions earlier in the day.

"How come no one's ever mentioned *this* before?" Tessa demanded.

Aunt Susannah glanced at Michelle, frowning slightly. "It was a long time ago, sweetie."

"All you said was that you met Dad when you lived in that condo building in downtown Seattle."

"That's how we did meet." Susannah called upstairs again. "Nate!"

"I'll be right down," Nate shouted from the landing.

"Michelle?" Tessa asked, looking to her for the explanation that wasn't being offered by her mother.

"I'll tell you all about it," Michelle whispered.

"Us, too," Emma Jane said.

"Of course," Michelle promised.

Nate Townsend bounded down the stairs, looking as handsome and debonair as always. He really was a wonderful uncle—energetic, funny and a terrific cook.

"Honey, we need to leave right now."

"I know." He opened the hall closet and took out Susannah's coat and his own. He helped Susannah on with hers, then reached over to kiss each of the kids.

"Be good," he said. "And Michelle, if you're going to tell them the story of your aunt and me, don't leave out the part about how you nearly ruined my reputation at the Seattle Bachelor Auction."

"Or the fact that I spent far too much money to buy

you," Susannah muttered. "I could've got you for half of what I paid."

Nate chuckled. "That's what you think. And, hey, I was worth every penny."

"Honey, we—"

"Have fun," Michelle interrupted, steering her aunt and uncle toward the entrance. Once they were on their way, she closed the door—and found her three cousins watching her expectantly.

"Now, where were we?" she murmured.

"Tell us everything," Tessa insisted.

"Can we have dinner first?" Junior asked.

"No," Tessa answered.

"Can you tell us while we eat?" Emma Jane asked.

"I do believe I can," Michelle said and the three followed her into the kitchen. "This is one of the most romantic and wonderful love stories I've ever heard—and to think it all started because of me."

* * * * *